Anthony Lewis discovered his passion for writing in middle school, inspired by a love of storytelling and big ideas. Focused on science fiction, he explores themes of choice and destiny, reminding readers, "Every choice matters. We are writing our own futures make it count."

Born in New Jersey, Anthony has travelled across the U.S. and now resides in the Netherlands with his girlfriend and their four dogs. With a background in IT, he combines analytical thinking with boundless creativity. A gamer and outdoor enthusiast, Anthony brings curiosity and depth to his work. This is his debut novel.

For Mandy,
My greatest constant in a world of shifting timelines. You've shown me that love defies time and space, grounding me when everything else felt uncertain. This book exists because of you.

And to you, dear reader,
Thank you for daring to step into the unknown. Every choice matters even the smallest ones. May this story inspire you to shape the future in ways you never imagined.

Anthony Lewis

HELP WANTED: BREATH OF TIME

AUSTIN MACAULEY PUBLISHERS
LONDON * CAMBRIDGE * NEW YORK * SHARJAH

Copyright © Anthony Lewis 2025

The right of Anthony Lewis to be identified as author of this work has been asserted by the author in accordance with sections 77 and 78 of the Copyright, Designs and Patents Act 1988.

All rights reserved. No part of this publication may be reproduced, stored in a retrieval system, or transmitted in any form or by any means, electronic, mechanical, photocopying, recording, or otherwise, without the prior permission of the publishers.

Any person who commits any unauthorised act in relation to this publication may be liable to criminal prosecution and civil claims for damages.

This is a work of fiction. Names, characters, businesses, places, events, locales, and incidents are either the products of the author's imagination or used in a fictitious manner. Any resemblance to actual persons, living or dead, or actual events is purely coincidental.

A CIP catalogue record for this title is available from the British Library.

ISBN 9781035892822 (Paperback)
ISBN 9781035892839 (Hardback)
ISBN 9781035892846 (ePub e-book)

www.austinmacauley.com

First Published 2025
Austin Macauley Publishers Ltd®
1 Canada Square
Canary Wharf
London
E14 5AA

This book wouldn't have been possible without the incredible support and patience of those around me.

First, to my girlfriend, Mandy, for your unwavering belief in me and for standing by my side throughout this journey. Your love and encouragement have been my greatest constants, and this book is as much yours as it is mine.

To our family, thank you for your patience as I disappeared into this world of words and timelines. Your understanding and support mean more to me than I can express.

A special thanks to Karen, my British sister, whose encouragement and determination kept me on point and motivated through every stage of this journey. Your belief in me has been invaluable.

To Tjim, my first reader and trusted sounding board. Your thoughtful feedback and keen observations helped me shape this story into something I could be proud of.

To Austin Macauley Publishers, thank you for believing in this book and for helping me bring it to life. Your guidance and expertise have been indispensable.

Finally, to you, the reader: thank you for choosing to step into this world I've created. Your time and imagination bring these words to life, and I am endlessly grateful. Always remember: every choice matters.

Chapter One

The worn leather of the ancient book creaked as John turned another page, his eyes scanning the yellowed paper with the intensity of someone searching for answers. This book, like the orphanage he'd always called home, was old and full of secrets. But tonight, something felt different. Tucked between the pages, something fluttered—a slip of paper, almost as old as the book itself. John's breath caught as he unfolded the note, the ink still bold against the fragile parchment: *You are destined for greater things, John. Be ready.*

Living in the bustling city, the orphanage was the only home John had ever known. The constant buzz of activity around him had become as familiar as the creaky floorboards and the faded wallpaper. Despite the chaotic environment, John found solace in books and history, often losing himself in tales of the past.

The orphanage, nestled between tall buildings and bustling streets, was a large, old structure with a long history, having served over the years as a hospital, a school, and now, an orphanage. It housed around one hundred children, ranging in age from infancy to late teens. John, now 19 years old, lived in the oldest dormitory, which had seen better days. The walls were covered in graffiti, and the furniture was worn, but it was home.

Each day after finding the note felt like a fever dream. John's hands would twitch towards the hidden pocket where he kept it, his thoughts spinning with every mundane task. The orphanage, once a chaotic but familiar home, now felt alien. Shadows seemed to stretch longer, faces lingered in his periphery, and objects—had that painting always been there?—shifted subtly, unsettlingly. Strangers in the street caught his eye more often than usual; their glances lingering just a bit too long.

After tossing and turning all night, John gave up on sleep and snuck out to the orphanage's rooftop to clear his mind. The door to the roof creaked open, sounding like steel girders breaking in an earthquake. He paused, collecting his thoughts, before he finally managed to push it open with a grunt of effort. The early morning rays burst through the stairwell, nearly taking the wind out of him. Or was it the pushing of the door? Hard to say after the night he had. Maybe he should have stolen that bourbon. At least it would have made the trip more pleasant.

Shielding his eyes from the morning sun, John leaned back against the rooftop door, gazing up at the clouds, their shapes and forms constantly shifting like the sands of time. A flock of birds passed overhead, their cries piercing the quietude of the morning. The air was alive with the sounds of the city, but here on the roof, he was alone with his thoughts. The sun continued its relentless climb towards the zenith, its warmth beginning to seep into his bones.

The city below buzzed with life, but up here, time seemed to slow. He closed his eyes, trying to recall the events that had brought him here. This seemed as good a time as any. At this point, no one would miss him. Hell, most people who knew him would probably throw a party.

As he looked around the small rooftop, he spied his purloined red ashtray in his favourite spot on top of the orphanage. It was the only reason he kept coming back to this spot. All those early mornings, sitting on the edge of the roof, just above the eastward-facing clock, watching the sunrise. John walked to the edge of the roof and sighed. He then leaned further over the edge, counting the floors down to the ground. It all looked so simple, so easy. As he pondered, he could feel something else in the air. Something electrifying. Looking down at his feet, he noticed a book that he hadn't remembered leaving up there.

He then sat down beside the tray and gently placed the book on his lap, his fingers tracing the familiar grooves in the red ashtray. He took out a worn pack of cigarettes and shook one loose. The silver and red design caught the sunlight, a brief flash that tugged at the edges of a memory something from a time before the orphanage, before the endless cycle of grey days and restless nights. He fumbled for his lighter, feeling the weight of the years in his bones as he struggled to click it open. The flame flared to life, and he brought it up to the tip, inhaling deeply as the smoke filled his lungs. He exhaled slowly, and the smoke curled up into the air, dissolving into nothing, much like his thoughts. A slight breeze kicked up, rustling through his medium-length brown hair.

As the wind picked up a bit more, rustling through the pigeons on the ledge beside him. He glanced at the birds, feeling a pang of something he couldn't quite place. Was it envy? Admiration? Something else entirely? He took another drag off his cigarette, watching the smoke dance in the air before him. Maybe it was all of those things and more. He sighed, feeling the weight of the book in his lap. He looked down at the book and read the title: *"The Rise and Fall of an Empire."*

As the wind continued to blow, the book suddenly flew open, revealing a folded piece of paper tucked inside. John's curiosity was piqued; he carefully unfolded the note. The paper was yellowed with age, and the ink faded, but the words were still legible. It was a letter, written in a flowing script that seemed to dance across the page. The letter spoke of a great adventure, of a world beyond John's wildest dreams. A world where he could make a difference, where he could be more than just a footnote in someone else's story. Unable to shake the memories of his past, John threw the letter aside and continued with his daily routine, watching the sunrise and smoking.

The cigarette ashes danced in the air as he exhaled, carried away by the gentle breeze. The smoke filled his lungs, and he felt a sense of peace wash over him. But beneath the surface, there was a restlessness that refused to be ignored. Something about that letter, about the adventure it spoke of, tugged at his heart.

Through the smell of the river and the exhaust of the cars, he caught a faint whiff of a cigar. Wait, a vanilla-flavoured cigarillo. He froze in place, not from fear, but from anticipation. His mind began to race. **Who the hell is up here? No one knows that I come up here. Derek doesn't smoke, and why did it have to be vanilla?** With another big, deep breath, Cris and John relaxed again. Who cares? He thought it was not like my life was that exciting anyway.

The stranger's chuckle was low, almost lost in the morning breeze. He took a measured step closer, his boots scraping against the gravel. "John, if I wanted to harm you, we wouldn't be having this conversation," he said, his voice carrying a drawl that hinted at a time long past. His stance was casual, but his eyes sharp, calculating betrayed a readiness that set John's nerves on edge.

John slowly turned his head, trying to make out the stranger's features. The man was tall and broad-shouldered, dressed in a long, black trench coat that flapped in the breeze. His face was shadowed by a fedora hat, tilted rakishly to one side. He wore a black suit, a crisp white shirt, and a deep burgundy tie. His salt and pepper hair was slicked back, revealing a handsome face with a strong jawline. Even though John couldn't see his eyes, he had a feeling that he was studying him intently. He didn't look like a threat, but there was something about him that made John uneasy.

"Thought you could lose me, huh?" the stranger asked with a grin. He took another drag from his cigarillo before flicking it away. It arced through the air, disappearing into the mist.

"No, sir," John replied, swallowing hard. "I just didn't expect to see anyone else up here."

The stranger chuckled, taking another step closer. "Well, you've got me all wrong. I'm not here to harm you, John. In fact, quite the opposite," he said, his voice like steel wrapped in velvet. The stranger shifted his stance slightly as if he were expecting something to happen.

"You never could handle my cigarillos," the stranger continued. "What's it been now, ten years? Fifteen maybe?"

Panic began to sink in. Who is this person and how did he know me? John tensed up, grabbed the last cigarette he had and placed it in his mouth. He reached back into his pocket for his trusty Bic. Shaking, he tried to spark it up. Just another smoke and all will be fine. One spark, fail. Two sparks, still no good. His hands were shaking so much, on the third strike, the lighter slipped from his hands and began the long, slow journey to the ground.

John swallowed hard, not knowing what was happening, knowing that he had no way of retrieving the little piece of sanctuary that was now at least ten flights beneath him, still flipping end over end, heading to the cold, hard pavement below. He turned around to meet this unfamiliar stranger from his past. Not knowing was the worst for him. No one had stayed too long in his life, and now he had a presence here, someone who knew about his past, his smoking habit, even the fact that he had been up here for so long.

"I'm not here to hurt you, John," the man said with a smile, his voice smooth as silk. "I'm here to help you. You see, I've been watching you, waiting for the right moment to approach you. And I think now is as good a time as any."

John looked down and saw the strange man's boots. Old and worn, still covered with fresh mud. Not sure how he found mud in the middle of the city, but there it was, nonetheless. As he started to look up, searching for the stranger's eyes, he stopped. Cigarillos…boots…. Could it be? John's eyes met the stranger's stare head-on. A spark and a wisp of air and right in front of his face was a lit match. John lit his cigarette off the free fire and drew it deep into his lungs. The smoke filled his chest, calming his nerves and soothing his soul.

The stranger took another step closer, his boots leaving deep impressions in the gravel. "You don't remember me, John?" he asked, his voice barely above a whisper. John didn't say anything, but his eyes never left the man's face. The stranger chuckled.

"It's been so long I didn't expect you to remember me." He paused, looking out over the cityscape. "You were just a kid back then, full of hope and dreams."

The man smiled warmly, revealing a toothy grin. "Like I said, I'm not here to hurt you, John. I'm here to offer you a chance to change your life. I work for the Lennox Time Corporation. We know what you're going through. You have a gift, John. A gift that very few people in this world have. A gift that could change everything for you."

"What the hell, man?" was all that John could mutter. Anger was clearly visible on his face, all the stranger could do was chuckle again.

"Look, John. I understand that this might not be what you were expecting. But I'm telling you, this could be your chance at a new life. A better life. A life without pain and regret."

John slid off the roof edge towards the strange man, keeping his sights locked on the other man's copper eyes. After another full inhale, he spoke.

"Dude, I don't even know you and you come up here, telling me about a new life and this LTC bullshit. Who the hell do you think you are?" John said, his anger growing with each word. He took another drag, the smoke dancing around him like a protective shield. The stranger smiled again.

"Yep, it's you alright. It's me, too. I know what you're about to do. That's why I'm here. Get your stuff. It's time." The stranger's words were soft, almost comforting.

John's eyes narrowed, a mix of anger and confusion clouding his face. He took another drag from his cigarette, the smoke swirling around him. "What the hell are you talking about?" he asked, his voice barely above a whisper. "Who are you, and why do you know so much about me?"

All the pleasantness that was visible in the stranger's face melted away to a non-expression. He spoke again, this time with force behind his words. "You know damn well who I am. We're running out of time. In five minutes, you're going to meet that pavement. A minute after that, the headmaster will come up here because you left the door open this time. The longer you wait, the greater the chance you'll be an obit. C'mon," he barked, grabbing John's arm. John stepped to the side, slipping out of the stranger's grasp.

The stranger sighed, shaking his head. After removing his hat, he ran his hand through his hair, mussing it slightly, before he straightened up again. He fixed his gaze on the horizon. "Look, I don't know what else to tell you. You know what's coming. You know what you're going to do if you don't come with me. But I can give you a chance at a better life. A life where you're not always running from the past." The stranger put his hat back on and waited for an answer.

"Wait. Just wait. What is going on? There's no other place to go; it's either the stairs or the pavement and if Derek's on his way up, that's it." The stranger handed John what looked like a small button off a shirt. When John looked at him, confused, the stranger continued, his expression serious.

"This is a hopper. Put it in your pocket and follow me," he said walking off towards the opposite edge of the roof. Still unsure of what was going on, John followed slowly behind. Once at the other side of the roof, behind the stairwell entrance, they could hear footsteps. John looked at the stranger and opened his mouth to speak. Before air could escape his lips, a heavy hand sealed his mouth, and the stranger mouthed the words: "Be quiet."

John nodded and stood motionless as the stranger whispered something into his ear. The stranger let go of his mouth and took a step back. With a look of surprise, John turned his head towards him but then looked back to the stairwell entrance. He could see Derek's silhouette through the light coming from below. The stranger smiled and put his finger to his lips, urging him to be quiet.

Looking around for cover, the stranger noticed some crates just to their right. They crouched behind the crates and waited for the opportunity to make their move. The stranger glanced over at John, who was still trying to process everything that had happened.

The stranger leaned in closer, his intense gaze boring into John's eyes. Sweat beads formed on his brow, and his jaw tightened as he spoke. "Look, I know this is a lot to take in, but you need to trust me," he whispered urgently. "Those men are from the future. They are here to kill you." He paused, taking a shaky breath before continuing. "But I'm here to protect you."

Shadows danced across the roof as the light from below shifted, casting eerie shapes across the crates they hid behind. John felt his heart racing, the adrenaline coursing through his veins making it difficult to think straight. He nodded, struggling to process everything the stranger was saying.

As if in response to their silent conversation, the footsteps coming up the stairs grew louder, echoing through the empty space around them. The wind picked up, howling across the rooftop, making it harder for them to hear and see clearly. John felt a bead of sweat roll down his spine, chilling him to the bone.

"Look, John, I get it. This all seems crazy," the stranger whispered, his voice barely audible over the noise. "But I swear to you, I'm not here to hurt you. Those men, they're dangerous. They'll stop at nothing to get what they want." He glanced over at Derek's silhouette, visible through the dim light from below. "And right now, they want you."

John swallowed hard; his throat dry. He looked at the stranger, his eyes filled with doubt and fear. "But how do I know I can trust you?" he managed to ask.

The stranger smiled reassuringly, putting a hand on John's shoulder. "Because I'm the only one who can protect you from them."

As the footsteps grew closer, the stranger whispered, "Stay low and follow my lead." He then reached under his jacket, revealing a Remington 1858 revolver hidden in a holster. The stranger's six-shooter was a well-worn but still deadly weapon. It had seen countless battles and had proven its worth repeatedly. When Derek and the other men rounded the corner, they were greeted by the sight of the stranger aiming his weapon at them.

Derek, his face contorted with anger and betrayal, took a step forward, and his hand reached for the holster at his hip. But before he could draw his own weapon, the stranger spoke: "Now, Derek, you don't want to do that," he said calmly, his voice cold as American West Steel. "Put your hands up where I can see them."

The men behind Derek exchanged glances, uncertainty flickering in their eyes. But it was Derek who finally complied, slowly raising his hands into the air. "What do you want, cowboy?" he asked, his voice quivering with rage. "You think you can just take him from me?"

The stranger's expression remained unchanged as he kept the gun trained on Derek. "I'm not here to take anything from you, Derek," he said softly. "I'm just here to make sure John gets out of this alive." He paused, then added, "And if that means putting an end to your little operation, well so be it." As the tension in the air thickened, John looked back and forth between the two men. His heart pounding in his chest, not sure what to believe, or who to trust.

The stranger glanced at John, then turned back to Derek. "Let's discuss this like adults, shall we?" he said, his voice low and threatening. "Because if we don't, things are going to get ugly real quick."

Derek, a man in his late thirties with a muscular build and a scar running down the left side of his face, glared at the stranger from behind his raised hands. He was dressed in a black suit and tie, the same suit and tie as his associates.

"Derek," the stranger continued, his tone softening just a bit, "I'm not here to cause any more trouble than I already have. I just want what's best for John. But if you force my hand, if you try to hurt him or anyone else involved in this, I won't hesitate to put a bullet in you."

The stranger lowered his gun but kept it nearby as he watched Derek carefully. Derek's face twisted in anger and fear, his hands still raised in the air. The men behind him shifted uneasily, unsure of what to do next.

"Now," the stranger said, "why don't you and your boys head on back to wherever it is you came from? And don't think about coming after John or anyone else connected to him. Because if you do, you'll be signing your own death warrants."

Derek's eyes narrowed as he looked at the stranger and pulled his weapon to fire.

The stranger's eyes widened in surprise as he saw Derek draw out a futuristic-looking weapon. It resembled a handgun but had an unfamiliar design, and emitted a soft blue glow instead of a muzzle flash. It seemed to be some sort of energy-based weapon, and it was clearly not something the stranger had encountered before.

Indeed, Derek's henchmen also had futuristic weapons similar to their boss'. As the gunfight escalated, they took cover behind various objects on the roof and began to fire at the stranger. With the instincts of a seasoned gunslinger, the stranger deftly evaded most of the incoming shots, ducking and weaving as he fired back at his attackers.

He quickly realised he was outmatched in firepower and decided to use his environment to his advantage. The stranger ducked behind a crate and rolled out of the way as Derek fired his weapon. The blue energy bolt sizzled harmlessly through the air where the stranger had been only a second before. He returned fire, but Derek had already found cover behind another air conditioning unit. Bullets whizzed past John's head and shattered some crates nearby.

The gunfight continued, with both men using the various objects on the roof as cover while they exchanged fire. As the bullets whizzed past, shattering crates, and sending debris flying through the air, John crouched behind a large trash can, terrified and confused. He didn't know who to trust or what to believe anymore.

The stranger reacted instinctively, ducking low as Derek's gunshot rang through the air. The bullet ricocheted harmlessly off the wall behind the stranger.

He didn't hesitate, returning fire as he rolled to the side. Derek and his men scattered, taking cover behind air conditioning units on the roof.

The stranger crawled back to where John was crouched, pressing himself against the wall. "Stay down!" he whispered urgently. "They're going to be looking for us." He reached out and helped John up, then pulled him into a crouch behind a large plant. "We need to find someplace to hide, quick."

The stranger ducked behind a stack of crates, using them for cover as he fired back at the other time travellers. He glanced at John, who was still crouched down, terrified. "Stay down!" he yelled over the gunfire. "But if you want to help, you can throw these at them." He handed John a handful of heavy metal objects, which turned out to be old-fashioned cell phones.

John crouched low, his heart pounding as the gunfight raged around him. The stranger ducked behind a stack of crates, using them for cover as he fired back at the other time travellers. John watched in horror as the stranger's handgun seemed to malfunction, jamming after only a few shots. The stranger cursed under his breath and tried to clear the jam, but the other time travellers were closing in fast.

"Stay down!" the stranger shouted, glancing at John briefly before returning his attention to the fight. "But if you can, throw those phones at them! It might buy us some time!"

Taking a deep breath, John grabbed a handful of the old-fashioned cell phones and carefully peeked over the edge of the crate. The other time travellers were only a few feet away now, their guns trained on the stranger. He took aim and threw one of the phones as hard as he could, aiming for the closest man. It hit him square in the back, causing him to stumble forward momentarily. The other time travellers looked confused, as the stranger finally cleared the gun jam. He fired his gun once more, hitting one of the other time travellers in the leg. The man cried out in pain, stumbling backwards. The other time travellers looked around to see where the bullet had come from. Taking advantage of the chaos, the stranger fired again, hitting another one of them in the arm. The man dropped his weapon, yelling in agony.

The remaining time travellers looked at each other in disbelief as the stranger managed to take down two of their comrades in quick succession. One of them took a deep breath and began to edge away slowly, trying to retreat down the stairs. The other two exchanged glances before finally deciding to follow suit.

As they backed away, the stranger gave John a nod of encouragement before turning his attention back to the fleeing time travellers.

The stranger aimed his gun carefully, taking into account the distance and the angle to Derek. As he squeezed the trigger, the gun responded with a powerful cracking sound and sent a ball of lead flying towards Derek's chest. Derek dove through the open stairwell door and into the darkness of the building.

The stranger glanced at John, his expression had a mix of amusement and concern. "You did good, kid," he said, clapping the younger man on the shoulder. "You were born to be a part of this."

Taking advantage of the calm after the gunfight, the stranger took this as his cue to explain the situation. "Look, I know this is all pretty confusing, but you need to understand that not everyone here has your best interests at heart. In fact, some of them are downright dangerous. I've been trying to protect you from them, but it looks like I'm going to need your help."

John shook his head, still trying to process everything that's happened. He looked at the stranger, then back at the stairwell where the other time travellers escaped, and finally back at the stranger again. He took a deep breath and nodded slowly. "I'm in," he said, his voice quivering slightly. "I want to know what's going on and why they're after us."

As the stranger pressed the hopper on his lapel, a blinding light enveloped them, and they were hurled back through time. The world spun around them, the sensation of being hurled through the void of time and space leaving them disoriented and nauseous. As their surroundings stabilised, they both realised that something was wrong. The stranger's time travel device was still glowing brightly, but it didn't seem to be functioning properly.

They were still on the roof of the orphanage as the stranger slumped against the wall, struggling to catch his breath. "It's damaged," he wheezed. "My time hopper it's not working right." He looked at John, his eyes wide with fear and desperation. "I think I think it might be sending me somewhere else."

The stranger's button pulsed with an unearthly glow, casting strange shadows across his face as he pressed it again with his thumb. The hopper nestled in John's pocket began to heat up, vibrating gently against his thigh. A sense of growing urgency filled the air as they both felt the power building up within their buttons.

The stranger's face twisted into a determined grin; his eyes locked on John's. The light from his button intensified, becoming brighter and brighter until it engulfed them both in a blinding flash. The sphere of light expanded rapidly, enveloping their bodies and the surrounding area in its searing radiance.

As the light grew stronger, John felt himself being pushed back against the metal frame of the air conditioning unit. The world spun around him, the ground rushing up to meet him as he struggled to keep his balance. He tried to fight the dizziness, but it was of no use. He felt as if he were falling, plummeting through the darkness, his stomach lurching uncomfortably. The stranger, too, seemed to be affected by the disorientation, his body swaying wildly as he fought to keep his footing.

Just as John thought he could bear the sensation no longer, the world vanished in a brilliant flash of light, replaced by an impenetrable void of inky blackness. The silence that followed was deafening, punctuated only by the distant ringing of his ears. John struggled to regain his bearings, feeling disoriented and disconnected from reality. He reached instinctively for his hopper, only to find it gone. The stranger, too, seemed to have vanished into thin air. The only evidence that they had ever been there at all was the faint warmth emanating from the metal frame of the air conditioning unit, where John's arm had brushed against it just moments before.

Chapter Two

John awoke to darkness, the creak of wood, and the rhythmic jolt of an old stagecoach as it rumbled down a dirt road. His limbs felt heavy and restricted, and as his eyes adjusted to the dim light of the full moon, he realised his arms and legs were bound, tethered to the door of the coach. The silhouettes of two others loomed opposite him one clearly feminine, given the heels, short dress, and long hair; the other figure was more ambiguous, though the build suggested a man.

As the stagecoach lurched, John strained to see his fellow passengers. The young woman, barely in her twenties, had long, dark hair that framed a pale, soot-streaked face. Her dress, once fine, was now rumpled and dirty, riding up to reveal her legs, marked with scratches. Her eyes met John's wide, fearful, and uncertain.

The man sat rigidly, his fine clothes dishevelled and soiled, as though he'd just come from a brawl or a fire. A silver pocket watch dangled from his vest; its chain caught on a loose button. He glanced at John briefly, then turned away, deep in thought.

Outside, the driver smoked a cigarillo, urging the horses onward through the thick mud. John noticed the man's clothes were also torn and stained, the signs of someone who'd been through something violent and chaotic. A sick feeling churned in John's stomach, a gnawing certainty that whatever was happening, it wasn't good.

"Where am I?" John croaked, his voice rough and unfamiliar to his own ears.

The woman leaned forward, her face catching a sliver of moonlight. She offered him a small, almost sad smile. "You're in a stagecoach, dear. We're taking you to the orphanage at Epsilon," she whispered.

John's gaze darted to the man, who looked at him briefly before returning his attention to the road. "Who are you people? What do you want with me?" John's voice trembled; the fear evident.

The man inclined his head slightly, acknowledging the question with an air of calm authority. "We're here to see you safely to your destination," he replied, his tone crisp and unmistakably British. "Certain people have taken an interest in you. It's our job to ensure you get where you need to go."

A shiver ran down John's spine. "What do you mean by 'taken an interest'?" he whispered, his voice barely audible.

The man hesitated, carefully choosing his words. "Let's just say you're important to some very influential people. We're part of a larger effort to ensure your safety."

John's mind raced with questions, but he sensed these strangers wouldn't reveal much more. He shifted uncomfortably, trying to make sense of his situation. The creaking of the stagecoach and the steady clip-clop of the horses' hooves were the only sounds breaking the stillness of the night.

The woman's face emerged more clearly as she leaned closer, the moonlight reflecting off her rounded glasses. Her fair skin and sculpted nose were illuminated briefly before she held a finger to her lips, signalling him to remain silent. The other figure remained cold and still, watching John struggle to sit upright. With a painful sigh, John gave up and stared out the window, feeling a wave of helplessness wash over him.

Through the window, he could see the first light of dawn breaking over the horizon, casting long shadows through the dense forest that surrounded them. Trees lined the narrow, well-worn path the coach travelled, their branches reaching out like skeletal fingers. The growing light only deepened his sense of dread.

"I don't understand what's going on. Why did you have to bring me here? Where are my parents?" John's voice trembled with fear and confusion.

As more sunlight filtered into the carriage, the woman's presence became more imposing. She was tall, thin, and well-proportioned, her elegant figure intimidating in the confined space. John's gaze drifted up her body, pausing as something struck him from the side—a strong, hard backhand. It wasn't enough to knock him out, but it rattled him, sending him crashing to the floor with a grunt of pain.

"I apologise for that, but it was necessary," the woman with the glasses said, her tone even and calm. "You must understand, John, you're in a precarious position. We're here to make sure you get to the orphanage safely." She tilted her head slightly, scrutinising him. "Do you understand?"

"NO!" a gravelly, harsh voice barked from the other figure. Undeniably male, his voice was edged with menace. As John tried to rise, a heavy boot pressed into his back, tightening the ropes painfully around his body.

Tears streamed down John's face as he struggled to comprehend the situation. Just hours ago, he had been with his parents, their comforting presence was now a distant memory. The image of the fire flashed in his mind—heat, smoke, panic. His parents' faces blurred, lost in the chaos. Now he was alone, surrounded by strangers who offered no solace.

"Please, where are my parents? I want to go home!" John's voice cracked with desperation.

The woman with the glasses sighed softly, her expression one of controlled patience. "Your parents are gone, John. We're here to ensure you reach the orphanage safely. That's our only concern."

John's heart pounded, the weight of her words sinking in. Gone. His parents were gone. His world had crumbled, leaving him with nothing but fear and uncertainty.

The man with the gravelly voice pressed his boot harder into John's back, making him wince. "Stay down, boy. You're safer this way."

John sobbed quietly, the reality of his situation crushing him. He didn't understand why this was happening or what these people wanted. All he knew was that he was terrified, trapped in a nightmare with no escape.

The carriage came to a sudden halt. "I understand this is overwhelming, John. But you must trust us. My name is Amelia, and this stiff gentleman is Malcolm. Wait until we get to Epsilon." Malcolm glanced at Amelia; concern etched on his face.

John heard someone dismount from the stagecoach above. Pressed to the floor, he could only see the bottom half of the door and the woman's towering heels. More heavy boots hit the ground outside as the driver jumped down. The carriage swayed slightly from the weight shift. John listened as the boots approached, stopping just outside the door.

The handle turned, and the door swung open to reveal a tall man with a moustache, a Stetson hat, and long brown hair. He huffed slightly, noticing John on the floor, face down in the dirt. "We can't hurt him, Malcolm. You know that," the stranger said, staring down Malcolm with his copper eyes, demanding an explanation for why John wasn't still unconscious.

Malcolm's eyes flickered with irritation before he responded. "He woke up earlier than expected. Amelia and I had to make sure he stayed still. You know the protocols, Gabe."

Gabe's gaze softened as he looked down at John, trembling with fear. "Protocols or not, the kid's been through enough," he muttered, stepping into the carriage. He knelt beside John, gently lifting him back onto the seat and brushing the dirt from his face. "It's alright, son. We ain't gonna hurt ya. We're here to keep ya safe."

John's wide eyes took in the rugged, yet kind features of Gabe's face. Despite the harshness of his appearance, there was something reassuring about him. The fear and confusion were still there, but the sense of impending danger lessened with Gabe's presence.

Amelia leaned forward, her expression genuinely concerned. "John, we're taking you to a place where you'll be safe. Epsilon's an orphanage, yes, but it's also a sanctuary. You'll be taken care of there."

John's mind raced, but he managed to ask the question that burned the most. "Why me? Why did you take me?"

Gabe exchanged a look with Malcolm and Amelia before answering. "You've been chosen, kid. You're special, even if ya don't know it yet. There are things happening in the world that you're a part of, things that you're meant to do."

Malcolm nodded, his earlier irritation replaced by a solemn, stoic expression. "Your parents were part of something much larger, something important. We can't explain everything now, but you need to trust us."

Tears filled John's eyes as the reality of his situation began to sink in. His parents were gone, and his life as he knew it was over. But there was a glimmer of something else, something that made him hold on to a sliver of hope. The promise of safety, a place where he could belong, was enough to keep him from breaking completely.

Gabe stood up and turned to Malcolm. "We should get movin'. The longer we stay here, the more dangerous it becomes."

Ignoring Malcolm's muttered curse, Gabe climbed back onto the stagecoach and took the reins, urging the horses forward. The coach lurched back into motion, the rhythmic clatter of hooves filling the tense silence.

John tried in vain to move out from under Malcolm's boot. Gabe shot a glance back, and Malcolm reluctantly lifted his foot, allowing John to sit up.

John sighed softly, still overwhelmed by the situation. He closed his eyes, wishing he could wake from this nightmare. The sound of Gabe's voice brought him back to the present. "We'll be there in no time, boys and ma'am." Gabe shot a sideways glance at Malcolm, who nodded grimly and tipped his hat at Amelia.

As the carriage rounded a bend, the orphanage came into view. It seemed peaceful enough from a distance, but John knew better than to trust appearances.

The coach pulled up in front of the orphanage, and Gabe reined in the horses. Malcolm and Amelia exchanged a brief look before opening the carriage door. Gabe reached in, grabbed the ropes around John's chest, and pulled him from the stagecoach. Lifting him with ease, he set John on his feet at the steps of a large, imposing building.

"Where are we? Why did you take me? My parents will come after you all!" John yelled, tears streaming down his face. He looked left to see a woman dressed in all black, much older than him but still youthful. Her green eyes shone like jewels in the early morning light. She smiled slightly at John and then turned to Gabe.

"Thank you for bringing him. I know it must have been a hard journey. Come, get some rest, Gabe," she said, reaching for John's rope.

John stepped back, shouting, "Get away from me! Wait till my parents…" Gabe pulled the rope, cutting it off. He turned to Malcolm, who was still in the carriage, and nodded. Then, Gabe looked back at John, trying to appear reassuring.

"John, your parents are gone. That's why you're here. They asked me before we left St. Louis to get you safe passage to Epsilon, and this, this is Epsilon." Gabe knelt to untie the ropes around John. He reached into his pocket and handed him a piece of paper. "There's too much to explain now." Gabe pointed to the woman in black. "Janice will take care of you. I'll be back to get you later. For now, take this note. Hold on to it; it will help you later in life."

Gabe stood and turned to leave. John's jaw dropped as he looked up at Gabe, tears streaming down his ghostly pale face.

"You can't just leave me here! How dare you! I'll find you, and I'll…I'll kill you!" John's voice broke with rage and fear. Gabe stopped, turning slightly. He looked back at the scared, and angry boy and sighed.

"Stay out of trouble, John." As Gabe's words faded, the world around John began to melt. The sky liquefied, trees running like water into the ground. John felt a sudden rush of air, and darkness crept in around him. He tried to run but found himself paralysed, the earth crumbling beneath his feet. Disoriented and terrified, he glanced down at his hand, where the paper Gabe had given him began to disintegrate, crumbling to dust.

As everything around him vanished into an inky void, the last thing he noticed was the sharp scent of antiseptic filling his nostrils.

Chapter Three

John opened his eyes to find himself somewhere else entirely. **Damn, I hate that dream.** The thought echoed through his mind as he tried to shake off the lingering confusion. The antiseptic smell, the drop-down ceiling, and the flickering fluorescent lights all screamed "doctor's office." His heart sank, a sickening déjà vu washing over him. He tried to sit up, only to find his limbs restrained, strapped down tightly to the bed. Panic bubbled up in his chest as he scanned the dimly lit room, struggling to make sense of his surroundings.

He noted the frosted window that let in a gloomy, grey light, the dull metal door, and the faint drone of unseen equipment that made the room feel unnervingly alive. **European?** The thought flitted across his mind as he noticed the unfamiliar plug sockets, their design alien to him, and the cold, clinical feel of the place. The air was thick with the sterile, sharp scent of disinfectant, mingling with something more metallic that made his stomach churn. His heart pounded harder as the door handle clicked, and the door swung open, revealing a woman in a lab coat.

"Hello, John. My name is Doctor Becker," she said, her thick German accent slicing through the sterile air with an eerie precision. She moved with a practiced, almost mechanical grace as she approached him, her expression a mask of calm. Her skin was unnaturally pale, almost faded, her eyes glinting coldly under the harsh fluorescent light, giving her an unsettling, otherworldly appearance. "I'll be taking care of you from now on."

John's stomach twisted as she sat down on the edge of his bed, crossing her legs casually as if she had all the time in the world. She seemed to drink in his fear, her eyes flicking over him with a clinical detachment that made his skin crawl. "I know you're confused right now, so why don't you try to relax? Whenever you're ready to talk, I'm here to listen."

John's mind raced his thoughts a chaotic jumble as he tried to piece together what had happened. He remembered being on the rooftop with Gabe, the city spread out beneath him like a map of possibilities, and then nothing. The sterile environment, the harsh lights it all felt too real to be a dream, but too disjointed, too surreal to be reality.

"Where am I?" he finally managed to ask, his voice hoarse and shaky, barely more than a whisper.

"You're at our local clinic," Doctor Becker replied smoothly, her voice a calculated mix of authority and reassurance. "You were brought in a few days ago after being found unconscious in an alleyway. We're running some tests to figure out what happened to you."

John's heart raced, fear gnawing at the edges of his mind like a hungry animal. He could feel his pulse hammering in his temples, each beat loud and insistent. "Who would do this to me? Why am I here?"

Doctor Becker's smile was almost sympathetic, but there was something off about it, something that made John's blood run cold. "That's what we're trying to figure out. But for now, just focus on getting better. We'll keep you safe here."

John's eyes narrowed, suspicion flaring as he searched her face for any hint of truth, any clue that might help him understand. **Help me? How can you help me?** The memories of the dream, of the rooftop and Gabe, blurred with his current reality, leaving him dizzy and disoriented. Everything felt wrong like he was trapped in a waking nightmare.

"Save me?" John stammered, the words catching in his throat as his chest tightened. "How can you save me when you're the one who… who…"

Doctor Becker's eyes gleamed with a twisted amusement, her smile curling at the edges in a way that made John's skin prickle. "You think I did this to you? Drugged you? Kidnapped you?" She laughed softly, the sound low and unnerving, shaking her head as if he had just said something amusingly naive. "No, John, I'm not here to hurt you. I'm here to help you understand what's happening to you."

She leaned in closer, her voice dropping to a conspiratorial whisper, the kind that made his heart skip a beat for all the wrong reasons. "You see, John, those dreams you've been having? They're not just dreams. They're memories. Fragments of a past life you've forgotten."

John's blood ran cold. His breath hitched as he tried to shake his head, to deny what she was saying, but the straps held him fast, the restraints biting into his skin. "That's… that's impossible. How do you…? I don't have any memories like that." His voice trembled, the words barely holding together under the weight of his fear.

Doctor Becker's smile widened her expression a mix of pity and condescension that made John's stomach turn. "Oh, John, you don't remember anything right now. But I can help you. I can show you the truth." She reached into her pocket and pulled out a small vial, the clear liquid inside catching the light with a sinister gleam. "This serum will help you remember. It will bring back the memories that were stolen from you."

John's heart pounded as he stared at the vial, his mind screaming for him to fight, to escape. Every instinct he had was shouting at him to get away, to run as fast and as far as he could, but he was trapped, helpless. "I don't understand. What are you talking about?" His voice was almost pleading as if he could will her to stop with his desperation alone.

Doctor Becker's gaze hardened, her smile fading as she became all business. "This is the only way for you to know the truth, John. But it's going to hurt. It's going to feel like your mind is being torn apart, like you're reliving every pain, every fear, all over again." There was a dark, almost sadistic edge to her words like she was savouring the anticipation of his suffering.

She placed the vial gently on his chest, the cold glass sending a shiver through him, a sick promise of what was to come. "When you're ready, just take it."

John's breath came in ragged gasps, the weight of the decision crushing him, squeezing the air from his lungs. **Do I trust her? Do I take the serum?** The room seemed to close in around him, the walls pressing in, the air thick with a sense of impending doom that made his skin crawl.

Doctor Becker watched him with detached interest, her eyes glinting in the dim light as if she were waiting for him to break. "There's no need to be afraid, John. I'm here with you every step of the way." Her words were meant to be comforting, but they only served to heighten the dread that coiled around his chest like a vice.

John felt the panic rising, a hot, suffocating wave that threatened to drown him. His heart hammered in his chest; each beat was a desperate plea for escape. He strained against the restraints, his muscles burning with the effort, but the straps held firm, cutting into his wrists and ankles. Sweat trickled down his back, stinging his skin as it mingled with the bindings. **I have to get out of here. I have to get out.**

The door suddenly burst open, splintering under the force of the impact. The sound was deafening, a sharp crack that echoed through the room, freezing Doctor Becker in place. She gasped, her eyes widening as her glasses slipped from her nose and clattered to the floor. Gabe, dressed in his black long coat and Stetson, strode into the room, his presence a jarring contrast to the sterile, controlled environment. He moved with the calm, deadly precision of someone who had done this a thousand times before.

Before Doctor Becker could react, Gabe closed the distance between them, his movements swift and sure. With a single, severe blow to the head, he knocked her out cold. She crumpled to the floor, her white coat billowing around her like a fallen ghost, her lifeless form an eerie echo of the controlled, calculating figure she had been just moments before. Gabe barely spared her a glance before turning to John, his expression softening with concern as he took in his friend's condition.

"You alright, buddy?" Gabe asked his voice a steady, reassuring drawl that cut through the fog of fear clouding John's mind.

John sagged with relief, the tension draining from his body in a rush that left him dizzy. His heart was still racing, the adrenaline pulsing through his veins, but for the first time since he had woken up, he felt a flicker of hope. "I'm okay," he managed to croak, his voice barely audible, the words rough and raw from disuse. "Just get me out of here."

Gabe nodded, his movements efficient and controlled as he unbuckled the straps and helped John to his feet. John swayed unsteadily, his legs weak and shaky from the adrenaline crash and the stress of the ordeal. Gabe caught him, his grip firm and steady as he supported him, guiding him towards the door.

As they reached the hallway, Gabe glanced back at Doctor Becker's unconscious form, his brow furrowing in concern. "I don't know what her angle was," he muttered, more to himself than to John, "but we need to move."

John nodded, still trying to process everything that had happened, the questions swirling in his mind like a storm. "She said I had a past life. That I was taken from them."

Gabe frowned, his expression darkening as he led John down the hallway. The silence was oppressive, the air heavy with the weight of unanswered questions. "We'll figure it out later," Gabe said, his tone resolute. "Right now, we need to get out of here."

They moved quickly, Gabe's senses on high alert, his eyes scanning their surroundings for any signs of danger. The hallway stretched out before them, long and ominous, each step echoing loudly in silence. As they rounded a corner, they spotted a group of armed guards ahead, blocking their path.

"Stay close," Gabe whispered, his tone urgent as his hand tightened around John's arm. "We'll get through this."

Chapter Four

Gabe's eyes narrowed as the sound of footsteps echoed closer, the rhythmic clatter of boots on the cold tile floor sending a fresh wave of adrenaline coursing through him. He glanced at John, who was still struggling to regain his strength, his breath coming in ragged gasps. The strain was clear in his eyes, but so was the willpower. "Here's the plan," Gabe murmured, his voice low and steady. "You keep movin', find a way to distract 'em, and I'll take care of the rest."

John swallowed hard, his throat dry and tight. He nodded, the weight of the world pressing down on him, but there was no time for hesitation. The fear gnawed at him, but the need to survive pushed him forward. Gabe darted out from behind the cover of a nearby wall, his movements smooth and practiced as he opened fire on the approaching guards with precise, lethal shots.

The sharp crack of gunfire echoed through the narrow hallway, mingling with the panicked shouts of the guards as they scrambled for cover. John's heart pounded in his chest, each beat a drumroll of fear and urgency. This was no longer a nightmare he could wake from it was terrifyingly real. He saw his chance and sprinted forward, his legs burning with the effort as he ducked low to avoid the hail of bullets whizzing past him. The acrid smell of gunpowder filled his nostrils, burning with a harshness that made him wince as he reached for the scattered weapons on the floor.

John dropped to his knees, the cold tile pressing against his skin as he grabbed a rifle and rolled to his feet in one fluid motion. He'd never fired a gun before, the weight of it unfamiliar and intimidating, but desperation sharpened his focus. He aimed and fired, his shots wild and erratic, but enough to provide the cover Gabe needed.

Gabe moved like a shadow, his movements fluid and purposeful, weaving between pillars and overturned gurneys. Together, they created a deadly crossfire, systematically taking down the remaining guards with brutal efficiency. The chaos of the battle slowly ebbed away, leaving behind a hallway littered with bodies, the only sound was their ragged, heavy breathing.

The silence that followed was oppressive, the air thick with the stench of blood and burnt gunpowder. They exchanged a brief nod, the adrenaline still coursing through their veins, their minds racing with the need to keep moving. Gabe scanned the corridor, his eyes sharp and calculating, ensuring no more threats were lurking in the shadows, while John took a moment to catch his breath, his mind reeling from the intensity of the confrontation.

"We need to keep movin'," Gabe said, his voice steady despite the chaos they had just survived. The calmness in his tone was almost unnerving as if he had done this a hundred times before. "The stairwell should be just around the corner."

John nodded, steeling himself for whatever lay ahead. His muscles ached, and his nerves were frayed, but there was no turning back now. They moved quickly, their footsteps echoing in the deserted hallway, a stark reminder of how isolated they were. As they rounded the corner, they saw the stairwell door, guarded by two more soldiers.

Gabe and John exchanged a look, silently communicating their next move. The unspoken understanding between them was palpable, a testament to the trust they had forged in such a brief time. With a final nod, they sprang into action, ready to fight their way to freedom.

A furious exchange of gunfire erupted in the narrow corridor, the sound deafening in the confined space. Gabe and John moved with practiced precision; their movements synchronised as they took down the guards one by one. The air was thick with the acrid smell of gunpowder, the harsh fluorescent lights casting eerie shadows on the walls.

As the last guard fell, Gabe quickly reloaded his weapon, his eyes scanning the corridor for any additional threats. The stairwell loomed ahead, a potential escape route, but also a potential trap. Gabe approached it cautiously, his senses on high alert. He peered down the staircase, listening for any sounds of movement below.

"Clear for now," Gabe whispered, nodding at John. "Let's move."

They descended quickly, the stairwell echoing with the sound of their hurried footsteps. The scent of fresh air grew stronger with each step, a promise of freedom that spurred them on. When they finally emerged into an alleyway, the cool breeze against their faces was a welcome relief, washing away the stale, metallic taste of fear that had clung to them.

Blinking in the bright sunlight, they spotted a parked motorcycle, its chrome gleaming in the midday light. Gabe swung his leg over the bike, his movements quick and practiced, and kicked the stand up with a sharp snap. "This will have to do," he muttered, tossing John the spare helmet.

John caught it awkwardly, his hands still trembling from the adrenaline. For a moment, he stood there, staring at the classic motorcycle in awe, the sheer absurdity of the situation hitting him all at once. It was a brief moment of surreal clarity in the midst of chaos. But reality snapped back into focus as Gabe cleared his throat, the urgency in his gaze pulling John back to the present.

"Hang on tight," Gabe said, gunning the engine. The roar of the motorcycle filled the alleyway, the vibrations reverberating through John's chest as he climbed onto the back, his grip tightened around Gabe's waist.

They sped through the streets of Berlin, the world around them a blur of colours and sounds. The wind whipped through John's hair, tugging at the helmet, the cool air biting at his skin as they weaved in and out of traffic, the city a maze of narrow streets and sharp corners. The occasional patrol car passed by, but Gabe's skilful manoeuvring kept them out of sight, their path winding through the hidden corners of the city.

Finally, Gabe spotted an abandoned building with boarded-up windows and a *Keine Eintritte* sign hanging crookedly on the door. "This should do," he muttered, pulling up to the building and cutting the engine. The sudden silence was jarring, the stillness almost deafening after the rush of the ride. They dismounted quickly, hurrying inside and ducking into a dusty corner to catch their breath.

John wiped the sweat from his brow, his mind still racing. "I keep having these strange dreams or maybe they're memories. Of this place, but not like this. It's all twisted and wrong."

Gabe glanced at him, concern etched into his face. The shadows in the dimly lit room played tricks with the contours of his expression, making him look older and wearier. "Twisted and wrong, huh?" Gabe mused, his voice softening. "Sounds like you're havin' a rough time, partner. But right now, we need to stay sharp."

John nodded, trying to push the thoughts away, but the images lingered in the back of his mind, unsettling and persistent. "Yeah, you're right. Let's just get out of here."

Gabe peeked out through the cracked door, scanning the area with a practiced eye. The alleyway was still, the air thick with tension, the silence almost palpable. In the distance, he noticed a small building with a sign that read "*Gartenhau*s," the faint glow of a streetlamp casting eerie shadows across its façade.

"Over there," Gabe whispered, nodding towards the building. "That might be our ticket out."

They ducked behind a low wall, their movements cautious and deliberate as they made their way to the building. Inside, they found an elderly woman knitting by a small fire, the warm glow of the flames was a stark contrast to the coldness they had just escaped. Gabe approached her cautiously, his tone respectful as he spoke in German.

"*Ich hoffe, wir stören dich nicht. Mein Name ist Gabe und das ist mein Freund John. Wir sind amerikanische Soldaten und wir ähm nun, wir stecken irgendwie in der Klemme,*" Gabe said, his voice steady but carrying a note of urgency. ("I hope we're not disturbing you. My name is Gabe, and this is my friend John. We're American soldiers, and we well, we're in a bit of a bind.")

The woman looked up from her knitting, her sharp, knowing eyes taking in the two men with a quick, assessing glance. She nodded slowly, setting her knitting aside as if she had been expecting them all along.

"*Sie sind also endlich hier,*" she murmured, her voice thick with a German accent but soft and calm. "*Ich wurde gewarnt, dass Sie kommen würden.*" ("So, you've finally arrived. I was warned that you would come.")

Gabe's expression tightened, but he nodded, understanding that they were treading in dangerous waters. "*Wir brauchen Ihre Hilfe. Irgendwelche Informationen oder Dokumente, die Sie haben, könnten unser Leben retten,*" he said, his tone serious. ("We need your help. Any information or documents you have could save our lives.")

The old woman nodded again and rose slowly from her chair. She moved with the deliberate slowness of age but with an air of purpose, as if she knew that every second counted. She handed Gabe a small stack of papers, her hands steady despite her years.

"Sie sagten mir, dass Sie beide auftauchen würden. Ich weiß, dass er kein Deutsch spricht, also werde ich Ihnen das sagen. Stellen Sie sicher, dass er dieses Papier sieht, nachdem Sie an Ihrem Ziel angekommen sind. Alles andere ist Müll. Beide Seiten warten darauf." ("They told me you two would show up. I know he does not speak German, so I'll say this to you. Make sure he sees this paper after you reach your destination. Everything else is garbage. Both sides are waiting for it.")

Gabe's eyes widened slightly, but he nodded. *"Danke, Fräulein. Wir werden jetzt gehen. Wir sehen uns in der Zukunft,"* Gabe replied, taking the papers carefully. ("Thank you, ma'am. We'll go now. We'll see you in the future.")

The woman smiled slightly, a sad but knowing smile that hinted at more than she was letting on. She returned to her seat and resumed her knitting, the soft click of needles filling the silence as if nothing had happened.

As they moved deeper into the building, Gabe sifted through the papers, his expression focused, tossing aside old bills and ledgers that meant nothing in the grand scheme of things. Finally, he handed John a folded piece of paper, the edges worn, the ink smudged in places.

"This one is for you. Have a look before we try time hopping again."

John unfolded the note, his heart pounding in his chest as he read the cryptic message: **"Seekers of temporal order, the hourglass turns. Join us at the crossroads of past and future, where destiny awaits. Apply within."**

John frowned, the words swirling in his mind, incomprehensible and foreboding. "This doesn't make any sense, Gabe. Who knew we were here?"

Gabe placed a hand on John's shoulder, his grip firm and reassuring, a small smile playing at the corners of his lips. "I'll keep a hold on you this time before we get started."

With a practiced motion, Gabe pressed the hopper on his lapel. A bright light engulfed them both, the world around them twisting and warping as they were pulled through time, the fabric of reality unravelling and reweaving itself around them.

The sky above darkened, replaced by a swirling vortex of colours, a kaleidoscope of time and space. The buildings of Berlin melted away, their solid forms dissolving into the chaos of history itself. The ground beneath their feet seemed to disappear, replaced by the infinite void of the time stream, a place where past, present, and future collided in a violent, beautiful storm.

"We're doing it, John," Gabe said, his voice firm, a steady anchor in the chaos. "This feels right this time."

Time seemed to slow, the world around them a blur of colours and light, the sensation of weightlessness giving way to a pressure that pressed against their skin, a reminder of the forces at work. And then, with a final lurch, the world snapped back into focus.

They stood in a dimly lit corridor, the sterile white walls and gleaming metal surfaces a stark contrast to the war-torn streets they had just left behind. The buzz of machinery filled the air, a testament to the bustling activity of the time travel operation, the sound both familiar and alien.

Gabe smiled warmly, the tension of the jump fading as he looked at John. "Well, kid, you did it. You made it through your first real jump."

A nearby time agent, dressed in the crisp uniform of the Lennox Time Corporation, gestured for them to follow, his expression professional but curious. Gabe handed John the small-time travel device, the weight of it heavy in his hand, a symbol of the journey he had just undertaken.

"Here you go, kid. You're one of us now," Gabe said with a grin, the pride in his voice unmistakable.

John took the hopper, feeling a mix of awe and responsibility settle over him like a mantle. They continued down the corridor, the atmosphere growing more surreal with each step, the walls lined with banks of computers and holographic displays that flickered with data from across time. Outside, the shadows of something massive moved across the sky, unnoticed by those inside, a reminder that the world they had entered was vast and full of mysteries.

Inside the debriefing room, a team of scientists and researchers waited, their faces eager, curious, and perhaps a little wary. As they took their seats at the long, polished table, Gabe leaned in close to John, his voice low but steady.

"Just remember, kid. I won't give you the 'with great power comes great responsibility' speech, but it is kinda true. You've got a lot riding on those shoulders now."

John nodded, his heart racing with excitement and anticipation for the adventures that lay ahead, completely unaware of the true nature of their new surroundings, and the trials that awaited him.

Chapter Five

The debriefing room hummed with the energy of controlled chaos. Scientists and researchers around the table were engrossed in their discussions, their voices a mix of excitement and tension. The familiar sterile environment offered some comfort, but John's unease only deepened as he noticed subtle, unsettling details: the strange, unfamiliar plants that seemed to thrive just outside the windows, and the shadows that moved in ways that defied logic. It was as if the world outside had shifted, slightly but unmistakably, into something else.

The debriefing proceeded, and the room bathed in the cool glow of monitors displaying data and schematics. Charts and maps were projected on the walls, highlighting key points and objectives from their mission in Berlin. Dr Morrison, the lead scientist, spoke with meticulous precision, his sharp, analytical eyes scanning the room to ensure every detail was understood. His voice, though calm, carried an underlying urgency that added to the tension in the room.

John tried to focus on the discussion, his thoughts still tangled with the chaos and danger of 1944. He answered questions about their encounters with the German soldiers, the layout of the hospital, and the obstacles they had faced. His voice was steady, but his mind kept drifting, the stark contrast between the war-torn past and the clinical present disorienting him further. The more he tried to ground himself in the now, the more he felt as though the ground beneath him was slipping away.

As the meeting finally wrapped up, John felt a strange dissonance between the sterile environment of the debriefing room and the chaotic, visceral memories of Berlin. The room's quiet hum of technology contrasted sharply with the gunfire and fear that still echoed in his mind. Following Gabe out of the room, he couldn't help but wonder how they had gone from dodging bullets to this controlled, almost surreal world.

"Come on, let's get you settled in," Gabe said, his voice steady and reassuring as they stepped into the corridor. The sleek, polished floors and walls, illuminated by a soft ambient glow, seemed almost too perfect, too untouched by the reality John had just experienced.

As they walked, John's curiosity got the better of him. The large leaves and vibrant colours of the plants outside caught his attention, and the vague shapes in the sky were those really pterosaurs? "Gabe, did you notice anything strange outside?" he asked, his voice tinged with both awe and confusion.

Gabe's smile was cryptic, almost amused. "You've got a keen eye, kid. There's a lot more to this place than meets the eye."

They continued walking, the odd tranquillity of the place doing little to ease the tension still coiled in John's chest. His mind kept flashing back to the shootout on the orphanage roof, to Derek's betrayal, and to the strange, disorienting leap through time that had dumped them into Berlin. The memories felt both immediate and distant, like a bad dream that clung stubbornly to the edges of his consciousness.

"Hard to believe we got through all that," John murmured, shaking his head as if to clear it.

Gabe nodded, his expression serious. "Yeah, but we did. And we'll figure this out too. Just gotta stay sharp."

John took a deep breath, feeling a bit more grounded by Gabe's steady presence. "Thanks, Gabe. For everything."

Gabe tipped his hat slightly, his eyes softening. "Anytime, partner."

They stepped outside into an open courtyard, and John's breath caught in his throat. Towering plants with massive leaves surrounded them, and the sky was dotted with the unmistakable silhouettes of pterosaurs gliding gracefully through the air. The world around them was both alien and strangely beautiful, a place where ancient history and futuristic technology coexisted.

"Gabe, where are we?" John asked, his voice filled with awe.

Gabe's knowing smile widened. "Welcome to the Yucatan Peninsula, 65 million years in the past," he announced. "This is the LTC Training Division. I remember my first time here; it's a lot to take in."

John tried to absorb the scale of what he was seeing. The facility itself was a marvel, with sleek, futuristic buildings that looked out of place in this ancient world. It was as if he had stepped into a different dimension, one where the rules of time and space had been rewritten.

"This is incredible," John said, still trying to wrap his mind around the reality of where he was. The advanced technology and the pristine, untouched environment were a stark contrast to the war-torn streets of Berlin they had just left behind.

Gabe walked beside him, a reassuring presence amidst the unfamiliar surroundings. "Yeah, it's a whole different world here. You'll get used to it," he said with a hint of a smile.

As they approached the main entrance to the LTC Training Division, the gates slid open with a soft hiss, revealing a woman who radiated both authority and warmth. Her auburn hair was tied back in a ponytail, and her bright green eyes sparkled with a mixture of professionalism and friendliness.

"Welcome to the Lennox Time Corporation Training Division," she said, her voice clear and confident. "I'm Sarah Thompson, the facility's director. I'll be overseeing your training."

Gabe nodded in acknowledgement; his posture relaxed yet respectful. "Sarah, this is John. He's the recruit we picked up in the late 20th century."

Sarah extended her hand to John, who shook it, feeling a bit more at ease with her welcoming demeanour. "It's a pleasure to meet you, John. I understand you've been through quite an ordeal. We're here to help you get settled and prepare you for the challenges ahead."

John nodded, grateful for her kindness. "Thank you, Dr Thompson. I'm still trying to process everything."

"That's perfectly normal," Sarah assured him with a warm smile. "We'll take it one step at a time. For now, let me show you around and explain what you'll be doing here."

As Sarah led them through the gates, John couldn't help but feel a sense of anticipation mixed with unease. The high-tech surroundings were almost overwhelming in their sophistication, and the glimpses of the prehistoric landscape beyond the facility's walls were both awe-inspiring and unsettling.

But as they walked, the tension between Sarah and Gabe became more apparent. Just outside the orientation room, Sarah stopped, her eyes narrowing as she turned to Gabe. "What the hell are you thinking, Gabe? John can't be here! Do you have any idea what this might do to?"

Gabe cut her off, his voice calm but firm. "His recruitment comes straight from the top. I'm here to help monitor his training and participate in any time travel missions concerning him. Trust me, he's here for a reason."

Sarah's eyes flashed with frustration as she jammed a finger into Gabe's shoulder. "I still don't think he should be here. He doesn't fit the criteria for recruitment."

Gabe's expression remained neutral, but his voice was edged with a quiet authority. "Like it or not, he's here now. And he needs our protection. Make sure he doesn't have any accidents."

Sarah sighed, her anger simmering just below the surface. "Alright, but we'll keep a close eye on him."

As they resumed their tour, John couldn't shake the feeling that he had just witnessed the surface of a much deeper conflict. Sarah's tension and Gabe's quiet resolve lingered in his mind, but he pushed those thoughts aside, focusing on the information Sarah was providing. The facility was vast, each new section revealing advanced technology and resources that far surpassed anything he had ever imagined.

Finally, they came to a stop near the entrance to the orientation room. Sarah gestured towards the door, her voice still carrying the professional warmth she had maintained throughout the tour. "This is where you'll begin your formal orientation, John. It's crucial that you familiarise yourself with the protocols and expectations here. We want you to succeed."

John nodded, feeling a mix of anticipation and unease. The sheer scale of what he was about to undertake was daunting, but he was determined to face it head-on.

Gabe, who had been quietly observing, stepped forward, his expression softening just a bit. "Good. John, go start your orientation. I'll be down in the cantina having a drink," he said, his voice calm but with a hint of something unspoken. He gave John a brief, reassuring nod before turning away, his long coat catching a slight, invisible breeze as he walked slowly towards the cafeteria.

John watched Gabe Walk away, feeling a pang of uncertainty but also a growing sense of resolve. He took a deep breath and turned back to the orientation room, ready to face whatever came next.

Dr Thompson's eyes followed Gabe's retreating figure, narrowing with a mix of frustration and concern. "Gabe, this is highly unprofessional," she called after him, her tone sharp with disapproval. "Your presence is required during the orientation."

Gabe paused mid-step, turning slightly to glance back at her. "Ma'am, the kid's in good hands with you. I reckon I need a moment to clear my head," he replied, his voice steady but tinged with his signature cowboy drawl.

Dr Thompson sighed, clearly frustrated but resigned. "We can't afford any laxity, especially not now. The integrity of our operations is key."

Gabe tipped his hat slightly, acknowledging her concern. "I'll be back soon, ma'am," he said, before continuing on his way, his long coat trailing behind him as he walked with deliberate calm towards the cafeteria.

Dr Thompson turned to John, her expression softening slightly, though the tension remained in her eyes. "I apologise for that, John. Let's get you started with your orientation. There's a lot to cover, and we need to make sure you're fully prepared."

John nodded, sensing the underlying tension but appreciating Dr Thompson's professionalism. "It's alright. I'm ready to get started," he said, trying to sound more confident than he felt.

They entered the orientation room, where a large holographic display flickered to life, casting a soft glow over the faces of the new recruits. Sarah walked down the aisle, her posture straight and authoritative as she took her place behind the podium. The room quieted; all eyes fixed on her as she began to speak.

"Hello, everyone," she began, her voice clear and commanding. "I'm Sarah Thompson, the director of the LTC Training Division. Welcome to your new home. We have an incredible journey ahead of us, and I can't wait to see what you all accomplish."

The room erupted into polite applause, and Sarah nodded graciously before continuing. "Before we begin, I want to make something very clear: This is not an ordinary training facility. You have been handpicked for this program because of your unique abilities and backgrounds. You are here because we believe in you and because we believe that you have what it takes to make a difference."

As she spoke, John found himself drawn in by her words, but his mind still buzzed with thoughts of Gabe and the strange tension between him and Dr Thompson. The undercurrents of conflict he had sensed earlier lingered in his thoughts, making him even more determined to prove himself worthy of being here.

"The Lennox Time Corporation's mission is to maintain an unpolluted timeline," Sarah explained, her tone growing more serious. "Time travel, while powerful, comes with great responsibility. Our job is to ensure that history remains unchanged and that any anomalies are corrected swiftly."

One of the recruits raised a hand. "How does the recruitment process work?" they asked, breaking through John's thoughts.

Sarah smiled, clearly prepared for this question. "Good question. Recruitment occurs when a specific person on the timeline exhibits skills that match LTC's criteria. This person is then recruited moments before they are supposed to expire on the timeline and brought here for training."

Another recruit looked puzzled. "Doesn't that pollute the timeline? I mean, if you take someone out of their time right before they die, doesn't that change history?"

Sarah shook her head confidently. "It doesn't. History still records that person's passing as it was supposed to happen. Their removal is so close to their moment of expiration that it leaves no ripple in the timeline. This is why everyone who works at LTC has gone through the same recruitment process. Security and secrecy are paramount to maintaining the integrity of our operations as well as the timeline itself."

As Sarah continued the introductions, pointing out key staff members, John found himself intrigued by the faces she highlighted. Dr Alexander Smith's piercing green eyes met his with a spark of recognition, though John couldn't quite place him. Dr Amelia Johnson, with her regal features and warm golden undertones, seemed vaguely familiar as well. The more he saw, the more questions bubbled up in his mind questions that only deepened his resolve to uncover the truth about this place.

By the time the orientation concluded, John was more determined than ever to make the most of this opportunity, even as the mysteries around him continued to grow. Sarah's final words echoed in his mind as she turned to him directly.

"As soon as Gabe is done at the cantina, I'll have him give you a detailed tour of the facility. It's crucial you get familiar with every part of it."

John nodded in agreement, just as Gabe reappeared behind her, looking more composed but no less serious. As they moved on to explore the facility, John couldn't help but marvel at the seamless integration of advanced technology into the natural surroundings. The corridors, lined with smooth, metallic panels that emitted a soft, ambient glow, felt like a bridge between worlds between the ancient and the futuristic, between the familiar and the unknown.

As the tour progressed, John's initial apprehension began to fade, replaced by a growing sense of purpose. The dormitories, the recreation centre, the cafeteria, the library each space was a testament to the level of care and planning that had gone into creating this place. But it was the simulation lab, with its mind-blowing technology and immersive training environments, that truly captured his imagination.

John's mind buzzed with possibilities as they moved from room to room, each new discovery only deepening his fascination with the world of time travel. Yet, amidst all the excitement, the lingering tension from earlier stayed with him, a subtle reminder that beneath the surface of this pristine facility, there were secrets still waiting to be uncovered.

As the tour concluded and they made their way back to Sarah's office, John couldn't shake the feeling that this was just the beginning both of his training and the mysteries he would have to unravel. Sarah reiterated her confidence in his abilities, her words echoing in his mind as they parted ways.

Chapter Six

John's first training session was a gruelling physical workout led by Jack Banks. The obstacle course was designed to mimic the challenges of a prehistoric environment, complete with uneven terrain, simulated predator attacks, and dense vegetation. The ground beneath John's feet was a mix of hard-packed earth and loose gravel, making each step a test of balance and strength. Ancient trees with thick, knotted roots created natural barriers that the recruits had to navigate around or climb over.

The first obstacle was a series of high walls that they had to scale. John's hands slipped on the damp surfaces, but he gritted his teeth and forced himself upward. The walls were covered in a thin layer of moss, making them slick and challenging to grip. He could hear the distant calls of prehistoric birds, adding to the surreal atmosphere of the training environment.

Next, they had to navigate through a maze of thick vines and underbrush. The vegetation was dense and tangled, creating a labyrinth that tested their agility and problem-solving skills. John's arms were scratched, and his uniform was covered in dirt, but he felt alive, every sense heightened by the challenge. The air was filled with the scent of damp earth and crushed leaves, grounding him in the intensity of the moment. Jack barked orders, his voice carrying over the sounds of their exertion, pushing them to their limits.

During a particularly challenging drill, John found himself struggling with a complex climbing wall. No matter how hard he tried, he couldn't seem to find the right handholds, his frustration growing with each failed attempt.

Gabe watched John struggle with the training exercise, a frown creasing his brow. "Hey, kid, you're overthinking it," he called out, walking over to him.

John looked up, frustration etched on his face. "I just don't get it," he muttered.

Gabe crouched down next to him, his voice lowering. "It's not about getting it right the first time. It's about persistence. You've got the guts, John. Use them."

John nodded, the tension easing slightly. Gabe's words were rough, but there was a kindness in his eyes that gave John a flicker of hope. He took a deep breath, refocusing his energy. Determined to conquer the wall, he approached it again, this time with renewed determination.

With Gabe's encouragement echoing in his mind, John found a rhythm. He moved more instinctively, letting go of his frustration and trusting in his ability. Hand over hand, he pulled himself up, finally reaching the top. He paused for a moment, catching his breath, a triumphant smile spreading across his face.

As he descended the other side, he saw Gabe watching him with a nod of approval. "Good job, kid," Gabe said, his voice carrying a note of pride. "Now keep that fire burning. There's more to come."

John felt a surge of confidence. The challenges ahead seemed less daunting with Gabe's support. He knew he had a long way to go, but for the first time, he genuinely believed he could rise to the occasion.

The rest of the training session was gruelling, but John faced each obstacle with determination. The encouragement from Gabe and the drive to prove himself pushed him forward. By the end of the day, he was exhausted but exhilarated, every muscle aching but his spirit unbroken.

As they regrouped at the training area's exit, Sgt Jack Banks approached them. "Impressive work today, John," he said, a rare smile crossing his face. "You've shown great resilience."

John smiled back, feeling a sense of accomplishment. "Thank you, Sgt Banks."

Gabe clapped a hand on John's shoulder. "Go get cleaned up and get ready for the next phase," he said, pointing John towards the showers. "You've earned it."

In the afternoons, John attended specialised sessions with Dr Tanaka, who delved into the intricacies of genetic adaptations and their impact on time travel missions. Her lectures were comprehensive, covering both the scientific and ethical aspects of genetic modifications. Dr Tanaka's passion for her work was infectious, her eyes lighting up as she explained the enhancements that made their missions possible.

During a break from physical training in the Yucatan Peninsula, John found a moment to sit with Dr Tanaka under the shade of a large tree. The humid air was thick with the sounds of ancient wildlife, and the towering trees provided a welcome respite from the intense sun. John wiped the sweat from his brow and joined Dr Tanaka, who was reviewing some data on a tablet.

"Dr Tanaka, I've been wondering about the genetic modifications we've received. How exactly do they help us in our missions?" John asked, curiosity evident in his voice.

"They enhance your physical and cognitive abilities, tailored to the specific challenges of different eras," Dr Tanaka replied, her tone both informative and reassuring.

"Isn't it risky, altering our genetics?" John pressed a hint of concern in his eyes.

Dr Tanaka smiled, appreciating his caution. "Every modification is carefully tested. We prioritise safety and ethical considerations above all," she explained, her eyes reflecting the seriousness with which she approached her work.

As they resumed training, John felt more aware of the genetic enhancements that made their missions possible, appreciating the science and care behind them. The complexity of the modifications fascinated John, and he found himself eagerly anticipating each session with Dr Tanaka, despite the steep learning curve. The more he learned, the more he understood the delicate balance required to ensure their missions did not disrupt the timeline.

One evening, as John wandered the quiet halls of the facility, unable to sleep, he stumbled upon a secluded corner of the library. Moonlight streamed in through the transparent walls, casting eerie shadows on the floor. His eyes were drawn to a particular book on a nearby shelf titled "The Rise and Fall of an Empire." Its worn leather cover and faded lettering hinted at its age, but it was the message hidden within that caught his attention.

The message was written in an ancient script, one that John had seen in his dreams but couldn't quite place. It seemed to be another cryptic help-wanted ad, calling out for someone with his unique skills and experiences. The more he read, the more he realised that the message was meant for him.

Discreetly, John copied the message into his notebook, determined to decipher its meaning. The script was intricate and filled with symbols that seemed to pulse with a hidden energy. It spoke of "the coming storm" and "the chosen path," phrases that resonated deeply with John's growing sense of purpose. Over the next few days, John approached Dr Johnson and asked for her assistance. She examined the symbols with a furrowed brow, her keen intellect quickly recognising the significance of the script. "This is extraordinary, John," she said, her voice filled with awe. "These symbols suggest a link between your presence here and pivotal events in history."

As John continued his training, he couldn't shake the feeling that the message was somehow connected to his purpose within the time travel program. He became more focused and determined than ever before, pouring himself into his studies and training, driven by the knowledge that the answers he sought lay hidden within the ancient script.

In the combat training centre, Jack Banks took a personal interest in John's progress, pushing him harder than ever before. He told John that he had the potential to become one of the facility's greatest assets, if only he could unlock his full potential. In the research lab, Dr Smith, and Dr Davis both began involving John in discussions about the time travel technology, seeking his insights and observations. It was clear that they valued his unique perspective and experiences.

As John lay in bed one night, his body sore from the day's exertions, his mind raced. The cryptic message haunted his thoughts, its meaning just out of reach. He couldn't help but feel that everything he was experiencing in the training—the camaraderie, the trials was all leading up to something monumental. But what? And why him? He had never considered himself special, but the more he learned, the more he realised that his role in the time travel program was far from ordinary.

The burden of his newfound responsibilities weighed heavily on him. The pressure to live up to the expectations of the LTC, to uncover the secrets of his past, and to decipher the cryptic messages was immense. Yet, amidst the uncertainty, there was a growing sense of resolve within him. He was no longer just a recruit; he was a crucial piece in a puzzle that spanned centuries.

As he stared up at the ceiling, the faint glow of the moon casting shadows across his room, John made a silent vow. He would uncover the truth, no matter the cost. He would rise to the challenge and prove that he was worthy of the trust that had been placed in him.

The facility's alarm system blared one evening, jolting John from his thoughts. Red lights flashed, and a voice over the intercom announced an emergency drill. The recruits scrambled, their training kicking in as they moved with practiced precision. John's heart pounded as he followed the protocols, his mind racing with the possibilities.

As they gathered in the main hall, the tension was palpable. Sarah Thompson addressed the group, her expression calm but serious. "This is a drill," she assured them, "but we must treat it as if it were real. Remember your training and stay focused."

John's eyes darted around the room, taking in the determined faces of his fellow recruits. The emergency procedures were complex, and designed to simulate various scenarios they might encounter. The atmosphere was charged with adrenaline, every sound amplified in the heightened state of alert.

The drill began with a warning siren, indicating that the facility was about to enter lockdown mode. The team was divided into two groups: one responsible for securing a vulnerable section of the perimeter, and the other for dealing with any intruders who managed to breach the defences.

As the drill progressed, John couldn't shake the feeling that something was amiss. The intensity of the exercise seemed disproportionate; the stakes were higher than usual. His instincts screamed that this was more than just a routine drill. He glanced at Gabe, standing nearby, smoking a cigarillo. Their silent exchange confirmed their mutual suspicion.

Just as they got into position, the lights flickered, and the alarm fell silent. The abrupt change sent a ripple of confusion through the group.

Sarah's voice cut through the silence, her tone urgent. "Attention, everyone. This is not a drill. We have a real breach." Panic threatened to overtake the recruits, but Sarah's leadership held them together. "Follow the protocols and stay calm," she instructed. "We will handle this."

John's mind raced as he processed the revelation. A real breach meant real danger, and the stakes had never been higher. He felt a surge of determination, his training kicking in as he prepared to face the unknown threat. The cryptic messages and the growing sense of destiny fuelled his resolve, his purpose clearer than ever.

As the facility braced for the unknown, John knew that this was just the beginning of his journey. The challenges ahead would test his limits, but he was ready. With his friends by his side and the wisdom of the past guiding him, he faced the future with unwavering resolve.

The intruders revealed themselves to be rival time travellers from a competing organisation known as Voskos Temporal Initiative (VTI). They had managed to breach the defences using advanced technology and were now attempting to steal sensitive information and sabotage the reactor core.

The facility's security staff quickly realised who was attacking. The intruders wore distinctive shoulder patches with the letters "VTI" prominently displayed, making it clear they were the source of the breach. The staff recognised the initials immediately and knew they were dealing with a serious threat. All resources were diverted to contain the situation.

John and his team were reassigned to help defend the perimeter while the staff worked to secure the reactor room. The atmosphere was tense as they took up their positions, the air crackling with the urgency of the impending battle. Gabe, ever the steady presence, gave John a firm nod. "Stay sharp, kid. This ain't no drill."

John crouched behind a barricade and turned to Gabe with a puzzled look. "Gabe, who are these VTI guys?"

Gabe's eyes narrowed as he surveyed the battlefield. "They're trouble, kid. But they shouldn't have been able to get in here, not without some serious inside help."

The first wave of VTI operatives hit them hard. They were highly trained and well-equipped, using advanced weaponry and tactics that tested the limits of the facility's defences. John ducked as energy blasts sizzled past him, the air filled with the acrid smell of burning metal and ozone.

"Here they come!" Jack barked, his voice carrying over the din of the firefight. The team responded with precision, returning fire and holding their ground. John's heart pounded in his chest, adrenaline surging through his veins as he squeezed off shots, each one finding its mark.

The VTI operatives were relentless, but so was the defence. The facility's security systems kicked in, automated turrets whirring to life and targeting the intruders. Explosions rocked the perimeter as grenades were thrown, the shockwaves sending debris flying.

"Watch out!" Gabe shouted, pulling John down just as a VTI operative fired a high-tech plasma rifle in their direction. The blast hit the barricade, melting part of it instantly.

John peeked over the edge, his eyes widening as he saw the VTI team deploying a small drone. The drone buzzed towards the reactor room, carrying a payload that could spell disaster. "We have to stop that drone!" he yelled.

"On it!" Gabe replied, aiming with his revolver. With a steady hand, he fired, hitting the drone dead centre and causing it to explode in a shower of sparks.

Despite their efforts, the VTI operatives continued to push forward. John's team fought valiantly, but the sheer number of attackers and their advanced technology made it a brutal struggle. The air was filled with the sounds of gunfire, shouts, and the hum of energy weapons.

Amidst the chaos, John noticed one of the VTI operatives trying to hack into a terminal. He sprinted towards the intruder, tackling him to the ground. They grappled fiercely, John using every ounce of his training to subdue the operative. "You're not getting away with this," he growled, landing a decisive punch that knocked the intruder out.

As the VTI operative slumped to the ground, barely conscious, he sneered at John. "You think you can stop her? You have no idea what you're up against."

John's eyes narrowed. "Who's 'her'? What does she want?"

The operative coughed, a cruel smile spreading across his face. "You'll find out soon enough. She's not one to be trifled with."

Before John could press further, the operative's eyes rolled back, and he passed out. The mention of a female leader sent a chill down John's spine. He had heard whispers of VTI's ruthlessness, but now, with this ominous warning, the threat felt all too real.

"Good job, John!" Jack shouted, providing cover fire. "But stay alert. There's more of them."

The battle raged on, both sides sustaining heavy casualties. The facility's corridors were littered with debris and the wounded; the walls scorched from the intensity of the firefight. John's uniform was torn, his face smeared with dirt and sweat, but he refused to back down.

Eventually, the staff managed to contain the intruders and secure the reactor core. The last of the VTI operatives were either captured or forced to retreat, their mission a failure. John and his team stood among the wreckage; their breaths heavy but victorious. Jack clapped a hand on John's shoulder, his usual stoic expression softened by a rare smile. "You did good, kid."

After the battle, John found a secluded spot in the courtyard to decompress. The adrenaline had faded, leaving behind an overwhelming sense of exhaustion. He sat on a bench under a massive tree, the ancient branches swaying gently in the breeze. The sounds of the jungle around him birdcalls, rustling leaves, and distant animal cries helped calm his racing mind.

He pulled out the notebook where he had copied the cryptic message from the library. The symbols seemed to swirl on the page, their meaning elusive yet tantalizingly close. The words of the VTI operative echoed in his mind: "You'll find out soon enough. She's not one to be trifled with." The connection between the message and the larger conflict with VTI felt undeniable, but the pieces were still scattered.

John closed his eyes, trying to let the tension seep out of his body. He focused on the rhythmic rustling of the leaves, grounding himself in the present moment. It was a rare quiet amid the chaos, and he allowed himself to breathe deeply, clearing his mind of the battle's intensity.

As he sat there, John couldn't help but reflect on how far he had come. The cryptic messages, the brutal training, the fierce battles everything was building towards something greater. But what? The weight of the responsibility pressed down on him, but so did a growing sense of purpose. He was no longer just a recruit; he was a key player in a much larger game.

The encounter with the VTI operative had shaken him, but it had also steeled his resolve. Whoever this mysterious leader was, John knew he had to be ready. The answers he sought were out there, scattered across time and space, waiting to be uncovered.

As the days passed, the adrenaline of the battle gave way to a sobering reality. The breach had exposed vulnerabilities within the facility that couldn't be ignored. The leadership wasted no time in launching a thorough investigation to determine how the VTI operatives had managed to penetrate their defences so easily. Tensions ran high as suspicions of internal compromise surfaced, leading to a thorough review of staff members and protocols.

John, still processing the events, watched as the facility buzzed with renewed urgency. Meetings were held behind closed doors, and the atmosphere was thick with a mix of anxiety and determination. The gravity of what had occurred weighed heavily on everyone, reinforcing the dangerous nature of their work.

It wasn't long before the investigation bore fruit. Several staff members were discovered to have been compromised by the rival time travellers, either through coercion or subtle manipulation. The news sent shockwaves through the ranks, leading to immediate reassignment or dismissal of those involved. It was a stark reminder of the lengths VTI would go to achieve their objectives and the constant threat they posed.

Dr Thompson, as always, stood at the helm, addressing the team with a mix of relief and resolve. "We've learned a lot from this attack. We'll strengthen our defences and be better prepared for any future threats," she declared, her voice carrying the weight of authority and the promise of action.

John stood among his peers; his resolve hardened by the experience. The battle had shown him just how high the stakes were and how vigilant they needed to be. "We won't let them catch us off guard again," he said, his voice firm with conviction.

Throughout it all, John's unique perspective and experiences continued to make him an invaluable asset to the facility. His ability to adapt to new historical contexts and navigate the complexities of time travel earned him the respect of his superiors and colleagues alike. As the facility began to rebuild and strengthen its defences, John knew that his journey was only just beginning.

Exhausted after another intense day of training, John made his way back to his quarters. His mind was racing, trying to piece together everything he had learned about time travel, the timeline, and himself. As he lay down on his bunk, his body heavy with fatigue, the sounds of the facility began to fade.

The soft vibration of machinery and the quiet murmur of voices outside his room became distant until they disappeared completely. His eyelids grew heavy, and the darkness of sleep came swiftly, pulling him under.

Chapter Seven

John's eyes blinked open to the blinding light of the midday sun. A sharp pain shot through his limbs as he tried to move, his muscles were stiff as if they hadn't been used in days. His mouth felt dry, a metallic taste lingering on his tongue, and for a moment, he struggled to remember where he was supposed to be. *A barracks? The training room? No... this wasn't right.*

The smells hit him first dust, sweat, and something oddly familiar. Cooked meat, seasoned with unfamiliar spices, wafted in the air, mingling with the pungent scent of livestock and the acrid tang of burning wood. Disoriented, John pushed himself upright, blinking against the sunlight that streamed down, harsh and relentless. As his vision cleared, his surroundings became more defined.

But they didn't make sense.

Around him, the world was alive with chaos. People moved everywhere, dressed in flowing robes, their sandals slapping against uneven cobblestones. The streets were narrow and lined with stone buildings that seemed ancient yet teeming with life. The clattering of metal on stone rang out, competing with the relentless hum of conversation and the cries of animals—oxen, goats, and something else that he couldn't place. His head whipped back and forth, trying to orient himself, but the scene felt more like a fragment of a dream, or a long-lost memory, than anything real.

Where the hell am I?

He stood slowly, his legs unsteady, and felt the grit of the earth beneath his bare feet *bare feet?* His heart started pounding. His uniform was gone, replaced by a tattered tunic, rough against his skin. Instinctively, he reached for his belt, where his communicator should have been. His fingers fumbled, finding only empty fabric.

No communicator. No gear. Nothing.

"What the hell?" he muttered under his breath, panic bubbling up from the pit of his stomach. His voice felt foreign in his own throat, swallowed up by the cacophony of the world around him.

A vendor nearby caught the sound of his voice, glancing at him with a mixture of curiosity and disdain. He barked something in a language that scratched at John's ears, harsh syllables that sounded like they were spoken through gravel. John's brow furrowed he didn't understand a word. The vendor spat on the ground, gesturing dismissively before turning back to his customers.

John's heart raced. He opened his mouth to call out again, this time louder, more desperate. "Where am I?" His voice cracked, panic seeping into every word. But no one paid him any mind. The people around him moved like a tide, indifferent as if he were invisible.

He tried to focus, to slow his breathing, but his thoughts were a whirlwind. *Think, John, think!* He scanned the crowd again, watching their movements, their gestures, trying to find something *anything* familiar. But it was all wrong. The language grated against his ears, completely foreign. The buildings, the clothing, the sounds… everything was alien.

And then, through the noise, a thought formed at the back of his mind, chilling and cold.

Ancient Rome.

His pulse thundered in his ears, and his eyes darted from face to face, hoping no, praying that this was some kind of trick, a mistake, a nightmare. But the smells, the sounds, the heat of the sun on his skin everything was too real. He tried to swallow, but his throat was too dry.

He was alone. No gear. No backup. No explanation. Just John, standing in the middle of a civilisation that shouldn't exist, surrounded by people who didn't know him, couldn't understand him.

And he had no idea how he got there.

"I don't know where I am! Can you help me?" John's voice cracked, louder now, a plea drenched in desperation as he took a step towards the vendor.

The vendor's face twisted, eyebrows pulling together in something between anger and annoyance. His lips curled back as he spat a harsh reply in that same jagged language John couldn't understand. The man waved him off, gesturing wildly with his hand as if John's very presence was a nuisance, a pest to be shooed away.

John's stomach clenched. The man's dismissive glance, the way his eyes never lingered on John for more than a second, sent a wave of cold realisation through him. He was nothing here. Just another face in the crowd, no more significant than the animals being herded down the street.

"Please, I just need—" John's words were cut short as the vendor turned his back, muttering to himself in the same incomprehensible tongue, as though John's plea for help had been nothing more than the buzzing of a fly in his ear. The man's calloused hands busied themselves with arranging goods on the stall, already moving on as if John had ceased to exist.

John felt the world tilt beneath him, his pulse thudding in his temples. A wave of nausea crashed over him, his legs wobbling beneath the weight of his growing fear. His eyes darted around the street, searching for someone anyone who might offer a shred of recognition, a lifeline in this unfamiliar world. But all he saw were more strangers, more unfamiliar faces moving in a world that felt impossibly far from his own.

His mouth went dry, heart hammering in his chest. It wasn't just the language barrier it was the cold indifference. No one cared. No one even saw him.

What's happening to me?

His vision blurred for a moment, and he pressed a hand to his forehead, fighting the rising panic. The sounds around him grew louder, the clamour of the street crashing into his mind, chaotic and disorienting. The smell of sweat, dirt, and smoke mixed with the scent of cooking meat turned his stomach again.

John staggered backwards, his breath coming in short gasps, a growing sense of dread gnawing at him. *I have to get out of here. I have to figure this out.* But every direction felt the same alien, unknowable, hostile.

His head throbbed with the weight of it all, and he swallowed hard, trying to push down the fear that threatened to overwhelm him. But it was there, just below the surface, gnawing at his resolve.

I'm trapped.

He pushed through the crowd, his movements frantic, weaving between clusters of people who seemed oblivious to his struggle. His eyes darted from one unfamiliar face to the next, searching for anything or anyone that made sense. But each face was a stranger, each voice had an unintelligible hum in the overwhelming din of the marketplace. His heart raced, pounding in his ears, the weight of the situation pressing down harder with each passing second.

John's steps quickened, his shoulders brushing past people who didn't give him a second glance. The crowd closed in around him, bustling, indifferent, swallowing him whole. His breath came in shallow bursts, panic gnawing at the edges of his mind. He was alone, utterly alone, in a world where no one understood him.

A group of young boys darted past, their laughter loud and carefree as they shouted to one another in a rapid stream of words. The cadence was familiar, just barely, a garbled mess of Latin. John strained to catch fragments, his mind struggling to recall the ancient dialects he'd studied at the academy. But without his translation gear, the words slipped through his fingers like sand, their meaning lost in the whirlwind of sounds.

Come on, focus. You've trained for this. You know Latin, John reminded himself, but it was no use. His training felt distant, useless here without the tools he had come to rely on. The language swirled around him, mocking in its familiarity yet unreachable, like trying to grab at smoke.

He turned sharply into a narrow alley, hoping to find a moment of quiet to think, but the walls seemed to close in on him, the space suffocating. His breath came faster, the tightness in his chest making it harder to stay calm. Every step he took echoed off the stone walls, amplifying the sense that he was trapped, enclosed in a world he couldn't navigate.

Suddenly, a fruit vendor at the end of the alley shoved a basket of dates towards him, speaking rapidly, his hands motioning for John to buy. The vendor's face was a mask of impatience, his words blending into the incomprehensible noise that filled John's head.

"I don't want anything," John tried to say, shaking his head, and raising his hands in a universal gesture of refusal. But the vendor wasn't deterred. He stepped closer, his tone sharp and insistent, gesturing emphatically at the dates as if John were just being difficult.

"I don't want anything!" John shouted, his voice hoarse, the panic slipping into his words. His eyes darted around for an escape, but the alley felt too narrow, the walls pressing in on him. He could feel eyes on him now curious, suspicious and the weight of his isolation crashed over him like a wave.

The vendor's expression darkened. His words grew louder, angrier, as he shoved the basket towards John again, almost thrusting it into his chest. People were starting to notice, their eyes flicking towards the commotion. John's pulse quickened, the din of voices around him growing louder, a cacophony that threatened to drown him.

"I said no!" John barked, taking a step back, his heart hammering in his chest. But the vendor didn't back down. He kept speaking, his tone rising, the crowd around them beginning to slow, to stare. The alleyway that had once felt narrow now felt like a trap, with no way out.

John's mind raced. *Get out. Move. You have to keep moving,* he told himself, but his legs felt heavy, weighed down by the unfamiliarity of everything. He took another step back, his head spinning as the reality settled into his gut: there was no one here he could communicate with, no one who understood him. He was on his own.

Before John could back away further, a loud crash erupted from the vendor's stall. The vendor's angry shouts escalated, his words turning into a furious tirade. John's heart leapt into his throat, and before he could process what was happening, an earthenware jug hurtled through the air, spinning wildly past his head. The jug shattered against the stone wall behind him, the shards raining down with a sharp, piercing sound.

John ducked instinctively, his pulse pounding in his ears, the world around him narrowing into sharp focus. He didn't need to understand the words anger was universal. The vendor's frustration had boiled over, and the growing tension in the air signalled that this confrontation was far from over. John's mind screamed at him to move.

The crowd seemed to sense the escalation, their murmurs rising into a low hum of anticipation. People stopped, their eyes narrowing on the foreigner who had unknowingly ignited the vendor's wrath. More voices joined the fray, harsh and accusing. John's chest tightened as the space around him grew smaller, the people pressing in, their curious stares shifting to something more threatening.

Go. Now. The thought cut through his panic like a knife.

Without a second thought, John bolted.

His feet pounded against the cobblestone, his breath coming in short, ragged gasps as he weaved through the narrow streets, his heart hammering in his chest.

Behind him, he could hear the vendor's continued shouts and the sound of heavy footsteps in pursuit. The alleyways twisted and turned, the maze-like streets of the ancient city offering no clear escape route.

The smell of dust and sweat filled his lungs as he sprinted, his boots slipping slightly on the uneven ground. His vision blurred with the sweat pouring down his face, but he didn't dare stop to wipe it away. He pushed through groups of people, his shoulder brushing against cloaks and tunics as he barrelled past. Each glance back confirmed his worst fear: they were following.

John's muscles screamed for relief, but he couldn't stop he wouldn't. The urgency was primal, survival instinct kicking in as he raced down a narrow alley, hoping to lose his pursuers in the winding streets. His heart thundered in his chest, and his breath laboured, as he spotted a narrow gap between two buildings.

Without thinking, he slipped into it, the space barely wide enough for him to squeeze through. The cool shadows of the alley provided momentary shelter, the noise of the marketplace fading behind him. He crouched low, his chest heaving as he pressed himself against the cold stone wall. He wiped the sweat from his brow with a shaky hand, willing his breathing to quiet. The adrenaline still coursed through him, making his limbs feel jittery and weak.

His mind raced, trying to piece together what had just happened. *What the hell is going on?* He had trained for disorientation, for chaotic situations but this was something entirely different. He didn't know where he was, he didn't have his gear, and no one could help him.

John risked a glance back towards the alley entrance, his ears straining to catch any sound of pursuit. The footsteps had faded, the angry shouts replaced by the distant hum of the marketplace. His pulse began to slow, but the tension in his body remained coiled, ready to spring again if necessary.

He crouched behind a pile of discarded pottery shards, trying to gather his thoughts. His chest rose and fell rapidly, the aftershocks of fear still gripping him. Every nerve in his body was on edge, waiting for the next threat, the next danger to present itself.

The weight of his isolation hit him like a wave. He had no idea where he was, no idea what had triggered that hostile encounter, and worst of all, no idea how to communicate with anyone. It was as if the world had suddenly closed in on him, leaving him trapped and powerless. He needed answers, but the only thing that surrounded him was uncertainty.

As he caught his breath, John ran his hands through his hair, his mind racing with questions. *Why am I here? Is this a test?* If it was a training simulation, it had gone off the rails, and if it wasn't the alternative was even more terrifying.

The alleyway remained quiet, the muted sounds of the bustling city drifting in from the streets beyond. John leaned back against the rough stone wall, trying to calm his racing heart. But deep down, the gnawing sense of dread only grew stronger.

He was alone. And for the first time in a long while, John had no idea how to find his way out.

John's thoughts swirled in a chaotic mess. *Where was Gabe? Where was the team?* His fingers absentmindedly brushed the empty spot where his communicator should have been, the absence a cold reminder of his isolation. He had no backup, no gear, and no clue how he had ended up here. The more he tried to piece it together, the more it unravelled. *This isn't right.*

The academy's training simulations were always challenging, pushing him to his limits, but they never left him this vulnerable. He was always equipped with a fail-safe, a way to communicate or at least the reassurance that someone was watching. This time, though, there was nothing. No safety net. No invisible hand guiding him.

It felt too real. The grit of the streets beneath his feet, the noise of the bustling marketplace, the sun baking his skin it was all too vivid, too raw. A creeping thought began to gnaw at the edges of his mind. *What if this wasn't a simulation?*

The hours ticked by, each one more torturous than the last. Without his gear or any means to communicate, he was truly alone trapped in a world he barely understood. His training had prepared him for survival, but not for this not for the utter helplessness that was starting to settle into his bones.

Survive, he reminded himself, *adapt.*

John positioned himself in the shadow of a large archway, watching, waiting. His eyes darted from one person to the next, analysing every gesture, and every interaction. If he couldn't understand their words, he would have to rely on the universal language of body movement and facial expression. Romans moved with a confidence that belied the chaos of their daily lives. Their gestures were sharp and purposeful. He observed the way they bartered, the way they held themselves with authority when speaking, the subtle nods and hands extended in exchange for goods. They communicated with their entire bodies, and after a few hours, John felt like he was starting to understand the rhythm of it.

When the sun began to dip lower in the sky, casting long shadows across the stone streets, hunger gnawed at him. He hadn't eaten since waking up in this strange place, and his stomach was beginning to cramp. He decided to test what he had learned, cautiously stepping away from his hiding spot. Blending into the crowd, he navigated the streets until he came across a small food stand.

The vendor, an elderly man with a long grey beard and weathered skin, didn't seem as hostile as the others John had encountered. His movements were slow but deliberate as he arranged loaves of bread and other modest foodstuffs on display. John stood back for a moment, observing the other customers. He noticed how they interacted through short exchanges, brisk gestures, and a quick trade of coins for food. He had to mimic that if he wanted to avoid trouble.

With deliberate, careful steps, John approached the stand. His heart pounded in his chest as he pointed to a small loaf of bread, his movements slow and non-threatening. The vendor stared at him for a moment, eyes narrowed as if assessing whether John was a friend or foe. A tense silence hung between them, but finally, the old man gave a slight nod and handed over the loaf.

John exhaled quietly, grateful for the small victory. He glanced around, noticing another patron show a coin to the vendor before walking off with their purchase. Mimicking the gesture, John held out his palm, displaying that he had no coin. The vendor's eyes darkened with suspicion, his gaze flicking between John's face and his empty hand. For a moment, John braced himself for a confrontation and prepared to bolt if things turned sour.

But instead, the old man huffed, muttering something under his breath, and waved John away dismissively. The tension left John's body in a slow release as he clutched the loaf to his chest. It wasn't much, but it was a start. He offered a nod of gratitude before quickly melting back into the crowd, disappearing among the sea of faces.

As the days passed, John's survival instincts took over. Each dawn brought new challenges, but also new lessons. He learned how to navigate the labyrinth of narrow streets and bustling markets, his eyes constantly scanning for opportunities. He became a ghost in the city, moving unnoticed among the Romans, blending in with the throngs of people. He scavenged what he could, picking up scraps of food and observing the routines of the city's underbelly.

His clothes became dust-covered and worn, his body leaner from the constant physical strain and sparse meals. His hair, once neatly cropped, grew shaggy, blending with the dirt that clung to his skin. But survival was more than just physical it was mental. And John's mind was constantly on edge, teetering between hope and desperation.

The nights were the worst. Alone in whatever dark corner he could find to rest, his thoughts raced. Each crack of a twig, each distant shout would send his heart racing, his body tensing for a fight or flight. Sleep became a luxury he couldn't afford, and even when exhaustion claimed him, his dreams were filled with fleeting images of the academy, of Gabe, of the team he'd left behind. He would wake up drenched in sweat, disoriented and gasping for breath.

Each day, a new hope would rise with the sun that he would see someone familiar, that this would all turn out to be part of some elaborate test. But as the days stretched into what felt like an eternity, that hope began to dwindle.

His isolation gnawed at him. No one was coming for him.

At first, John had told himself that it was just a delay. Maybe the team was having trouble tracking him down. Maybe they were facing their own challenges in this unfamiliar timeline. But as the days dragged on with no sign of rescue, a deep, sinking feeling settled into his chest.

What if no one's looking?

The thought made his stomach turn, a pit of dread opening inside him. He was trained to handle the impossible, but this being completely cut off, no communication, no sense of time or place was beyond even the academy's worst-case scenario drills. The loneliness gnawed at him, a constant, hollow ache.

He couldn't give up. *There had to be a way out.*

Every now and then, John thought he saw something out of place, a flicker of technology hidden in the folds of history. A faint reflection in the corner of his eye, a strange hum that seemed to vibrate through the air moments that made his pulse quicken with hope. But every time he turned to investigate, it was gone. Vanished. Just like his chances of escape.

The days dragged on, and John felt more and more like a ghost trapped in a world that wasn't his. His grip on time itself felt slippery, his sense of reality fraying at the edges. His training had prepared him for tough missions, but nothing like this. He was beginning to lose hope.

Until the note.

It appeared one morning and slipped into the folds of his cloak as he woke under the archway where he'd taken shelter. John nearly dismissed it as a piece of trash, but the faint weight of paper so out of place in this period caught his attention. Heart pounding, he unfolded the rough parchment.

The handwriting was sharp, precise yet familiar in its mystery:

John, you're being watched. Adapt or perish. The key is beneath your feet.

He stared at the note, his breath catching in his throat. A flood of memories washed over him memories of notes from his childhood, from his time in the orphanage, those same cryptic, seemingly omniscient clues left by someone who knew far more than they should. Those notes had guided him through some of the darkest moments of his life, always appearing just when he needed them. But this note felt different. There was something colder, more urgent about it.

Whoever had sent the previous messages had never been this direct, this pointed. The cryptic tone was the same, but the stakes felt higher now. His heart raced with a mix of dread and curiosity. *Watched? By who? And what did they mean, "adapt or perish"?* The words lingered in his mind like a warning, each syllable heavy with the threat of his situation.

John's fingers tightened around the note as he read it again, his eyes scanning the message for any hidden meaning. But it was clear far too clear for comfort.

The key is beneath your feet.

He lowered his gaze, eyes scanning the dusty ground beneath him. His mind churned with possibilities. *Was this literal? Was there something buried beneath him? Or was it metaphorical, a clue, an instruction to pay attention to something he'd missed?*

The thought that someone was watching him tracking his every move made his skin crawl. He wasn't just alone; he was under surveillance. His instincts screamed at him to find out who was behind this, but with no communicator, no gear, and no backup, the idea of uncovering this mystery on his own felt impossible. Still, if this note was anything like the ones he'd received in the past, it wasn't just a taunt. It was a lifeline.

But why now? Why here?

John's gaze swept the surrounding streets, searching for anything unusual, any indication that someone might be following him. The city moved as it always had no signs of anything out of the ordinary. But that only made the note more unsettling. Whoever had placed it there had done so with precision, without leaving a trace.

Kneeling, John brushed the dirt and debris beneath him, as if the ground might hold some hidden secret. His fingers brushed over the rough stone, feeling for any inconsistencies, any sign of a hidden compartment or clue. But there was nothing but the cold, unyielding stone beneath his hands.

Frustration bubbled up inside him. He was being played. Again.

But if the note was right if the key to getting out of this was somehow beneath his feet he couldn't afford to give up. He'd seen this kind of game before. Whoever was behind the notes had always known more than they let on, and every time, those messages had led him through the maze. This one would be no different. It had to be.

Taking a deep breath, John stood, slipping the note into his pocket. His mind whirred as he mentally replayed every interaction, every place he'd been since arriving in this timeline. Something had to connect. Something had to make sense.

Because if it didn't, he was as good as dead.

Chapter Eight

The days continued to blur together, a relentless battle for survival in a world that seemed both ancient and alien. John's body ached from sleeping on hard stone floors, his muscles stiff and sore from the constant strain. Hunger gnawed at his insides, his stomach a near-constant reminder that he hadn't had a proper meal in days. Every bite he managed to scrounge from the markets or beg from a vendor was barely enough to keep him moving. He was surviving, but only just.

But worse than the physical exhaustion was the sense of disconnection from time itself. He wasn't just stuck in the past he was lost, cut off from everything and everyone he knew. It was as if reality had frayed at the edges, and he was caught in the strands. Each day that passed only deepened the isolation, the nagging feeling that this wasn't a simple simulation but something more insidious. He was being tested and pushed to his limits in ways he couldn't fully understand.

His mind kept returning to the note. *"The key is beneath your feet."* The words echoed in his head, maddening in their simplicity. *What key? What was beneath him?* Every cobbled street, every alley, every stone he passed seemed to mock him, offering no answers. He had walked the roads of Rome for days, scouring the ground beneath his feet, searching for anything—*anything*—that would make sense of the message. But the city offered only more questions and more frustration. The note felt like a cruel riddle, one he couldn't solve no matter how hard he tried.

The weariness weighed on him like a physical burden, his mind fraying at the edges as the days passed. How much longer could he keep this up? How much longer before he simply couldn't push forward anymore?

And then he saw it.

At first, it was nothing just another uneven patch of cobblestone in a city filled with such imperfections. He almost missed it entirely. But something in the way the stones sat caught his eye, something in the pattern that seemed off. John's gaze lingered on the ground, narrowing in suspicion. Slowly, he crouched down, his fingers tracing the surface.

A crack.

It was barely noticeable at first glance, just a hairline fracture in the cobblestone. But as he looked closer, his heart began to race. The line was too straight, too deliberate to be a natural part of the street. It wasn't random like the rest of the cracks and seams in the weathered stones it had a purpose.

John's pulse quickened; the weariness of days spent searching momentarily forgotten. His hands trembled as he pressed his fingers against the crack, feeling along the edges of the stone. The cobblestone was rough beneath his fingertips, but as he pressed harder, it shifted ever so slightly. His breath caught in his throat.

He glanced around quickly, his eyes scanning the streets for any signs of onlookers. The Romans moved about their day, as usual, oblivious to him and the strange discovery beneath his feet. No one seemed to notice or care about the lone foreigner crouching in the street. But John had learned enough in his time here to know that appearances could be deceiving. He couldn't afford to draw attention.

Satisfied that he was alone, John's fingers dug into the gap between the stones, prying at the edges. His heart pounded in his chest as the stone shifted beneath his grip. It was heavy, and his fingers scraped against the rough surface, but after a few agonising moments of effort, it lifted.

Beneath the stone was a small hatch, hidden in plain sight. It was unremarkable at first glance just a flat, metal panel, weathered by time and dirt. But to John, it was everything. His hands trembled as he wiped away the dust and grime, revealing a simple latch.

His breath came in short, shallow bursts, the rush of adrenaline making his hands shake. Could this be it? Was this what the note had been referring to? The key beneath his feet?

There was no time to hesitate. His instincts screamed at him to open it, to see what lay beneath. Without a second thought, John pulled the latch.

The hatch creaked open, revealing a dark, narrow tunnel that descended into the earth. The air that rose from below was cool and damp, carrying the faint scent of stone and earth long undisturbed. The darkness beckoned, silent and foreboding.

John stared down into the void, his pulse racing. This was it. The answer, or at least the next step. But something about the tunnel felt wrong, as though it was waiting for him expecting him. He swallowed hard, the weight of the moment pressing down on him.

He was trapped in the past, lost in a world that didn't belong to him. But maybe just maybe this was his way out.

Taking a deep breath, John steeled himself and lowered his foot onto the first rung of a hidden ladder. With a final glance around the street above, he descended into the unknown.

Was this the key?

John's heart pounded as he began his descent into the darkness. The ladder creaked beneath his weight, each step echoing in the enclosed tunnel as the world above faded from view. The air around him grew colder, heavy with the scent of damp earth and stone. The walls, rough and uneven, pressed in on him from all sides, adding to the growing sense of claustrophobia. Every breath felt louder in the confined space, each exhale bouncing off the narrow stone walls like a whisper from the past.

He kept descending, deeper and deeper, the tunnel twisting and turning in ways that made it impossible to gauge his direction. Disoriented, he forced himself to keep moving, the memory of the note pushing him forward: *"The key is beneath your feet."* But what kind of key? And where did it lead?

The cold seeped into his bones as he reached the bottom of the ladder. His feet touched solid ground, but the oppressive darkness still clung to him, making it hard to see more than a few feet ahead. John hesitated for a moment, his instincts screaming at him to turn back, to climb up to the relative safety of the city above. But nothing was waiting for him in Rome, no answers, no allies. He had to press forward. This was the only lead he had.

The tunnel opened into a narrow passage, barely wide enough for him to walk through. The walls were uneven, ancient, and wet with condensation. He moved cautiously, his fingers grazing the stone as he navigated the winding path, his every step measured, deliberate. His breath formed a fine mist in the cold air, the silence around him broken only by the occasional drip of water echoing from somewhere deep within the tunnel system.

And then, after what felt like an eternity of walking, the passage widened. The walls drew back, and John stepped into a small chamber.

His breath caught in his throat.

The chamber was simple, its rough stone walls illuminated by a faint, unnatural glow. At the centre of the room, surrounded by dirt and ancient debris, was something that had no place here something that didn't belong. A machine.

It sat there, humming faintly, its sleek, metallic surface starkly out of place amid such an ancient setting. John's eyes widened in disbelief. The machine was far too modern, too sophisticated to exist in the Rome he had been wandering through. Its polished metal gleamed in the dim light, the smooth edges and intricate mechanisms looking more at home in a futuristic lab than in a forgotten underground chamber.

A glitch in the simulation.

John's heart raced. His mind buzzed with a dozen conflicting thoughts. *Was this real?* It had to be part of the simulation as nothing else made sense. But why was it here, hidden away, buried beneath the city like some kind of secret relic? Was this his way out?

His feet moved before his mind had fully processed the situation, carrying him closer to the machine. He reached out, his fingers trembling as they hovered just above the surface. The metal was cool to the touch, smooth, almost unnaturally so. It vibrated faintly under his fingertips, like a pulse alive in a way that set John's nerves on edge.

As he touched it, the machine reacted, humming louder. Lights flickered across its surface, small digital readouts blinking to life. Symbols and numbers flashed in rapid succession, too fast for John to make sense of. His pulse quickened as the machine's energy seemed to fill the chamber, the hum growing more intense, vibrating through the ground beneath his feet.

And then, without warning, the machine spoke.

The voice was mechanical, cold and flat, but there was something disturbingly human about it. "John. You have found the key."

John froze, his hand still resting on the machine, heart thudding in his chest. The voice knew his name. How? He swallowed hard, his mouth dry, trying to steady his breath. "Who—who are you?" he asked, his voice barely above a whisper.

There was a long pause, the hum of the machine intensifying. The symbols on the display shifted again, forming strange, alien patterns before disappearing.

"We are watching."

The words sent a chill down John's spine. He pulled his hand away from the machine, stepping back instinctively. His mind raced. *Who was watching? Was this still part of the simulation, or had he stumbled onto something far more dangerous?*

He glanced around the chamber, the oppressive silence returning as the machine's voice faded. The sense of being watched was overwhelming now, the hairs on the back of his neck standing on end. He felt exposed and vulnerable. The machine was more than just a tool it was a message, a warning.

"Adapt or perish," the voice added, the finality in its tone sending a wave of dread through him.

John's mind reeled. *Adapt or perish? What did that mean? Was he supposed to solve something, survive some kind of test?* The cryptic message echoed in his thoughts, offering no answers, only more questions. His gaze flicked back to the machine, the display now blank, the hum quieter but still present a constant reminder that this wasn't over.

He took another step back, breathing hard, trying to gather his thoughts. *This was all part of the simulation.* It had to be. But why did it feel like something far more real, far more threatening than a simple training exercise?

The machine offered no further answers, its silence as unnerving as its words. John knew one thing for certain this was a test, but it was no ordinary one. Someone, or something, was pulling the strings. Watching. Waiting to see what he would do next.

The cold darkness pressed in around him, but his path was clear. There was no turning back now. He had to adapt. Or perish.

"Simulation integrity compromised. Initiating fail-safe."

The machine's voice was cold and detached, a stark contrast to the rising panic in John's chest. The room around him shuddered as the walls flickered and warped, the stone crumbling like a mirage breaking apart. The ground beneath his feet rippled unnaturally as if the very fabric of reality was being torn apart at the seams. He stumbled backwards, his pulse racing as the flickering grew more violent, the ancient chamber dissolving in jagged bursts of light and shadow.

John's eyes darted to the machine, its display flashing in rapid succession, numbers spiralling out of control. He could hear the faint hum of its systems reaching a fever pitch, the energy it emitted distorted everything around it. His breath caught in his throat as the machine's final words echoed in the chamber, sending a shockwave of fear through him: "Fail-safe activation imminent. Countdown initiated."

Panic gripped him. *The key...* He had found it, but instead of granting him an escape, it was unravelling everything the simulation, the reality, and him.

He tried to move, to run, but his legs felt like they were made of lead, his body rooted to the spot as the room convulsed. The air around him seemed to twist and bend, creating strange ripples that distorted everything in his vision. It was as if the world was collapsing in on itself, folding into impossible shapes. His head throbbed with the sheer impossibility of what he was seeing.

The machine's countdown reached its final moments.

Three.

John's heart pounded against his ribcage, his breath coming in short, desperate gasps. He could feel the pull of something unnatural a force yanking at him from all directions.

Two.

The walls disintegrated, becoming nothing but streaks of light and shadow, the solid ground beneath his feet splintering like glass.

One.

There was no time left. John's body was torn apart by the force, his mind screaming as he felt himself being stretched in every direction at once. Time itself seemed to shatter around him, the sensation like being trapped in a vortex, spinning uncontrollably. Every cell in his body burned with the impossible strain of being ripped through the collapsing simulation. He could feel the remnants of ancient Rome, of the life he had been forced to survive in, slipping away like sand through his fingers.

And then, in a blinding flash of light

Zero.

Chapter Nine

The world exploded around him.

The brightness was overwhelming, erasing everything in its path, obliterating the twisted remnants of the simulation. John felt himself hurtling through the void, every sense overwhelmed by the sensation of being pulled and compressed, twisted and stretched beyond what his mind could comprehend. He couldn't scream couldn't even think as he was swept up in the storm of collapsing time and space.

And then, just as suddenly as it began, it was over.

John hit the ground with a bone-jarring thud, the impact knocking the wind from his lungs. His body ached as he gasped for air, the sudden stillness of his surroundings a stark contrast to the violent chaos he had just been ripped from. His ears rang, the world around him muted, distant as if he were trapped underwater.

Gasping, he slowly lifted his head, his vision swimming as he tried to focus on his surroundings.

Gone were the streets of Rome, the crowds of strangers, and the ancient stone walls that had confined him for days. In their place were sterile white walls, the hum of machinery, and the cool, antiseptic air of the academy. John blinked against the harsh lights overhead, his mind struggling to reconcile the jarring transition.

The simulation pod. He was back in the simulation pod.

The hiss of hydraulics filled the room as the pod's door slid open, releasing a gust of cool air that hit his face like a slap. John winced, his body protesting as he slowly sat up, his limbs were heavy and sore from the days and weeks he had spent trapped in the simulation. His hands shook as he gripped the edges of the pod, his breath still ragged as the adrenaline coursed through him.

It's over. The thought echoed in his mind, but it didn't feel real. Rome, the vendors, the cold nights sleeping in the streets it had all felt so vivid, so real. His heart was still racing, the phantom sensations of running, of hiding, of survival thrumming through his veins. He could still smell the dust and sweat of the ancient city, still hear the distant chatter of a language he didn't understand.

John dragged himself out of the pod, his feet unsteady as they touched the cold metal floor. His head spun as he tried to make sense of what had just happened. How long had he been in the simulation? Why had it felt so different so much more real than any other training exercise he'd ever experienced?

His eyes darted around the room, searching for someone anyone who could explain. But the chamber was empty, save for the gentle hum of the pods lining the walls. The familiar environment felt alien in the wake of what he had just been through.

John took a deep breath, trying to steady his thoughts, but his mind wouldn't stop racing. *Who had left the note?* The cryptic message about adapting or perishing still echoed in his head, the final piece of the puzzle that had set everything in motion. And yet, even back in the academy, the sense of being watched hadn't disappeared.

Shaking his head, John wiped the sweat from his brow and slowly made his way towards the door, his legs still shaky from the transition. He needed answers, answers that the academy, or someone within it, was withholding.

As the door slid open, the sterile corridor stretched out before him, its fluorescent lights a sharp contrast to the chaos of the simulation. But even as he stepped out of the pod room, he couldn't shake the feeling that the real test had only just begun.

Something wasn't right.

The academy should have been alive with activity. The constant murmur of voices of recruits discussing strategy, instructors barking orders, and the distant hum of machinery was always present. Yet now, the silence was oppressive, thick and unnatural. John's footsteps echoed too loudly against the cold, sterile floor as he glanced around the empty chamber. The control panels, usually glowing with data, were dark. The familiar chatter of cadets prepping for their next training session was nowhere to be heard.

John frowned. *Where is everyone?*

His eyes scanned the room, searching for any sign of life. That's when he saw it a folded note sitting on the control panel, its crisp edges almost too deliberate, too perfectly placed in the stark emptiness of the room. His heart skipped a beat as he approached it, the familiar handwriting sending a cold jolt through his veins.

No... it couldn't be.

He hesitated, his hand hovering over the note for a moment before snatching it up. The words were simple, but their weight settled heavily in his chest.

"Welcome back, John. The test is far from over."

John's pulse quickened as he clenched the note, the paper crinkling under his tightening grip. *The test? What test?* His thoughts scrambled for answers, but none came. His eyes darted around the empty room again, every shadow feeling more sinister, every flicker of the overhead lights making his skin crawl.

Had it all been real?

Suddenly, the lights flickered.

The room twisted before his eyes, distorting like a mirage, the walls warping as if reality itself was bending. The very air around him shimmered unnaturally, as though it were rippling beneath some unseen force. John staggered backwards, his pulse pounding in his ears, a sharp pain spiking behind his eyes.

No, no, no

He reached out blindly, steadying himself against the edge of the pod. His breath came in short, panicked bursts, his vision swimming as the world around him twisted into impossible shapes. The sensation was all too familiar, the same sickening feeling he'd had in the simulation as it began to collapse.

"Focus, John," he whispered through gritted teeth, forcing himself to take deep, steady breaths. He clenched his eyes shut, willing the nausea and confusion to pass.

Slowly, the flickering stopped.

He opened his eyes, cautiously, half-expecting the room to still be unravelling. But the walls had settled. The lights overhead were steady, and the room's cold, clinical air returned to its usual staleness. The pod's earlier hiss had faded, leaving behind only the quiet, persistent hum of the academy's systems.

But something still felt off.

John's gaze darted around the room, searching for any clue anything to explain what was happening. His eyes landed on the clock on the far wall. He squinted at it, but something was wrong. The time displayed didn't make sense it was a number that felt impossible. It was as though hours, maybe even days, had passed while he was in the pod, yet he couldn't remember any of it.

A knot formed in his stomach. His hand instinctively reached for his communicator, fumbling to activate it. He tapped it, waiting for the familiar chirp of a signal connecting him to the facility's network.

Nothing.

John stared at the device in disbelief, shaking it slightly as if that might fix the issue. He tapped it again, harder this time, but the result was the same no signal, no connection.

"What the hell?" he muttered under his breath, a cold chill creeping up his spine.

Panic stirred in his chest as he looked around the room again, his mind racing. There were no signs of life. No voices, no footsteps in the distance. The stillness of the room pressed in on him, the silence deafening.

Where was everyone?

His grip tightened on the folded note still in his hand. The mysterious benefactor's message repeated in his mind: *"The test is far from over."* What did it mean? Was this still part of the simulation? Had the fail-safe triggered something else?

John's thoughts spiralled as the weight of the situation pressed down on him. He couldn't trust anything. Not the time on the clock, not his communicator hell, grant even his senses anymore.

He took a step back towards the pod, his mind screaming for answers. But before he could make sense of anything, the overhead lights flickered again, casting the room in brief flashes of darkness. This time, they didn't stabilise. The walls groaned as though under immense pressure, and the air seemed to hum with tension. The sensation of unreality washed over him again, a warning that something was deeply wrong.

John's heart hammered in his chest as he clutched the note tighter, the paper damp from the sweat on his palm.

Who is doing this?

A low, distant rumble echoed through the room, and the ground beneath him trembled.

The test is far from over…

He turned on his heel, mind buzzing with questions, and made his way to the exit, determined to find out what was going on. As he reached for the door, a flicker of movement caught his eye in the periphery of his vision. He froze, his muscles tensing. Spinning around, his eyes darted across the room, scanning every shadow, every corner.

Nothing.

The room was empty.

John's breath came in shallow, ragged bursts as he strained to catch any sound, any hint of movement. *Was it real?* His mind raced, trying to piece together the last few moments, but the lines between reality and the simulation blurred. *Was this still part of the test?*

He took a deep breath, steadying himself, his heart pounding in his ears. Shaking off the unease, he stepped out of the chamber and into the hallway, the door sliding shut behind him with a final *hiss*. The corridor felt too quiet at first, but then, slowly, the familiar sounds of the academy began to filter back in. Footsteps echoed down the hall, voices of recruits carried from a distance, and the low hum of machinery filled the air.

The normalcy of it all felt like a splash of cold water, startling him from the chaos he had just escaped. But even as his surroundings grounded him, the unsettling sensation gnawed at the back of his mind.

John shook his head, rubbing his temples as if to clear away the lingering disorientation. *It had to have been a dream,* he reasoned. *A glitch, maybe. Just a messed-up simulation. Nothing more.* But the explanation didn't sit right. No simulation had ever felt so vivid, so personal, and yet so unhinged.

The corridors stretched before him, illuminated by the soft, artificial glow of the overhead lights. As he made his way towards his quarters, the unease wouldn't let go. It clung to him like a shadow, something intangible but heavy. His footsteps quickened, almost reflexively, as though the answers he sought were waiting for him at the end of the hallway.

Reaching his room, the door slid open with the same familiar *hiss* it always did. He stepped inside, his gaze immediately sweeping across the small space.

Everything was in its place. The bed was neatly made, his belongings exactly where he had left them. The same orderly room he had known for months.

But something was still... off.

John's eyes flicked over the room again, slower this time, trying to pinpoint what was wrong. The air felt different and stale, as though the room had been untouched for far longer than it should have been. His bed, though neatly made, looked too perfect, like it hadn't been slept in for days. His belongings, though in place, felt distant, foreign, as if they belonged to someone else.

A chill ran down his spine.

He walked towards the bed and pressed a hand to the mattress. Cold. Too cold. It was as if the warmth of his presence had been erased, replaced by something sterile and artificial.

What's happening? The question echoed in his mind, growing louder with each passing second. He moved to his desk, fingers tracing the edge of his datapad. The screen blinked to life with a swipe, showing the usual logs and academy updates. But something about the timestamps felt wrong. His schedule and his assignments didn't match what he remembered.

Was it just fatigue? John's mind raced to rationalise the discrepancies. *Maybe I'm just shaken up from the simulation. It has to be that.*

But deep down, he knew it wasn't that simple.

The feeling of being watched crept over him again, like a weight pressing against the back of his skull. He spun around, eyes narrowing at the door as though someone might be standing on the other side, observing him. But the hallway outside was silent, devoid of life.

John exhaled sharply, dragging his hand through his hair. *I need to clear my head,* he thought, pacing the small room. The sterile, mechanical hum of the academy felt claustrophobic, the walls closing in on him with each step.

He caught sight of the mirror on the wall, his reflection staring back at him. He looked tired. His eyes, once sharp and focused, now seemed haunted by something he couldn't quite grasp. The face looking back at him was familiar but in a strange, disjointed way. He leaned closer to the glass, studying his features, searching for the part of him that still made sense.

The lights flickered again.

John snapped his head towards the ceiling, his breath catching in his throat. The flicker was brief, but in that split second, everything seemed to distort again the walls, the bed, the reflection in the mirror. He stumbled backwards, gripping the edge of his desk for support. The room wavered, reality-bending at the edges like it had in the simulation.

No... not again.

He stood frozen, muscles tensed, waiting for the flicker to pass, waiting for the room to stabilise.

But the dissonance lingered this time. The air seemed to hum, as though the fabric of his surroundings was unravelling just out of reach. A faint ringing filled his ears, drowning out the hum of the machines, and John found himself gripping the edge of his desk tighter, his knuckles white.

Then, as quickly as it began, the flickering stopped.

The room snapped back into focus, everything in its place once more. But the unease remained, thrumming under the surface, threatening to break through again at any moment.

John's breathing was shallow as he stared down at the desk, his pulse pounding in his temples. He knew now this wasn't just disorientation from a simulation. Something was wrong. Deeply wrong.

And it was getting worse.

John collapsed onto the bed, his body sinking into the mattress like it was pulling him into the earth. Every muscle ached, weighed down by exhaustion, but his mind refused to slow. He stared up at the ceiling, eyes tracing the familiar contours of the room, yet his thoughts kept dragging him back to Rome.

The simulation. The note. The machine. The explosion.

Too real.

The memory of it gnawed at him, replaying in fragmented loops. The rush of the ancient city, the crowd, the crack in the cobblestones. He could still feel the heat of the Roman sun on his skin, the distant hum of the marketplace buzzing in his ears. His fingers twitched involuntarily as if expecting to feel the rough texture of the ancient stones beneath them.

John glanced down at his hands, half-expecting to see the dirt and grime of Rome still clinging to his skin. His fingers flexed, brushing against his palms. But there was nothing. No dust, no marks. Just clean, unblemished skin.

No proof. No evidence that any of it happened.

But it *had* happened. He was sure of it. His heart quickened as doubt began to claw at the edges of his mind. How could it feel so vivid, so tactile, and yet leave no trace behind?

And yet John shifted, his hand brushing against something under the pillow. His pulse spiked as he froze. There shouldn't be anything there. Slowly, cautiously, he reached beneath the pillow, his fingers grazing something rough and unfamiliar.

His breath caught.

He pulled it out, his eyes widening as he stared at the small, crumpled scrap of parchment in his hand. The ink was faded, the edges frayed, but the words were unmistakable.

"Adapt or perish."

John's heart hammered against his ribs, his mind spinning. The note from Rome was the same note that had been hidden in his cloak. But how? How was it here, now, in his quarters?

He sat up quickly, gripping the note tightly in his hand, as though it might disappear if he let go. His eyes darted around the room, half-expecting the walls to start flickering again, for the world to twist and bend like it had before. The silence of the academy pressed in on him, but it felt too still, too controlled like something was watching, waiting.

The note was real. He could feel the coarse parchment between his fingers, and smell the faint mustiness of aged paper. His mind screamed for an explanation, but none came. Was he still in the simulation? Had it bled over into his reality? Or was his reality the simulation now?

John ran a hand through his hair, his pulse thundering in his ears. Every inch of him screamed that something was wrong, but he had no way to confirm what it was. He looked down at the note again, reading the words over and over.

"Adapt or perish."

He'd seen those words before, cryptic messages left behind during his training, little breadcrumbs that had led him through difficult situations. But this felt different. The stakes were higher. The consequences are more immediate.

Had someone placed the note under his pillow? Or had it somehow followed him from the simulation, bending the rules of time and space to remain in his reality?

He stood up abruptly, pacing the small room, the note still clenched in his hand. His thoughts raced, trying to find logic in the madness. But there was no logic. Not this time.

He turned, eyes scanning the room for answers, but it was the same sterile, unyielding space it had always been. The neatly folded blanket at the foot of his bed, the desk with its organised datapads, the mirror reflecting the unease etched into his face.

He glanced at the door, half-expecting another flicker, another twist in reality. But everything was still.

Too still.

John's hand gripped the note tighter, the words burnt into his mind like a brand. What did it mean? Was it a warning? A clue? And who had left it?

With a surge of determination, he folded the note and tucked it into his pocket. He couldn't stay here, trapped in this suffocating uncertainty. He needed answers. Now.

He turned towards the door, but before he could take a step, the lights flickered again just for a heartbeat. Long enough to make his stomach drop. Long enough to remind him that nothing was as it seemed.

John froze, his eyes locked on the door.

Am I still in the simulation?

The question lodged in his throat, unspoken, but it echoed through his mind, louder and louder. The room felt like it was closing in on him, the walls too close, the air too thick. He had to move. He had to know what was real.

John took a deep breath, steadying himself. He pushed the doubt down, burying it deep, and strode towards the door with purpose.

Adapt or perish.

The words echoed in his mind, but he was done playing this game. He would find out the truth. No matter what.

John glanced around the room, the shadows stretching long as the evening light filtered through the window. The dying sun cast an eerie, golden hue over everything, elongating the silhouettes of familiar objects, and making them feel foreign and distorted. The air itself felt heavier, as though it carried an unspoken weight, a tension he couldn't quite place, pressing down on his chest.

His eyes flicked towards the note on the desk. *"Adapt or perish."* The words seemed to mock him, their presence as out of place as his unease in the room. He rubbed his temples, trying to will away the creeping sense of dread that had settled into the pit of his stomach.

Maybe I'm just tired, he reasoned. *Maybe I just need to sleep it off.*

But even as he thought it, he knew it wasn't that simple.

His hand trembled slightly as he turned down the light. The room, once a haven of routine and normalcy, now felt hostile. Foreign. The shadows seemed to shift in the corner of his eye, like they were moving when he wasn't looking, bending under a logic he couldn't grasp.

He lay back down, his body sinking into the bed, but it didn't bring the usual comfort. The pillow was cool against his cheek, the sheets neatly tucked, but he felt no sense of safety. Exhaustion tugged at his limbs, but his mind raced, playing the day's events on a loop Rome, the machine, the explosion, the note.

His eyes fluttered shut, and for a brief moment, it felt like everything was still. His heart slowed, and his breath evened. But just as the calm began to settle, the flicker of a question one he'd been trying to avoid rose to the surface, stubborn and insistent:

Was any of this real?

The thought clung to him, refusing to be dismissed. It whispered in the corners of his mind, weaving through every memory, every doubt. The simulation had been too real. The pain, the fear, the note. It all felt like more than just a test.

And yet, here he was back in the academy, back in his quarters, as if nothing had happened.

His eyelids grew heavier, but the question lingered, haunting him as the darkness crept in. The air seemed to pulse, just slightly, like a shift in pressure, the sensation so subtle it could've been imagined. But John's breath hitched, his body tensing as if sensing something he couldn't name.

What if I'm still there?

He swallowed hard, his pulse quickening even as sleep began to pull him under. His muscles relaxed despite his mind's protests, sinking deeper into the bed as exhaustion finally overtook him.

But the last thing he felt before slipping fully into unconsciousness wasn't relief.

It was fear.

The darkness closed in, but the question remained, gnawing at the edges of John's mind until sleep finally overtook him.

Chapter Ten

When he awoke the next morning, the lingering unease from the dream still clung to him, a shadow he couldn't shake. The bed beneath him was familiar and solid, but his mind remained clouded with uncertainty. Was it all just a nightmare? Or had it been something more?

As he lay there, trying to make sense of the blurred lines between reality and simulation, his communicator beeped, pulling him back into the present. He glanced at the screen, blinking away the remnants of sleep. The message was clear and direct: **Meet Jack Banks at the combat arena.**

John sat up slowly, the disorientation fading but not disappearing entirely. The world around him felt more grounded now, more real, yet a part of him still questioned everything. He moved through the now-familiar corridors, noting the change in atmosphere at the facility. There was a new tension, a weight in the air that hadn't been there before. The recent breach had left its mark.

Recruits and staff moved with a renewed sense of urgency. Their expressions were hardened, their movements sharper. As the facility underwent a thorough security overhaul, John couldn't help but feel that the intensity in their eyes mirrored his own internal struggle. Was it the breach that had heightened this sense of reality or something else?

Whatever the case, it didn't matter now. His training had resumed, and with it came the familiar rhythm of combat drills and tactical briefings. But as he made his way towards Jack Banks, one thought lingered in the back of his mind, still unresolved: **Was it really just a dream?**

In the combat arena, John joined a group of recruits who were already assembled. Jack Banks stood at the centre, his presence commanding respect. "Listen up," Jack barked, his voice carrying over the sounds of the training facility. "Today, we're going to push you harder than ever. The exercises will be gruelling, but they're designed to prepare you for any situation you might face in the field."

John steeled himself for the challenges ahead. The obstacle course had been tough, but he knew that the training would only get more demanding. Jack's words echoed in his mind as he approached the first station, a series of high walls that they had to scale. His muscles ached, but he forced himself to keep going, driven by a mix of determination and the desire to prove himself.

As the day progressed, John found himself pushed to his limits. The training was relentless, with each exercise designed to test their physical endurance, mental acuity, and teamwork. Despite the exhaustion, John felt a sense of camaraderie with his fellow recruits. They encouraged each other, their shared struggles forging bonds of friendship and mutual respect.

During breaks, John took the opportunity to finally get to know his fellow recruits better. He struck up conversations with Lisa Brown, a tall and athletic woman with short, curly hair and an infectious laugh. Her deep brown eyes held a spark of adventure and curiosity that drew John in. Lisa had a passion for uncovering the secrets of the past, and her enthusiasm was contagious. She was eager to learn more about the time travel technology and was determined to make a difference in protecting the timeline.

One afternoon, as they rested between exercises, Lisa nudged John as they both caught their breath. "So, what got you into this crazy time travel gig?" she asked, her tone light but genuinely curious.

John smiled, thinking back to the series of events that had led him here. "Long story," he replied, wiping the sweat from his brow. "But let's just say I wasn't exactly given a choice."

"Aren't we all," Max Johnson chimed in, adjusting his glasses as he joined them. Max was a young man with piercing blue eyes and an unruly mop of dark hair. His lean frame was accentuated by a pair of stylish glasses, and he had an air of confidence that came from being a tech genius. Max could hack into any system with ease, and he was eager to use his skills to protect the facility and ensure the integrity of the timeline. He had a quick wit and a knack for making even the most mundane situations seem exciting. "I got roped in after hacking into what I thought was just a top-secret government file. Turns out, it was a little more complicated."

Lisa laughed, a sound that cut through the tension of the day. "You always have to poke around where you don't belong, don't you, Max?"

"Hey, curiosity never killed the cat," Max retorted with a grin. "It just sent him on an epic adventure through time."

John couldn't help but admire Lisa's unwavering enthusiasm. Even after a brutal workout, she seemed energised by the challenge, her eyes bright with a determination that mirrored his own. Max, on the other hand, was a different kind of force. His sharp intellect and quick wit brought a sense of levity to the group, but beneath that lay a fierce loyalty to their mission something John was beginning to feel himself.

Later that day, the three of them were paired up for a team exercise. As they navigated through the simulated jungle, Lisa took the lead, using her agility to scout ahead. Ancient trees with thick, knotted roots created natural barriers that the recruits had to navigate around or climb over, and Lisa moved through them with the ease of someone who had done this all her life. Max, meanwhile, tapped away at his handheld device, hacking into the simulation's control panel to give them a tactical advantage.

John covered their flank, trusting his teammates' skills as they moved as one unit. "Got it," Max whispered, holding up a fist. "We've got a clear path to the objective."

"Good work, Max. John, keep an eye out. Let's move," Lisa directed, her voice calm but authoritative.

As they continued, John found himself reflecting on his teammates. Lisa mentioned her past almost offhandedly during a lull in the training. "Back home, I used to be a competitive climber. Nothing like scaling ancient ruins, though," she added with a wry smile. "Guess that's why they picked me."

Max smirked, adjusting his glasses again. "I was always more comfortable behind a screen, but now I'm here, diving into the action. Who would've thought?"

John realised even more now that each of them had been chosen for a reason, their unique skills and backgrounds making them invaluable assets to the team. As the day progressed and they faced the gruelling challenges together, John felt a growing sense of camaraderie with Lisa and Max. Despite the hardships, their shared struggles were forging bonds of friendship and mutual respect, bringing them closer as a team.

In the evenings, John attended lectures by Dr Johnson and Dr Davis. These sessions offered a welcome respite from the physical demands of training, yet they were no less challenging. Dr Johnson's lectures were immersive, delving into the intricacies of historical contexts and cultural nuances. Her words painted vivid pictures of ancient civilisations, revealing the delicate balance that maintained the timeline's integrity. Dr Davis, with his dry wit and vast knowledge, provided a steady counterpoint, emphasising the crucial importance of cultural sensitivity and deep understanding.

John found himself captivated by their teachings. The lectures were more than just lessons; they were windows into the past, revealing the complexities of history and the interconnectedness of events. He took copious notes, determined to absorb as much knowledge as possible. The cryptic messages he had received only heightened his sense of urgency, fuelling his desire to uncover the truth.

As the weeks passed, John's skills improved, and he began to feel more confident in his abilities. The training sessions grew increasingly advanced, introducing new challenges designed to push them beyond their limits. In the simulation lab, they practiced using time machines and portals, learning how to navigate different periods while avoiding the creation of paradoxes. Dr Tanaka's meticulous guidance underscored the importance of precision and caution, ensuring they understood the gravity of their work.

John's favourite part of the training was, without a doubt, the time travel lab. The room itself was a marvel of technology, filled with sleek, futuristic devices that hummed with latent power. The walls were lined with consoles and interfaces, each one a gateway to another time, another world. The air buzzed with a sense of possibility, and John couldn't help but feel a thrill of excitement every time he entered the lab.

The time travel devices, known as Chronoverges, were intricate machines that required both precision and a deep understanding of temporal mechanics. Their surfaces were smooth and metallic, with panels that glowed softly in various shades of blue and green. The interfaces were touch-sensitive, reacting instantly to the slightest movement of the user's fingers. John quickly learned that these machines were as much about finesse as they were about raw power; one wrong move could send a traveller to the wrong century or worse, create a ripple in the timeline.

During his first few sessions, John made several mistakes. The Chronoverges were unlike anything he had ever encountered, and their complexity was daunting. He fumbled with the controls, struggling to align the coordinates correctly, often resulting in miscalculations that would have been catastrophic in a real mission. The first time he incorrectly calibrated a destination, the holographic simulation displayed an apocalyptic vision of a ruined city, a stark reminder of what was at stake.

But Dr Smith was there, always patient and composed, guiding John through each step with a calm, methodical approach. Dr Smith was an expert in the craft, his understanding of the machines seemingly infinite. He never raised his voice or showed frustration, even when John struggled. Instead, he would offer a quiet word of encouragement, his steady hands demonstrating the correct procedure with precision.

"Remember, John," Dr Smith would say, his voice as smooth as the polished surface of the Chronoverge, "time travel is not about force. It's about understanding the flow of time and working with it, not against it. Let the machine guide you, and trust in the process."

John began to grasp the nuances of the devices, learning to respect their power. Dr Smith introduced him to the finer points of temporal navigation, explaining how to interpret the delicate readouts on the screens that indicated the stability of the timeline. They delved into the importance of aligning not just spatial coordinates but temporal markers that ensured their presence wouldn't disrupt historical events.

As they worked through another session, John smiled and said, "You know, Gabe calls it a 'time hopper'." He couldn't help but chuckle at the nickname, which seemed so much simpler and less intimidating than the official term.

Dr Smith raised an eyebrow but smirked in amusement. "Trust Gabe to simplify things," he replied, shaking his head. "Though I can see the appeal. Time hopper. It does have a certain charm to it, doesn't it?"

John nodded. "It's stuck with me now. Every time I'm using one of these, I think of that."

Smith's smirk faded into his usual seriousness. "Well, whatever you call it, just remember this isn't a game. The consequences of even a small misstep can be catastrophic."

John sobered at the reminder, his fingers hovering over the controls. "Yeah, I know."

He inhaled deeply, grounding himself in the moment. Dr Smith's words echoed in his mind as he steeled himself for the next challenge, aware that each lesson was a step closer to mastering the Chronoverge.

One particularly challenging lesson involved navigating through a temporal vortex, a phenomenon that could occur when two timelines intersect. The simulation showed a swirling mass of light and energy, and John's task was to guide the Chronoverge through it without being caught in the distortion. His hands hovered over the controls, fingers twitching with tension as the vortex loomed closer on the screen.

"Steady now," Dr Smith advised, his eyes fixed on the display. "Watch the flux readings. Keep them in the green zone. The moment they shift to yellow, adjust the stabilisers gently. It's all about subtlety."

John followed the instructions, his heart pounding as he carefully adjusted the controls. The readings flickered, and for a moment, the vortex seemed to pull them in, the screens flashing warnings in bright red. But John didn't panic. He took a deep breath, recalled Dr Smith's calm demeanour, and made the necessary adjustments. Slowly, the readings stabilised, and the Chronoverge glided smoothly through the vortex, emerging on the other side unscathed.

When the simulation ended, Dr Smith placed a hand on John's shoulder, a rare gesture of praise. "Well done, John. You're beginning to understand. It's not just about the mechanics; it's about the feel of it. The machine is an extension of your will. Trust it, and it will take you where you need to go."

The complexity of the Chronoverges continued to fascinate John. Each session revealed new layers of intricacy, from the way the machines calculated temporal drift to the safeguards in place to prevent paradoxes. The more he learned, the more he realised how much there was still to understand. Yet, instead of feeling overwhelmed, John felt invigorated. He eagerly anticipated each lesson, driven by a desire to master the technology that held the key to their missions.

With every mistake, he grew more adept, his hands moving more confidently over the controls, his mind attuned to the rhythms of the machines. The steep learning curve that had initially intimidated him now served as a challenge he was determined to conquer.

One evening, as the facility teemed with the quiet activity of recruits and staff winding down for the night, John found himself once again drawn to the library. It had become his refuge, much like the small, dusty library at the orphanage where he used to escape the world. Here, surrounded by the vast expanse of history and knowledge, he felt a sense of calm amidst the chaos of his life. The air was thick with the musty scent of old paper and leather, a comforting aroma that grounded him in the familiar even as he ventured into the unknown.

The dim lighting cast long shadows between the towering rows of shelves, creating a maze of knowledge that seemed to stretch endlessly into the darkness.

The soft rustle of pages being turned, and the occasional creak of old wood were the only sounds that accompanied his solitary exploration. This was a place where time itself seemed to slow, where the past and present coexisted in a delicate balance, and where John could lose himself in the pursuit of answers.

He had become a regular visitor here, spending hours poring over ancient texts and manuscripts, searching for any clue that might shed light on the mysterious messages that had been haunting him. The cryptic notes had become a driving force in his life, propelling him forward in his quest for the truth. Each message seemed to pull him deeper into a mystery that he felt compelled to solve as if an invisible hand was guiding him towards a destiny he couldn't yet comprehend.

As he wandered through the library, his eyes scanning the spines of the books, he noticed a familiar figure sitting at one of the large oak tables, hunched over a tablet. It was Max, his attention fully absorbed in whatever he was working on. The faint glow of the screen illuminated his face, casting soft shadows over his features. John hesitated for a moment, not wanting to disturb him, but curiosity got the better of him.

"Max," John whispered as he approached, "I didn't expect to see you here."

Max looked up, surprised but pleased to see him. "John! Yeah, I'm just digging through some old systems manuals, trying to figure out a few things." He gestured to the books and tablets scattered around him, filled with schematics and codes. "What about you? Still hunting for those mysterious messages?"

John nodded, feeling a mix of relief and unease at the mention of the messages. "Yeah, it's been consuming me lately. I found another one tonight."

Max's eyebrows shot up in interest. "Seriously? That's what, the third one now?"

"Fourth," John corrected, pulling the delicate parchment from his pocket to show Max. "This one was hidden in a book up on the top shelf. It's just as cryptic as the others."

Max took the parchment carefully, his analytical mind already at work. "These symbols they're ancient, but there's something almost digital about the way they're arranged, like a code within a code." He glanced at John; his curiosity piqued. "You think it's leading you somewhere specific?"

"That's what I'm trying to figure out," John said, the frustration creeping into his voice. "I feel like I'm being watched, like someone's testing me, pushing me towards something. But I don't know who or why."

Max frowned thoughtfully, handing the parchment back. "Have you considered that maybe it's not just a person behind this? Maybe it's something else, something bigger. The timing, the patterns it's almost like an algorithm."

"An algorithm?" John echoed, intrigued by the idea. "You mean like a program?"

"Or a directive," Max suggested, his mind racing through possibilities. "We're dealing with time travel, right? What if these messages are coming from a different point in time, sent back to guide you?"

The idea sent a chill down John's spine. It made sense, in a way that was both fascinating and terrifying. "But what am I supposed to do with that? How can I trust something I don't even understand?"

Max leaned back in his chair, his expression serious. "You can't. Not entirely, at least. But you can trust yourself, your instincts. Whatever this is, it's targeting you for a reason. Maybe it sees something in you that you don't even see in yourself yet."

John mulled over Max's words, feeling a strange mix of fear and purpose. The idea that these messages were guiding him perhaps even shaping his future was daunting, but also strangely empowering. "I just need to keep digging, I guess," he said finally, slipping the parchment back into his notebook. "Whatever it is, I'll find the answers."

Max nodded, giving him an encouraging smile. "You will. And if you need help, you know where to find me. I'm always up for cracking a mystery."

With that, John left Max to his research and continued his exploration of the library. As he wandered through the aisles, his thoughts kept returning to their conversation. Max's insight had opened up new possibilities, but it also left John with more questions than answers.

Finally, he reached the shelf where he had originally found the parchment. He reached for the dusty old tome again, half-expecting something else to fall out, but nothing did. Still, he couldn't shake the feeling that he was on the verge of something significant. As he carefully slid the book back into place, he made a silent promise to himself: whatever this was, he wouldn't stop until he uncovered the truth.

The room seemed to close in around him as he pondered the implications of the message. Every rustle of paper and creak of wood seemed amplified, his senses heightened by the tension that hung in the air. The silence was oppressive, pressing in on him from all sides as he stood alone in the vast, shadowy library.

He knew he had to find out who was behind these messages, and why they were so insistent that he seek the truth. The realisation settled heavily on his shoulders his journey was far from over, and the path ahead was fraught with uncertainty and danger.

But John was no longer the scared, uncertain boy he had once been. The training, the challenges, the experiences he had faced had begun to forge him into something stronger. He was still scared how could he not be? but he was also determined. He couldn't afford to ignore the warnings, nor could he trust anyone fully. The stakes were too high, the consequences too dire. With a deep breath, he carefully copied the symbols into his notebook, each stroke of the pen feeling like a step further into the unknown. The weight of the mystery bore down on him, but so did the fire of his resolve.

As he slipped the parchment back into the book and returned it to the shelf, he made a silent promise to himself. He would uncover the secrets that lay hidden in the shadows of time, no matter the cost. The answers were out there, waiting to be discovered, and he would stop at nothing to find them.

John left the library, the cryptic message still burning in his mind. The night was dark, the corridors silent as he made his way back to his quarters, but he felt a new strength within him. He was no longer just a passive observer in this strange, unfolding drama. He was a player, and he was ready to take control of his fate.

The next day, John approached Sarah Thompson's office, his mind swirling with questions. The library encounter with Max had left him with more doubts than answers, and the cryptic message from the night before lingered like a shadow over his thoughts. He needed clarity, and he hoped that Sarah, with her authority and knowledge, could provide some.

As he reached her door, he paused, taking a deep breath to steady himself. The corridor was quiet, the usual hum of the facility muted, as if the building itself held its breath in anticipation. John raised his hand and knocked, the sound echoing slightly in the stillness.

"Come in," Sarah's voice called from inside, her tone brisk yet inviting.

John stepped into the room, immediately noticing the organised chaos surrounding her desk. Stacks of documents were neatly piled next to holographic displays that floated in mid-air, each showing a different piece of critical information. The room was a blend of the past and the future, much like the facility itself, and it always left John feeling slightly out of place.

Sarah looked up as he entered, her expression warm and welcoming, but the smile quickly faded when she saw the seriousness etched on his face. Her eyes, usually so calm and collected, now reflected a hint of worry.

"Sarah, can we talk?" John asked, trying to keep his voice steady despite the turmoil inside him.

"Of course, John," she said, gesturing to the chair in front of her desk. "Please, sit. What's on your mind?"

John lowered himself into the chair, his hands clasped tightly in his lap, the tension evident in the way his knuckles whitened under the pressure. He hesitated for a moment, gathering his thoughts. "I found another encrypted message," he began, his voice tinged with frustration. "Another one of those 'Help Wanted' notes telling me to seek the truth and trust no one. What does it mean, Sarah? Why am I being singled out?"

Sarah's expression shifted from concern to something more guarded, her brows knitting together as she considered his words. She leaned back in her chair, her fingers steepling as she weighed her response. "John, I understand your concerns," she began slowly, her tone careful. "But you have to understand that time travel is still a realm filled with unknowns. Even with all our technology and knowledge, there are elements that remain mysterious, even to us."

"But why me?" John pressed, his frustration bubbling to the surface. He leaned forward, his voice edging on desperation. "Why am I the one getting these messages? What makes me so special?"

Sarah sighed deeply, her gaze dropping to the papers on her desk as if searching for answers among them. When she looked back at him, her eyes were filled with a mix of empathy and something else something she was keeping hidden. "John, I wish I could give you all the answers you're looking for. The truth is, I don't know why you're being targeted specifically. But what I do know is that you're here for a reason. You've been chosen because we see potential in you, because we believe you can handle the challenges that come with this responsibility."

John nodded slowly, her words doing little to ease the gnawing anxiety in his gut. He could sense that there was more she wasn't telling him, something deeper that she was holding back. But how could he press her without overstepping? The last thing he wanted was to alienate one of the few people he trusted.

"I promise you, John," Sarah continued, her voice softer now, "we're doing everything we can to understand these messages and why they're reaching out to you. In the meantime, it's crucial that you stay focused on your training. We need you to be prepared for whatever lies ahead."

John forced a smile and nodded, but inside, he felt no comfort. He appreciated Sarah's reassurance, but he couldn't shake the feeling that she knew more than she was letting on. The words "trust no one" echoed in his mind, amplifying his unease. He left her office with a resolve that was stronger than ever, knowing that if he wanted answers, he would have to dig deeper, even if it meant going against the advice of his mentors.

As he stepped back into the corridor, the soft click of the door closing behind him felt like a finality a reminder that, despite the camaraderie he had begun to feel with his fellow recruits, he was still very much alone in this mystery.

As he continued his training, John couldn't shake the lingering unease that had taken root since his conversation with Sarah. He began to pay closer attention to his surroundings, his senses attuned to the subtle nuances of the facility. What had once seemed like the normal hustle and bustle of a highly advanced training program now appeared in a different light one tinged with suspicion and doubt.

It started with trivial things, almost imperceptible at first. A conversation between two staff members that abruptly ended when he entered the room, their smiles tight and forced as they quickly changed the subject. Or the way certain doors remained locked no matter the time of day, with security measures far more advanced than seemed necessary for a simple training facility.

John also noticed the surveillance cameras more acutely, their lenses always seeming to track his movements. He couldn't shake the feeling that he was being watched, not just for his progress in training but for something more. Whenever he passed a camera, he felt a prickling sensation on the back of his neck, as if unseen eyes were scrutinising his every move. Even in the communal areas, where recruits gathered to relax or study, he felt the weight of those invisible eyes.

The inconsistency of the information he was given began to gnaw at him as well. During a lecture, Dr Johnson might emphasise the importance of preserving the timeline, only for Dr Davis to later suggest that certain "necessary adjustments" were sometimes unavoidable. The more John observed, the more these contradictions stood out, leaving him with a growing sense of unease about the true nature of the Lennox Time Corporation's mission.

He began to question everything why were they so secretive? Why did certain details about the training feel deliberately vague, as if they were keeping him in the dark? And why, despite their reassurances, did it seem like he was always being watched?

John tried to push these thoughts aside during his training, but they lingered in the back of his mind, whispering doubts and suspicions that grew louder with each passing day. The camaraderie he had begun to feel with his fellow recruits now felt like a fragile veneer, easily shattered by the creeping paranoia that had taken hold.

Even the cryptic messages, which had once been a source of confusion and frustration, now took on a new significance. Were they warnings? Or were they part of some larger manipulation, designed to push him in a specific direction? The question gnawed at him, adding to the growing weight of his suspicions.

As John's awareness of these inconsistencies grew, so did his resolve to uncover the truth. He knew he had to tread carefully one wrong move could expose his suspicions and put him in even greater danger. But he couldn't ignore the signs any longer. The more he observed, the more he began to question the true motives of the Lennox Time Corporation. What was their real purpose? And what role was he truly meant to play in their plans?

With each passing day, John's resolve to find answers solidified. He realised that the truth, whatever it was, wouldn't be handed to him. He would have to seek it out, piecing together the fragments of information he could gather, all while navigating the increasingly complex web of secrecy and deception that surrounded him.

One night, unable to sleep, John found himself lying in bed, his mind churning with thoughts he couldn't quiet. The cryptic messages, the subtle inconsistencies he had noticed, and the growing sense of unease gnawed at him. Deciding he needed some air to clear his head, he quietly left his quarters and began to wander the silent corridors of the facility.

The halls were dimly lit, the usual bustle of the day reduced to an eerie stillness. The soft hum of the facility's systems provided a low, constant background noise, occasionally interrupted by the distant sound of footsteps or the faint murmur of voices. The solitude was comforting in a way, giving John a chance to process everything without the pressure of training or the watchful eyes of the staff.

As he walked, his thoughts drifted back to the messages he had been receiving. *Seek the truth. Trust no one.* The words echoed in his mind, adding weight to the suspicions he had been harbouring. Why was he the only one receiving these messages? What truth was he supposed to find?

Lost in thought, John almost missed the faint light spilling out from a door left slightly ajar down a side corridor. He paused, curiosity pulling him closer. The door was one he hadn't noticed before, tucked away in a part of the facility he rarely visited. As he approached, he heard voices two people deep in conversation, their tones hushed but urgent.

He stopped just outside the door, careful not to draw attention to himself. The voices inside were tense, and though he couldn't make out every word, the snippets he caught sent a jolt of alarm through him.

"…concerned about the recent breaches…"

"…unusual activity around the Epsilon facility…"

John's breath caught in his throat. He had never heard of this Epsilon facility before, but the way they spoke about it with a mix of anxiety and secrecy suggested it was something important, something potentially dangerous.

He leaned in closer, straining to hear more.

"…keep an eye on the new recruits, especially John…"

A chill ran down his spine. They were talking about him. The realisation hit him hard, confirming his fears that he was being monitored more closely than he had thought. But why? What was it about him that warranted such attention?

Backing away slowly, John felt his pulse quicken. He needed answers, but he knew he had to be careful. Whatever was happening, it was bigger than he had imagined, and he couldn't afford to make a wrong move.

As he made his way back to his quarters, John felt a new sense of urgency settle over him. The pieces of the puzzle were starting to come together, but the picture was far from clear. He had to stay sharp, gather more information, and, above all, keep his suspicions to himself.

Sleep didn't come easily that night. John's mind raced with questions and possibilities, but eventually, exhaustion overtook him, and he drifted into a restless sleep.

The next morning, John awoke with a renewed sense of purpose. He couldn't let this go, not after what he had heard. After getting ready, he headed to the training yard, where Gabe was overseeing drills in Jack's absence. The morning air was crisp, the sounds of recruits grunting and shouting as they pushed through their exercises filling the yard. Gabe's sharp eyes tracked their progress, his presence a steady anchor in the chaotic environment.

John waited patiently, watching as Gabe directed the recruits with his usual calm authority. When there was a break in the activity, he approached, his heart pounding with a mix of anticipation and apprehension.

"Gabe, can I talk to you for a minute?" John asked, trying to keep his voice steady despite the turmoil inside.

Gabe turned to him, a flicker of curiosity in his eyes as he noticed the serious expression on John's face. "Sure, kid. What's up?"

John hesitated, the weight of his discovery heavy on his shoulders. But he knew he had to say something. Taking a deep breath, he plunged ahead. "I overheard some staff members talking about breaches and something called the Epsilon facility. They mentioned keeping an eye on me. What is Epsilon and why does it sound familiar?"

The question hung in the air between them, and John could see the slight narrowing of Gabe's eyes as he processed the information. Gabe glanced around, ensuring they weren't being overheard, before he spoke again, his voice low and measured.

"Epsilon is not something you need to worry about right now, John," Gabe said, his tone firm but not unkind. "Focus on your training."

John felt a surge of frustration. He had expected this kind of response, but it didn't make it any easier to accept. "But Gabe, they specifically mentioned me," he pressed, his voice rising slightly with the intensity of his emotions. "How can I focus on my training when I know there's something going on that involves me?"

Gabe sighed, his stern expression softening just a bit. He looked at John, a mixture of sympathy and caution in his gaze. "Look, kid, I get it. But there are things at LTC that are above our pay grade. Epsilon is complicated. Trust me when I say it's best to keep your head down and do what you're here to do. When the time is right, you'll get the answers you need."

The words were meant to reassure, but they only deepened John's frustration. Still, he knew pushing further wouldn't get him the answers he wanted. He forced himself to nod, biting back the questions that still burned in his mind. "Alright. Thanks, Gabe."

Gabe clapped him on the shoulder, the gesture both comforting and dismissive. "Stay focused, John. You've got potential, but don't let curiosity get you into trouble."

John managed a small, tight-lipped smile, but as he walked away, the tension in his chest didn't ease. Gabe's advice was clear, but John couldn't shake the feeling that whatever was happening at LTC whatever the Epsilon facility was, was something he needed to understand.

Despite Gabe's advice, John couldn't shake the nagging feeling that there was more to the story more that he needed to understand. The unanswered questions gnawed at him, but he channelled his frustration into his training, pushing himself harder, staying vigilant. Every detail, every conversation took on new significance as he sought to piece together the truth. The facility, which had once seemed like a beacon of hope and purpose, now felt like a labyrinth of secrets, each corridor hiding another layer of mystery.

That night, sleep eluded him. Restless, John lay in bed, his thoughts spiralling back to the orphanage. The cold, damp nights under a thin blanket, the constant sense of being an outsider, unwanted and alone. Even Derek angry, accusatory, but the closest thing to a father figure he'd ever known had kept his distance. The gunfight on the roof flashed in his mind. What had really happened to Derek? Who were those men? Gabe had never fully explained, and there hadn't been time to ask.

His thoughts drifted further back to a night at the orphanage he would never forget. The night he'd snuck out to watch the stars, seeking solace in the vast, silent sky. In that moment, under the endless expanse of stars, he had felt a rare sense of peace, a fleeting glimpse of something greater than his small, troubled world. That sense of wonder, of longing for something beyond the orphanage walls, had driven him then, and it still drove him now, propelling him forward on this strange, dangerous path.

Chapter Eleven

Still unable to sleep, John slipped out of bed, his restless energy pushing him to move. The facility was eerily quiet, the usual hum of activity silenced by the late hour. He wandered the halls, his mind churning with questions and half-formed theories. The polished floors and sterile walls, once a source of comfort, now seemed cold and oppressive.

His feet carried him almost unconsciously to the section of the building where he knew the Epsilon facility was housed. As he approached, his heart quickened, and he hesitated at the edge of the corridor. The area was dimly lit, and a heavy silence hung in the air, amplifying the sound of his own breathing. Just as he was about to turn back, thinking better of it, he saw movement a shadowy figure slipping through a doorway.

John froze, his breath catching in his throat. The figure was quick, almost ghostly in the way it moved, but John had seen enough to know it was no ordinary staff member. Curiosity flared, mixed with the fear that had been gnawing at him for days. He knew he should turn around, go back to his quarters, and pretend he hadn't seen anything. But something inside him wouldn't let it go. He needed to know.

Slowly, carefully, John crept closer to the doorway, keeping to the shadows. His mind raced, weighing the risks, but the pull of the unknown was too strong to resist. He had come this far, and turning back now would mean living with even more unanswered questions. And John was done with unanswered questions.

He peered through the small window in the door, just in time to see the figure disappear deeper into the Epsilon facility. The door clicked shut behind them, leaving John alone in the dimly lit corridor, his heart pounding in his chest. What is Epsilon, really? The question echoed in his mind, louder and more urgent than ever.

John lingered in the shadows, debating his next move. He could feel the weight of the decision pressing down on him one wrong step, and everything could unravel. But the need to understand, to find the truth that seemed to elude him at every turn, was too powerful to ignore.

Taking a deep breath, he made a decision. He would find out what Epsilon was, and why it seemed to be at the centre of the facility's secrets. He would do it carefully, discreetly, and most importantly, alone.

John's breath hitched as he observed the figure from his hidden vantage point. There was something unsettlingly familiar about them, though he couldn't quite place where he had seen them before. The figure's silver eyes seemed to scan the room with a predatory awareness, and John instinctively pressed himself further into the shadows.

The two staff members continued their conversation, their voices dropping to hushed tones, but John strained to catch their words.

"We have to make a decision soon. The longer we wait, the more dangerous it becomes," the first staff member insisted, his voice barely above a whisper.

"Agreed," the second replied, glancing nervously towards the figure with silver eyes. "But if the higher-ups find out we've been discussing this…"

"They won't, as long as we keep it quiet. But we can't keep patching the timeline like this. We need a permanent solution."

The tall figure with the silver eyes turned suddenly, as if sensing John's presence, and he barely had time to duck back out of sight. His heart pounded in his chest, and he willed himself to stay still, every muscle tensed. For a moment, there was only silence, broken only by the distant hum of machinery and the faint echo of footsteps as the staff members moved on.

John exhaled slowly, his mind racing with the fragments of conversation he had overheard. Anomalies? Patching the timeline? None of it made sense, but it all sounded like it was far more serious than anything he had encountered in his training.

The silver-eyed figure's presence weighed heavily on him, lingering in his mind as he debated his next move. They clearly held some kind of authority within the facility possibly even within the broader structure of the Lennox Time Corporation itself. But who were they, and what role did they play in this increasingly tangled web of secrets?

John knew he had to be cautious, but he also knew that this might be the only chance he had to gather more information. He waited until he was certain the staff members and the mysterious figure had moved on before quietly slipping further into the Epsilon facility.

As he ventured deeper, the atmosphere grew colder, the buzz of machinery more pronounced, as though the facility itself were alive, pulsing with hidden energy. The dim lights flickered overhead, casting ominous shadows that danced along the walls. John kept close to the edges of the corridor, his senses on high alert for any signs of movement.

He came across a door marked with a symbol he didn't recognise a complex geometric design that seemed to twist and shift as he stared at it. Hesitating only for a moment, John reached for the handle, steeling himself for whatever lay beyond.

The door creaked open, revealing a dimly lit room filled with monitors and strange, humming devices. At the centre of the room stood a large console, its surface covered in buttons and dials that John couldn't begin to comprehend. The monitors displayed timelines his timelines intersecting, overlapping, and fraying at the edges. He recognised snippets of his own past, mingled with scenes from what looked like possible futures.

His pulse quickened as he approached the console. Whatever this place was, it was tied directly to him, to his past and his future. The cryptic messages, the anomalies, the secrecy it was all connected. He had stumbled upon something that the facility was desperately trying to keep hidden, and it terrified him as much as it intrigued him.

But before he could examine the console further, he heard the sound of footsteps approaching, and he knew he had to leave now. Quickly, he backed out of the room, pulling the door closed behind him as silently as possible. He turned and hurried back the way he had come, his mind racing with the implications of what he had just seen.

He barely made it back to his quarters before his legs gave out, and he sank onto his bed, his heart still pounding. The encounter had shaken him, but it had also steeled his determination. Whatever was going on in the Epsilon facility, whatever secrets they were hiding he was going to find out. And he was going to make sure that he wasn't just a pawn in their game.

As he lay there, trying to calm his racing thoughts, he couldn't shake the memory of the figure he had seen. His heart skipped a beat as he replayed the moment in his mind. Who was that person? They didn't look like any of the staff he had seen before. The way they moved, the way their gaze had swept the corridor with a sense of awareness that seemed to cut through the shadows it sent a chill down his spine.

He pressed himself deeper into the shadows in his mind and the creases of his bed, recalling how he had held his breath, watching as the figure paused, almost as if they sensed his presence. There was something unsettlingly familiar about them, but no matter how hard he tried, he couldn't place it. It gnawed at him, adding another layer of intrigue to the growing mystery surrounding the Epsilon facility.

John's curiosity was piqued, but he knew he needed to be cautious. This was bigger than he had imagined, and diving in recklessly could be dangerous potentially deadly. As his breathing slowly returned to normal, one thing became clear: he couldn't trust anyone completely. Not yet. Not until he had all the answers.

With that thought lingering in his mind, he finally drifted into a restless sleep, knowing that the path ahead was fraught with uncertainty and danger.

The next morning, still haunted by the previous night's revelations, John realised he couldn't tackle this alone. He began spending more time with his fellow recruits, particularly Lisa and Max both sharp and resourceful in their own ways. If anyone could help him dig deeper into the facility's secrets, it was them.

As days passed, John carefully fostered his relationships with the two. Over casual conversations during training sessions and shared meals, he subtly probed for hints of what they knew or had noticed. He needed to know if they were seeing the same inconsistencies, sensing the same hidden tensions.

It wasn't long before their subtle glances and quiet, cryptic comments told him that Lisa and Max, too, were beginning to pick up on the same irregularities. The bond between them grew, cemented by the unspoken understanding that something about the facility was off.

One morning over breakfast in the bustling mess hall, John decided it was time to take the next step. Leaning in closer to Lisa and Max, his voice low but steady, he casually asked, "Have you guys noticed anything strange going on around here?"

Lisa paused, a thoughtful expression crossing her face. "Well, I did hear some of the staff talking about increased security measures. They mentioned something about the Epsilon facility, but I didn't catch all the details."

Max, who had been quietly stirring his coffee, looked up with a frown. "Yeah, I've picked up on similar things. There's definitely something going on, but they're keeping it under wraps. I thought it was just standard protocol, but now... I'm not so sure."

John glanced around the room to make sure no one was listening, then leaned in closer. "I think there's more to it. I've been receiving cryptic messages, and I believe they're related to the breaches and the activity around Epsilon."

Lisa raised an eyebrow. "Messages? Like what?"

"*Seek the truth. Trust no one,*" John recited quietly, his voice tinged with frustration. "It's like they want me to find something, but I have no idea what. And I'm starting to think it has everything to do with this place."

Max's eyes narrowed thoughtfully. "That's not something you ignore. If someone's going through the trouble to send you those messages, there's a reason. But why the secrecy? And why you?"

John shook his head. "I don't know yet. But I think we need to find out what's really going on, starting with the Epsilon facility."

Lisa and Max exchanged glances, their curiosity clearly piqued. "Alright, we're in," Lisa said, a determined look in her eyes. "What's the plan?"

Max leaned in, his voice lowering conspiratorially. "We'll need to be careful. If they're hiding something, they'll be watching us too. We can't raise any suspicions."

John nodded, feeling a sense of relief that he wasn't alone in this. "Agreed. Let's gather what we can without drawing attention, and we'll meet up tonight to figure out our next move."

Lisa smirked. "Looks like we're going on a little adventure."

John outlined his strategy: they would keep a low profile, discreetly gather information, and share their findings only with each other. Meanwhile, they'd continue their training, staying sharp and ready for whatever challenges might come their way.

As they worked together, John felt a deepening sense of purpose. The cryptic messages, the breaches, and the activity around Epsilon all pointed to something bigger than any of them. He knew they had to uncover the truth something wasn't right, and he was determined to get to the bottom of it.

As they finalised their plan, Lisa leaned in, her voice hushed. "Are we going to let Gabe in on this?"

John and Max exchanged a quick glance before both shook their heads emphatically. "No," they said in unison.

"Not yet," John added, his tone firm. "We need to figure out what's going on before we involve anyone else."

With that settled, the group went back to their routine, blending in as best they could. The training sessions were as intense as ever, and John pushed himself harder, his focus sharper than it had ever been. The truth was out there, and he was getting closer to it with every passing day.

Ever since the breach, the facility ramped up its security measures. The heightened alert was palpable; recruits and staff moved with a cautious edge; their senses sharp for any sign of trouble. Despite the increased vigilance, John, Lisa, and Max continued their investigation with a growing sense of urgency.

One evening, while John was combing through ancient texts in the library, he stumbled upon a passage that seized his attention. It described a temporal anomaly that had occurred centuries ago an anomaly eerily similar to the recent breaches. The text was dense and cryptic, but John managed to piece together fragments of the story. The anomaly had been linked to a powerful artifact, one rumoured to manipulate time itself. Though the artifact had been lost to history, its impact on the timeline was undeniable.

John's mind raced as he considered the implications. Could the recent breaches be connected to this long-lost artifact? And if so, what could that mean for the present and the future?

Eager to explore this new lead, John shared his findings with Lisa and Max the next morning. The mention of a powerful time-manipulating artifact caught their attention immediately. "This could be the key to everything," Max mused, his mind already churning with possibilities.

Lisa nodded, her expression serious. "If the breaches are linked to this artifact, it explains why they're so desperate to keep everything under wraps. We need to find out more."

Their investigation now had a sharper focus: the Epsilon facility, a heavily guarded research centre specialising in temporal displacement studies. Getting inside would be risky, but they all agreed it was the only way to get the answers they needed.

Over the next few days, the trio meticulously gathered information. They observed the facility from a distance, noting the security protocols, the timing of shifts, and the movements of key personnel. Every detail was scrutinised and recorded, their plan slowly taking shape. It was dangerous, but the stakes were too high to back down now.

One evening, under the cover of darkness, John, Lisa, and Max made their move. The night was still, the only sounds came from the distant rumble of machinery and the occasional rustle of leaves in the breeze. They had spent days preparing, memorising the facility's security systems and timing their approach to avoid detection. Now, it was time to put their plan into action.

The trio moved with silent precision, their footsteps barely making a sound on the cold, concrete floor as they bypassed the perimeter defences. Max, with his tech expertise, effortlessly disabled the security cameras, creating a brief window of opportunity. Lisa kept watch, her sharp eyes scanning the shadows for any sign of movement. John led the way, his heart pounding in his chest, a mix of fear and excitement propelling him forward.

The corridors inside the Epsilon facility were dimly lit, the sterile, industrial atmosphere adding to the unease that hung in the air. The faint hum of machinery reverberated through the walls, creating a sense of oppressive confinement. They moved cautiously, every turn and intersection bringing them closer to the heart of the facility and, potentially, the answers they sought.

After what felt like an eternity of navigating the maze-like hallways, they finally arrived at the end of a long, narrow corridor. There, looming before them, was a giant steel elevator with a single button beside it. The metal doors were polished to a cold, reflective sheen, casting distorted reflections of the three of them as they approached.

John hesitated for a moment, his hand hovering over the button. This was it the point of no return. With a deep breath, he pressed the button, and the elevator doors slid open with a low, mechanical hiss. The interior was stark and unwelcoming, its metallic walls gleaming under the harsh overhead light.

They stepped inside, the doors closing behind them with a sense of finality that sent a shiver down John's spine. The elevator was small, barely enough room for the three of them, and the air felt thick with tension. On the panel before them, there were only two buttons and a keyhole. One button was marked "ST," and the other had a large, ominous red "E" emblazoned on it.

John stared at the buttons, his mind racing. "ST" likely stood for "Surface Transport" or something similar perhaps a safer option. But the big red "E" was clearly the one that led deeper into the facility, likely to the restricted areas they were seeking. His fingers twitched with indecision. Which button would lead to the answers they sought? And which one could lead them into a trap?

Before John could voice his thoughts, Max suddenly reached out and pressed the red "E" button without hesitation.

"Big red 'E,' must be Epsilon," Max said with a shrug. "So, I pushed it. Sue me."

John blinked in surprise, the words caught in his throat. Lisa giggled softly and shot John a shrug, as if to say, *Why not?*

All three of them braced as the elevator jolted into motion, beginning its descent deeper into the unknown. John turned to Max, his voice a mix of concern and irritation. "Wha Max, are you sure about this?"

Max met John's gaze with a determined look, his expression resolute. "If we're going to find out what's really going on, we need to go all the way. No turning back now."

Lisa nodded in agreement, her eyes steely with resolve. "We're in this together, John. Let's see where this takes us."

The elevator had shuddered to life, descending rapidly as the floor beneath them seemed to drop away. The hum of the machinery grew louder, the walls vibrating slightly as they plunged deeper into the unknown. The three of them exchanged tense glances, each of them bracing for whatever awaited them below.

After a few minutes, the elevator came to a stop with a soft ding, the doors sliding open with a grating metallic screech. John peered around the corner, searching for guards, his breath held in anticipation. Oddly enough, there weren't any in sight. The corridor beyond was dimly lit, the walls lined with steel and illuminated by flickering, pale lights. The air was frigid, carrying with it a faint, acrid scent that set John's nerves on edge.

Unbeknownst to the trio, two figures watched their every move through the glowing screens in the facility's security control room. One, a technician, glanced nervously at the man standing beside him tall, composed, and cloaked in the same quiet authority that John had felt in Epsilon. It was him the same man who had been watching John before.

"Sir, they're moving deeper into Sector E," the technician murmured, his voice tight with uncertainty. "Should we alert security?"

The man, his face partially hidden in the shadows of the dimly lit room, leaned forward, studying the screen with the same unsettling calmness. "No," he replied, his voice a smooth, calculated whisper of control. "Let them continue. I want to see how far they'll go. John's been curious… but we'll learn more if we don't intervene yet."

The technician hesitated, fingers hovering over the controls. "But, sir, they're not authorised to be in Epsilon. Shouldn't we—"

"They're no threat," the mystery man interrupted, his tone soft but decisive. "I've watched John before. He knows more than he lets on. Let him lead his friends a little further."

Back in the corridor, John, Lisa, and Max continued navigating the labyrinthine passages. John's heart pounded in his chest, a blend of fear and exhilaration coursing through him. Every step they took seemed to pull them deeper into the unknown, the weight of their decision settling heavily on their shoulders. The corridors twisted and turned, a maze of sleek, metallic walls that reflected the dim light, casting eerie shadows that danced along the floor.

The air grew cooler as they descended, a stark contrast to the warmth of the upper levels. It was as if they were venturing into the very heart of the facility, a place where secrets were buried, and truths were obscured by layers of security and deception. The faint hum of machinery reverberated through the walls, a constant reminder of the technology that powered this place, and the potential dangers that lay ahead.

Their journey led them to a particularly ominous corridor, the walls narrowing as if funnelling them towards something significant. The dim lighting flickered intermittently, casting brief moments of darkness that heightened their anxiety. John exchanged a glance with Max and Lisa, both of whom appeared as tense as he felt. But there was no turning back now; they were committed to uncovering whatever lay ahead.

Finally, they arrived at a secure chamber, the door looming before them like a sentinel guarding its secrets. The door was marked with symbols that John immediately recognised from the cryptic messages he had received. His pulse quickened, his breath hitching as he stepped closer, drawn to the door by an inexplicable force.

The symbols were etched deeply into the metal, their patterns complex and ancient, each line and curve meticulously crafted. They seemed to glow faintly, a soft luminescence that pulsed in rhythm with his heartbeat. John's fingers hovered over the designs, almost as if they were inviting his touch. When he finally allowed his fingers to trace the intricate markings, he felt a subtle vibration emanating from the door, as though it were alive with a hidden power, waiting to be unlocked.

Lisa and Max watched silently, their expressions a mixture of awe and apprehension. "What do you think it means?" Lisa whispered, her voice barely audible in the stillness of the corridor.

"I don't know," John replied, his voice equally hushed, "but I think we're about to find out."

Max stepped forward, his eyes narrowing as he examined the door more closely. "There has to be a way to open it," he murmured, his mind already working to solve the puzzle. "Maybe something in the symbols or a hidden mechanism."

John nodded, his mind racing. The symbols seemed familiar, yet their meaning eluded him. He focused on the patterns, trying to recall anything from his studies or the cryptic messages that might give him a clue. The realisation struck him suddenly these symbols were more than just markings. They were a code, a key to unlocking whatever lay beyond the door.

Taking a deep breath, John pressed his hand flat against the centre of the door, where the symbols converged into a single, intricate design. For a moment, nothing happened. Then, slowly, the door began to respond, the vibrations intensifying as the symbols glowed brighter. The metal beneath his hand grew warm, the heat spreading through his fingers and up his arm, until the door finally slid open with a soft, mechanical hiss.

Beyond the threshold lay a room bathed in a soft, ethereal light. The chamber was unlike anything they had seen before, its walls lined with advanced technology interspersed with artefacts that appeared ancient, their origins a mystery. The air inside was cool, almost cold, and carried a faint metallic scent, tinged with something that felt ancient and powerful.

John, Max, and Lisa stepped inside, their eyes wide with wonder and trepidation. The room seemed to hum with a life of its own, the energy within it palpable, almost overwhelming. In the centre of the chamber stood a pedestal, and on it, a small, glowing object that radiated an intense, otherworldly energy.

"Is that?" Lisa began, her voice trailing off as she stared at the object in awe.

John nodded slowly; his eyes locked on the glowing artifact. "I think it is," he whispered, the weight of their discovery settling over him. This was what they had been searching for an artifact of immense power, connected to the very fabric of time itself.

With a deep breath, John activated the access panel. The door slid open with a soft hiss, revealing a chamber that was both awe-inspiring and intimidating. A rush of cool air greeted them, carrying the sharp scent of ozone and something distinctly metallic. The atmosphere inside was different, almost charged with an unseen energy that made the hairs on the back of John's neck stand on end.

As they stepped inside, the chamber revealed itself in all its technological splendour. The walls were lined with an array of screens, each displaying streams of complex data and holographic interfaces that seemed to float in mid-air. The floor was made of a smooth, dark material that absorbed the ambient light, giving the room an otherworldly feel, as if they had stepped into a realm beyond the ordinary.

The air hummed with energy, a vibration that resonated deep within their bones, making each breath feel both invigorating and daunting. At the centre of the room, suspended within a protective field, was the artifact. It was a crystalline structure, its surface shimmering with a kaleidoscope of colours that shifted and danced like the Northern Lights. The artifact pulsed with a rhythmic energy, sending out waves of power that were palpable even from a distance.

The chamber was bathed in the artifact's glow, the shifting colours casting ethereal shadows on the walls. The ceiling arched high above them, lined with conduits and intricate wiring that seemed to pulse in time with the artifact's energy. The entire room felt alive, as though the very technology surrounding them was a part of the artifact's power, responding to its rhythm.

John's eyes widened as he took in the sight, his mind racing with possibilities. The artifact was unlike anything he had ever encountered, its beauty and power mesmerising in a way that defied explanation. He could feel its energy reaching out to him, a connection that was almost tangible, as if the artifact itself recognised him and sought to communicate.

Lisa and Max joined him, their expressions mirroring his awe. "This is it," Lisa whispered, her voice barely audible over the hum of the artifact. "This is what we've been searching for."

John nodded, his heart pounding in his chest. The artifact held the key to understanding the breaches, the cryptic messages, and perhaps even his own place in this complex web of time. It was a beacon of knowledge and power; a nexus point that connected them all to the greater mysteries of the timeline.

The room seemed to hold its breath as they stood before the artifact, the enormity of their discovery settling over them like a heavy shroud. They had found what they were looking for, but the implications of this discovery were far greater than they could have ever imagined. The artifact was not just a key it was a doorway, one that could lead to answers or to untold dangers.

John felt a mix of fear and excitement as he reached out towards the artifact, the pull of its energy irresistible. This was the moment they had been building towards, the culmination of their search. But as his fingers hovered just above the crystalline surface, he knew that whatever happened next would change everything.

This moment was filled with anticipation, every breath charged with the awareness that touching the artifact could have significant consequences. The air around them seemed to thrum with energy, and John felt a pull deep within him, as if the artifact was calling to him, urging him to reach out and make contact. The weight of the moment pressed down on him, his heart pounding in his chest as his hand inched closer to the crystalline structure.

But just as his fingers were about to make contact, a voice echoed through the chamber, startling them. The voice was calm but commanding, carrying a weight of authority that made John pause mid-motion. "Step away from the artifact," it said, the words cutting through the charged silence like a blade.

As they turned to face the figure, John's breath caught in his throat. The figure's piercing silver eyes, cold and commanding, seemed to bore into him, and for a brief moment, something flickered in John's mind a vague, distant sensation, like a memory just out of reach. It was as though he should recognise this person, but the connection was hazy, buried deep within the recesses of his mind. The feeling was unsettling, sending a shiver down his spine, but he couldn't place it.

The figure's gaze swept over them, their expression unreadable. "You are not authorised to be here," the voice repeated, firm but calm. The words carried a hint of warning, yet also something else a note of finality that made John hesitate, as if the figure knew far more than they were letting on.

John's hand, which had instinctively reached out to the artifact, now fell to his side. The pull he felt from the artifact was still strong, almost magnetic, but the unease he felt from this strange, commanding figure was stronger. His mind raced, questions piling up one after another, but he knew this wasn't the time for answers.

As he motioned for Lisa and Max to step back, that flicker of recognition twitched again in the back of his mind. There was something disturbingly familiar about this person, something that tugged at the edges of his consciousness, but it was buried too deep for him to grasp. John frowned, pushing the feeling aside, knowing they couldn't risk a confrontation not yet.

The figure stayed rooted by the artifact, their presence a silent but powerful barrier between them and the answers they sought. With a final, reluctant glance at the glowing crystal, John turned and led Lisa and Max out of the chamber. The door slid shut behind them with a final hiss, sealing the artifact and the enigmatic figure away.

As they made their way back through the labyrinthine corridors, John's mind churned with thoughts. The encounter had only solidified his drive to uncover the truth. There was more at stake here than he had realised, and he couldn't shake the feeling that the figure in the chamber was somehow connected to him in a way he didn't yet understand.

But for now, that understanding eluded him, buried in the depths of his subconscious, waiting for the right moment to surface.

The trio raced back to the elevator, their hearts pounding in unison. John's hand slammed onto the button labelled "ST," and the elevator responded immediately, hurtling upward with a speed that made their stomachs lurch. The confined space felt like it was vibrating with the intensity of their emotions fear, adrenaline, and the lingering sense of the artifact's power still crackling in the air around them. The elevator's ascent was rapid, a stark contrast to the ominous descent they had just made. Each second felt like an eternity, the walls closing in as they silently prayed for a clean getaway.

After several tense minutes, the elevator jolted to a halt, and the doors slid open with a soft hiss. Relief was short-lived as John's face was met with the cold, unyielding barrel of a large weapon. His breath caught in his throat as he looked up to see Jack Banks, the no-nonsense combat trainer, on the other side, his expression a mix of disappointment and restrained anger.

Jack kept his weapon trained on them, his eyes narrowing as he reached up with his free hand to touch the communication device on his neck. "I have them," he said, his voice clipped. "They were in the elevator." There was a pause, the tension in the air thick enough to cut. "No, it's just the three of them. Security footage only shows them. We'll be in your office when you arrive."

With a practiced motion, Jack lowered his hand back to steady his weapon, his gaze never leaving the trio. "Alright," he commanded, his voice brooking no argument, "out of the elevator and sit here on the couch. Dr Thompson will be here shortly."

The three recruits, their earlier bravado now replaced by a heavy sense of impending consequence, followed his direction without protest. The couch felt like the seat of judgment as they sat, the weight of their actions pressing down on them. John's mind raced, trying to anticipate what would come next, while Lisa and Max exchanged anxious glances.

Moments later, the doors to Sarah's office burst open with a force that made all three of them jump. Sarah strode into the room, her steps quick and purposeful, each one a testament to the fury simmering beneath her composed exterior. Behind her, Gabe sauntered in, the familiar curl of a cigarillo hanging from his lips. He glanced at the scene, then looked down, spitting a small stream of tobacco juice onto the floor. Sarah's head snapped towards him, her eyes flashing with even more rage. Gabe, unperturbed, simply offered a sly smile and took a few steps back, distancing himself slightly as if to let Sarah handle the matter.

As Sarah began her reprimand, Jack stood by the door, his expression unreadable. After a brief exchange of glances with Gabe, Jack gave a small nod and silently exited the room, his role in the confrontation complete. Gabe, still leaning against the wall, continued to puff on his cigarillo, ignoring Sarah's earlier admonishment.

With Jack gone, Sarah's attention snapped back to the three recruits. She crossed her arms, her piercing gaze locking onto them. "You shouldn't be down there," she began, her voice icy and controlled, barely concealing the anger bubbling beneath the surface. "That area is restricted for a reason."

John swallowed hard, his earlier resolve wavering under the weight of her stare. "We had to find out the truth," he managed to say, his voice weaker than he intended. But Sarah cut him off sharply, her words like a whip.

"And another thing you shouldn't be anywhere near that elevator either," she continued, her tone brooking no excuses. "How did you get past security?"

Max shifted uncomfortably in his seat, a sheepish grin tugging at his lips as he met Sarah's gaze. The mischievous spark in his eyes did little to lighten the tension in the room. Sarah's shoulders slumped slightly as she sighed, shaking her head as if she had expected better but wasn't entirely surprised by their audacity.

Gabe, leaning against the doorway, finally spoke up, his voice casual but tinged with a hint of amusement. "Kids these days, always poking their noses where they don't belong." He took another drag from his cigarillo, the smoke curling lazily around his head as he watched the scene unfold.

Sarah shot him a withering look, her patience clearly wearing thin. "Gabe," she snapped, her voice sharp, "how many times do I have to tell you? No smoking on facility grounds."

Gabe's smile widened, the corners of his mouth curling up in a roguish grin. He tipped his hat slightly, a gesture of mock respect, and took another slow drag from the cigarillo, the embers glowing bright. "I'll keep that in mind, ma'am," he drawled, the smoke escaping his lips in a deliberate, leisurely exhale.

Sarah's eyes narrowed, but she knew better than to waste her energy arguing with him. With a frustrated shake of her head, she turned back to the trio on the couch, her focus shifting back to the matter at hand. "You're in deep trouble," she said, her voice now tinged with disappointment as much as anger. "But more than that, you've crossed into territory that could have serious repercussions. You don't know what you're dealing with."

John met her gaze, his mind racing. He knew they were in trouble, but the encounter with the artifact and the mysterious figure was too important to ignore. "We didn't go down there just for kicks," he said, his voice steady but firm. "The breaches, the messages they're all connected to this artifact."

Sarah's eyes softened, her anger giving way to something more complex concern, perhaps even fear. "I understand your need for answers, John," she said, her voice quieter now. "But there are things about this artifact that even we don't fully comprehend. It's powerful, and it's dangerous."

John leaned forward, his expression intense. "We can't just leave it alone. We need to know what it is and how it's impacting the timeline."

Sarah sighed, her shoulders slumping slightly as she weighed the situation. "You're right that this is important, but you went about it the wrong way. This isn't just about breaking the rules what you did could have serious repercussions, not just for you, but for the entire timeline."

Gabe, who had been quietly observing the exchange, finally spoke up. "Sarah, they were wrong to go down there, but you and I both know there's more at play here. The kid's been getting those messages for a reason, and they're tied to that artifact. If we shut them out now, we might lose our best shot at figuring out what's really going on."

Sarah shot Gabe a sharp look, but there was a hint of understanding in her eyes. "I know, Gabe. But we can't just let this slide. They need to understand the gravity of what they've done."

Gabe nodded, stepping forward. "They do. And they will. But if we punish them now without addressing the bigger issue, we're just putting blinders on. We need to face this head-on, together."

Sarah hesitated, the conflict clear on her face. Finally, she sighed again, her resolve softening. "Alright. But understand this," she said, turning to John, Lisa, and Max. "You're still in trouble. There will be consequences for breaking protocol. But..." she paused, her gaze softening slightly, "we need to proceed with caution. I'll help you, but we must do this together. No more going off on your own."

John nodded; relief mixed with the weight of responsibility. "Thank you, Sarah. We won't let you down."

Sarah nodded, her expression firm. "Good. But first, I'm going to have another talk with Gabe," she added, shooting him a look that promised a serious conversation later.

Turning back to the recruits, Sarah's expression softened slightly, but her tone remained firm. "You three are dismissed. Go back to your quarters and stay out of trouble. We'll discuss your next steps in the morning."

John, Lisa, and Max nodded, a mix of relief and lingering tension in their expressions. Without another word, they quietly exited the room, their footsteps echoing down the corridor as they made their way back to their quarters.

As the door closed behind them, Sarah turned to Gabe, her arms crossed. "We need to talk."

Gabe tipped his hat slightly, his usual grin tempered by the seriousness of the situation. "I figured as much," he said, leaning back against the wall. "But you know as well as I do that those kids are onto something. We can't just ignore it."

As soon as the recruits were out of earshot, Sarah's posture relaxed just a fraction, but the tension between her and Gabe was palpable. She moved to her desk, her fingers tracing absent patterns on the surface, clearly gathering her thoughts.

Gabe watched her, his hat tipped back slightly, eyes narrowing as he studied her. "So, what's the plan now, Sarah? We keep dancing around this, or are we finally going to face it head-on?"

Sarah's eyes flicked up to meet his, a mix of frustration and something more vulnerable flashing in her gaze. "You know we can't just come out with it, Gabe. Not yet. There's too much at stake."

"Yeah, but how long do you think we can keep this up before it all blows up in our faces?" Gabe asked, his voice softer now, as if the fight had gone out of him. He pushed off from the wall and walked closer to her, the usual swagger in his step subdued. "John's smart, too smart. He's going to start connecting the dots, and when he does…"

"He'll need us more than ever," Sarah finished, her tone almost resigned. She leaned against the desk, crossing her arms tightly, as if trying to hold herself together. "But we can't overwhelm him. If he learns too much too fast… it could be disastrous."

Gabe nodded slowly, understanding but not entirely agreeing. "It's not just about protecting him, though, is it? It's about protecting what he means to all of this… and what he means to you." The last words carried a weight that was hard to ignore, laden with unspoken history.

Sarah flinched slightly, not at the mention of Alexander Voskos, but at the way Gabe's words tugged at their shared past. They had once been close closer than either would admit now, given the layers of professionalism and secrets that had piled up between them. "I know, Gabe," she said quietly, her voice almost breaking. "But we're playing a dangerous game here. One wrong move, and it's not just John who could suffer."

Gabe reached out, placing a hand on her shoulder, the gesture somewhere between comforting and conflicted. "We'll handle this, Sarah. We have to. For John's sake… and for everything else that's riding on this."

Sarah looked at him, her gaze softening, though the walls she'd built between them over the years remained firmly in place. "Just promise me we won't push him too hard, Gabe. He's been through enough already."

Gabe nodded, his hand lingering for just a moment longer before he stepped back, the distance between them returning. "I promise, Sarah. We'll do it your way. But we can't keep this up forever."

"No," Sarah agreed, a hint of sadness in her voice. "We can't. But for now, we do what we have to. For John."

Gabe tipped his hat, his smile returning but with a trace of melancholy. "For John."

With that, the tension between them settled into something more manageable, a shared understanding that, despite everything, they were in this together. For John, for the secrets they guarded, and for the future that was rapidly approaching one that neither of them could fully control.

As they worked, John felt an increasingly strong connection to the artifact. It was as if it resonated with something deep within him, its energy calling out in ways he couldn't fully explain. The cryptic messages that had led him here now seemed to take on new meaning, their words guiding him towards a deeper understanding of both the artifact and himself.

The investigation also brought the team closer together. Sarah's knowledge and experience proved invaluable, her insights steering their efforts with precision. Lisa's background in archaeology provided a unique perspective on the artifact's ancient origins, while Max's technical prowess ensured they could navigate the complex systems within the facility.

Together, they uncovered startling revelations. The artifact had been created by an ancient civilisation that had mastered the art of temporal manipulation. Its original purpose was to safeguard the timeline, preventing anomalies and ensuring the continuity of history. But over time, its power had been corrupted, leading to the very breaches they now faced.

John's mind raced as he processed the implications. The artifact was both a blessing and a curse, its power capable of shaping the course of history for better or worse. They had to find a way to control it, to harness its energy for the greater good.

Their efforts culminated in a plan to stabilise the artifact and prevent further breaches. It was a complex and risky endeavour, one that required precise coordination and unwavering focus. But they were determined to succeed, their determination undeterred by the challenges ahead.

The night of the operation arrived, the facility buzzing with a tense anticipation. John, Sarah, Lisa, and Max gathered in the chamber; their expressions set with strength of mind. The artifact pulsed with a rhythmic energy, its power palpable in the air.

"Are you ready?" Sarah asked, her gaze sweeping over the team.

John nodded, his heart pounding. "Let's do this."

They moved with precision; their actions guided by weeks of preparation. John focused on the artifact, feeling its energy resonate within him. The connection was undeniable, almost magnetic, pulling him towards a destiny he was only beginning to comprehend.

As they initiated the stabilisation process, the chamber was bathed in a blinding light. The artifact's energy surged, its power threatening to overwhelm them. But they held their ground, each one drawing on their inner strength.

John's mind whirled with a mix of fear and determination. The artifact's energy coursed through him, both exhilarating and terrifying. They were on the brink of something monumental a moment that would shape the course of history.

With a final surge of effort, they completed the process. The artifact's energy stabilised, its rhythmic pulsing slowing to a steady, controlled beat. The blinding light dimmed, leaving the chamber bathed in a soft, radiant glow.

John's breath caught as he took in the sight. The artifact was transformed, its energy harmonised and controlled. He could still feel its power, but now it was something he could understand and, perhaps, even command.

"We did it," Sarah whispered, her voice filled with awe. "We've stabilised the artifact."

John nodded, a sense of relief and triumph washing over him. They had faced the unknown and emerged victorious, ensuring the continuity of the timeline.

As they stood in the chamber, bathed in the artifact's radiant glow, John knew their journey was far from over. The challenges ahead would be formidable, but they were ready. With their newfound understanding and unwavering commitment, they faced the future with confidence and determination.

In the days that followed, the facility buzzed with renewed purpose. The stabilisation of the artifact brought a fresh sense of urgency to their work, as they focused on safeguarding the timeline and preventing further breaches.

John, Lisa, Max, and Sarah worked tirelessly; their bond strengthened by their shared experiences. Each day brought new challenges, but they faced them together, united by a common goal.

As they stood in the chamber once more, gazing at the artifact, John felt a deep sense of fulfilment and anticipation. The cryptic messages had guided him to this moment, revealing a destiny intertwined with the fate of the timeline.

Taking a steadying breath, John let his fingers hover just above the artifact. The energy radiating from it was almost tangible, humming with a power that both humbled and emboldened him. He could feel the weight of what lay ahead, a path fraught with challenges and uncertainties.

"We've made a lot of progress," Lisa said softly, the pride in her voice tinged with the awareness of the work that still remained. "But we're just getting started."

John nodded, his gaze still fixed on the artifact, its rhythmic pulse matching the beat of his own heart. "There's so much more to uncover," he murmured, the determination in his voice clear. "We've only scratched the surface. But no matter what comes next, we're in this together. We'll protect the timeline, no matter what it takes."

Chapter Twelve

The hum of machinery and the soft buzz of conversations filled the air of the research facility. The room was a hive of activity, with scientists and technicians moving about, their faces illuminated by the glow of computer screens and holographic displays. Rows of advanced equipment lined the walls, humming with energy as they processed vast amounts of data. The sterile, metallic scent of the facility mixed with the faint, tangy aroma of ozone from the constantly running high-tech devices.

Without warning, a blinding light erupted in the centre of the facility, forcing everyone to shield their eyes. Conversations halted mid-sentence, the hum of machinery seemed to fade, and the air itself grew thick with tension. The light was so intense that it seemed to pierce the very fabric of the room, casting stark, jagged shadows across the polished surfaces. As it dimmed, the silhouette of a tall, imposing figure emerged, their presence dominating the room even before the last flicker of light faded.

When the light finally subsided, the figure stood there, a commanding presence in the sterile environment. Their androgynous face was set in a stern, unreadable expression, and their piercing silver eyes scanned the room with a gaze that seemed to cut through the very air. Sarah's usually composed demeanour faltered for a split second just long enough for those closest to her to notice. She quickly masked her surprise, but the slight widening of her eyes betrayed her unease. Gabe shifted uncomfortably, a hand twitching towards the weapon at his side before thinking better of it.

The figure's mere presence was enough to silence the entire facility. The scientists and technicians, normally so absorbed in their work, found themselves frozen in place, their faces reflecting a mix of awe and fear. Even the constant hum of the advanced machinery seemed to quiet, as if in deference to the authority that had just appeared in their midst.

"I need to speak with Sarah Thompson and Gabe Welles immediately," the figure demanded, his voice calm yet commanding. His voice carried a weight that made it clear he was not to be questioned, resonating with a depth that seemed to reverberate through the room.

The room remained silent as everyone stared in shock at the newcomer. John, standing nearby with Lisa and Max, felt his heart skip a beat. He had seen this person before, outside of Epsilon, though he couldn't quite place where. The figure's presence stirred something deep within him, a flicker of recognition that he still couldn't quite grasp. Was it St. Louis? Was it more? The answer was just out of his reach, in the far recesses of his memory.

Lisa and Max exchanged bewildered glances. "Who is that?" Max whispered, his eyes wide with curiosity and a hint of fear. The glow from the various screens cast an eerie light on his face, emphasising his wide eyes and furrowed brow.

"No idea," Lisa replied, her voice tinged with awe. "But he doesn't look like someone you'd want to mess with." She kept her gaze fixed on the figure, her posture tense and ready to react.

John's mind raced. He had seen this man before; he was sure of it. But where? The image was fleeting, like a shadow in his memory, always just out of reach. His curiosity and anxiety grew with each passing second. The room's usual background noise seemed to fade away, leaving only the pounding of his heart and the low hum of the machinery.

Sarah stepped forward; her expression composed but her eyes betraying a hint of unease. The normally confident and authoritative director seemed momentarily taken aback by the figure's sudden appearance. "Follow me," she said, her voice steady despite the tension in the air. She led the figure to a secure conference room away from prying eyes and ears, her movements purposeful but slightly hurried, as if eager to get the encounter out of the public eye.

The scientists and technicians slowly returned to their tasks, but the air was thick with a mix of curiosity and apprehension. Whispers spread through the room, the sudden arrival of the mysterious figure leaving a palpable sense of unease. John, Lisa, and Max exchanged glances, their thoughts racing with questions and concerns about what had just transpired.

Inside the conference room, the atmosphere was tense. The walls were lined with advanced technological interfaces, each one displaying real-time data from various points in history. Holographic projections floated in mid-air, showing detailed maps and timelines. A large, polished table occupied the centre of the room, its surface embedded with interactive screens.

Sarah, Gabe, and the figure took their seats, the weight of the situation hanging heavy in the air. The figure's presence dominated the room, his piercing silver eyes observing everything with an intensity that was almost palpable. The air was thick with unspoken tension, a blend of professional urgency and unresolved history.

Sarah broke the silence, her voice steady but carrying an undercurrent of tension. "What's the situation?" She shot a glance at Gabe, who returned it with a barely perceptible nod an unspoken acknowledgment of the seriousness of the moment.

The figure's silver eyes locked onto hers as he began to speak. "The stabilisation of the artifact has disrupted the temporal flow. We're seeing anomalies events that were supposed to happen are being altered or erased altogether. If this continues, the consequences could be catastrophic."

Gabe leaned forward; his brow furrowed. "What kind of anomalies?" His tone was professional, but there was an edge to it, something that hinted at more than just concern for the mission.

"Temporal distortions," the figure said, his tone sharp and precise. "The timeline is attempting to correct itself, but it's only causing further damage. Additionally, the stabilisation may have awakened something ancient, something we're not fully prepared to confront."

Sarah's face grew pale, her mind racing. She glanced at the holographic displays showing erratic spikes and deviations in the timeline, her gaze flicking to Gabe, noticing the tightness in his jaw. For a brief moment, memories of their past flickered in her mind their heated debates, the way they used to challenge each other's decisions. But this was different. This was about more than just them.

"How did we miss this?" she asked, her voice more controlled now, though the underlying tension was evident. She was always the one to think ten steps ahead, to plan for every possibility. That she hadn't seen this coming stung more than she cared to admit.

"The artifact's power is beyond even our understanding," the figure admitted, a trace of frustration slipping through his otherwise controlled demeanour. "Stabilisation was necessary, but we underestimated the fallout. We need to act now."

Gabe, sensing Sarah's frustration, softened his tone. "What's the plan?" he asked, a subtle attempt to bridge the gap between them. But there was no denying the undercurrent of blame in the room, hanging between them like unfinished business.

The figure leaned back slightly, his fingers steepled under his chin, his gaze unwavering. "We need to isolate the affected points in the timeline and correct the distortions. Precision is crucial one misstep could make things worse. And keep John away from Epsilon. His training must continue, but he cannot be involved with Epsilon, not yet."

Sarah took a deep breath, her professional demeanour slipping back into place. "We'll need our best operatives on this. Gabe, can you assemble a team?"

"Consider it done," Gabe replied, his voice steady. But there was a brief pause before he continued, a hesitation that only Sarah would notice. "But what about the ancient presence? How do we deal with that?"

The figure's eyes narrowed, and he spoke with a grave certainty. "For now, we focus on stabilising the timeline. If what has been awakened becomes a threat, we will deal with it accordingly. It's crucial that we proceed with caution."

Then the figure turned his intense gaze directly at Gabe. "It is imperative that you continue to mentor John closely. His development is critical to our efforts. Ensure that he remains unharmed. His role is more important than he knows."

Gabe met the figure's eyes and nodded solemnly. "Understood. I'll keep a close watch on him." He felt Sarah's gaze on him, but he didn't turn to meet it. The unspoken tension between them crackled in the air, a reminder of the complicated history they shared and the decisions that had driven them apart.

As the figure's presence faded, the room was left in a charged silence. Sarah stood first, her posture rigid, betraying none of the turmoil she felt inside. "Good. Gabe, you and I will need to have another chat, and soon," she added, shooting him a look that promised a serious conversation later.

Gabe watched her go, his expression unreadable. He could feel the old familiar tension simmering between them, a mixture of unresolved feelings and professional respect. There was so much left unsaid, but now wasn't the time to address it. Their priority had to be the mission.

As Sarah walked away, Gabe let out a breath he didn't realise he'd been holding. There was too much at stake to let their past cloud the present, but that didn't make it any easier to ignore. He turned back to look through the glass at the recruits, ready to focus on the task at hand, but his thoughts lingered on Sarah a moment longer than he would have liked.

Back in the main training area, the recruits were still abuzz with speculation about the mysterious figure and the intense meeting. John, Lisa, and Max exchanged curious looks; their training momentarily forgotten.

"Who do you think that was?" Max asked, his voice barely a whisper.

"No clue, but did you see the way everyone reacted?" Lisa replied, her eyes wide. "He must be someone really important."

John remained silent, his mind racing. He had seen that figure before, but where? The memory was elusive, slipping through his grasp like sand.

Gabe entered the room, his expression serious but calm. He clapped his hands to get everyone's attention. "Alright, listen up!" he called out, his voice carrying authority.

The room fell silent as all eyes turned to him. Gabe scanned the faces of the recruits, noting their mix of curiosity and apprehension. "We need to move back upstairs. There's a situation that requires immediate attention, and we need to be prepared."

John stepped forward, a hint of confusion on his face. "What's going on, Gabe?"

Gabe met his gaze, his expression softening slightly. "I can't give you all the details right now, John. Just know that it's critical, and we need to be ready for anything. Follow the procedures and stay sharp."

Lisa frowned, her curiosity getting the better of her. "Is it related to that figure who just appeared? What's happening?"

Gabe sighed, rubbing the back of his neck. "All I can say is that we're dealing with some serious temporal anomalies. That's why we need to act quickly and efficiently. Trust me, the less you know right now, the better."

Max nodded slowly; his usual playful demeanour replaced by a rare seriousness. "Got it, Gabe. We'll do our part."

"You heard him," Lisa said, nudging Max. "Let's get moving."

As the recruits began to file out of the training area, John lingered for a moment, his mind racing with questions. He wanted to press Gabe for more information, but he could see the determination and urgency in the older man's eyes.

Gabe placed a reassuring hand on John's shoulder. "Stay focused, John. Trust that we're doing everything we can to handle the situation."

John nodded, swallowing his questions for now. "Got it, Gabe."

Together, they made their way upstairs. The hallways, with their soaring ceilings and gleaming surfaces, felt more like a labyrinth today, each turn filled with the tension of the unknown. The air was thick with tension and anticipation, but there was also a sense of resolve. Whatever challenges lay ahead, they would face them together.

The recruits assembled in a larger briefing room upstairs, a space designed for rapid dissemination of information. The walls were lined with screens displaying various historical data points and real-time feeds from various parts of the facility. John, Max, and Lisa sat at the front, with the rest of the class sitting in the rows behind them. Gabe stepped to the front of the room, addressing the group with a steady voice.

"Listen up, kids. We're dealing with some serious anomalies that need our immediate attention. This is a high-stakes situation, and we need all hands on deck. Stay alert and be ready to move at a moment's notice."

John exchanged glances with Lisa and Max. The gravity of the situation was clear, and the mystery of the figure's appearance only added to the urgency. As they settled into their seats, the room buzzed with a mix of nervous energy and determination.

Sarah entered the room, her presence commanding attention. "We've identified key points in the timeline that need intervention," she announced, her voice calm but firm. "Teams will be assigned specific tasks, and you'll be briefed on your roles shortly. Remember, precision is crucial. We cannot afford any mistakes."

The recruits nodded, their focus intensifying. John felt a surge of resolve. Whatever lay ahead, he was ready to face it with his team. The cryptic messages, the training, and the enigmatic figure they were all pieces of a larger puzzle, one that he was determined to solve.

"John, Lisa, Max," Sarah continued, turning her gaze to them. "Return to your training exercises for now. Further orders will be issued later."

John, Lisa, and Max exchanged glances, then nodded. "Understood," John said. They turned and left the briefing room, heading back to the training area.

Gabe watched them go, then turned to Sarah. "I'll keep an eye on them. Make sure they stay focused."

Sarah nodded. "Thank you, Gabe. I'll be in my office, coordinating everything from there. Keep me updated."

"Will do," Gabe replied, and with that, they parted ways.

Sarah made her way back to her office, her mind a whirlwind of activity. The facility was more hectic than ever, with staff hurrying through the corridors, their faces marked by a clear sense of purpose. She reached her office, a sleek, modern space filled with screens and communication devices. She sat down at her desk and began issuing orders, her fingers flying over the keyboard as she coordinated the complex operation.

Meanwhile, John, Lisa, and Max returned to their training exercises. The training area was a large, open space filled with various obstacles and equipment designed to push them to their limits. Despite the challenges he faced, John's mind was elsewhere. The cryptic messages, the enigmatic figure, and the sense of something larger at play gnawed at him, refusing to be ignored.

"Come on, John," Lisa called, snapping him back to the present. "Focus! We need to be ready for anything."

John nodded, shaking off his distractions. "You're right. Let's do this."

They threw themselves into their exercises with a fresh resolve. They climbed walls, navigated through intricate mazes, and practiced combat techniques with simulated enemies. They trained in high-intensity drills, dodged laser-guided obstacles, deciphered complex codes under pressure, and honed their marksmanship using state-of-the-art holographic systems. Each task pushed their endurance and adaptability, from mastering zero-gravity manoeuvres to engaging in virtual time-jump scenarios where split-second decisions could alter entire timelines. Yet, even as he pushed his body to the limit, John's mind remained focused on the mysteries he had yet to unravel.

In his downtime, John continued to notice small inconsistencies and peculiarities within the facility. He sensed a growing tension among the staff, though he couldn't quite pinpoint the cause. The feeling of being watched and manipulated only intensified his resolve to seek answers.

One evening, after a particularly difficult training session, John wandered through the quiet halls of the facility. The air felt charged, almost electric, and he couldn't shake the feeling that something significant was happening behind the scenes. He caught glimpses of hurried conversations and staff members exchanging worried looks, further fuelling his curiosity.

As he passed by a closed door, he overheard a snippet of conversation. "…the anomalies are getting worse. We need to act fast."

John's heart raced as he pressed himself against the wall, straining to hear more. But the voices faded, and the door remained closed.

Frustrated but more determined than ever, John returned to his quarters. He knew he had to find out what was going on, not just for his sake, but for the sake of the entire mission. The cryptic messages, the mysterious figure, and the strange occurrences all pointed to something bigger, something that he was now a part of.

As he lay in bed that night, John's mind raced with thoughts of the day's events. He was tired, his body aching from the intense training, but sleep eluded him. He knew that whatever was happening, it was only the beginning. The challenges ahead would test him in ways he couldn't yet imagine, but he was ready to face them head-on.

Eventually, exhaustion overtook him, and he drifted into a restless sleep. His dreams were vivid and unsettling, pulling him back to memories of his past. In his dream, he was a child again, standing outside the charred remains of a grand building. The air was thick with the acrid stench of burning timber and brick, the night sky faintly glowing with the last embers. He could hear the distant clatter of horse-drawn fire wagons and the cries of children, their faces smeared with soot. John wandered through the ruins, his boots crunching over shattered glass and scorched debris, feeling the weight of its lost importance. In the shadows, a figure stood, watching him silently.

It was Gabe, but younger and dressed in his western attire complete with a Stetson, longcoat, and a six-shooter on his side. He stepped forward, his face illuminated by the flickering light of the fire. In his hand, he held a piece of paper, and as he approached, he handed it to John.

John looked down at the paper with trembling hands and unfolded it. The message was clearer this time, written in neat, precise handwriting:

HELP WANTED. SEEK THE TRUTH. TRUST NO ONE.

Gabe's voice echoed in his mind, calm and reassuring. "You have a purpose, John. Remember that. You must find the truth."

The dream shifted, and John found himself sitting in a stagecoach, the leather seats worn but comfortable. The rhythmic clatter of hooves on cobblestones filled his ears. He looked out the window and saw the countryside rolling by, the coach heading towards an unknown destination. He knew this was the journey to the Louisiana orphanage, the place where he had spent his childhood after the fire.

The scene changed again, and he was standing in a long, dark corridor. The walls were lined with doors, each one slightly ajar, revealing glimpses of different moments in time. He walked slowly, peering into the rooms, each scene more confusing than the last.

He saw himself training at the facility, talking to Sarah, and even the enigmatic figure who had appeared earlier that day. Each scene felt significant, but he couldn't quite piece together the connections. The overwhelming sense of urgency pressed down on him, and he felt the weight of his mission more acutely than ever.

Suddenly, one of the doors slammed shut, jolting him awake. John sat up in bed, his heart pounding and sweat trickling down his forehead. The dream lingered in his mind, the message from Gabe echoing in his thoughts.

The next morning, John woke with a clear sense of direction, the weight of uncertainty from the previous days replaced by a sharp resolve. He met up with Lisa and Max, and together they continued their training. The exercises were gruelling, but John persisted, driven by a newfound strength.

Gabe watched them closely, his eyes never leaving John. He had promised to keep an eye on the young recruit, to mentor him and ensure his safety. He saw the grit in John's eyes, the fire that burned within him, and he knew that John was destined for something great. Gabe's mind often wandered back to his own early days with the Lennox Time Corporation, the challenges he faced, and the mentors who guided him. He saw a reflection of his younger self in John, and it strengthened his resolve to help the boy succeed.

As the days passed, the tension within the facility grew. The sense of urgency was palpable, and everyone was on edge. Conversations were often hushed, eyes darting around as if expecting something to happen at any moment. The usually bustling corridors were now filled with an undercurrent of anxiety. The mission to address the temporal anomalies was weighing heavily on everyone's minds.

But through it all, John remained focused. He trained harder, pushed himself further, and continued to seek the answers that eluded him. He spent hours in the library, poring over ancient texts and manuscripts, looking for any clues that could help him understand the cryptic messages. The whispers he had overheard, the strange occurrences, and the enigmatic figure's appearance all pointed to something significant, and he was determined to uncover the truth.

As they wrapped up the day's exhausting activities, the sun dipped low on the horizon, casting long shadows across the field. John looked up from his book and saw Gabe approaching, his silhouette framed by the setting sun. The recruits were sweaty and exhausted, but the bond forged through shared hardship created an unspoken camaraderie. "You're doing great, kid," Gabe said, a rare smile crossing his face. "Keep it up."

John nodded, wiping the sweat from his brow with the back of his hand. His muscles ached, but there was a fire in his eyes that hadn't been there before. "Thanks, Gabe. I won't let you down."

"I know you won't," Gabe replied, clapping him on the shoulder with a reassuring firmness. "Just remember, we're in this together. Trust your instincts and stay focused."

John nodded again, feeling a surge of confidence. Gabe's words meant a lot to him. Despite the gruff exterior, he knew Gabe cared deeply about his recruits. He knew that whatever lay ahead, he was ready to face it. With Gabe's guidance and the support of his team, he felt unstoppable.

John gazed across the quieting training grounds, now cloaked in the lingering glow of dusk. Shadows stretched long over the landscape, and a new sense of purpose settled within him. As night fell, John couldn't shake the feeling that the challenges ahead would test them in ways they hadn't yet imagined. Every cryptic message, every training exercise, had led to this point. They were being prepared for something, but what?

The next morning, John, Lisa, and Max were summoned for their most difficult simulation yet. As the briefing concluded, they knew they had their work cut out for them. A massive time rift had opened in the heart of a futuristic city, its volatile energy threatening to tear apart timelines and destabilise the fabric of reality.

"Remember," Gabe said, his voice firm, "your objective is to neutralise the time breach and stabilise the timeline. No backup, no do-overs. You're on your own out there."

The simulation initiated, and the three found themselves in a world where time had begun to fracture. The city was teeming with chaos buildings flickered between different eras. One moment, towering skyscrapers dominated the skyline, and in the next, medieval fortresses and crumbling Roman aqueducts stood in their place. Citizens from various historical periods walked among them in confusion: soldiers from different eras stumbled through the streets, cavemen ran in terror from self-driving cars, and futuristic drones zipped through the skies.

"Whoa," Lisa breathed, taking in the chaotic scene. "This is worse than I imagined."

John's wrist device flashed a warning a critical instability zone, growing larger by the second. "We've got twenty minutes to stop this thing," he said, his voice strained. "Let's get to work."

They made their way through the debris-laden streets towards the central rift, carefully navigating around cracks in the ground where prehistoric lava seeped up. Max scouted ahead, using his brute strength to clear debris and fend off aggressive holographic soldiers who mistook them for invaders.

"Careful," Lisa warned as they crossed a bridge that appeared to be in two places at once. Half of it was solid stone, the other half translucent metal. The transition was so unstable that it caused ripples in the air around them. "One wrong move, and we'll be stuck in another time."

They reached the first stabilisation point, a pulsating energy conduit that ran from the ground to the rift. It sparked and flickered, overloaded by the chaotic energy. John and Lisa hurriedly set up their stabiliser, attaching it to the conduit's base. "We need to bring the temporal flow under control," Lisa said, her fingers working quickly to adjust the device's settings.

Max kept watch, fending off holographic invaders from every corner of history. "We're out of time, guys!" he called, knocking away a holographic Roman legionnaire before ducking to avoid a flying drone.

"Just a few more seconds," John muttered, his hands flying over the control panel. Sweat beaded on his forehead as he tried to isolate the temporal distortion. The rift crackled and flashed overhead, growing more unstable by the second.

"Got it!" Lisa announced as the stabiliser came online, emitting a steady hum. The rift shuddered, its growth slowing for a moment before stabilising.

But as they moved to the second location, things quickly spiralled out of control. A sudden earthquake rocked the city, knocking them off their feet. The rift swelled, pulling in energy from both past and future. A nearby skyscraper transformed into a medieval tower, its base flickering in and out of existence.

"We're losing control!" John shouted over the roar of the collapsing buildings.

Max struggled to his feet, glancing up at the widening tear in the sky. "We've got to shut it down now, or it's going to swallow everything."

The second stabiliser was malfunctioning the energy readings were off the charts. Lisa cursed under her breath, frantically adjusting the settings. "The rift's too strong. It's drawing from multiple timelines at once. We need to sever the connection!"

John scanned the area and spotted the source a glowing artifact suspended in mid-air at the rift's core. It pulsed with energy, warping everything around it. "That artifact is feeding the rift. We need to cut the flow directly."

The team advanced cautiously towards the artifact, dodging incoming debris and holographic figures that appeared out of thin air. Time flickered all around them prehistoric jungles gave way to futuristic cities, ancient battlefields dissolved into peaceful meadows. The sensory overload made it difficult to focus, but John kept his eyes on the prize.

They reached the artifact, and Lisa quickly attached the stabiliser to it, but the moment she did, the device overloaded with a loud crack. Sparks flew, and the stabiliser's circuits shorted out. Lisa cursed. "It's not holding! The energy's too unstable."

John raced to her side, pulling out a backup stabiliser. "We need to redirect the energy manually," he said, hooking the backup device to the artifact. His hands trembled as the energy surged through the stabiliser, nearly shorting it out again. But with Lisa's help, they managed to siphon off just enough energy to weaken the rift.

The artifact flickered and dimmed as the rift finally began to shrink. The simulated world around them flickered as well, the clashing timelines fading one by one until only the futuristic city remained. The drones stopped buzzing, the holographic soldiers disappeared, and the chaotic energy in the air began to dissipate.

They stood in the eerie silence, catching their breath as the final remnants of the rift closed. The simulation flickered for a moment, and then the city disappeared, replaced by the familiar walls of the training facility.

"Simulation complete," a robotic voice announced as the three of them collapsed onto the ground, exhausted but relieved.

John sat up, wiping sweat from his brow. "That was insane."

Lisa let out a long breath. "We just barely managed to stabilise it. If we'd been any slower…"

Max chuckled weakly, lying flat on the ground. "I don't know about you guys, but I could use a break."

John smirked, glancing at his teammates. "Yeah, well something tells me this was just the warm-up."

They exchanged knowing looks, each of them realising that the real challenges still lay ahead. But as the tension of the simulation began to fade, so did their exhaustion. For now, they had won. But the rift had been just a taste of what was to come.

As the simulation faded, Gabe approached them with a look of approval on his face. "Well done, team. That was tough, but you handled it well. Remember, it's not always about physical strength. It's about mental resilience and working together."

John nodded, breathing heavily. "Thanks, Gabe. That was intense."

Gabe chuckled. "That's the point, kid. Real missions will test you in ways you can't even imagine. Better to be prepared."

Lisa sat down next to John, wiping sweat from her brow. "That building that became a tower I thought it was going to give way."

Max nodded in agreement. "Yeah, the simulation felt so real. It's amazing how they can create such an immersive experience."

Gabe's expression grew serious. "And that's why we push you so hard here. You need to be ready for anything. Out there, there's no room for hesitation."

John looked around at his teammates, feeling a deep sense of camaraderie. They had been through so much together, and he knew that they would continue to support each other, no matter what challenges lay ahead.

As the sun rose high in the sky and everyone filed out for lunch, John found a quiet spot to reflect. The training was tough, but he felt himself growing stronger, both physically and mentally. The cryptic messages still haunted him, but he was more determined than ever to uncover the truth.

He thought back to the dream he had had the night before. The image of Gabe handing him the "Help Wanted" note was etched in his mind. What did it all mean? How was it connected to the anomalies and the mysterious figure who had appeared in the facility?

John's thoughts were interrupted by the sound of footsteps. He looked up to see Gabe approaching, his expression thoughtful.

"Penny for your thoughts, kid?" Gabe asked, sitting down beside him.

John shrugged. "Just thinking about everything that's happened. The training, the messages, that figure. It's a lot to take in."

Gabe nodded, his gaze distant. "Yeah, it is. But you're handling it well. Better than I did when I first started."

John looked at him, surprised. "You mean you struggled too?"

Gabe chuckled. "Of course. Everyone does at first. But it's the challenges that shape us, make us stronger. You've got the fire, John. I see it in you. Just keep pushing forward."

John nodded, feeling a renewed sense of determination. "Thanks, Gabe. I won't let you down."

Gabe clapped his hand on John's shoulder. "I know you won't. Now get some rest. Tomorrow's another day, and there's more training to be done."

As Gabe walked away, John took a deep breath, feeling the weight of his responsibilities. He looked up at the bright midday sky, the sun hanging high, casting sharp shadows over the grounds. The path ahead was uncertain, but he knew he wasn't alone. With Gabe's guidance and the support of his team, he felt ready to face whatever came his way.

The next morning, the team assembled in the operations centre, a room abuzz with a mix of anticipation and anxiety. The room was a marvel of modern technology. Large holographic screens projected detailed maps of different time periods, each flickering with live data points and potential anomalies that demanded their attention. The hum of machinery and the soft beeping of computers processing information created a symphony of organised chaos. The walls were lined with advanced consoles, each staffed by technicians whose fingers danced over touchscreens with hawk-like precision, eyes glued to the fluctuations in the timelines.

Gabe stood at the centre of the room, his presence commanding attention like a general before a crucial battle. He wore a tactical suit that seemed to enhance his already imposing stature. Before beginning the briefing, he gestured to a nearby table where period-appropriate clothing and equipment were laid out.

"Alright, team, here's the mission. We've identified several anomalies in the timeline occurring in the late 18th century, specifically around the French Revolution. These anomalies are causing significant disruptions, and we need to correct them to stabilise the timeline."

He pointed to a holographic map of Paris in 1792, where several points were highlighted in red. The map was a detailed representation of the city, showing bustling marketplaces, narrow alleyways, and prominent landmarks. "Our primary objective is to prevent a key figure from being assassinated. This individual's survival is crucial to maintaining the correct flow of events. We'll be working in pairs to ensure we cover all possible threats."

Gabe's eyes scanned the team, his expression serious. The light from the holographic displays cast a blue hue on his face, emphasising his determined look. "Remember, stick to the plan, and watch each other's backs. We can do this. John, you're with me. Lisa and Max, you'll handle the eastern quadrant. Stay alert and keep your communicators on at all times. While this mission is crucial, it is still considered a training mission, just don't fuck up."

He motioned to the table. "Everyone, grab your period clothing and equipment. The time hopper will integrate seamlessly into your attire. If anything goes wrong, use the emergency recall button on your hopper. It will bring you back to the facility immediately."

After Gabe mentioned the "time hopper," Lisa furrowed her brow and leaned towards John. "Time hopper? What's that?"

John smirked slightly. "It's what Gabe calls the Chronoverge. Same thing, just his way of making it sound less technical."

Lisa nodded, understanding. "Figures he'd have his own name for it."

Smiling, John stepped forward, picking up a neatly folded set of clothing. The material felt authentic to the touch, a testament to the meticulous preparation of the mission. He quickly changed into a simple tunic, trousers, and a cloak, blending in perfectly with the common folk of 1792 Paris. He attached the Chronoverge to his cloak's inner lining, its sleek design hidden from view.

John felt a surge of delight as he nodded along with the others. He was ready, they all were. This was his chance to prove himself and make a difference. The gravity of the mission weighed on him, but he was determined to rise to the challenge. The room seemed to buzz with a collective sense of purpose, each team member mentally preparing for the task ahead.

As they prepared to time travel, John couldn't help but feel a mix of excitement and apprehension. Gabe handed each team member a small, sleek device. "Remember, this is your time hopper," Gabe said as he winked at Lisa. "John already has his. Keep it secure and hidden. It will also translate local languages for you. This is the recall button, remember where it is, always." Gabe pointed to the back of the Chronoverge as he explained.

With their period-appropriate clothing on and Chronoverges secured, they gathered in a circle. Gabe looked around, making sure everyone was ready. "Alright, everyone, activate your hoppers."

John pressed the button, and immediately a bright light engulfed him. The familiar surroundings of the facility dissolved into a vortex of colours and lights. The sensation was disorienting, like being pulled apart and reassembled in an instant. He felt as if he were falling through time, the air around him charged with energy.

The transition was both instantaneous and overwhelming. When the light faded, John found himself standing in a narrow alleyway. The stone walls on either side were covered in moss and grime, a stark contrast to the clean, advanced environment of the operations centre. The air was filled with the sounds of market vendors calling out their wares, the clatter of horse-drawn carriages over cobblestone streets, and the distant murmur of political discourse. The scent of freshly baked bread mingled with the more pungent smells of a city that was alive with activity.

John took a deep breath, trying to steady himself. The translation function in his Chronoverge turned on, and he could hear and understand the bustling conversations around him as if he were a native speaker.

Next to him, Max and Lisa materialised, looking equally disoriented but quickly regaining their composure. Max adjusted his cloak, making sure his Chronoverge was hidden but accessible, while Lisa did a quick check of her surroundings, her eyes sharp and alert.

Gabe immediately took charge, scanning their surroundings and motioning for the group to follow. "Stay close, everyone. We need to blend in and make our way to our positions."

John nodded, adjusting his cloak again. The streets were crowded, and the energy was electric with the fervour of revolutionary change. As they moved through the throngs of people, John's senses were on high alert, every noise and movement scrutinised for potential threats.

Lisa and Max stayed close; their expressions focused. Lisa whispered to John, "Remember the plan. Keep an eye out for anything suspicious."

Max added, "And don't forget to use the emergency recall if things go south. We need to be ready for anything."

John appreciated their words of caution. They navigated through the bustling streets, moving seamlessly among the locals. The historical authenticity of 18th-century Paris was striking, from the ornate architecture to the lively market stalls.

They reached a bustling square, where Gabe pulled John, Lisa, and Max aside to brief them further. "Our target is Jean-Luc Fournier, a moderate revolutionary whose ideas are key to stabilising the new government. We've intercepted information that an extremist group plans to eliminate him tonight. We need to ensure that doesn't happen."

John's heart pounded as the reality of their mission sank in. This wasn't just about protecting a man it was about safeguarding the ideals he represented. Fournier's survival could mean the difference between a revolution that upheld justice and one that spiralled into chaos. The gravity of their task pressed down on him, sharpening his focus. "How do we make sure he's safe?" he asked, his voice firm but tinged with the weight of the responsibility now resting on his shoulders.

Gabe's gaze was unwavering, his voice calm yet charged with the seriousness of the task ahead. "Stick to the plan and get to your checkpoints around the square. This will be where Fournier is set to address the crowd. You need to be vigilant watch for anything that feels off, any movement that doesn't belong. The moment you identify a threat, act quickly. Don't hesitate, don't second-guess."

John exchanged glances with Lisa and Max, a silent understanding passing between them. This mission was more than just saving a life; it was about preserving the future. Gabe's calm confidence anchored them, fuelling their resolve. As they took their positions, blending into the crowd, the weight of the mission settled over them. With Gabe's leadership bolstering their determination, they began to scan the area for any signs of danger.

As the sun set, casting a golden glow over the square, Fournier took the stage. Applause filled the air, but John's focus locked onto a man cutting through the crowd, his movements sharp, his expression tense. Every instinct screamed this was their threat.

"Gabe, I've got eyes on a suspect," John murmured into his communicator, never losing sight of the man.

"Stay on him. Wait for my signal," Gabe's voice came through, calm but urgent.

John watched as the man's hand slid into his coat. His pulse raced. "He's reaching for something. I'm moving in."

"Go," Gabe commanded.

John surged forward, tackling the man just as he drew a pistol. The weapon clattered to the ground. The crowd gasped, chaos rippling through them, but John's focus was pure: neutralise the threat.

Within seconds, Max and Lisa were at his side, subduing the would-be assassin. "Nice work, John," Lisa said, pride in her voice.

Max swiftly retrieved the fallen pistol, ensuring it was out of harm's way, while Lisa remained vigilant, her senses still on high alert. As the crowd began to settle and Fournier resumed his speech, John could feel the weight of responsibility still pressing on them. They had succeeded in stopping one threat, but complacency wasn't an option. Together, they had safeguarded a key moment in history, but this was only the beginning of their larger mission.

Gabe approached, his eyes reflecting both pride and caution. "Not bad, but don't let this go to your heads," he said, his voice steady. "This was just one mission. The anomalies, the messages, and that figure they're all pieces of something bigger. Keep that in mind."

John nodded, the adrenaline fading as the weight of their mission settled in. "We get it," John replied, his voice firm. "We'll be ready for whatever's next."

Gabe's gaze softened slightly, a rare moment of unguarded emotion passing between mentor and protégé. "I know you're ready, but don't let your guard down just yet. We're in for a helluva ride, and these ain't your everyday rodeo clowns we're up against."

As they made their way out of the square, the weight of their mission hung heavy over them, a constant reminder of the stakes involved. The success of today was a step forward, but the path ahead was long and filled with unknown dangers. The cryptic messages, the artifact, and the mysterious figure these were pieces of a puzzle that still eluded them, and they knew that the answers wouldn't come easily.

Back at the facility, the debriefing was quick, but the atmosphere was thick with the unspoken understanding of what lay ahead. The mission had been a success, but the sense of unease that had settled over them in Paris lingered, a shadow that would not easily be dispelled.

That evening, as John sat alone in the quiet of his quarters, his thoughts drifted back to the cryptic messages and the figure's haunting presence. The memory of those silver eyes and that commanding voice echoed in his mind, a stark reminder that their mission was far from over. The day's success had not brought the clarity he had hoped for; instead, it had deepened the unease that had settled over him. The more they uncovered, the more questions seemed to arise, and he knew that their journey was just beginning.

John exhaled slowly, bracing himself for the unknown. The nagging sense that something far greater was at play gnawed at him, as though their mission was just a piece of a far more intricate puzzle one that could tear apart the fabric of time itself. He was ready to dive into the mysteries that surrounded them, no matter how far he had to go to uncover the truth.

John lay back, exhausted but restless, his mind swirling with the day's events. The cryptic messages, the artifact, the shadowy figure they all weighed on him, creating more questions than answers. He knew their mission had only just begun.

As sleep overtook him, he had a fleeting sense that whatever lay ahead, it would be more dangerous and complex than they could imagine.

Chapter Thirteen

The facility buzzed with a renewed sense of urgency. The success of the previous day had only deepened the tension. As John, Lisa, and Max made their way to the operations centre, the memory of the Paris mission lingered. On one of the monitors, the subdued suspect from 1792 appeared in another room, awaiting interrogation. His face was still etched with defiance and anger as he glared at the camera.

Sarah was already there, reviewing the mission data with a team of analysts. She looked up when John, Lisa, and Max entered, her expression serious. "Good, you're here," she said, motioning for them to join her at the large conference table. Holographic displays floated above the table, highlighting key points from the mission.

"The mission was a success, but we still have a lot of unanswered questions," Sarah began, her voice steady but weighted by the situation. "Gabe, can you walk us through the key events?"

Gabe, standing with his arms crossed, nodded. "Fournier was protected, and John's quick thinking neutralised the threat before it escalated. The suspect is in custody, and preliminary scans suggest he's not from our timeline."

John's curiosity spiked. "Not from our timeline? How is that possible?"

Sarah exchanged a glance with Gabe before replying. "This isn't the first time we've encountered someone from a different timeline. It could mean a lot of things, but we need more information before drawing conclusions."

Max leaned forward, his analytical mind already working. "If he's from another timeline, that complicates things. We need to know who he is, where he's from, and why he targeted Fournier."

Lisa nodded. "And how he even crossed into our timeline without us detecting it."

Sarah gestured towards the holographic display, which now showed a series of anomalies similar to those in Paris. "We'll begin the interrogation soon. In the meantime, I need all of you on high alert. This mission may have been a success, but it's clear the challenges we're facing are far from over."

Gabe turned to the team, his expression serious but supportive. "You all did well, but we have to stay sharp. This was just one piece of a much larger puzzle."

John nodded, feeling the weight of Gabe's words. The mission had been successful, but it had also opened the door to more questions more mysteries that needed unravelling.

As they were dismissed to rest and recover, John's thoughts lingered on the figure they had encountered in Paris, the cryptic messages, and the looming presence of VTI. The sense that they were on the brink of something much larger potentially catastrophic gnawed at him. But he took solace in knowing he wasn't facing it alone.

Later that evening, as John settled into the quiet of his quarters, trying to push the day's events from his mind, a knock at the door interrupted his thoughts. He opened it to find Gabe standing there, a mischievous grin lighting up his face.

"Get dressed, kid," Gabe said. "We're heading out."

John blinked in confusion. "Where to?"

Gabe's grin widened. "To blow off some steam. We're going back to 1867, New Mexico. I'll explain on the way."

John quickly gathered his gear, excitement and curiosity replacing his earlier exhaustion. This wasn't just another mission this was something different. As he joined Lisa and Max in the operations centre, a new sense of anticipation filled him. Whatever lay ahead, they would face it together, united by the trials they had already overcome and the challenges yet to come.

"Where exactly are we going?" John asked, catching up to Gabe, who was already checking his gear.

Gabe gave him a quick nod. "New Mexico, 1867. Time for a good old-fashioned bonfire. Meet us in ten minutes."

John's fatigue evaporated, replaced by adrenaline. "A bonfire? In 1867?"

Gabe nodded. "Yep. You, me, Lisa, and Max. Consider it a reward for today's success."

With his Chronoverge secured, John felt the familiar rush of excitement as he headed back to the operations centre, where Lisa and Max waited, equally intrigued.

Gabe stood there, cowboy hat perched on his head, long coat draped over his shoulders looking every bit the rugged cowboy. "Ready, everyone? This is going to be fun."

The team activated their Chronoverges, and a bright light engulfed them. The familiar sensation of falling through time returned, and when the light faded, they found themselves standing in the rugged, open terrain of New Mexico in 1867. The night sky stretched overhead, clear and filled with countless stars.

Gabe led them to a secluded spot, where a pile of firewood was already set up. The landscape, framed by rolling hills and the distant silhouette of mountains, was breathtaking. The air was crisp and clean a refreshing change from the sterile environment of the facility.

"Welcome to New Mexico, 1867. Let's get this bonfire started," Gabe said, his enthusiasm palpable as he began arranging the firewood.

As they worked together to light the fire, John couldn't help but feel a sense of camaraderie and adventure. The intensity of their missions melted away as they laughed, shared stories, and soaked in the warmth of the fire under the vast, starry sky.

Max, ever the tech enthusiast, looked around in awe. "It's amazing how different it feels out here. No tech, no distractions. Just us and the stars."

Lisa nodded, her face illuminated by the flickering flames. "It's peaceful. I get why you brought us here, Gabe."

Gabe smiled, tipping his hat. "This is the real deal. Where I grew up, out in West Texas, nights like these made you appreciate the simple things. Sometimes you've just got to step away from all the tech and remember what it's like to be out here."

John felt a warmth spreading through him that had nothing to do with the fire. For a moment, they were just a group of friends, celebrating their successes and enjoying each other's company. It was a welcome respite from the intensity of their missions, and John felt a renewed sense of purpose.

As the fire crackled and the night wore on, Gabe began sharing stories from his past, weaving tales of the Wild West that mesmerised them.

"You know, I wasn't always this comfortable with time travel," Gabe said, his tone thoughtful as he gazed into the flames. "I was born in a small town called Dustbowl, Texas, back in 1850. Doesn't exist anymore it got swallowed up by time."

John leaned in. "What happened to it?"

Gabe's expression darkened, a distant look in his eyes. "Dustbowl was rough, lawless. I was a peacemaker by sixteen, and a bounty hunter by eighteen. It was a dangerous life, but it taught me resilience."

He paused, letting the crackling fire fill the silence. "One day, Dustbowl just disappeared. One minute it was there, the next it wasn't. I've pieced together parts of the puzzle, but some questions don't have answers."

John frowned, absorbing Gabe's story. "Is that what brought you to LTC?"

Gabe shook his head, a faint smile playing on his lips. "Not exactly. I was recruited while hunting down a bounty Jebediah Barker. Thought it was just another job, but Barker was always one step ahead, like he had the devil's luck."

He poked at the fire with a stick, watching the embers rise. "When I finally tracked him down in Arizona, we had a shootout. Barker was a better shot than I expected. I was bleeding out in the dust, and I knew it was the end. History records that I died that day."

John's eyes widened. "But you didn't."

Gabe nodded. "Someone intervened. Pulled me out of that moment, brought me into LTC. To everyone else, I was dead, but in reality, I'd been recruited."

Lisa leaned forward, intrigued. "Who recruited you?"

Gabe hesitated, his face half-hidden in the firelight. "A man…" He trailed off, his gaze shifting to John. "Let's just say someone knew exactly when and how to find me." His eyes lingered on John for a moment, something unspoken passing between them, but he didn't elaborate further.

A tense silence followed until Lisa broke it. "Well, my recruitment was a bit less dramatic. I was on a deep-sea expedition when things went south equipment failure. By the time they pulled me out, I wasn't breathing anymore. That's when LTC stepped in. Right before I expired."

Max nodded, joining in. "Yeah, they got me too, but in a server room accident. Fire trapped me, and there was no way out. I was about to burn to death when LTC swooped in. They do have a knack for recruiting right at the last second."

John raised an eyebrow. "So, you both got recruited right before things went bad?"

Max smirked. "Seems like their standard operating procedure scoop you up right when you're about to kick the bucket."

Lisa smiled faintly. "They always step in when you're on the edge, don't they?"

John looked down at the fire, letting their words sink in. "Guess that makes me no exception."

Gabe's gaze stayed fixed on John, his silence more telling than words. He knew more than he was letting on, and John felt the weight of that unspoken connection between them.

Gabe lit a cigarillo, exhaling as the smoke curled up into the night, blending with the flickering firelight. John watched him, feeling a familiar twinge of longing. It had been a while since he'd smoked a habit he'd picked up at the orphanage to cope with the stress, and only recently kicked.

Catching the look, Gabe raised an eyebrow. "Gave it up, huh? Good on you. That's no easy feat."

John nodded. "Yeah, wasn't easy at all. I used to smoke constantly helped me handle everything. But when training got serious, I knew I needed every advantage I could get. Smoking didn't exactly help with that."

Gabe offered a nod of approval. "Smart choice. But don't be too hard on yourself if you miss it sometimes. We've all got our vices."

Gabe offered a nod of approval. "Smart choice. But don't be too hard on yourself if you miss it sometimes. We've all got our vices."

John smiled faintly, feeling the weight of the conversation settling in as silence stretched between them. The fire crackled softly, and after a long pause, Gabe exhaled a cloud of smoke, his tone shifting to something more contemplative.

"There's something about the West," Gabe said, his eyes distant. "It teaches you resilience, how to face down the worst life has to offer and come out the other side stronger. Remember that, kids. No matter what the future throws at you, stand tall and face it head-on."

John looked around at his friends and mentors, feeling an overwhelming sense of gratitude for the journey that had brought them together. Not long ago, he had felt alone, unsure of his place. But now, surrounded by people he trusted, he knew he wasn't facing the unknown by himself. There would be challenges ahead, but with this group by his side, he felt ready for whatever came their way.

"Gabe," John began, breaking the comfortable silence that had settled over them. "I've got some questions, if you don't mind."

Gabe looked up, his eyes reflecting the firelight. "Shoot, kid. What's on your mind?"

John took a deep breath, organising his thoughts. "Back at the facility, during the debriefing, Sarah mentioned VTI and that the suspect might be from a different timeline. What did she mean by that? What exactly is VTI?"

Gabe's expression darkened slightly, and he glanced at Lisa and Max before responding. "VTI stands for Voskos Temporal Initiative. They're another time travel organisation, but their goals differ from ours." He paused, choosing his words carefully. "They operate across multiple timelines. Sometimes, they shift people or events from one timeline to another, all to serve their own agenda."

John's curiosity deepened. "So, that guy we captured in Paris he's not from our timeline?"

Gabe nodded slowly. "That's a possibility. We've seen VTI operatives come from other timelines before. They don't follow the same rules we do. For them, a timeline is just another tool to manipulate. We're still figuring out exactly where he's from, but it's likely he was brought here by VTI."

Max raised an eyebrow. "So, they're the bad guys?"

Gabe gave a shrug. "Depends on who you ask. In their eyes, they're doing what needs to be done. But their methods well, they don't care about the damage they leave behind."

John nodded, digesting the information. "And the suspect we brought back do you think he's from VTI?"

Gabe sighed. "It's possible. We've encountered their operatives before, but we'll know more once the interrogation is done."

Lisa leaned forward, her curiosity piqued. "Why hasn't LTC taken more direct action against VTI if they're such a threat?"

Gabe looked into the fire, his expression thoughtful. "It's not that simple. Time travel makes things complicated. Direct confrontations can lead to unintended consequences. We have to be careful, strategic. Our goal is to protect the timeline, not escalate conflicts."

Max nodded in agreement. "Makes sense. If we start fighting them openly, we could end up causing more damage than we prevent."

John felt a surge of frustration, coupled with a flicker of worry. "So, we're just supposed to let them keep going?"

Gabe shook his head. "No, John. We stop them whenever we can, but we have to be smart about it. Every action we take has consequences, especially when you're playing with time. That's why your training matters so much. You need to see the bigger picture."

John nodded, though the weight of it all pressed heavily on his shoulders. "I get it. It's just hard to wrap my head around."

Lisa offered him a reassuring smile. "You're doing great, John. We've all been there trying to make sense of it all. Just remember, we've got each other's backs."

Max leaned back, glancing at the stars. "Yeah, man. We're a team. We'll figure it out together."

Gabe smiled, a hint of pride in his eyes. "You're doing fine, kid. This isn't easy work, but you've got the guts and the smarts for it."

As the conversation lulled, they sat in comfortable silence, the fire crackling softly in the still night air. John's mind raced, swirling with thoughts of VTI, timelines, and the burden of protecting the future. But amidst the chaos in his head, a sense of clarity emerged. He wasn't in this alone.

As the night grew colder, Gabe handed out blankets from a pack he'd brought along. "Alright, it's getting late. Get some rest. Tomorrow's another day, and who knows what it'll bring."

John wrapped himself in the blanket, lying back to stare up at the stars. His mind buzzed with the evening's revelations, and despite the overwhelming nature of it all, he found comfort in the steady crackle of the fire and the presence of his team nearby. Gradually, exhaustion claimed him, pulling him into a deep, dreamless sleep.

Chapter Fourteen

The warmth of the campfire faded into the stark, clinical atmosphere of the conference room. John blinked, adjusting to the harsh lighting and the cold edges of the advanced technological interfaces lining the walls. The sense of camaraderie from the previous night was replaced with tension. The large table at the centre of the room stood as a silent witness to the gravity of what was about to unfold.

John, Lisa, and Max took their seats alongside Gabe and Sarah. The air buzzed with anticipation and apprehension.

Sarah tapped a few keys on the console, and a holographic image of the suspect appeared above the table. "We've identified him as an operative from the Voskos Temporal Initiative," she said, her voice steady and controlled. "His name is Samuel Taron. We believe he has critical information about the recent anomalies and the artifact we recovered."

Gabe leaned forward; his brows furrowed. "What do we know about his mission?"

Sarah sighed, glancing at the holographic image. "Not much, unfortunately. He's been trained to resist interrogation, and so far, he hasn't given us anything useful. But we've discovered a few things that might help us break through his defences."

John listened intently; his curiosity piqued. "What kind of things?"

Sarah met his gaze. "We found a communication device on him. It's encrypted, but our tech team is working on cracking it. We're hoping it will give us some insight into his mission and the larger plans of the VTI."

Max, always eager to contribute, chimed in. "What about the anomalies? Do we know if he's directly responsible for them?"

Sarah nodded. "We believe he played a part, but it's still unclear how. The anomalies are widespread and seem to be connected to multiple events throughout history. Our main goal is to find out what he knows and how we can stop these disruptions."

Lisa leaned back in her chair, her expression thoughtful. "If he's been trained to resist interrogation, how do we plan to get the information we need?"

Sarah exchanged a look with Gabe before answering. "We have a few strategies. Psychological tactics, truth serums, and if necessary, more advanced techniques. But we need to be careful. We can't risk causing any more damage to the timeline."

John felt a surge of urgency. "What can I do to help?"

Sarah offered a small, appreciative nod but raised a hand. "Right now, we're waiting for more intel. Get some rest, John. We'll need everyone at full strength for what's coming next." With a reluctant nod, John left the conference room, his thoughts still racing with unanswered questions.

Later that night, exhaustion finally pulled him into a restless sleep. The dream returned familiar yet always unsettling. This time, John found himself once again in that endless corridor, the walls lined with doors slightly ajar, showing fragmented moments of his past. He recognised them immediately: his training, interactions with Sarah, moments in the orphanage, and flickers of his mission. He had been here before, in this strange place where time seemed to twist on itself.

As he walked further, the door at the end of the corridor swung open. This time, instead of glimpses from his past, he found himself inside the stagecoach. The figures from his previous dream were there the woman and the ambiguous man silent, their faces obscured by shadow. The woman, who had told him they were headed to the orphanage at Epsilon in a prior dream, now reached into her coat and handed him something.

A Help Wanted note, crumpled and worn; the writing familiar: **"Help Wanted: Seek the truth. Trust no one."**

John's breath hitched. He had seen this message before first in the real world, then in dream after dream. The note's meaning remained elusive, but its repetition nagged at him, pulling at a deeper truth he couldn't yet reach.

As the stagecoach rumbled down the path, the walls began to flicker again. The scene outside the windows blurred, morphing into **an explosion in New York** the one that hadn't happened yet but kept appearing in his dreams. The note fluttered in his hand as the woman whispered, "Time is not your ally."

Then, suddenly, the corridor reappeared, the transition jarring. The walls warped and twisted, pulling him back to where he had started. **More notes appeared**, pinned to the walls: **"Every choice ignites the future"** and the final message, **"It's almost time."**

John's pulse quickened. He was being shown something. The dream, once cryptic and fragmented, now seemed to push him towards something inevitable.

The cloaked figure, its face obscured as always, emerged from the shadows at the far end of the corridor. Its voice echoed, clear and cutting: "You think you understand time, but time will break you."

The walls began to close in, warping into a spiral of shattered memories and future glimpses the orphanage, the explosion, the ticking clock, the Help Wanted notes scattering in the wind. The figure stepped closer, and John caught sight of something in the distance an older version of himself, standing at the edge of something vast, dangerous, and unknown.

The final note fluttered before his eyes: **"The truth is right in front of you."**

His Chronoverge chirped, jerking him awake. Groaning, John reached for it, his heart still racing as the remnants of the vision clung to him the corridor, the stagecoach, the notes, the warnings.

Sarah's voice came through, calm but urgent. "John, meet Gabe in the atrium."

Rubbing his eyes, John swung his legs out of bed, the fragments of the dream still vivid. **The notes.** "Help Wanted: Seek the truth. Trust no one." **It was all connected but to what?** He dressed quickly, the cold air of the night doing little to shake the weight of the dream as he headed to the atrium, his mind swirling with questions.

Gabe was waiting, his usual confident demeanour slightly subdued. "We've got a situation, kid," he said. His gaze softened for a moment. "But first, are you alright? You look like you've seen a ghost."

John shook his head, trying to clear the lingering images from his mind. "Just a bad dream, I guess. What's going on?"

Gabe's eyes narrowed, and for a brief moment, it seemed like he wanted to pry further into John's answer, but he held back. "We'll get into that later. Right now, we have a problem with the suspect we brought back. We've been working on decrypting the device we found on him, and we're starting to piece some things together."

John's curiosity sharpened. "What kind of things?"

Gabe gestured towards the hallway, his expression serious. "Come on. We've intercepted some strange signals something we weren't expecting. The encryption is deep, layered, like it's designed to shift with time. It's VTI tech, no doubt, but Sarah's got the details. There's more some of it might tie into those anomalies you saw in the field."

As they moved through the quiet halls of the facility, John couldn't shake the feeling that the dream was more than just a figment of his imagination. The notes, the figure's warnings, the corridor they gnawed at him. There was something hauntingly familiar about it all something that felt less like a dream and more like a memory, a warning.

They entered the conference room, where Sarah and the rest of the team were already gathered. The atmosphere was tense, weighed down by the gravity of their mission and the looming questions that hung in the air.

Gabe stopped near the centre of the room, glancing towards the large holographic display. "I'll let Sarah get into the technical stuff, but what we've found could change everything."

Sarah looked up as they entered, her expression unreadable but serious. "We've got a lead on the suspect. It's time to find out who he is and what he knows."

The silence in the room was palpable as John, Lisa, and Max took their seats alongside Gabe and Sarah. The walls, lined with advanced technological interfaces, hummed softly, casting an eerie glow across the room. The large table at the centre displayed a holographic image of their recent mission's key points, casting shadows that danced across the surface.

Sarah, her expression set with a mix of focus and concern, tapped a few keys on the console. A holographic image flickered to life above the table, revealing the face of the suspect they had apprehended. His sharp features and cold, calculating eyes sent a chill down John's spine. **Samuel Taron**. The name echoed in his mind.

"This is Samuel Taron," Sarah began, her voice calm but edged with tension. "We've confirmed that he's an operative from the Voskos Temporal Initiative. His mission appears to be tied to the recent anomalies, and possibly to the artifact we recovered."

Gabe leaned forward, his posture tense as the weight of the situation pressed down on the room. "What do we know about his objectives?"

Sarah exchanged a glance with Gabe, frustration tightening her expression. "Not as much as we'd hoped. Taron has been trained to resist interrogation so far, he hasn't given us anything useful. But we've uncovered a few things that might help us break through."

John leaned in, unable to fully contain the frustration creeping into his voice. "What have we found?"

Sarah met his gaze, her eyes reflecting both concern and determination. "We discovered a communication device on him. It's encrypted, but our tech team is working on cracking it. We're hoping it'll give us insight into his mission and, more importantly, into VTI's larger plans."

Max, studying the hologram, chimed in, his voice thoughtful. "If he's been trained to resist, then whatever he knows is crucial. The fact that he's not talking suggests it's big something VTI can't afford to lose."

Lisa, ever the strategist, added, "And if standard methods aren't working, we need to look at other options. What's the plan?"

Sarah exchanged a look with Gabe before responding. "We're considering a few approaches psychological tactics, truth serums, and if necessary, more advanced methods. But we have to be careful. One wrong move could cause untold damage to the timeline."

John felt frustration bubble up, though he tempered it. "How can I help?" He wasn't a rookie anymore he wanted to be involved.

Gabe's hand settled firmly on John's shoulder, his voice steady. "I know you're eager, but right now, your job is to keep training. You're learning fast, but interrogation? Let us handle that for now."

John nodded, though the feeling of being sidelined stung. "Alright. Just let me know if there's anything I can do."

Sarah offered a brief smile. "Stay sharp, John. We may need your input once we crack the encryption. For now, let's focus on getting through Taron's defences."

A contemplative silence settled over the room, the gravity of the situation hanging in the air. The hologram of Taron's face flickered above the table, a constant reminder of the ticking clock and the answers they desperately needed.

Just then, the door to the conference room slid open, and a technician entered, holding a small device. "We've cracked the encryption on Taron's communication device," he announced, his voice carrying a mix of triumph and urgency.

Sarah's eyes widened slightly, her professional demeanour briefly giving way to surprise. "That was fast. What did you find?"

The technician placed the device on the table, and the holographic display shifted, revealing a series of coded messages and complex diagrams. The room fell silent as everyone leaned in; their attention locked on the unfolding data.

"It appears to be a series of communications between Taron and his superiors within the VTI," the technician explained, his fingers dancing over the controls as he highlighted key sections of the messages. "There's a lot of data here, but we've managed to decode some of it. It looks like he was coordinating with other operatives to create the anomalies we've been tracking."

Gabe's frown deepened as he studied the messages. "What's their endgame?"

The technician shook his head, frustration creeping into his voice. "We're still piecing that together. But from what we've decoded, it seems they're trying to alter key events in history to their advantage."

Sarah's expression hardened, her focus narrowing on the holographic display. "We need to stop them. Whatever their plan is, it's causing massive disruptions. Our priority is to figure out when and where the next anomaly will occur and prevent it."

Before Sarah could continue, Max cleared his throat from the other side of the table. "Actually, I should probably mention something."

All eyes turned to him as Max tapped his tablet casually. "I hacked LTC's network earlier, just a little, you know, to see if I could speed things up. And, uh, turns out I hacked the device from here. So you can thank me for the decryption."

The technician froze mid-sentence, his triumphant expression faltering as his gaze flickered between Max and the tablet. His frustration was almost palpable. "Wait what? You hacked it from here? Without going through our system?"

Max shrugged, a slight grin playing on his lips. "Yeah, I figured it would take too long, and we needed results. So, I bypassed the network protocols. No big deal."

Sarah blinked, clearly impressed, though her face remained composed. "Max, you!"

"Broke every security rule in the book," the technician interrupted, his voice tinged with annoyance. "That was supposed to be an authorised operation. You could've compromised."

"Yeah, yeah," Max cut in, waving a hand dismissively. "We'll have that talk later. But hey, I got us the data, didn't I?"

Sarah fought to suppress a smile, finally giving Max a nod. "Good work. Let's focus on what we've got."

The technician muttered something under his breath, clearly less amused, but the tension in the room shifted back to the information they now had.

John felt a renewed sense of urgency, but underneath it, frustration simmered. He wanted to do more to be more involved but felt sidelined again. "What's our next move?" he asked, trying to keep his voice steady.

Gabe sighed, noticing the tension in John's voice. "We'll split up. Sarah's going to oversee the interrogation. I'll stay here with you three. We need to dig through this data and see if we can find any patterns or clues that point to the next anomaly."

Sarah immediately raised an eyebrow. "Gabe, I don't think…"

But before she could continue, Gabe shot her a disarming smile, the kind of effortless charm he always managed to pull off. "Sarah, you know me. Trust me on this one. Let them handle the data. They've got it under control."

She hesitated for a moment, clearly still unsure. But with a sigh and a faint, reluctant smile, she relented. "Alright. But I'll hold you accountable for this one." She gave a quick nod to the group. "Do what you can. I'll be overseeing the interrogation. I'll check in after."

With that, she turned on her heel and exited the room, leaving John, Lisa, Max, and Gabe to focus on the data. John, Lisa, and Max exchanged glances. Despite John's lingering frustration, he knew Gabe was doing his best to keep him engaged.

Max was already tapping furiously on his tablet. "Since I already hacked the network, decrypting the rest of this data should be a breeze. Let's see what we find."

Hours slipped by as they combed through the holographic messages. Lisa's sharp mind caught key phrases, while Max cross-referenced the data with known historical events. John, despite his frustration, focused on piecing together the timeline of VTI's activities.

Lisa suddenly tapped the screen. "Here! Look at this," she said, tracing a line of text. "It mentions a specific date Vienna, 1814. The Congress of Vienna."

Max's eyebrows shot up. "That lines up perfectly with one of the anomalies we detected earlier. This might be their next move."

John nodded, his focus sharpening. "We need to act fast. If we can intercept them in Vienna, we might stop another disruption."

Before they could delve deeper, Max paused again, his attention drawn to something unusual. "Wait there's another file here. It's on you, John."

John's eyebrows furrowed in confusion. "On me? How can that be?"

Max, curious, tapped the screen, but as soon as the file opened, the entire device flickered, and lines of code began to erase themselves. Max's eyes widened as he watched the data vanish.

"Whoa," he muttered. "That's some serious fail-safe. The whole thing just wiped itself."

Lisa's mouth dropped slightly. "Self-deleting files? What the hell could that be about?"

Max set the now-useless device down, shaking his head in disbelief. "Whoever set this up didn't want anyone digging into that file. It's gone completely."

John's mind raced, unsettled by the thought of VTI having information on him information that had just vanished. A chill ran through him as the reality of the situation sank in.

Before they could dwell on it, Gabe and Sarah re-entered the room, their expressions a mix of tension and hope. "Did you find anything?" Sarah asked, her voice carrying the weight of the mission.

John pointed to the highlighted text on the display. "Vienna, 1814. We think it's their next target."

After leaving the conference room, Sarah returned to her office, pulling up the live feed of the interrogation. Samuel Taron sat across from the LTC agents, unmoving, his posture rigid and defiant. Sarah scrutinised his every move through the screen, but Taron hadn't cracked yet.

Her datapad hummed softly beside her, the decryption progress slow but steady. She kept one eye on Taron's interrogation and another on the data being pulled from his device. Suddenly, a soft comm chirp broke the silence.

It was Gabe.

"Sarah, we've found something," Gabe said, his voice low but urgent. "Vienna, 1814 it looks like that's their next target."

Sarah's fingers hovered over the datapad as she processed the information. "That fits with the anomalies we've been tracking. Any further progress on Taron's datapad?"

"We're working through it," Gabe replied. "Max has decrypted part of it, and we're starting to piece together more about the timeline of these disruptions. But it's a slow process."

Sarah's eyes remained on Taron through the feed. "Keep at it. I'm overseeing the interrogation, but Taron's not giving anything up yet. I'll stay on him from here and coordinate with you once we get more from the datapad."

"Got it. I'll keep you updated," Gabe responded before the comm line clicked off.

Sarah took a deep breath, her mind shifting gears. The feed of the interrogation room continued to display Taron, still resistant to the agents' questioning. Her focus remained sharp, but she knew the next step was to make contact with Alexander.

Tapping the screen of her secure datapad, Sarah initiated the communication protocol, her fingers moving swiftly over the controls. The holographic image of Alexander materialised before her desk, his silver eyes piercing as ever.

"Sarah," Alexander greeted her, his voice calm but charged with urgency. "What's the latest?"

Sarah straightened in her seat. "We've identified the next anomaly target Vienna, 1814. Gabe and the team are working through the data now, but I've been overseeing Taron's interrogation. He's been resistant so far, but we're not done."

Alexander's expression remained neutral, but a flicker of concern passed through his eyes. "Good. Keep the pressure on. The Congress of Vienna is critical. Any disruption could have far-reaching consequences."

Sarah nodded, already thinking about the next steps. "We understand. We're doing everything we can to ensure the timeline remains stable. But there's something else…" She hesitated, choosing her words carefully. "The suspect, Samuel Taron, he's proving difficult to crack. We've managed to decode some of his communications, but it's clear he's highly trained. He's been resistant to all our interrogation techniques so far."

Alexander leaned back slightly, his gaze thoughtful. "That's not surprising. The VTI has always been thorough in their training. Taron's resilience is expected. Continue with your efforts. Use whatever means necessary to extract the information we need."

Just as Sarah was about to respond, her comm chirped again. It was Max this time.

"Sarah, we've run into something strange," Max said, his voice carrying a note of unease.

Sarah frowned. "What kind of strange?"

Max hesitated. "We found a file on Taron's datapad. It was about John but the moment we accessed it, the entire device wiped itself. The file just vanished."

Sarah's heart skipped a beat. She leaned forward in her chair. "The entire device?"

"Yeah," Max replied, clearly still puzzled. "It's completely bricked now."

Sarah sat back, processing the new information. The idea that Taron's datapad had data on John was disturbing enough, but the fact that it self-deleted? That changed things.

"I'll need to loop in Alexander," she said, already pulling up the secure channel. "Keep working with Gabe and the team. I'll handle this."

Once Max confirmed, Sarah took a deep breath and refocused on Alexander, who was still watching her, his silver eyes sharp and focused.

"Alexander, there's something new," Sarah began. "Max found a file on Taron's datapad about John. But the moment he accessed it, the entire device wiped itself. The file is gone, and the datapad is useless now."

Alexander's eyes narrowed, his expression darkening slightly. "A file on John, you say?"

Sarah nodded. "It seems VTI had data on him. The self-deletion it wasn't something I've seen before. What does this mean?"

Alexander didn't hesitate. "It means John is even more important than we realised. The fact that they would go to such lengths to protect this information tells us something."

Sarah's unease deepened. "Is there something about John we don't know? Something that VTI does?"

Alexander's voice remained calm, though a flicker of tension passed through his eyes. "I know exactly how important John is. The VTI does too, apparently. His role in all of this is more significant than he or any of us fully understand. But for now, focus on the mission at hand. The datapad's destruction is unfortunate, but we can't let it distract us."

Sarah absorbed the information, the weight of Alexander's words sinking in. "There's something else," she added, almost hesitantly. "John has been having vivid dreams that seem to blend his past and our current missions. I'm not sure what to make of them."

For the first time, Alexander's composure seemed to falter slightly. His eyes narrowed, his tone becoming more introspective. "Dreams, you say? Given John's unique connection to the timeline, it's possible these dreams are more than just subconscious manifestations. They could be memories or even glimpses of possible futures."

Sarah sighed softly, rubbing her temples as she processed this. "That's what I was afraid of. We'll keep a close eye on him. He's shown great potential, but I'm worried about the pressure he's under. He's still new to all of this, and I don't want him to be overwhelmed."

Alexander's expression softened, a rare sign of emotion crossing his otherwise stoic features. "John is stronger than you realise. He's proven his resilience time and again. Continue his training and keep him close. His role in all of this is more significant than even he knows, and perhaps, more than any of us fully understand."

Sarah absorbed his words, feeling the gravity of the situation deepen. "We'll do our best, Alexander. Is there anything else we should be aware of?"

Alexander paused, a flicker of something almost like hesitation crossing his face a stark contrast to his usual unflappable demeanour. "There is one thing," he began slowly, his voice tinged with a hint of caution. "The leadership of the VTI is more connected to us than you might realise. Be cautious of their tactics. They are personal."

Sarah frowned, her mind racing to decipher his cryptic warning. "Personal? What do you mean?"

Alexander's gaze grew distant, as if recalling memories he'd rather leave buried. But then he refocused on Sarah, his voice firm but carrying a weight of unsaid emotions. "Just be careful. The lines between friend and foe are not always clear."

Sarah could see the depth of his concern, a subtle hint of sadness in his eyes, but she didn't press him further. There was an unspoken understanding between them a recognition that some truths were too dangerous to fully uncover just yet. "Understood, Alexander. We'll proceed with caution."

Alexander nodded, his demeanour returning to its usual calm authority. "Good. Focus on the mission in Vienna. I'll be monitoring the situation closely. Keep me updated on your progress."

"We will," Sarah replied, her voice steady as she ended the communication.

As Alexander's holographic image faded, Sarah remained seated at her desk for a few moments, staring at the empty space where his figure had been. His words echoed in her mind, a mixture of guidance and veiled warnings. She couldn't shake the feeling that the stakes were even higher than she had initially realised. Whatever personal connections Alexander had hinted at, they were clearly tied to something deeper, something that could have a profound impact on their mission.

Pushing herself from her chair, Sarah left her office with her mind already working on the next move. There was no time to dwell on uncertainties. The mission had to move forward.

Chapter Fifteen

The team assembled in the operations centre, anticipation and anxiety thick in the air. Holographic displays filled the walls, showing various timelines and critical points of intervention. The hum of machinery and the soft beeping of computers created a symphony of organised chaos. The tension was palpable, underscored by the memory of a previous mission that had nearly ended in disaster a subtle reminder of the risks they faced. Yet, despite the tension, there was a powerful sense of determination; they were ready to face whatever challenges lay ahead.

Gabe stood at the centre of the room, his presence commanding attention. He wore a tactical suit that enhanced his already imposing stature. Beside him, Sarah held her datapad, her expression focused. She occasionally glanced at the device, aware that Alexander was discreetly monitoring the situation. Gabe's eyes swept the room, his mind briefly flashing to the weight of the mission. This wasn't just another operation it was a moment that could change everything.

Gabe gave a final briefing, his voice steady and reassuring. "Alright, team, here's the mission. We've identified several anomalies in the timeline occurring around the Congress of Vienna in 1814. These anomalies are causing significant disruptions, and we need to correct them to stabilise the timeline."

He pointed to a holographic map of Vienna in 1814, several points highlighted in red. The map detailed the city's bustling marketplaces, narrow alleyways, and prominent landmarks. "Our primary objective is to intercept and recover a stolen artifact crucial to maintaining the timeline's integrity. If altered or used improperly, it could cause significant disruptions in history."

Gabe's eyes scanned the team, his expression serious, the blue light from the holographic displays casting shadows on his face. He felt the gravity of the mission pressing on him like never before. He needed to lead with confidence not just for the team, but for history itself. "Max and Lisa, you'll stay here. Your job is to help Sarah oversee the operation and provide us with real-time updates. John, you're with me."

Max and Lisa exchanged glances, their frustration evident.

"Why do we have to stay behind?" Max asked, his voice tinged with annoyance. "We've trained just as hard as everyone else."

Lisa nodded in agreement. "We want to be out there, making a difference."

Gabe smiled, a hint of his cowboy charm shining through, but inside he understood their frustration. He had felt the same way once, eager to be in the thick of things. But he also knew the importance of their roles. "I get it, believe me. But this mission needs coordination, and you two are the best we've got at that. We need sharp eyes and quick minds to keep everything running smoothly. Think of it as being the backbone of the operation. Without you, the whole thing could fall apart."

Sarah stepped forward, her voice firm yet understanding. "Max, Lisa, your roles are vital. Trust me, we wouldn't ask this of you if it wasn't crucial."

Max sighed but nodded. "Alright, we'll do our best."

Lisa smiled slightly. "Just make sure you come back in one piece, okay?"

As John prepared to leave, he couldn't help but reflect on how far he'd come. This mission felt like a turning point a chance to prove not only his worth to the team but to himself. He had trained, studied, and fought hard to reach this point, but in the quiet moments, when no one was looking, he still wrestled with the fear that he wasn't good enough. That he would make a mistake. That he might not live up to the expectations Gabe had for him.

The memory of his first failed mission still lingered in the back of his mind. He had been impulsive then, overconfident in his abilities. It had cost him, cost others. But Gabe had taught him patience, focus. Today, he would be patient. He would listen, watch, and strike only when the time was right. No more mistakes.

John took a deep breath, feeling the weight of the mission settle over him. He glanced at Gabe, who stood ready and confident. Gabe believed in him. And that, more than anything, gave him strength.

"Alright, team," Gabe said, breaking the silence. "Let's move out."

They made their way to the portal room, where they were handed period-appropriate clothing and small communicators that fit discreetly in their ears. The time travel devices were activated, and a bright light enveloped them. The familiar sensation of falling through time washed over John, and when the light faded, they found themselves standing in the bustling streets of Vienna in 1814.

The portal deposited them in a narrow alleyway, its stone walls covered in moss and grime. Gabe immediately took charge, scanning their surroundings and motioning for John to follow. "Stay close. We need to blend in and make our way to the rendezvous point."

John adjusted his clothing, trying to look as inconspicuous as possible. The streets were filled with people going about their daily business, the air alive with the sounds and smells of a vibrant city. The scent of freshly baked bread mingled with the more pungent smells of horse-drawn carriages and street vendors.

As they moved through the crowds, John's excitement mixed with apprehension. The city was alive with activity, and the political tensions of the Congress of Vienna were palpable. John's thoughts briefly flashed to his past, remembering a time when impatience had cost him dearly a lesson learned the hard way. Today, he would be patient, just as Gabe had taught him.

Gabe led them to a discreet vantage point near the location where the artifact was believed to be held. "Remember," he whispered, "we need to stay sharp and act quickly. No mistakes." John nodded; his senses heightened as he took in the surroundings.

Back at the training facility, Max and Lisa monitored the operation closely, their eyes fixed on the holographic displays, tracking Gabe and John's movements while relaying critical information through their communicators.

"John, we're picking up some unusual activity near your location," Max's voice crackled through John's earpiece. "Be on alert. We're detecting possible VTI operatives in the vicinity."

"Copy that," John replied, glancing at Gabe, who nodded in acknowledgment.

Lisa's voice followed. "There's a café nearby. It seems like a good spot to observe without drawing attention. Head there and keep a low profile."

Gabe led the way, and soon they were seated at a small café, blending in with the patrons. John sipped his coffee, his eyes scanning the street for any sign of their target or potential threats.

"Anything on your end?" Gabe asked quietly.

"Not yet," Lisa responded. "Stay put for now. We'll let you know if we see any changes."

The café was modest, filled with locals engaged in lively conversations. The clinking of glasses and the soft murmur of voices created a comforting background noise. Sunlight streamed through the large windows, casting a golden hue on the wooden tables and the patterned tile floor. Outside, the streets of Vienna were alive with activity. Horse-drawn carriages clattered over cobblestone streets, and vendors called out to passersby, hawking their wares. Elegant women in flowing dresses strolled past, arm in arm with gentlemen in top hats and tailcoats.

John grew restless as minutes stretched into an hour. He glanced at Gabe, who seemed perfectly at ease, sipping his coffee and watching the world go by. Gabe caught his eye and gave a reassuring nod.

"Patience, kid. In our line of work, waiting is half the battle," Gabe said, his voice calm.

John smirked. "And here I thought knowing was half the battle."

Gabe chuckled. "Whoever said that probably didn't spend much time waiting for VTI operatives to show up."

John laughed softly, feeling some of the tension ease. "So, what's the other half, then?"

Gabe leaned back in his chair, a playful glint in his eye. "Making sure you don't get caught sneaking cookies from the mess hall. Sarah's got eyes like a hawk."

John chuckled, shaking his head. "I'll keep that in mind."

Before Gabe could respond, Sarah's voice crackled through the communicator. "You two know I can hear you, right?"

John straightened, the seriousness of their task settling over him once more. "Understood, Sarah. We're on it."

Gabe gave John a reassuring nod. "Right. Let's keep our eyes peeled."

The café around them was bustling with life, a deceptive calm that belied the tension of their mission. The minutes stretched into an agonising crawl until Max's voice snapped through the communicator, bringing John back to reality. "John, Gabe, we've got movement," Max's voice came through, tense and urgent. "Two individuals matching the description of VTI operatives just entered a building across the street from your location."

John's heart rate quickened. "Copy that, Max. We're on it," he replied, glancing at Gabe.

Gabe finished his coffee and set the cup down with deliberate calm. "Let's move," he said, standing up and adjusting his coat.

They exited the café and blended into the flow of pedestrians, making their way towards the building Max had indicated. It was a stately townhouse, its façade adorned with intricate carvings and large windows that reflected the late afternoon sunlight.

John and Gabe approached cautiously, sticking to the shadows as they assessed the situation. Gabe motioned for John to follow him down a narrow alley that ran alongside the building. They found a service entrance, partially concealed by a stack of barrels.

"This way," Gabe whispered, pushing the door open just enough for them to slip inside.

The interior was dimly lit, and the air was thick with the scent of old wood and dust. They moved silently through the narrow corridors, their footsteps muffled by the worn carpet. Gabe led the way, his movements precise and deliberate.

They reached a staircase and began to ascend, their ears straining for any sound that might indicate the presence of the VTI operatives. As they reached the landing, they heard voices coming from a room at the end of the hall.

Gabe held up a hand, signalling John to stop. He leaned closer, trying to make out the conversation. The voices were muffled, but one thing was clear: they were discussing the artifact.

"We need to secure it before the LTC operatives find us," a voice said, urgency evident in their tone.

"Agreed. The artifact's power is too great to fall into their hands," another voice responded.

Gabe turned to John, his expression serious. "This is it. Stay close and be ready."

They moved forward, careful to avoid making any noise. Gabe positioned himself by the door, signalling John to take the opposite side. With a quick nod, Gabe pushed the door open, and they burst into the room, weapons drawn.

"Freeze! LTC!" Gabe shouted, his voice commanding and authoritative.

The two VTI operatives looked up in shock, their hands instinctively reaching for their weapons. The male operative, a burly man with a scar across his cheek, lunged towards Gabe, while the female operative aimed her weapon at John.

In a swift motion, the female agent fired a warning shot that whizzed past John's head, embedding itself in the wooden wall behind him. John ducked, his heart pounding as he rolled to the side, coming up with his weapon aimed at her.

Gabe sidestepped the male operative's charge, delivering a swift blow to his midsection that sent him sprawling to the ground.

"Drop it!" John yelled, his voice steady despite the adrenaline coursing through him.

The female operative hesitated, her eyes darting between John and Gabe. In that split second, Gabe moved in, disarming her with a precise twist of his wrist and pinning her against the wall.

"Nice work, kid," Gabe said, his voice low and tense.

The male operative, regaining his composure, sneered from his position on the floor. "You're too late. It's already on its way out of Vienna."

Gabe's eyes narrowed. "Who has it?"

The female operative, who had been silent until now, glanced at John and then back at Gabe. Gabe felt his heart skip a beat as recognition dawned on him. He knew her, though he kept his expression neutral to avoid giving anything away. She was someone from his past, someone significant.

"Do you remember me, Gabe?" the female operative said, her voice calm and eerily familiar. "You always were good at making quick decisions."

John felt a strange sense of déjà vu as he looked at her. There was something about her voice, her presence, which tugged at the edges of his memory, but he couldn't place her.

The male operative laughed, a harsh, mirthless sound. "You think I'm going to tell you?"

Gabe tightened his grip on the man's collar. "You'll tell me, or you'll regret it."

The female operative, who had been silent until now, glanced at John and then back at Gabe. Her eyes lingered on him for just a moment longer than necessary. Gabe felt his heart skip a beat as recognition dawned on him. He knew her though he kept his expression neutral, the memories from his past rushed back, crashing against the walls of his mind. Her presence here, now, was more than just coincidence.

"Do you remember me, Gabe?" she asked, her voice low but calm, almost as if she knew the weight her words carried. "You always were good at making quick decisions."

Gabe's mind flashed to a different time, a different mission one where their fates had crossed before. He knew this woman, and that knowledge made this encounter far more dangerous than he had anticipated. But he kept his focus, not allowing the others to see the turmoil roiling beneath the surface.

John's confusion deepened. There was a hidden meaning in her words, something just out of his grasp. He looked to Gabe for an explanation, but Gabe's face was a mask of controlled emotion.

Before the male operative could respond, Lisa's voice came through the communicator. "Gabe, we've intercepted a transmission. The artifact is being transported to a safe house on the outskirts of the city. I'm sending you the coordinates now."

Gabe released the male operative and glanced at John. "We've got our lead. Let's move."

They secured the male operative and immediately sent him back to the training facility using a portable time travel device. Gabe's attention was focused on ensuring the male operative was properly restrained and the device activated correctly. In the dimly lit room, his focus wavered just for a moment, enough for the female operative to act.

With a swift movement, she rolled back into the shadows, using the cover to her advantage. Gabe and John spun around, but she was already slipping away, her movements quick and silent. John caught a glimpse of her retreating figure, but the darkness concealed her escape route.

Gabe cursed under his breath, frustration evident in his voice. He knew exactly who she was, and her escape felt like a personal failure. As she made her way to the exit, she turned back and yelled, "Take care of him, Gabe! You'll know what to do when it's time."

John, still catching his breath, looked at Gabe. "Who was she? You seemed to recognise her."

Gabe's face was a mask of controlled emotion. "Just someone from my past, kid. Let's stay focused on the mission."

As the last words left her mouth, a bright flash of light illuminated the shadows where she stood, and she disappeared. The room fell silent, the only sound being the faint hum of the portable time travel device as it deactivated.

Gabe took a deep breath, his jaw clenched. "Damn it. We'll deal with her later. We need to focus on securing the artifact."

John nodded, filing the information away for later. They had more pressing matters to attend to now. The coordinates for the safe house were their next target, and the urgency of their mission pressed heavily on both of them as they prepared to move out.

They made their way out of the building, urgency driving their every step. The streets of Vienna blurred around them as they navigated through the city, following the coordinates Lisa had provided.

As they approached the outskirts of Vienna, the bustling city gave way to quieter, more secluded streets. The safe house was a nondescript building, its appearance blending seamlessly with the surrounding architecture.

Gabe and John approached cautiously, their senses on high alert. They circled the building, looking for any signs of security or surveillance. Finding none, they made their way to the back entrance.

"This is it," Gabe whispered. "Stay sharp."

They entered the building and found themselves in a dimly lit corridor. Moving silently, they made their way through the labyrinthine hallways, their eyes scanning for any sign of the artifact.

Finally, they reached a room at the end of the hall. Gabe pushed the door open, and they stepped inside. The room was filled with shelves and cabinets, all packed with various artefacts and historical items. In the centre of the room, on a pedestal, was the artifact.

John's breath caught in his throat as he approached it. The artifact was a crystalline structure, encased in a sleek, metal framework that formed part of a larger device. The device, with its intricate gears and levers, shimmered with a kaleidoscope of colours. It pulsed with a rhythmic energy, its power palpable even from a distance.

Gabe moved closer, examining the device. "This is the encryption machine they've been using for secure communications," he said, his voice low. "Without this, the Congress of Vienna can't finalise their treaties. The encryption ensures that all diplomatic communications are confidential and protected from tampering."

John nodded, understanding the gravity of the situation. "So, if this was stolen or tampered with…"

"Exactly," Gabe interrupted. "The entire conference could be compromised. Treaties could be altered or leaked, and history would be irrevocably altered."

The device's crystalline core was at its heart, radiating a soft, pulsating light. It was clear that this core was the source of its power, providing the encryption and decryption capabilities necessary for the diplomats to communicate securely.

John felt the weight of their mission more acutely than ever. "We need to secure this and make sure it stays in the right hands."

Gabe nodded. "We need to get this to the Congress right away. They can't continue without it."

They carefully retrieved the device, making sure not to damage its delicate components. As they prepared to transport it to the Congress of Vienna, John couldn't shake the feeling that this was just the beginning of a much larger conflict. The implications of their mission weighed heavily on him, but he knew they had to succeed.

The journey to the Congress was fraught with tension. They moved through the streets of Vienna with the device carefully concealed, avoiding any prying eyes or potential threats. The city was alive with activity, but every shadow and corner seemed to hold a potential danger.

As they approached the Hofburg Palace, the grand structure loomed before them, its impressive architecture a testament to the significance of the events taking place inside. The palace was heavily guarded, and they knew they couldn't simply walk in.

"We need a plan," John said, glancing at Gabe.

Gabe nodded and activated his communicator. "Max, Lisa, we're at the Hofburg Palace. The place is crawling with guards. We need a way in that avoids the main entrances."

Max's voice crackled through the device. "Give me a second to pull up the schematics. There has to be a less guarded entry point."

They waited in the shadows, tension thick in the air. Moments later, Lisa's voice came through. "Gabe, John, there's a servant's entrance at the rear of the building. It's less guarded, but you'll need to move quickly. Once inside, follow the corridor to the left; it should lead you to a back staircase."

Gabe relayed the information to John. "Alright, we head to the back. Stay close and keep an eye out."

They navigated through the narrow alleys, keeping to the shadows. As they approached the servant's entrance, they spotted two guards stationed by the door. Gabe and John exchanged a glance, knowing they needed to handle this carefully.

Gabe approached the guards with a confident stride, pulling a document from his coat. "We have urgent business inside," he said, his tone authoritative. "Diplomatic orders."

The guards eyed them suspiciously but, seeing the official-looking document, hesitated. "Wait here," one of them said, disappearing inside to verify the papers.

John's heart pounded in his chest as they waited. Moments later, the guard returned and nodded. "You may enter."

They slipped inside, moving quickly through the narrow, dimly lit corridors used by the palace staff. The sounds of the Congress echoed faintly through the stone walls, a reminder of the critical nature of their mission.

Gabe led the way with a surefootedness that spoke of experience, guiding John through the labyrinthine passages. They encountered a few servants along the way, but Gabe's presence and the urgency in their movements dissuaded any questions.

As they reached the back staircase, Gabe checked in with Max and Lisa again. "We're in. Any updates on our route?"

Max responded quickly. "You're on the right track. The secure room you're looking for is on the third floor. Once you get there, it should be the second door on your right."

"Got it," Gabe said, leading John up the stairs.

Finally, they reached the third floor and moved down the hallway, counting doors. The sounds of intense discussions from various rooms filled the air, underscoring the importance of their mission. They found the door they were looking for and Gabe knocked lightly before entering.

Inside, a group of officials were seated around a large table, their faces marked with concern and urgency. The room fell silent as Gabe and John stepped in, the tension palpable. The lead official, a stern-looking man with greying hair, stood up and eyed them suspiciously.

"Who are you and what are you doing here?" he demanded, his voice echoing in the room.

Gabe flashed a confident smile, tipping his hat slightly. "Good evening, gentlemen. Name's Gabe Welles, and this here's John. We're from a special envoy tasked with ensuring the safe delivery of this encryption device. There were some complications, and we had to make sure it arrived here unharmed."

The official narrowed his eyes. "Complications? What kind of complications?"

Gabe's mind raced, but he kept his demeanour relaxed. "Well, sir, we encountered some, let's say, less than reputable characters along the way. They seemed mighty interested in this here device. We had to take a few detours to avoid them. You know how it is."

Lisa's voice crackled in Gabe's ear through the communicator. "Gabe, mention the increased security protocols. It'll make your story more believable."

Gabe nodded slightly, continuing. "Due to the nature of these threats, the higher-ups decided to implement some increased security protocols. We were given direct orders to hand-deliver this device to ensure its safety. And here we are, unharmed."

The lead official's suspicion didn't waver. "And why should we believe you?"

John stepped forward, holding out the official document they had used earlier. "Here's the documentation. It has all the necessary clearances and signatures. We're just here to do our job and make sure everything goes smoothly."

The official took the document and examined it closely, his eyes scanning every detail. After a tense moment, he looked up, a hint of acceptance in his eyes. "Alright. Let's see the device."

Gabe and John carefully unveiled the encryption device, its crystalline core pulsing with a rhythmic energy. The officials gathered around, their expressions shifting from suspicion to relief as they inspected the artifact.

"This is it," the lead official said, his tone softening. "You've done well to get it here safely."

Gabe nodded. "Just doing our job, sir. Now, if you'll excuse us, we need to make sure it's installed properly. Can't have it failing at a critical moment, now can we?"

The officials quickly moved to install the device, their movements precise and practiced. John watched as the crystalline core was carefully connected, its pulsating light merging with the intricate workings of the machine.

As the device powered up, a sense of relief washed over the room. The officials exchanged nods, their expressions softening slightly.

"Thank you," the lead official said, turning to Gabe and John. "You've just ensured that the Congress can proceed without disruption."

Gabe nodded. "Just doing our job. Make sure it stays safe."

With their mission complete, John and Gabe stepped back, allowing the officials to continue their work. John felt a profound sense of accomplishment, knowing that they had played a crucial role in preserving the integrity of a pivotal moment in history. However, they knew that leaving the palace through the main entrance could draw unwanted attention.

Gabe glanced around the room, his eyes settling on a small door to the side. "We need to find a discreet way out," he muttered to John. "Let's see where that leads."

They moved quickly but quietly to the door and slipped through it. The door led to a narrow corridor, dimly lit and seemingly unused. They continued down the hallway, their footsteps echoing softly on the stone floor.

As they rounded a corner, Gabe spotted a small, empty storage closet. "This should work," he said, opening the door and peering inside. "It's secluded enough."

John followed him into the closet, the tight space barely accommodating them both. Gabe pulled out his time travel device and set the coordinates for their return.

"Ready?" Gabe asked, his voice low.

John nodded, the weight of their mission still heavy on his mind. "Ready."

Gabe pressed the button on his time travel device, and both of them reached up to touch their lapels. A bright light enveloped them, and John felt the familiar sensation of weightlessness as they were pulled through the fabric of time. Colours and shapes blurred around them, creating a dizzying kaleidoscope of movement.

The sensation of falling through time was both exhilarating and disorienting. John's mind raced with the rapid shifts, yet there was an underlying thrill in the journey. He could feel the energy of the time stream all around them, pulsating with a rhythm that seemed to sync with his heartbeat.

As quickly as it began, the light started to fade. The weightlessness subsided, and John felt solid ground beneath his feet once more. The blurred surroundings sharpened into focus, revealing the high-tech environment of the LTC training facility.

The room they left behind in 1814 stood empty, the air still humming with the residual energy of their departure. The only evidence of their presence was a faint, lingering glow that slowly dissipated, leaving the space quiet and undisturbed.

The room they left behind in 1814 stood empty, the air still humming with the residual energy of their departure. The only evidence of their presence was a faint, lingering glow that slowly dissipated, leaving the space quiet and undisturbed.

Moments after the light faded, a shadowy figure materialised in the room, stepping out of the darkness as if it had always been there. Cloaked in black, the figure moved with a predatory grace, scanning the room with a device that emitted a soft, ominous hum. His eyes, sharp and calculating, swept the space with cold efficiency. The device's readings flickered and danced, capturing traces of the temporal energy left behind by John and Gabe.

The figure's lips curled into a knowing smile as the readings stabilised, revealing a pattern that only he could understand. His fingers traced the data on the screen, and for a brief moment, his smile faded replaced by a grim, almost personal intensity.

"Almost found you, John," he muttered to himself, the name laced with a mix of bitterness and familiarity.

This wasn't the first time he had pursued John through the timeline. Each encounter brought him closer, each step through time tightening the noose. He had been watching, waiting, and soon very soon, their paths would cross again.

Satisfied with the data, the figure tapped a button on the device, and the room darkened further. Instead of the bright, enveloping light that accompanied John and Gabe's time travel, a swirling vortex of darkness began to form around the figure. The air seemed to bend and warp, sucked into the inky blackness like a miniature black hole.

With a final glance around the room, the figure stepped into the dark vortex, disappearing into the void. The room returned to its previous state, eerily silent and undisturbed, as if no one had ever been there.

Chapter Sixteen

Gabe and John landed back at the LTC training facility, the familiar surroundings of the operations centre slowly coming into focus as the bright light of their time travel faded. They stumbled slightly, adjusting to the sudden change in environment. The high-tech hum of machinery and the soft beeping of computers processing information surrounded them, a stark contrast to the historical ambiance of Vienna.

Max and Lisa were there, waiting anxiously. Max quickly approached them, his eyes scanning for any sign of trouble. "You made it," he said, relief evident in his voice. "Any problems?"

Gabe shook his head, a satisfied grin on his face. "Nothing we couldn't handle. The device is secure, and the Congress can proceed as planned." John felt a surge of pride and relief. They had done it. They had successfully completed their mission and preserved an important moment in history.

"Good work, team," Sarah said, stepping forward. "You've all done an excellent job. Take some time to rest and regroup. We'll debrief in the morning." John nodded, feeling the fatigue of the mission catching up with him.

"Sounds good," he responded. "I could use a break."

As they made their way out of the operations centre, John's thoughts drifted back to the mysterious message he'd seen in his dream the one that felt so urgent, so personal. He glanced at Gabe, considering whether to bring it up, but something stopped him. Maybe it was the way Gabe's expression had darkened when John mentioned the female VTI agent. Maybe it was just the weight of everything they'd been through. He decided to hold off, at least for now.

The next morning, the facility was abuzz with excitement and anticipation for the graduation ceremony. The newly trained recruits were about to take the next step in their journey as time travellers, and the atmosphere in the main hall reflected the significance of the occasion. The large space had been transformed into an impressive auditorium, with holographic banners displaying the LTC insignia and the names of the graduates.

John stood with Lisa and Max, their uniforms crisp and their expressions a mix of excitement and nerves. They had worked so hard for this moment, and it was finally here.

Sarah took the stage, her presence commanding respect and admiration. She smiled warmly at the gathered crowd before addressing the graduates. "Welcome, everyone, to the graduation ceremony of our latest class of time travellers," she began. "Today, we celebrate the hard work, dedication, and resilience of these remarkable individuals. They have faced countless challenges and have emerged stronger and more capable than ever."

The audience erupted into applause, and John felt a surge of pride. Sarah continued, outlining the importance of their roles in maintaining the integrity of the timeline and the responsibilities that came with their new positions.

"Each of you has shown exceptional skill and commitment," Sarah said, her eyes scanning the rows of graduates. "Today, you join the ranks of the Lennox Time Corporation as full-fledged time travellers. Your assignments have been carefully considered, and we have great confidence in your abilities."

As Sarah began calling out names and assignments, John's anticipation grew. He listened as his fellow trainees were assigned to various missions and departments, each one met with cheers and applause.

Sarah then introduced the heads of the departments, each stepping forward to acknowledge the graduates. Dr Alexander Smith, the head physicist, nodded solemnly. Dr Yukari Tanaka, the geneticist, stood with a serene expression. Jack Banks, the combat trainer, gave a thumbs up.

"Before we proceed with the individual assignments, I have an important announcement to make," Sarah said, her tone becoming more formal. "Dr Amelia Johnson, our esteemed historian, is moving on from the facility to a different assignment. Her contributions here have been invaluable, and while we will miss her, we know she will continue to make significant impacts wherever she goes."

There was a murmur of surprise and then applause for Dr Johnson, who smiled graciously but offered no further details.

"Additionally, Dr Malcolm Davis has also been reassigned. His expertise in cultural adaptation has been instrumental to our success, and we wish him the best in his new role."

Again, the audience responded with applause.

As Sarah called out Max's name and assigned him to the timeline analysis and anomaly detection team, a quiet sigh escaped John. They had been through so much together, but now their paths were diverging. When Max returned to the group, John gave him a tight smile.

Max grinned, trying to ease the tension. "Looks like I'm on desk duty from now on. I'll be the one keeping you out of trouble."

John chuckled, though the laughter didn't quite reach his eyes. "Don't worry. I'll make sure to give you plenty of anomalies to keep you busy."

Max's grin faded slightly, and he placed a hand on John's shoulder. "Hey, just because we won't be in the field together doesn't mean we're not still a team. You're still my brother in this, John. We'll always be working towards the same goal."

John nodded, feeling a lump in his throat. "Yeah. We'll make sure the timeline stays intact together, no matter where we are."

Next, Sarah turned to Lisa. "Lisa, you'll be assisting the new historian."

Lisa stepped forward, her expression a mix of pride and bittersweet resignation. After the ceremony, she walked back towards the group, meeting John's gaze. "Looks like I'll be more in the archives now, huh? Less action, more research."

John smiled softly. "You'll still be uncovering the truth, Lisa. And we'll need that just as much as we need boots on the ground."

Lisa nodded, her voice quieter now. "We might not be in the field together anymore, but that doesn't change what we've built. This team us we're stronger because of what we've been through. No matter where we go, that's not going away."

John reached out, giving her a reassuring pat on the arm. "And when we do meet again, we'll be even better."

Then Sarah called John's name, assigning him to work alongside Gabe in the field. John turned back to Max and Lisa. He swallowed hard, searching for the right words. "It's not going to be the same out there without you two."

Max smiled softly, and Lisa nodded, her eyes glistening with unshed tears. "We'll see each other again," Lisa said, her voice filled with hope.

"And when we do," Max added, "it'll be like old times, but with a few more stories to tell."

John nodded, feeling the weight of their shared history, but also the hope in their shared future. They were splitting up, but the bond between them was unbreakable. Wherever they went, they would always be connected by the mission, and by the moments they had survived together.

Gabe caught the look on John's face and, with a smile that held just a hint of that West Texas charm, said, "Don't you worry, kid. This isn't goodbye it's just the beginning. We've still got plenty of trails to blaze. You'll be out there doing what you were meant to do, and when you need us, you know where we'll be."

John felt a wave of relief and excitement. He turned to look at Gabe, who gave him an encouraging nod and a proud smile.

John nodded, feeling the weight of their shared history, but also the hope in their shared future. They were splitting up, but the bond between them was unbreakable. Wherever they went, they would always be connected by the mission, and by the moments they had survived together.

Gabe caught the look on John's face and, with a smile that held just a hint of that West Texas charm, said, "Don't you worry, kid. This isn't goodbye it's just the beginning. We've still got plenty of trails to blaze. You'll be out there doing what you were meant to do, and when you need us, you know where we'll be."

John felt a wave of relief and excitement. He turned to look at Gabe, who gave him an encouraging nod and a proud smile.

As the ceremony continued, dozens of other trainees were also called forward, each receiving their assignments and congratulations from the department heads. John watched as familiar faces he had trained alongside took their steps into the future. Each name called was a reminder of how far they had come and how much they had yet to accomplish. Though their paths were diverging, the bonds forged in those long hours of training, in missions where they had risked everything, were unshakeable.

John felt a sense of fulfilment and anticipation for the future. The bonds he had formed with his friends and mentors would carry them forward, and he knew they would face whatever challenges lay ahead together.

Unable to sleep, John found himself wandering through the quiet halls of the facility. Despite the excitement of graduation, a heavy mix of thoughts and emotions swirled in his mind. He eventually made his way to the training room, hoping that some physical activity might help clear his head.

As he entered, he found Jack Banks there, going through a series of combat drills. Jack moved with a fluid, almost mechanical precision, his muscles rippling beneath his shirt as he executed each movement with practiced ease.

"Couldn't sleep?" Jack asked, not pausing in his movements.

John shook his head. "Too much on my mind. Thought some training might help."

Jack nodded as he completed another flawless drill. "Training's good for that. Clears the head." He finished the set and turned to face John, wiping the sweat from his brow. "You know, you remind me a bit of myself when I first started with LTC. Lost, full of questions, trying to find my place."

John smiled slightly. "I didn't know you felt like that. You always seem so sure of yourself."

Jack laughed, a deep, easy sound that filled the quiet room. "Trust me, kid, everyone's got doubts. It's what you do with them that matters."

They began sparring, the familiar rhythm of training helping to ease John's mind. Each punch, each block, came naturally to him now his muscles responding with the reflexes he had honed during his training. Jack's movements were deliberate but restrained, as though he was testing John, measuring him.

As they moved, Jack started to share a story from his past. "Before I joined LTC, I was in the Special Forces. We had a mission in Afghanistan, deep in enemy territory. It was supposed to be a simple extraction, but everything that could go wrong, did. We were ambushed, outnumbered, and cut off from support."

John listened intently, fascinated by the story. "What happened?"

"We had to adapt. Improvise. The mission changed from extraction to survival. We lost good men that day, but we completed the mission. It taught me a lot about resilience and the importance of teamwork. Those lessons have stuck with me, even here at LTC."

John absorbed Jack's words, finding comfort in the shared experience. "I guess every mission has its challenges. It's how we face them that defines us."

Jack paused for a moment, studying John's face before giving a nod of approval. "Exactly. And you've got what it takes, John. Don't ever doubt that. You've already shown more guts than most."

They continued sparring for a while longer, the physical exertion helping John to clear his mind. Each strike, each movement, felt sharper now like the cloud in his thoughts was lifting, revealing clarity. By the end of it, he felt more focused, more ready to face whatever came next.

"Thanks, Jack," John said as they finished. "I needed this."

Jack grinned and gave John a firm pat on the shoulder. "Anytime, kid. Just remember, it's not about where you start it's about how you keep going. Now get some rest. Tomorrow's another day, and you'll need all the energy you can muster."

John nodded, feeling lighter as he left the training room. The conversation with Jack had given him a new perspective, a renewed sense of determination. Jack had been right everyone had doubts, but it was what you did with them that mattered.

As John lay down in his quarters, the adrenaline from sparring still coursing through his veins, he hoped to finally get some rest. But as his eyes fluttered closed, his mind was once again pulled into vivid dreams, dreams that felt more like memories or warnings than simple figments of his subconscious.

John found himself back in the stagecoach, feeling the familiar jostle of the wheels over rough terrain. The rhythmic creak of the wooden frame mingled with the thudding of hooves, and through the small window, he saw the endless expanse of wilderness. Dark, towering trees lined the road, their branches swaying ominously in the wind. Gabe sat at the reins, his grizzled face set in a determined frown. His eyes remained focused on the road ahead, but something in his posture told John this journey was more than it appeared to be.

"Hang on, kid," Gabe called back, his voice steady but edged with tension. "We're almost there."

John turned towards the inside of the stagecoach and saw the familiar man and woman from his previous dreams. They sat silently across from him, their faces strained with worry. The tension between them was palpable, though neither spoke a word.

"You'll be safe at the orphanage," the woman suddenly said, her voice low but firm. "It's where you need to be right now." She didn't look at him when she spoke, but her words weighed heavy on John, as though they carried a deeper meaning he couldn't grasp.

John glanced around the stagecoach, suddenly noticing Derek's absence. His seat was empty, replaced by an uneasy quiet that clung to the air. Confusion mixed with dread, but before John could speak, the landscape outside began to blur. The trees dissolved into shadows, and a creeping drowsiness tugged at John's mind. He fought to stay awake, but the pull was irresistible.

The scene shifted.

John stood now outside the training facility. The familiar halls stretched before him, dimly lit and eerily silent. His footsteps echoed in the emptiness as he wandered through the cold corridors. The air was thick with a sense of abandonment, as though the building itself held its breath in anticipation.

Rounding a corner, John froze. At the end of the hall stood a figure a shadowy presence from his previous dreams. It watched him, unmoving, a dark silhouette against the dim light. A chill crept down John's spine, and though every instinct told him to turn and run, he found himself drawn towards the figure.

His heart pounded as he approached, the distance between them shrinking with every step. But just as John reached out, the scene shifted again, blurring into darkness.

Now he was standing in a large, dark room filled with advanced technology. Rows of flickering screens cast a pale glow across the space, illuminating strange, shifting data. The hum of machinery buzzed in his ears, and the air was thick with tension.

In the centre of the room, John saw the female VTI agent from Vienna. She stood in deep conversation with someone, her voice low and urgent. Though he couldn't make out the words, a sense of impending danger clung to her tone. Whoever she was speaking to remained obscured in shadow.

Suddenly, the familiar figure from the hallway appeared beside her. Both of them turned towards John in unison, their eyes locking onto him with an intensity that made his blood run cold. The figure's gaze seemed to pierce through him, unravelling secrets John wasn't even aware of.

The figure raised a hand, and the room darkened further. The walls seemed to close in around him, pressing in from all sides. A crushing pressure weighed down on John's chest, and he struggled to breathe, as though the air itself had been sucked from the room.

"Almost found you, John," the figure whispered, their voice echoing in his mind, sending waves of dread through him.

The female agent stepped forward then, her face still hidden by shadows. "You're important, John. More than you know," she said, her voice filled with a strange mix of urgency and familiarity. As she spoke, she reached out and slipped a piece of parchment into his hand. John looked down, and there it was the same message he had seen before.

"Help Wanted: Seek the truth. Trust no one."

The crushing pressure intensified, and John felt himself being pulled towards the figure. Panic set in as he tried to break free, but it was like fighting against an invisible force. His limbs felt heavy, unresponsive, as though the very air had turned to lead. He struggled, his heart racing, but it was no use. The figure loomed closer, the shadows deepening around them.

Just as John felt himself slipping away, the scene shifted one last time.

He was back in the stagecoach, slumped against the seat, his body limp and exhausted. Gabe was still driving, the same grim determination etched on his face. The man and woman were talking now, their voices low and filled with worry. They seemed unaware of John's distress.

John tried to speak, to warn them about the figure, about the female agent, but no sound came out. His throat felt tight, his voice trapped. He wanted to scream, to shout, but his body wouldn't respond.

The stagecoach jolted as it hit a rough patch of road, and John's eyes snapped open. He was back in his quarters, his heart racing, his skin clammy with cold sweat. The dream had felt so real, so vivid, that for a moment he wasn't sure where he was.

His eyes darted around the room, taking in the familiar surroundings of the facility. Slowly, his breathing steadied, but the lingering sense of dread remained. The words from the dream echoed in his mind, the figure's warning chilling him to his core.

"Almost found you, John."

John sat up in bed, wiping the sweat from his brow, his heart still pounding. The dream had felt different this time more urgent, more ominous. And the message, that same cryptic warning, had resurfaced. It wasn't just a coincidence.

The images from the dream lingered in his mind, the familiar figure's words echoing in his ears. **"Almost found you, John."** He couldn't brush it aside any longer. There was something important in those dreams something he needed to understand.

His breathing was shallow, his mind racing. The sense of impending danger was too strong to ignore. As he lay back down, trying to calm his thoughts, John made a firm decision. He would talk to Sarah and Gabe about the dream in the morning. Whatever this was, it couldn't wait.

The next morning, John joined the team for the debriefing, the weight of his dreams still heavy on his mind. The atmosphere was calm but focused, everyone eager to hear the details of the mission and any additional information that had surfaced. The debriefing room was a state-of-the-art space, equipped with large screens displaying various data points and timelines. The soft hum of advanced technology filled the air, creating an environment of quiet efficiency.

Sarah stood at the head of the table, her expression serious. Beside her, a discreet console flickered, allowing Alexander to listen in without being seen.

"First, let me congratulate you all on a successful mission," Sarah began, her voice steady. "The Congress of Vienna is proceeding without a hitch, thanks to your efforts. But there's something we need to discuss."

She tapped a button on her datapad, and a holographic image of the shadowy figure from 1814 appeared in the centre of the table. The figure's dark cloak and menacing presence were clear, even in holographic form.

John leaned forward, his eyes narrowing as he studied the image. "That's the figure I saw in my dream last night," he said quietly.

Gabe shot him a sharp look, his voice taking on that unmistakable drawl. "Ya saw 'em, huh? Well, ain't that somethin'." But there was something beneath his tone a tension, maybe. The recent change in assignments weighed on them both, the separation of the team not yet fully felt but looming.

Before Gabe could say more, Sarah continued. "We've been monitoring the timelines closely, and this figure has appeared at several key events. We believe they are connected to VTI, but we don't have enough information yet."

Max, seated further from John than usual, exchanged a glance with Lisa, who now had her own set of new responsibilities. They both looked thoughtful, distant even, knowing their paths were no longer as intertwined with John's and Gabe's as they once were. Max leaned forward, breaking the brief silence. "What do we know about their objectives?"

Sarah sighed. "Not much, unfortunately. But what we do know is that they are targeting specific points in time that could have significant impacts on history. Their motives are still unclear."

Gabe cleared his throat, drawing everyone's attention. "We need to stay vigilant. John, ya mentioned a dream. Can ya tell us more 'bout it?"

John nodded, recounting the details of his dream: the stagecoach, the familiar figure, the female VTI agent from Vienna, and the cryptic message she handed him. As he spoke, he noticed Sarah's expression growing more intense.

"That message you received," Sarah said, leaning forward. "It's the same one you've seen before, isn't it?"

John nodded. "Yes, but it felt different this time. More urgent."

Sarah exchanged a brief look with Gabe, who gave John a steadying look before she continued. "We need to understand what these messages mean and why you're receiving them. It's possible they're connected to your role in the timeline."

Max shifted slightly, glancing towards Lisa, who sat quietly observing. Neither had been directly involved in the field as much since the assignments were finalised, and John could feel the distance. It wasn't just physical it was emotional too. Their roles had evolved, but they still cared.

Alexander's voice crackled through the console, startling everyone. "John's role is indeed significant, but we must tread carefully. The messages could be a double-edged sword."

John felt a chill run down his spine at the sound of Alexander's voice. There was something about it that seemed both familiar and unsettling. "What do you mean?" he asked.

Alexander paused before responding. "The messages could be guiding you towards something crucial, but they could also be leading you into a trap. We must decipher their true intent."

Sarah nodded in agreement. "For now, we need to stay focused on our missions and continue gathering information. John, keep us informed about any more dreams or messages you receive. They could be the key to unlocking this mystery."

John looked around the room, seeing the seriousness in everyone's faces, but his gaze lingered on Max and Lisa. Their expressions were supportive but more distant than he remembered. It was clear to him now that things had changed. Max would be buried in data analysis and timelines, while Lisa's new role as a historian would pull her away from the fast-paced missions they once shared.

"I will," John replied, his voice steady despite the uncertainty he felt inside. "I just want to make sure we're prepared for whatever comes next."

Sarah gave him a reassuring nod. "We all do, John. We're in this together. Remember that."

Max offered John a nod, though they both understood they wouldn't be working side by side as much anymore. "Keep me in the loop, man. I'll still be here," Max said, his voice lighter, but the weight of the shift in dynamics was clear.

Lisa smiled softly, her eyes reflecting a mixture of pride and a touch of sadness. "You know where to find me," she said. "I'll be knee-deep in historical records, but that doesn't mean I won't be paying attention."

With the meeting concluded, the team began to disperse. Max and Lisa exchanged a glance, silently acknowledging the gravity of what lay ahead, before turning their attention to their new roles. Gabe lingered a moment, giving John a thoughtful look before following Sarah out of the room.

As John made his way towards the exit, he couldn't help but feel that something was on the horizon something big. The cryptic messages, the dreams, the warnings they were all pieces of a puzzle he was only just beginning to understand. But with Max and Lisa shifting into their own worlds, John felt the subtle ache of separation from the people who had become his family. They weren't leaving his life, but they weren't going to be right by his side either. Still, they'd always be connected.

He paused at the doorway, glancing back at the now-empty conference room. The holographic image of the shadowy figure had faded, but its presence still lingered in his mind. With a deep breath, John resolved to stay vigilant, to continue piecing together the clues, and to trust his instincts as they ventured further into the unknown.

As John left the room, he found Gabe waiting for him in the corridor. The older man gave him a nod of understanding, his voice calm and full of that unmistakable drawl. "Looks like y'got a lot rattlin' around in that head'a yours," Gabe said, his voice steady as ever, that easy calm wrapped around the weight of what lay ahead.

John sighed. "Yeah, something like that."

Gabe straightened up, the soles of his boots making a soft tap on the floor as he stepped closer. "Ain't gonna be easy, John. But y'already knew that. What matters is we keep pushin', keep our eyes on the prize, and trust the folks walkin' this path with us."

John gave a small, grateful smile. Gabe had a way of making things seem manageable, no matter how heavy the weight on their shoulders.

"You're not in this alone, kid. We'll get through it. Now, let's get to steppin'. Tomorrow's gonna come whether we're ready or not."

John nodded, the weight of the conversation still pressing on him. The tension in his chest eased momentarily with Gabe beside him, but the echoes of the dream lingered. Whatever came next, he couldn't shake the feeling that it was already closing in on them.

And he wasn't sure if he was ready.

Chapter Seventeen

The next morning came quickly, the faint light of dawn filtering through the windows of the LTC facility's mess hall. John and Gabe sat in their usual corner, trays in front of them, their breakfast mostly untouched. The low hum of conversations and the clatter of dishes filled the room, but John's mind was miles away still caught on the shadowy figure from his dream and the weight of the mission ahead.

Gabe took a sip of his coffee, eyeing John with a smirk. "You're quieter than a rattlesnake in the grass, kid. That dream still got its claws in you?"

John shrugged, trying to shake it off. "Something like that. I'll figure it out. But we've got more immediate things to handle."

Before Gabe could respond, Sarah appeared, moving briskly through the crowd. She slid into the seat across from them, her datapad in hand, already all business.

"Morning," she greeted, her tone clipped but not unfriendly. "I'll keep this quick. I know you're due in the portal room soon."

John sat up straighter, pushing his thoughts aside. Gabe leaned back in his chair, watching Sarah with a practiced calm.

"We're sending you to England first," Sarah began, tapping on her datapad. "You'll use the safehouse in the countryside as your base. It's quiet, out of the way, and should give you enough cover to plan your next move."

She paused, her eyes flicking between the two men. "After that, you're crossing into Germany. Your target is Anna Müller she's a deep-cover operative working for the Allies, but our intel suggests she's about to walk into an ambush. She's critical to the timeline, and we believe she could be a valuable recruit for LTC."

John nodded, listening intently. "So, we're pulling her out?"

"If you can," Sarah replied, her expression serious. "She doesn't know about us. You'll need to approach carefully. Her mission is to sabotage a munitions depot, but enemy forces are already aware of her plans. If she goes through with it, she's not making it out alive."

Gabe raised an eyebrow. "What if she doesn't want to come with us?"

Sarah's mouth tightened into a thin line. "Convince her. If she refuses you may have to intervene. But tread lightly altering the timeline too much isn't an option."

The weight of the mission hung between them. Gabe glanced at John, then back to Sarah. "We'll handle it. Safehouse is stocked, I assume?"

"Fully," Sarah confirmed. "You'll have everything you need to lay low and plan the recruitment. The area should be clear of any major disturbances, but keep your heads down. You'll be entering one of the most volatile periods in history."

John exchanged a look with Gabe, the gravity of the task settling in. "We'll take care of it."

Sarah stood, satisfied. "Good. You leave in an hour. Head to the portal room when you're ready."

As she walked away, John exhaled slowly, the weight of the upcoming mission sinking deeper. Gabe tossed back the last of his coffee and stood, stretching out his arms with a casual ease that didn't quite match the tension in the air.

"Well," Gabe said with a slight grin, "guess we're headed to jolly ol' England first."

John smirked, shaking off the heaviness for a moment. "Can't say I'm looking forward to the weather."

Gabe chuckled, clapping John on the shoulder. "Could be worse. Now let's get a move on don't want to miss our ride."

With a shared nod, they made their way to the LTC transport hub, a central point for their journeys through time. The familiar, soft hum of the transport machinery buzzed in the background as the technicians checked their equipment. Gabe adjusted his hat, and John, still turning over thoughts about the dream, mentally prepared himself for what was to come.

Stepping onto the platform, they felt the familiar tingling sensation of the Chronoverge gearing up. A bright flash of light enveloped them, and in an instant, the sleek, advanced facility was replaced by the dense, quiet woods of the English countryside.

They trekked through the woods, the path uneven and covered in a thick carpet of foliage. The air was crisp, carrying the scent of damp earth and pine a smell that reminded John of long-forgotten camping trips from his youth. Gabe led the way with confident strides, his cowboy boots crunching on the fallen leaves, a sound that spoke of autumn's arrival. John followed closely, his eyes scanning the lush greenery for any signs of danger, his hand resting instinctively near the holster of his sidearm.

As they approached, the cottage appeared through the trees, a quaint, rustic building with ivy creeping up its stone walls. Sunlight filtered through the canopy above, casting dappled shadows on the moss-covered roof. To John, it looked like something out of a painting, serene and untouched by time an illusion that clashed with the weight of their mission.

"There she is," Gabe remarked with a nod towards the cottage, his voice tinged with a fondness reserved for a much-loved hideout. "Our little slice of history."

John took it in with curiosity. He hadn't been to this particular safehouse before, and while it seemed like a peaceful countryside retreat, he knew better than to take anything at face value. "Doesn't look like much from out here," he commented, his tone slightly sceptical.

Gabe chuckled. "That's the point, kid. It's what you don't see that counts. This place is a fortress disguised as a postcard."

They approached the wooden shutters that were slightly ajar, revealing glimpses of candlelight within a scene of calm that felt almost jarring given the war raging nearby. Gabe pushed open the creaky wooden door and stepped inside, holding it open for John to follow.

"Home sweet home," Gabe said with a grin. "At least for now."

John stepped in, immediately struck by the contrast between the rustic charm of the old wooden furniture and the subtle hints of modern tech. "You weren't kidding," John muttered, eyes scanning the room. The large stone fireplace was alight, its glow casting flickering shadows on the rough-hewn walls. However, it was the discreet panels and sleek equipment, artfully hidden behind oil paintings and tapestries, that caught his attention.

"Pretty cosy for a tech hub," John remarked, setting his bag down with a sigh of relief. He felt the weight of their journey lift, though the responsibility of the mission remained.

Gabe moved towards a table in the corner where a map of Western Germany lay spread out, its edges worn from use. "We've received intel about a skilled operative in this area. Could be a valuable asset to LTC. Our job is to find and recruit 'em."

John peered over the map, his brow furrowing as he studied the terrain. "You know who we're looking for?"

"Not yet," Gabe admitted, tapping a finger on a specific point marked with a faded 'X.' "They're operating deep under the radar. We'll need to gather intel locally and tread lightly. Last thing we want is to draw attention."

The room buzzed quietly as they prepared, the hum of hidden technology blending with the comforting crackle of the fire. Gabe double-checked the calibration of their communicators and time travel devices, while John adjusted his gear, his hands methodically securing his holster.

"Blend in and stay sharp," Gabe said, his voice low but firm. "This ain't one of our routine hops. Stakes are higher here."

John met Gabe's gaze, feeling the seriousness settle over him. "Understood." He adjusted his disguise, feeling the familiar weight of his gear settle on his shoulders. "We'll be careful."

By the time they finished their preparations, the late afternoon sun was casting a warm, golden hue through the windows, softening the tension in the room. Outside, the forest seemed peaceful, its whispers of leaves and distant birdsong a sharp contrast to the mission that awaited them.

"Let's move out," Gabe said, folding the map with a sharp snap. "Time to find our recruit."

The familiar rush of time travel enveloped them, a whirl of light and sensation. When the disorienting blur finally faded, they were met by the cold, biting air of rural Western Germany. Pines towered around them, swaying in the wind. The distant sound of artillery fire rumbled on the horizon, a reminder of the war-torn era they'd stepped into.

Gabe adjusted his hat, scanning their surroundings with a sharp, practiced eye. "Keep close," he said, his voice low but firm. Without further words, they moved forward through the dense undergrowth, their footsteps muffled by the thick carpet of fallen leaves.

The forest was alive with the sounds of nature a sharp contrast to the occasional rumble of distant conflict. John kept his hand near his sidearm, his senses heightened, aware of the weight of this mission. Every rustling branch and snapping twig seemed louder than usual, as if the forest itself was holding its breath.

They moved in tense silence, the forest canopy casting dappled light onto the ground, creating an ever-shifting pattern of shadows. Gabe walked with the confidence of someone who had navigated countless such terrains, his hand resting casually on his revolver, ready for any unexpected challenge.

Hours passed in quiet anticipation. Finally, through the rustling branches and shifting shadows, a figure emerged, moving with the grace and precision of someone who had been trained to survive in hostile environments. Their target.

Gabe shot John a glance, his expression unreadable beneath the brim of his hat. He nodded towards the figure, and John understood immediately. The way the figure moved controlled, alert this wasn't just any civilian. This was their operative.

"We've found her," Gabe muttered, his voice barely audible over the faint echoes of artillery in the distance.

They approached slowly, careful to remain unseen. The figure ahead paused, as if sensing their presence, before continuing her path deeper into the forest. Gabe signalled for John to crouch beside him, and they ducked behind a thick thicket of brush. The tension in the air was palpable.

John leaned closer to Gabe, his voice no more than a whisper. "What happens if we don't recruit her?"

Gabe's gaze remained locked on the figure. "She continues with her mission. Sabotaging a munitions depot tonight." His voice was low, tinged with the weight of what was to come. "Problem is, the enemy knows she's coming. They've cracked our codes and set an ambush. She won't make it."

The revelation hung heavily between them, the gravity of the situation sinking in. John's eyes flickered with a mixture of concern and determination. "So we offer her a way out."

Gabe's jaw tightened. "Right. She needs to know the stakes."

They crept closer, staying hidden in the shadows as they neared the operative. Her posture was tense, alert, her every movement betraying years of experience and wariness. Gabe called out in fluent German, his voice steady and calm despite the urgency of the moment. "We're not here to harm you," he said. "We're with LTC, and we've got a proposition."

The woman froze at the sound of his voice, her body rigid. Her eyes flicked towards them, sharp with suspicion. Her hand hovered near her concealed weapon, ready to react if needed. "LTC?" Her voice was cold, demanding. "What do you want from me?"

John stepped forward, his voice urgent but steady. "We intercepted enemy communications. They know you're coming. It's a trap."

The suspicion didn't fade from her eyes. "Why should I trust you?" Her voice was firm, challenging. The forest around them seemed to grow still, as if waiting for the outcome of this tense exchange.

Gabe met her gaze, his voice low and steady. "Because if you go through with your mission, you won't make it out. The enemy is planning an ambush, and we're offering you a chance to avoid that. Join us, and you can make a real difference on your terms."

Anna's jaw clenched, her eyes flickering with a mix of frustration and fear. "And if I join you? What's in it for me?"

John took a step closer, lowering his voice, his sincerity evident. "You'll have the resources and support to keep fighting. But you won't have to do it alone. You've been out here on your own, risking everything for a cause that leaves you vulnerable. We're offering you protection and a way to make a bigger impact."

A long silence followed, the weight of John's words sinking in. The forest around them remained eerily quiet, as if holding its breath. Anna looked between them, her mind racing as she considered the offer. Slowly, she lowered her weapon, though the tension in her posture remained.

"Alright," she said, her voice edged with caution. "I'll give you a chance. But if this is a trick, you'll regret it."

Gabe nodded, acknowledging the guarded trust she extended. "Fair enough. Let's get out of here and talk in a safer place."

As they began to guide her back through the forest, Anna's initial wariness didn't disappear completely, but there was a shift in her demeanour. Her posture remained tense, but her eyes softened ever so slightly. She exhaled a deep breath, the smallest hint of a smile breaking through the caution on her face.

"My name is Anna Müller," she said, her voice steady but still guarded.

"Nice to meet you, Anna," Gabe replied, his tone warm but measured. "We'll explain everything once we're back at the safehouse."

As they moved through the trees, the distant echoes of war faded, replaced by the quiet of the forest around them.

With Anna Müller now part of their team, John, Gabe, and their new recruit made their way through the dense forest. The lush greenery dampened the distant sounds of conflict, creating an almost eerie calm as they advanced. The forest floor, covered in a mosaic of fallen leaves and twigs, whispered softly under their boots, while dappled sunlight pierced the canopy, casting shifting patterns of light and shadow on their path.

Gabe broke the silence, his voice low but steady. "As much as I appreciate the peace, don't let it fool you. The woods can be just as dangerous as any battlefield."

Anna, still grappling with the abrupt shift in her circumstances, nodded in acknowledgment. Her trained eyes swept their surroundings constantly, scanning for any signs of trouble. "I'm used to danger," she said, her voice calm despite the uncertainty that flickered in her eyes.

The trio soon emerged into a small clearing, where their time travel device sat camouflaged against the backdrop of the forest. Gabe moved forward, checking the settings with the ease of routine, while John took the opportunity to explain the temporal travel process to Anna.

"Time travel can be a bit disorienting at first," John said, offering her a reassuring smile. "Just stick close to us. We'll guide you through it."

Anna gave a curt nod, her expression one of focused resolve as she prepared for the strange journey ahead. With a deep breath, she steeled herself as the hum of the device filled the air. In the blink of an eye, the clearing around them dissolved, replaced by a swirl of light.

Moments later, they landed at the LTC training facility. The sharp contrast between the serene forest and the sleek, high-tech environment hit them instantly. The air inside was cool, laced with the faint metallic scent of advanced machinery. The soft hum of technology surrounded them, a reminder of the vast temporal network that sprawled within LTC's walls.

Sarah met them with a brisk nod, her expression all business as she welcomed them back. She led them through the gleaming hallways, walls lined with intricate digital displays and maps of temporal activity. Anna followed closely, her eyes wide as she took in the vast scale of LTC's operations.

"This is where the real work happens," Sarah remarked as they walked, her voice cutting through the steady hum of the facility. Anna, who had lived through covert operations in a very different world, absorbed the futuristic surroundings with a mix of awe and cautious curiosity.

Sarah guided them to a conference room, where walls shifted between sleek screens and holographic displays, showcasing the ever-moving tides of time they were tasked with protecting. Anna's gaze flickered across the room, her mind racing to absorb the magnitude of what she was stepping into.

"Anna, welcome officially to the Lennox Time Corporation," Sarah said, her voice now carrying a formal, welcoming tone. "Your recruitment isn't just about filling a role; it's about embracing a cause that transcends time itself."

She handed Anna a tablet, its surface glowing with documents and procedures. "This contains everything you'll need your training schedule, security clearance, and protocols. We're strict for good reason, but your skills will fit right in."

Anna took the tablet, her eyes scanning it as Sarah continued. "Your background in covert operations is invaluable, but this work requires an even keener awareness. Even the smallest misstep can ripple through history. Starting tomorrow, you'll begin intensive briefings on temporal dynamics, ethics, and how to handle our tech."

Anna nodded slowly, the weight of her new reality settling in. As she listened, she occasionally asked sharp, pointed questions, a testament to her quick adaptability and tactical mind.

"Rest for tonight," Sarah concluded, her voice both firm and encouraging. "Tomorrow's orientation will be rigorous. Our timeline doesn't allow for slow adjustments."

With the briefing concluded, John and Gabe ensured Anna was settled with her integration plan, explaining the next steps. With everything in place, it was time to return to their mission in England.

As they moved through LTC's corridors, they reached the temporal departure zone a room humming with energy and vibrant with the glow of advanced transport technology. The soft, rhythmic pulses of light signalled the start of their journey back to 1940s England.

As the system engaged, the air around them shifted, and in the blink of an eye, they found themselves once again stepping into the quiet, leafy clearing outside the safehouse.

"Make sure your gear's set right, John. This isn't just another hop across the pond," Gabe remarked, his tone a blend of seriousness and his usual dry humour as they adjusted their time travel devices.

John checked his gear. The familiar rush of temporal energy enveloped them, and the stark contrast between the sleek LTC facility and the rustic 1940s countryside hit them as they reappeared in the dense forest surrounding their safehouse.

"Feels like stepping through history's back door," John remarked, taking a deep breath of the crisp, chilly air.

Gabe chuckled. "Every time."

As they approached the safehouse, the sound of the forest was suddenly interrupted by a series of rustling noises. Both men stopped, their instincts immediately on alert.

"Did you hear that?" John asked, his hand instinctively moving towards his sidearm.

Gabe nodded, his posture tensing. "I did. Let's check it out."

They followed the sound cautiously, moving towards the edge of the surrounding woods. The noise grew louder, a mix of whimpers and soft growls. Emerging from the trees, they found the source of the commotion a young Border Collie cowering under a bush, looking up at them with wide, fearful eyes.

"Looks like we've got a stray," John said, crouching down to get a better look. "Hey there, buddy. It's okay."

The dog, sensing John's calm demeanour, slowly emerged from his hiding spot. His fur was matted, and he looked both hungry and scared, but curious. John extended his hand slowly, allowing the dog to sniff him.

Gabe watched from a few steps back, assessing the situation. "We should take him in. He could be a good companion, and maybe he just needs a bit of care."

John nodded in agreement, reaching out to gently pat the dog's head. "You're right. Come here, boy."

The Border Collie, with a tentative wag of his tail, stepped closer to John. It was clear the dog was beginning to trust him. John carefully lifted the dog into his arms, noticing how the animal relaxed, pressing against him with a relieved sigh.

"Looks like he's found a friend," Gabe said, a hint of amusement in his voice. "Let's get him back to the safehouse and see if we can clean him up."

As they carried the dog back to the cottage, John spoke softly to him, trying to soothe the animal. The dog seemed to respond well, his anxiety easing with each step.

Back at the safehouse, they tended to the dog's needs, feeding him and giving him a much-needed bath to clean his matted fur. As John worked to scrub the dirt away, his hands brushed against something under the dog's tangled coat.

"Hey, looks like you've got a collar," John murmured, pushing the fur aside to get a better look.

The collar was worn and weathered; the leather cracked from age. As John inspected it further, his eyes widened in surprise. Stamped into the metal nameplate was a single word: *Joe.*

"Gabe," John called out, holding the collar up for him to see. "He's already got a name. Joe."

Gabe leaned in for a closer look, raising an eyebrow. "Huh. Looks like someone cared for him once, but I wonder how long he's been out here."

John gave the dog Joe an affectionate scratch behind the ears. "Well, Joe, I guess you've found your way back to someone who'll look after you again."

The Border Collie, as if recognising his name, wagged his tail and leaned into John's touch, the trust in his eyes growing.

By the end of the night, Joe was resting comfortably in a makeshift bed in the corner of the safehouse, his once fearful eyes now showing a glimmer of trust and familiarity.

"Looks like it was meant to be," Gabe said with a grin. "Joe, huh? Maybe he's been waiting for you all along."

John, sitting beside Joe and gently stroking his fur, smiled back. "Maybe. He was just waiting for someone to show him a bit of kindness."

The next morning, Joe moved around the safehouse with more confidence, his tail wagging as he explored the space. John watched him, his usual scepticism lingering at the edges of his mind. *Finding a dog, out here of all places?* It seemed too convenient, too perfect, and in any other moment, John would have questioned it. But the sight of Joe, with his name already etched into the worn leather collar, melted away any doubts.

"Still think it's a little strange, finding him like this," John admitted, glancing at the collar once more, the name *Joe* staring back at him. "But I can't say I'm not happy about it."

Gabe, leaning against the doorframe, gave a knowing smile. "Sometimes things line up right when we need 'em to, kid. Don't overthink it. Enjoy it."

John chuckled, scratching behind Joe's ears as the dog settled beside him. "Yeah, maybe you're right. He's a good boy. I guess we were meant to find each other."

For now, John let the joy of having Joe win out over his usual caution. The scepticism could wait at least for a little while.

As the team prepared for their day, Joe's presence provided a comforting sense of normalcy and companionship, grounding them in their hectic lives.

Gabe remained focused; his expression serious as he surveyed the surroundings. After giving Joe a quick, affectionate pat, he began a methodical inspection of the cottage's exterior. "Let's not get too comfortable just yet. We need to ensure no temporal anomalies have occurred during our absence," he called over his shoulder.

John nodded, following Gabe's lead. "I'll check the equipment inside to make sure everything's still running smoothly," he replied, his voice carrying a blend of professionalism and underlying concern.

Stepping back into the cottage, John was greeted by the familiar blend of old-world charm and modern technology. The wooden beams and stone walls were complemented by hidden high-tech equipment concealed behind panels and beneath floorboards. He approached the main console, which was cleverly disguised as a panel next to the fireplace. With a discreet press of a button, the panel slid away, revealing a series of monitors and controls that hummed quietly to life.

John systematically checked each system, his eyes flickering across the data displayed on the screens. The equipment monitored temporal fluctuations, maintained communications with LTC, and managed various security protocols. Everything appeared in order, with only the soft electronic hum of machinery and the occasional crackle from the fireplace breaking the silence.

Outside, Gabe completed his round of the perimeter, his keen eyes scanning for any signs of disturbance or unfamiliar tracks that might indicate unwelcome visitors or anomalies. Satisfied with the security status, he re-entered the cottage, brushing a few leaves from his jacket.

"All clear outside. How are things in here?" Gabe asked, glancing at the monitors over John's shoulder.

"Systems are stable, no breaches or anomalies detected. It's like we never left," John reported, his hand brushing against the cool metal of the console.

Gabe nodded approvingly. "Good. Let's keep it that way." He walked over to stoke the fire, adding a log to the gently burning embers. "Now, let's settle in and plan our next steps."

As they discussed their strategies, Joe lay contentedly by the fire, his presence a comforting constant amid the ever-shifting demands of their temporal duties. The cottage, a blend of past and future, provided a rare stability in the chaotic timeline they navigated, offering a temporary haven from their high-stakes missions.

In the soft glow of the dwindling fire, Gabe's demeanour relaxed, his voice taking on a reflective tone as he began to share more about his past. He refilled their cups with a practiced hand, the warmth of the drink matching the growing warmth in his expression.

Gabe stared into the fire for a moment, his eyes distant, as though sifting through memories that didn't quite fit together anymore. "You asked about my recruitment," he began, his voice steady, but carrying the weight of something deeper. "It was during a brutal winter in Arizona. I was hunting down Jebediah Barker, a notorious outlaw who had a knack for staying one step ahead of the law. I finally cornered him and his gang. We ended up in a firefight me against them."

John leaned forward, his interest piqued. "Jebediah Barker? I haven't heard of him."

"Not many have," Gabe admitted, his eyes narrowing as he recalled that day. "It was a hell of a fight. Barker's men were ready, well-armed, and there I was, outnumbered. The bullets came fast, real fast I remember the sting, the burn as they hit. Took more than I care to count." His hand subconsciously rubbed his side, the phantom pain still vivid.

John watched him closely, the image of Gabe standing alone in the desert, bloodied but unyielding, flashing through his mind.

"That's when the stranger showed up," Gabe continued, his voice quieter, almost distant. "Came out of nowhere, dressed in black, said he was from LTC. I was on the verge of bleeding out. Could barely stand, let alone fight." He shook his head, his eyes reflecting the flickering flames. "Gave me a choice join LTC or die right there in the sand. According to the timeline, I wasn't supposed to make it out of that shootout. I was meant to die that day, my death a message in some local dispute."

John felt the weight of Gabe's words, but something in Gabe's expression seemed off, like a subtle dissonance in the story he was telling. "So you joined," John said, his tone almost reassuring.

Gabe nodded slowly, though there was a flicker of hesitation in his eyes, as though the memory itself didn't quite align with what he knew. "Yeah, I joined. Didn't really have much of a choice at the time. But..." He paused, his hand gripping the edge of his cup a little tighter. "It felt like... like that wasn't the only time I'd been there."

The air between them thickened, the fire crackling in the silence. Gabe didn't explain further, taking a long sip of his drink instead, letting the unease pass. Whatever else he remembered or didn't remained unspoken.

"It was," Gabe agreed, though his voice was softer now. "But joining LTC gave me purpose. Working to correct anomalies, to mend what's broken it's not just a job; it's a second chance at life." His eyes flickered with a mix of regret and resolve as he continued. "As for Barker... well, that part of my story got left unfinished. After I joined, I couldn't go after him anymore. Jebediah Barker, me, the Dustbowl... all of it just faded into Old West lore."

John furrowed his brow. "So, you never caught him?"

Gabe shook his head slowly. "No. Barker became one of those legends, a name whispered in dark corners of saloons. And me? I became part of that lore too just another ghost in the dust. It's one of those things you learn to live with when you're part of this world."

John absorbed the weight of Gabe's words, feeling the layers of personal sacrifice beneath the surface. "And the stranger who recruited you? You ever learn more about him?"

A soft chuckle escaped Gabe's lips. "I asked, believe me. But some secrets remain locked up tighter than a sheriff's vault. All I know is he was with the recruitment division. Beyond that? Still a mystery."

The firelight flickered, casting long shadows as the conversation grew quiet. Gabe's stories had pulled back the curtain on the complexities of their work and the deep personal costs that came with it. John felt a newfound connection, not just to the mission but to the life Gabe had lived and the choices that haunted him.

As the night deepened and the fire reduced to glowing embers, Joe the Border Collie stretched lazily by their feet, tail thumping against the floor. John looked down at the dog, a small smile tugging at his lips. "Looks like Joe's found his place just fine," he remarked, giving the dog a gentle pat.

Gabe chuckled softly, nodding. "He's a good judge of character. Fits right in with us, doesn't he?" His hand reached out to scratch behind Joe's ears, eliciting a contented sigh from the dog.

"Seems like he does," John agreed, his hand joining Gabe's in offering affection to Joe. "Makes you wonder about his story before he joined us. Every one of us, even Joe here, has a tale to tell."

"True enough," Gabe said, his eyes twinkling in the firelight. "And Joe's no exception. Though with that collar, looks like someone gave him a name already. Maybe he's been waiting for the right time to find us just like we all do, one way or another."

The conversation gradually shifted from the intense narratives of time travel to lighter, more immediate topics Joe's playful antics and his quick adjustment to life with time travellers. They talked about training him to adapt to their unpredictable lifestyle, the possibility of him being more than just a companion perhaps a valuable part of their missions.

"As much as he's a comfort, he's got the makings of a fine working dog," Gabe observed thoughtfully. "Alert, intelligent, and loyal. Could help us out in a pinch."

John nodded, watching Joe roll over to expose his belly, inviting more affection. "Yeah, he's already proving to be a great addition. And who knows? His instincts might come in handy out there."

The rest of the evening passed with light-hearted banter and shared laughter. The bond between them deepened, not only through shared responsibilities but also through the presence of Joe, whose quiet companionship brought a sense of home, wherever they were.

As they decided to turn in for the night, they made sure Joe was comfortable, his calm presence a reassuring constant in their otherwise transient lives. With Joe curled up at the foot of his bed, John drifted off to sleep, a rare sense of peace settling over him despite the uncertain future.

But peace rarely lasted long for John.

As he slept, his mind was pulled into another vivid dream. He found himself back in the burning LTC facility in St. Louis, the fire's roar deafening, the heat unbearable. Desperate cries for help echoed through the halls as flames licked at the walls, consuming everything in their path. John stood frozen, watching the chaos unfold, his heart pounding with a sense of helplessness.

Then, just as suddenly, the inferno dissolved, replaced by the tranquil grounds of the Louisiana orphanage. The sounds of children playing filled the air, laughter and joy a stark contrast to the earlier devastation. Tall oak trees swayed gently in the breeze, casting long shadows on the brick paths. But the shadows began to stretch, twisting and darkening until they converged into the familiar figure cloaked in shadow.

The dark figure stood at the edge of the courtyard, watching silently as the children continued to play, oblivious to its presence. The peaceful scene was tainted by a growing sense of unease as the figure began to move towards John, its form blending with the darkening shadows of the trees. In its outstretched hand, it held a burnt and crumpled piece of parchment the same Help Wanted note John had seen before, though this one was charred around the edges, as if rescued from the flames.

The words blurred before John's eyes, but one line remained clear: **"Every choice ignites the future."**

As John reached for the paper, the figure pointed towards the orphanage, drawing his attention back to the children. The laughter slowed, becoming distorted, eerie echoes reverberating through the dream as the figure's shadow loomed larger. The boundaries between past and present blurred, connections John couldn't yet understand flickering just beyond his reach.

He jolted awake, heart pounding, his body covered in a cold sweat. Joe, sensing his distress, lifted his head, the dog's calm presence grounding him. John took a few deep breaths, the remnants of the dream still vivid in his mind the flames, the orphanage, and the cryptic message.

"Every choice ignites the future."

The words lingered in his mind as he stared at the dim glow of the fire, trying to make sense of it all. The dark figure had been appearing more frequently in his dreams, and its presence always brought a sense of urgency. There was something in the dreams that John needed to understand, a truth that eluded him but felt vital.

As Joe settled back down, John remained awake for a while longer, the mystery of the dream gnawing at him. The peacefulness of the cottage and the presence of Gabe and Joe offered some comfort, but John knew that the real answers still lay ahead waiting for him in the shadows of the timeline.

Chapter Eighteen

As the first light of dawn filtered through the small, grimy windows of the safehouse, John's eyes snapped open, his heart pounding erratically. The sharp, insistent barking of Joe, the Border Collie, pierced through the early morning stillness, pulling him from the depths of a restless sleep. The dog stood by the door, his body tense and alert, ears pricked up as if he sensed something John could not yet perceive.

John shook off the remnants of his unsettling dream, the shadows of the night still clinging to him like smoke from the fire that had raged uncontrollably in his mind. He sat up slowly, the chill of the floor seeping through his thin pyjamas as he rubbed the sleep from his eyes, trying to steady his erratic breathing. The dream had left him disoriented and troubled flashes of roaring flames, eerie screams echoing in his ears, and that same shadowy figure looming in the distance. It was as if his subconscious was grappling with something significant and deeply buried, tugging at the edges of his reality. A warning, perhaps. Or worse, a message.

The tension sat heavily on his chest as he made his way into the main living area, the cool morning air brushing against his face like a splash of cold water. "Gabe?" he called out, his voice rough and hoarse, betraying the unease that still gnawed at him. He found Gabe standing by the window, a steaming cup of coffee in hand, gazing out at the mist-laden English countryside. The landscape was bathed in the soft, early light of dawn, deceptively peaceful compared to the storm raging in John's mind.

"Morning, kid," Gabe said, turning to face him. His eyes, though tired, held a trace of concern as they took in John's expression. "You look like you've seen a ghost."

"It was another dream," John admitted, accepting the warm cup of coffee that Gabe handed him. He took a sip, the bitter liquid doing little to soothe the knot tightening in his stomach. He joined Gabe at the window, staring out at the tranquil but deceivingly serene landscape. "It was the same dark figure, but this time there was a fire and the orphanage. It felt like a warning, or maybe a message."

Gabe's expression grew more serious as he listened, his gaze shifting to the misty horizon before returning to John. "Dreams like that can be more than just random fragments of our subconscious. Given everything we're dealing with, they might be temporal echoes residuals from the timeline. We need to consider that they could be trying to tell us something important."

John frowned, the weight of Gabe's words adding to his mounting confusion. **Temporal echoes.** Could the timeline itself be trying to communicate? The sense of dread from the dream seemed to intertwine with his waking fears, blurring the boundaries between past and present. It was getting harder to tell where his own memories ended and the shadows of the timeline began. The safehouse, with its modest furnishings and utilitarian décor, suddenly felt smaller, more like a prison than a refuge. Every creak of the floorboards, every whisper of wind outside amplified his sense of vulnerability.

As if sensing the shift in his mood, Joe padded over to his side, offering a brief, reassuring nudge. John reached down to give the dog a gentle pat, grateful for the momentary distraction.

Before he could dwell further on the dream, Sarah's voice crackled through their comms, pulling him back to the present. "Gear up and familiarise yourselves with the technological specifics of the era," she instructed, her tone sharp yet tinged with empathy, especially when she addressed John. "We've detected a possible anomaly linked to VTI activity in 2075. You deploy in 24 hours. The temporal integrity of New York City is at risk. This could be the event that pushes everything over the edge. Make sure you're prepared for both the mission and the challenges it presents."

John blinked, his mind still catching up with the rapid shift from the surreal world of his dreams to the cold, hard reality of their mission. "What kind of anomaly?" he asked, his voice still rough with sleep but now laced with growing tension.

"Temporal disruption a major one," Sarah continued. "We've detected temporal tremors centred around a technology summit in New York. VTI has been laying low, but this spike is a warning. Our intel suggests that they're planning to deploy an advanced AI capable of manipulating timelines, and it's already embedded in the city's infrastructure. If this device activates, the ripple effect could devastate not only New York but multiple future timelines connected to key historical figures."

Gabe, who had been listening quietly, gave a low whistle. "Sounds like VTI's stepping up their game."

Sarah's voice hardened. "They are. And that's why we're sending you two. This mission requires precision. We need to find the source of the disruption, neutralise it, and prevent any further damage. There are no second chances here."

John exchanged a glance with Gabe, the gravity of their task settling heavily between them. This wasn't just another mission it was an operation with potentially catastrophic consequences. As much as his dream lingered in the back of his mind, the mission now demanded his full focus.

Sarah continued, her voice steady but urgent. "This won't be easy. New York in 2075 is a technological maze, full of advanced surveillance, autonomous systems, and the potential for temporal interference everywhere. You'll have to navigate the city, blend in, and track down VTI's operatives without alerting anyone to your presence. You'll be equipped with cutting-edge gear tech designed to give you a fighting chance but even that might not be enough. Keep your wits about you."

She paused for a moment before adding, "And John, I know you're still processing everything. But I need you sharp on this. Whatever's going on with your dreams, we'll deal with it when you return. Right now, the mission comes first."

The words hung in the air, a reminder that even with the weight of his personal struggles, there was no room for hesitation in their line of work. Not when the fate of the timeline hung in the balance.

With the briefing concluded, John and Gabe left the mission room, the weight of their task settling heavily on their shoulders. The urgency of the mission loomed large, pushing aside the lingering echoes of John's dream, at least for the moment. They poured over technical manuals, adjusting their gear with meticulous care, yet John's thoughts kept drifting back to the fire, to the orphanage, to the figure in the shadows.

But the mission came first. Always.

After returning to the LTC facility, their next stop was the armoury, where the heavy door sealed behind them with a decisive hiss. The room, lined with advanced weaponry and gadgets from various eras, offered a final opportunity to ensure they were fully equipped. Jack Banks was already there, checking over a newly arrived inventory. His usual hearty enthusiasm greeted them as they entered.

"Ah, if it isn't the dynamic duo! Ready to gear up for the future?" Jack asked, handing them sleek, compact energy-based sidearms.

"Always ready, Jack," Gabe replied with a smirk. "Especially if it involves better toys than you had in your heyday."

Jack chuckled, presenting the sidearms. "These beauties? They make your old six-shooters look like slingshots. See if you can handle that."

Gabe examined the weapon with an appreciative nod. "Looks like the kind of contradiction I can get behind. High noon meets high tech."

As they bantered, Anna Müller approached, her expression a mix of eagerness and professionalism. "Gabe, John, I've checked your equipment list for today's mission. Everything's calibrated to the mission specs."

John raised an eyebrow, amused. "Appreciate the diligence, Anna. How about coming with us? Could use an extra pair of hands, especially if you're as thorough in the field as you are here."

Before Anna could respond, Jack chimed in proudly, "Don't get any ideas. After a few *accidents* in training, we've discovered Anna's got a knack for explosions." He grinned at Anna, who rolled her eyes good-naturedly. "So, I'll be training her personally. She's still learning the finer points of controlled chaos."

Gabe shot John a look and turned to Anna. "He's not kidding. You've got your own training schedule to stick to. Can't have you running off on field missions just yet."

Anna masked her slight disappointment with a nod. "Understood. I'll make sure to learn as much as I can here."

"There's the spirit," Jack chimed in again, clapping her on the shoulder. "Besides, you keep us old-timers on our toes. Almost as good at this as I am."

Gabe rolled his eyes. "Almost," he says. Don't let him fool you, Anna. Jack's still trying to figure out how to work a digital watch."

Jack feigned offence, then grinned mischievously. "Just for that, I'm putting you two on extra inventory duty when you get back."

John and Gabe shared a laugh, finishing their preparations, the light-hearted banter a temporary reprieve from the serious nature of their mission.

As they were about to leave, Jack leaned in towards Gabe, a playful challenge in his voice. "So, Gabe, you still calling it a *time hopper*? Because *Chronoverge* just sounds like you know what you're doing."

Gabe shot him a look, but couldn't help the grin that tugged at his lips. "Time hopper's got character, Jack. Besides, who needs fancy words when you're riding the stream?"

John and Anna exchanged amused glances, trying not to laugh too loud as the friendly rivalry between Gabe and Jack simmered in the background.

With a final nod to Jack, John and Gabe exited the armoury. The serenity of the forest, where the temporal coordinates were hidden, offered a brief moment of calm before the next leap into the unknown. The transition point, a discreet platform camouflaged among the trees, awaited them.

Standing in the designated launch area, the air around them hummed with the energy of impending temporal displacement. Gabe glanced at John, giving a nod to proceed. "Ready for the ride, kid?"

"Ready as I'll ever be," John replied, touching the cool metal of his Chronoverge. With a deep breath, as he pressed the button, feeling the familiar tingle of anticipation as they prepared to hop through time.

The world around them began to blur as both men activated their pins. Brilliant white light flooded their vision, and they experienced the jolt of time travel a complex ballet of physics and technology. For a moment, they were suspended in the flow of history, surrounded by a tunnel of swirling colours and the sensation of weightlessness.

Gradually, the chaos of light and sound coalesced, revealing the futuristic skyline of New York City in 2075. Skyscrapers stretched towards the sky, adorned with greenery and shimmering with solar panels. The city was alive with hover vehicles and vibrant energy.

As their feet touched solid ground, the chill of the air contrasted sharply with the controlled climate of the LTC facility. They stood on a rooftop overlooking the sprawling urban landscape. John took a moment to steady himself as the final remnants of temporal disorientation faded.

"We're here," Gabe said, his voice a mix of relief and resolve. "New York, 2075. Let's get to work."

Stepping into the ultra-modern summit hall, John and Gabe were enveloped by a kaleidoscope of digital displays and neon lights. The hall was a technophile's paradise, with interactive holographic projections and AI-driven exhibits showcasing the latest advancements.

Gabe paused to marvel at a display where virtual reality met physical interaction. Attendees floated effortlessly in anti-gravity pods, their movements seamlessly syncing with the virtual environments projected around them. The entire setup created an ethereal spectacle of levitating bodies and shifting virtual landscapes. "Now, ain't that something?" he mused aloud, his cowboy drawl causing a few curious glances from passersby.

"Sure is," John agreed, his smart glasses flashing alerts and feeding him data on the attendees. "But remember, we're here for a reason. Eyes on the prize, Gabe."

They split up to cover more ground. John headed towards a cluster of tech entrepreneurs pitching their startups to potential investors. He mingled effortlessly, posing as a discerning investor. "So, what's the biggest challenge your startup faces today?" he inquired, his tone casual but laced with genuine curiosity.

The developer eagerly launched into a detailed explanation about cybersecurity threats and the need for robust temporal data protection. "Temporal data protection, you say? Sounds like the stuff of science fiction," John remarked, his tone light while mentally cataloguing every relevant detail. The developer's passionate discourse hinted at vulnerabilities that could be pivotal for their mission.

Meanwhile, Gabe wandered towards a quieter corner of the summit, where an exhibit honoured technologies from a decade past. He stood before a display showcasing early holographic tech a far cry from the sleek, immersive holograms of today. "Used to be you could see the pixels on these screens," he commented to a nearby attendee, his voice tinged with nostalgia.

The attendee laughed and agreed, enthusiastically explaining how display technology had rapidly evolved. Gabe's charm worked its magic as he joked, "Back in my time, we thought colour TV was a big deal." The attendee chuckled, assuming it was just a humorous exaggeration rather than a glimpse into Gabe's past.

John, catching sight of Gabe's engaging interactions, sent a quick, encrypted message via their communicators: "Making friends, cowboy? Any interesting leads?"

Gabe's reply came with a smirk: "Might just recruit a few of these folks for the ranch back home. But seriously, they're giving me some good intel."

As the day progressed, John and Gabe reconvened in a secluded corner of the summit a simulated garden designed to offer a serene escape from the high-tech storm raging outside. The garden's lush greenery and gentle ambient sounds of trickling water created a deceptive calm, perfect for their clandestine meeting.

"Found a couple of potential leads," John whispered, glancing around to ensure their conversation wasn't overheard. "There's chatter about an innovative AI that can predict temporal anomalies. It's the kind of breakthrough VTI would go to great lengths to control."

Gabe's expression darkened. "I've caught wind of a private meeting room where high-stakes deals go down. If VTI's involved, that's probably where they'd be."

"Looks like it's time to put our cowboy and investor personas to real use," John said, a determined glint in his eye as he mentally prepared for the next phase of their mission.

"Just another day at the rodeo," Gabe replied with a grin, his enthusiasm a stark contrast to the seriousness of their task.

Together, they ventured deeper into the heart of the summit, their interactions carefully calculated to gather the intelligence needed to protect the timeline. Every conversation, every observation brought them closer to uncovering the potential threats VTI posed. Their path was clear: find the AI, track down the VTI operatives, and prevent any disruptions to the timeline.

Gabe manoeuvred through the sea of technocrats and innovators, his gaze fixed on a commanding figure at the front of the conference hall. Emily, now the leader of the Voskos Time Initiative, exuded the same air of authority that had always drawn people to her. Her silver-streaked hair, coupled with her composed presence, only amplified the quiet power she held. To most in this crowd, she was an influential figurehead, but to Gabe, she was a reminder of unfinished business.

As the presentation concluded, Gabe slipped through the crowd towards her, calling out in his steady West Texas drawl, "Mrs Voskos. A moment of your time?"

Emily turned, her eyes narrowing slightly at the sound of his voice. For just a second, something passed between them a flicker of recognition, perhaps of the past they shared. "Mr Welles," she replied smoothly, though her expression remained guarded. "I assume you didn't come all this way just to reminisce."

Gabe tipped his hat slightly, keeping his tone light despite the undercurrent of tension. "Always straight to the point. But no, this isn't a social call."

Her gaze flicked to the crowd surrounding them. "Then I suggest we step outside for some privacy," she said, leading him towards a quieter corner, far from prying eyes.

Once they were alone, Gabe's demeanour shifted, his voice lowering as his familiar drawl took on a more serious note. "We need to talk about St. Louis, Emily. Things are starting to resurface, and I think you know exactly what I mean."

Emily's face remained impassive, though her eyes flashed with something darker. "St. Louis is in the past, Gabe. I have bigger concerns now. The VTI has its own future to shape."

Gabe's gaze hardened. "Yeah, but it's a future built on the ashes of decisions we made back then. And now it's catching up to us. Or maybe just to you."

She held his stare, her voice controlled but laced with an edge. "We all make choices, Gabe. You made yours. I made mine. I've moved on."

Gabe took a step closer, his voice dropping even lower. "Maybe you have. But that doesn't mean the timeline's done with us. And you and I both know it's coming to a head."

Her expression tightened, the composed mask slipping ever so slightly. "You've always been one to dig up old graves, Gabe. Some things are better left buried."

"Not when they start affecting the future," he shot back. His voice softened, but there was an intensity behind it. "John's future."

Emily's eyes flickered, a crack in her stoic demeanour. "What do you want from me, Gabe? You think dragging up St. Louis is going to change what's already in motion?"

Gabe nodded, his expression turning solemn. "I do. And I respect the burdens you carry. But there's someone else who deserves to know the truth. Someone deeply affected by your choices."

The weight of his words hung in the air between them, a subtle tension building as Emily's expression shifted to one of guarded concern. She opened her mouth to respond, but before she could utter a word, the sound of footsteps approached. Gabe stiffened slightly, recognising the familiarity of the steps, but kept his focus on Emily, who remained poised.

John had been moving through the crowded hall, scanning for Gabe, when something tugged at his attention. His instincts kicked in a sense of something off, a pull towards a conversation happening just out of sight. He slowed his pace, rounding the corner as snippets of dialogue reached his ears.

St. Louis?

That was all it took. His breath hitched, and his steps faltered. John's mind raced as he took in the scene before him Gabe and a woman standing close, their postures tense, their voices low.

For a moment, John couldn't place her. There was something about her presence, something he should know, but it lingered just out of reach, shrouded in the confusion swirling in his head. His eyes narrowed as he approached, catching more of the conversation. The mention of St. Louis and the tone between them heightened his suspicions.

He cleared his throat, stepping forward. The weight of the moment pressed down on him, though he hadn't yet fully understood why.

"St. Louis? What's this about?"

Both Gabe and the woman turned at the sound of his voice. John hadn't fully registered her yet just another figure talking to Gabe but something about her presence gnawed at him, something familiar. His eyes quickly moved to Gabe, sensing tension.

"John…" Gabe began, stepping forward.

But as John's gaze shifted back to the woman, the realisation hit him like a blow to the chest. His breath caught in his throat, and the ground seemed to tilt beneath him. The woman standing before him wasn't just another agent or leader in this temporal war. It was her.

His voice cracked, raw with emotion. "Mom?"

Emily, the leader of VTI, stood still, her composed mask faltering ever so slightly. The shock in John's voice cut through her usual air of authority. She didn't respond immediately, but the recognition, the acknowledgment, was in her eyes.

John's heart pounded; his breath uneven. His mother. Alive. Standing before him, when for so long he had believed she was dead, lost to him forever. His world spun.

"How?" He swallowed hard, unable to process the flood of emotions. "How are you why are you here?"

Emily's face remained calm, though her voice softened. "John."

But the anger rising in John's chest overwhelmed the disbelief. He took a step forward, the words tumbling out before he could stop them. "You've been alive this whole time? You let me think you were dead. You left me."

The words hung in the air, raw and heavy. Emily's gaze flickered with something guilt, maybe but she remained steady, choosing her words carefully. "I didn't have a choice. There are things you don't understand yet."

"Understand?" John's voice trembled with fury and pain. "I don't understand why my mother let me grow up thinking she was dead. I don't understand why you abandoned me."

Gabe moved slightly, trying to step in, but John shot him a glare, the betrayal deepening. "And you knew." His voice turned cold, accusing. "You've known all along, haven't you, Gabe?"

Gabe's face tightened with regret. "John, it's not that simple."

"Not that simple?" John echoed bitterly. His world was crashing down around him, the people he trusted the most suddenly strangers. "How long? How long have you been working with her?"

"I wasn't working with her, John," Gabe said, his voice steady but filled with remorse. "I found out later. After you were already with LTC."

"And you didn't tell me." John's voice was sharp, the hurt palpable. "You lied to me."

"I didn't lie," Gabe protested. "I was trying to protect you."

"Protect me?" John's voice cracked again, his emotions unravelling. "From what? From the truth? From knowing my own mother was alive?"

Emily stepped in then, her voice soft but firm. "John, this wasn't about you. There's more going on here than you realise. I had to leave. I had to protect the timeline."

"Stop talking about the timeline!" John snapped, his eyes burning with a mix of betrayal and grief. "This is about you and me. This is about you abandoning your son."

Emily's composure wavered, her eyes darkening with emotion. "It was never my choice to abandon you, John."

"But you did," John whispered, the weight of her decision crashing down on him. "You left me, and you never came back."

Gabe watched the exchange, his expression sombre. He knew that no matter what they said, no matter how much they tried to justify it, John's pain wouldn't be easily soothed.

Before Emily could respond, her communicator beeped sharply, cutting through the heavy silence. She glanced at it, the moment slipping away. "This conversation isn't over," she said, her voice steady but tinged with regret. She turned back to John, her eyes holding his for a beat longer. "We will talk about this. I promise."

And just like that, she was gone, disappearing into the crowd, leaving John and Gabe in the aftermath.

John turned to Gabe, his body rigid with tension. His voice was low, strained. "You knew. You kept this from me."

Gabe nodded slowly, his eyes filled with sorrow. "I didn't know how to tell you, kid. I thought I was doing what was right."

John clenched his fists, his voice barely above a whisper. "This isn't over."

Without another word, John turned on his heel and walked away, his mind reeling from the revelation. Anger, disbelief, and betrayal swirled inside him like a gathering storm, crashing against his already fragile sense of reality. He didn't know where to focus his rage on Emily for being alive and hidden all this time, or on Gabe for keeping the truth from him.

Gabe stood there for a moment, watching John's retreating figure. His chest felt tight with the weight of his decision to stay silent all these years. He hadn't known when, or how, to tell John the truth. But now, the time for hiding was over.

"John," Gabe called after him, his voice thick with emotion. "It's time we talked. No more secrets."

John hesitated but didn't turn back. Gabe saw the tension in his shoulders, the way his fists clenched at his sides. With a sigh, Gabe followed, leading him through the maze of conference rooms and bustling hallways. Finally, they slipped out into the quiet streets, where the city's hum seemed to fade into the background.

They found a small, dimly lit café on a quieter street corner. Gabe guided John inside, choosing a secluded table away from prying eyes. The air inside was warm, and the soft murmur of voices blended with the clinking of cups and the muted sounds of the city outside. But the weight of the moment made everything feel heavier, more real, as if the world had narrowed down to just this conversation

They found a small, dimly lit café on a quieter street corner. Gabe guided John inside, choosing a secluded table away from prying eyes. The air inside was warm, and the soft murmur of voices blended with the clinking of cups and the muted sounds of the city outside. But the weight of the moment made everything feel heavier, more real, as if the world had narrowed down to just this conversation.

John, his features tight with expectation and frustration, leaned forward. "Start talking, Gabe. I want the whole story. Now."

Gabe took a deep breath, steadying himself. The cosy ambiance of the café felt at odds with the gravity of what he was about to reveal. The hum of background chatter seemed distant, almost surreal, against the significance of the conversation. He sighed deeply, the lines on his weathered face deepening as he prepared to untangle years of hidden truths.

"Alright, John. It all started back when…" Gabe's voice trailed off as he searched for the right words. His eyes flicked momentarily to the bustling street outside, the mundane passing by in stark contrast to the storm of revelations he was about to unleash. He refocused on John, meeting his intense gaze. "There was a fire at the St. Louis branch a fire set to cover up more than just paperwork. It was designed to destroy records of experiments that could have jeopardised LTC, but it was also meant to protect you."

John's brows furrowed, his voice sharp. "Protect me? What are you talking about?"

Gabe held his gaze steady. "The decision to move you from St. Louis to the Louisiana orphanage wasn't random. After the fire, Anton Lennox ordered your transfer. You were only six years old, John. Even back then, the timeline was vulnerable, and you were at the centre of it. Anton wanted to keep you hidden, to shield you from the growing threats, but that decision… it didn't sit well with your mother."

John's confusion turned to anger, his eyes narrowing. "What do you mean? What did Anton do?"

Gabe sighed, leaning forward, his voice heavy with the weight of memory. "Your mother, Emily, fought Anton on the decision to move you. She wanted to protect you her way. She believed Anton was using you, that the orphanage was part of a bigger plan she didn't trust. When he refused to listen, she snapped.

That was the final straw, John. She stole a VT-5500, one of the early time travel machines, and disappeared into the timestream. She didn't just leave LTC she defected."

John stared at Gabe, disbelief and rage swirling in his chest. "She stole a time machine? And no one told me?"

Gabe's voice softened. "It wasn't just about the machine, John. She left because of you. She didn't trust Anton, didn't trust LTC anymore. She became a part of VTI soon after. Her actions created a rift one that's still affecting us today."

John clenched his fists, feeling the sting of betrayal deepening with every word. "She left me behind," he muttered, his voice filled with a mix of anger and sorrow. "And you knew all of this?"

Gabe's expression was filled with regret. "I knew she was gone, John. I knew she was involved with VTI. But I didn't know how to tell you. I thought I was doing what was right, keeping you safe from all of it."

John's voice broke through, raw and hurt. "And my father? Did he know? Was he part of this too?"

Gabe hesitated, his gaze shifting slightly. "Your father… it's complicated. He's been involved in ways you don't fully understand yet, but we'll get to him. Right now, what matters is that you know the truth about your mother."

John's fists unclenched slowly, but the weight of the revelation crushed him. His voice was barely above a whisper. "This isn't over."

Without another word, John stood and walked out of the café, his mind reeling from the flood of truths, the anger and confusion swirling inside him like a storm. The city around him felt both foreign and suffocating, the weight of his past pressing down with unbearable force.

Gabe watched him go, his own heart heavy with the consequences of choices made years ago. He whispered to himself, "No, it's not over, John. But you deserve to know the whole story."

The door of the café swung shut behind John, but the weight of the conversation clung to him, thick and suffocating. Outside, the world seemed to blur as the revelation of his mother's betrayal twisted through his mind. His thoughts felt jagged, sharp with anger and confusion, and the bustling streets of the city blurred around him, distant and surreal.

In the quiet aftermath, John walked aimlessly through the streets, the city life swirling around him as if he were a ghost among the living. His mind churned with a storm of emotions anger like a searing flame, fuelled by the betrayal of those he had trusted implicitly. Confusion tangled his thoughts, making it nearly impossible to grasp the enormity of the revelations about his mother and his own past.

The world around him felt off-kilter, as if the timeline itself had shifted beneath his feet, leaving him disoriented and uncertain. Each step felt heavy, his mind replaying the fragments of conversation Gabe's regretful confessions, Emily's unresolved words, and the weight of secrets that had been kept from him his entire life.

The revelation that his mother, Emily, might be a pivotal figure in rival operations against LTC added a new layer of personal conflict. He had spent years believing her to be gone, lost in time erased by a fire he could barely remember. Now, discovering she was not only alive but possibly working against everything he thought he stood for, shook the very foundations of his identity. Who had she become? And why had she left him behind?

As he wandered, his footsteps eventually led him to a small park, a green oasis amidst the urban chaos. The cool shade of an old oak tree provided a slight comfort against the turmoil inside him. He found a secluded bench and sat down, the soft rustling of leaves and distant sounds of laughter starkly contrasting his inner storm.

He pulled out a small device from his pocket a portable holo-projector from his training days at LTC. With a flick, images of his mother materialised in the air before him. Photos of her, some familiar and others new, rotated slowly. Her smile, once a source of warmth, now seemed to taunt him with the secrets she had yet to uncover.

He pulled out a small device from his pocket a portable holo-projector from his training days at LTC. With a flick, images of his mother materialised in the air before him. Photos of her, some familiar and others new, rotated slowly. Her smile, once a source of warmth, now seemed to taunt him with the secrets she had yet to reveal.

Gabe's words from their conversation echoed in his mind: *"I didn't know how to tell you, kid. I thought I was doing what was right."* The admission stung there had been time to tell him, time to prepare him for the truth about Emily. But they hadn't. They had waited, manoeuvring around his life like he was just another piece on a chessboard.

His mind drifted to his father, Anton Lennox. Emily's choices had been shaped by Anton's decisions, too his father had been the one who ordered John moved, the one who had shaped the path he was on now. But Anton was still a mystery, a shadow who had pulled the strings from behind the scenes. What had driven him to make those choices? And what role did Emily play in the rift between them?

Feeling a surge of resolve amid the fog of his emotions, John shut off the projector. He couldn't afford to let his feelings paralyse him. If answers about his mother and the decisions made for him were to be found, he would seek them out. He needed to understand Emily's involvement with VTI, the fallout from St. Louis, and how his own story fit into the grand scheme LTC had crafted.

The café seemed unchanged in the brief time John had been away. The steady hum of conversation and the clatter of dishes filled the air, patrons absorbed in their own worlds. Gabe was exactly where John had left him, his rugged face etched with lines of concern, steam rising from his untouched coffee.

As John approached, the weight of their earlier conversation still lingered between them. His mind churned with everything Gabe had revealed his mother, Emily, alive and leading the Voskos Time Initiative, the hidden truths about St. Louis, and the choices that had shaped his life without his knowledge. There was so much left unsaid, but before John could re-engage, both their communicators chimed simultaneously, cutting through the café's ambient noise.

Sarah's voice crackled through John's earpiece, her tone terse and urgent. "Where have you both been? I've been trying to reach you for the last two hours. We've had no telemetry, nothing. What's going on?"

John's frustration and sarcasm bubbled to the surface, masking the storm of emotions underneath. "Must've been sunspots messing with the signals," he muttered, though the gravity of the situation hung heavy between them.

"This isn't a joke, John," Sarah shot back, her voice sharp with stress. "I need you both back at the conference centre immediately. There's been a complication. The timeline shows an anomaly an explosion that takes down the building today, in 2075. It wasn't there before. Find out what's causing this and look for any device that might be linked to it. Time is literally against us."

Gabe shot up from his seat, the tension between him and John momentarily set aside as the new crisis took precedence. He met John's gaze with a grim nod, the usual warmth in his West Texas drawl replaced by a crisp, commanding tone. "Let's move, kid. We've got a timeline to save."

John's jaw clenched, a hard edge forming in his eyes. "We'll finish this later, Gabe." His voice was thick with suppressed anger, each word laden with the weight of betrayal and the unresolved conflict swirling within him.

Gabe flinched slightly, the sting of John's words cutting deeper than he let on. For a fleeting moment, the cowboy's usual stoic expression faltered, his eyes glossing over with unshed emotion. But his resolve held, and the hardened lines of his face returned as he pushed it all down, focusing on the mission ahead.

"Right," Gabe said, his voice now a controlled rumble. "Let's focus on the mission."

They quickly made their way through the bustling streets towards the conference centre. The weight of the coming task hung heavily between them, as unspoken words and lingering tension simmered beneath the surface. The towering structure of the conference hall loomed ahead a marvel of architectural genius, its dynamic, morphing facades designed to adapt to environmental conditions. Yet, the looming threat of catastrophe overshadowed its beauty, a stark reminder of the dangers they faced.

Gabe's communicator beeped again, the crackling sound pulling them back to the urgent task at hand. Sarah's voice filtered through, relaying the crucial data. "We've pinpointed the projected explosion's time and location. You need to find the device before it goes off. Stay vigilant, and don't get distracted."

Gabe glanced at John. "You heard her. Keep your eyes sharp. We're looking for anything that stands out, anything unusual."

John nodded, his training kicking in as his mind switched to operational mode. He scanned the area, cataloguing potential threats, his thoughts racing with possibilities. Who would stand to gain from such an attack? Was this a diversion, or a targeted strike?

And most importantly, where did Emily fit into all this? Was she involved, or was she yet another piece in the puzzle John was still trying to solve?

As they moved towards the entrance of the conference centre, the enormity of the moment settled between them. The stakes were higher than ever, the weight of the timeline pressing down on their shoulders. But the real question that lingered in John's mind as they stepped into the fray was this: Was this just the beginning of the truth unravelling, or had they already lost control of the story?

Chapter Nineteen

As he passed through the security checkpoint, John's focus sharpened, his senses heightened by the weight of the holster pressing against his side a constant reminder of the stakes. Each step he took reverberated with the weight of recent revelations, the answers he sought now entwined with dangers lurking in every shadow.

The sleek, futuristic lobby of the corporate summit loomed large as John and Gabe stepped through the shimmering portal. The contrast between the bustling activity of the event and the silent tension between them was palpable. John grabbed the communicator with a practiced motion, his voice tight with controlled anger. "We need to cover more ground. Split up," John's tone was terse over the comm, barely masking his frustration and simmering bitterness.

Gabe hesitated, concern flashing briefly in his eyes before giving a reluctant nod. "Alright, but be careful," he replied, his words laden with an unspoken apology that never reached the surface. After a pause, he added, "We've got a timeline to save."

John shot back, his words laced with cynicism. "You always say that." The phrase, once a motto they'd both lived by, now hung between them like a final crack in the foundation of their partnership.

Without waiting for a response, John turned towards the emergency stairwell leading down to the sublevels. Gabe sighed heavily, the sound an echo of the day's emotional toll, as he made his way to the staircase leading upward. The decision to separate was strategic, but the weight of their fractured relationship pressed against them with every step.

John pushed open the stairwell door with a clang, the harsh sound reverberating through the building as an alarm blared to life. The echo of Gabe's footsteps from above seemed to pound in unison with John's heartbeat rapid and unresolved.

Fuelled by the adrenaline of betrayal and duty, John descended quickly. The floors passed in a blur as the signs flashed by: "B1, B2, B3…" His mind raced faster than his feet, trying to piece together the fragments of his life that had been shattered by Gabe's revelations.

Meanwhile, Gabe ascended, his steps slower, burdened with the weight of personal grief. Each step pulled him further from John, not just physically but emotionally, as the wailing alarm mirrored the turmoil raging inside him.

Reaching the lower levels, John was greeted by flickering lights and the cold, robotic voice of the building's security system. "Please evacuate the building immediately," the voice droned, a clinical contrast to the human chaos unfolding.

Above, Gabe reached the executive floors, his eyes scanning the sleek, sterile offices for any sign of the device they were sent to find. His communicator crackled, Sarah's voice cutting through with urgency. "Status report?"

"Still searching," Gabe replied, pushing open the doors to the main conference area, now bathed in dim emergency lighting that cast long, ominous shadows.

Back in the basement, John burst through a door labelled "Engineering and Maintenance." The room was a maze of server racks and humming machinery. His training took over as he navigated the space, his eyes scanning for any sign of an anomaly. Amid the mechanical whirs, his mind couldn't shake the weight of the unresolved tension between him and Gabe.

His communicator buzzed, John's voice coming through in a clipped tone, thick with resolve. "We finish this mission, Gabe. But you and me we're not done. We'll talk after."

Gabe's grip tightened around his own communicator, his jaw clenching. He blinked hard, moisture gathering in his eyes something uncharacteristic for the usually stoic cowboy. "Understood, John. Let's save the timeline first."

As Gabe climbed the emergency stairs, his steps were swift and deliberate. The cold echo of his boots against the metal steps reverberated in his mind, each footfall carrying the weight of a mission far greater than either of them. The sterile emptiness of the stairwell only heightened the pressure, the gravity of the secrets they were about to unearth hanging heavy in the air.

Suddenly, John's voice, tense and urgent, crackled through the communicator, shattering the rhythmic monotony of Gabe's ascent. "I've found them, Gabe. It's VTI. My mother she's here, in the basement, with something big. Looks like it's about to go critical."

Gabe's heart stopped for a brief second, the words striking him like a punch to the gut. Emily. Alive, and now standing at the heart of another crisis. The adrenaline kicked in, surging through him, pushing aside the shock. His boots skidded against the metal steps as he halted mid-stride. Without a second thought, he pivoted sharply, every muscle tense with purpose.

His descent was swift, his actions fluid yet fuelled by a rising panic. Gabe took the stairs two at a time, his controlled drop accelerating with each passing level. His mind raced as fast as his feet thoughts of John, Emily, and the looming catastrophe mixing in a chaotic spiral. **Time was running out**, and the ticking clock wasn't just against the timeline, but against their fractured past as well.

The cool, sterile walls of the stairwell blurred past him as he closed in on the basement, John's discovery pushing him harder and faster with every step. There was no room for hesitation now; they were closing in on something far more volatile than just another anomaly. This was personal.

Below, John was a silent shadow, hidden behind a utility box, his heart pounding in rhythm with the ominous hum of the cylindrical device at the centre of the room. His eyes were locked on the tense tableau before him: Emily, alongside several VTI agents, frantically manipulating the device that crackled with unstable energy. The air in the basement was thick, saturated with the electric buzz of imminent danger.

Through his earpiece, John whispered, "It looks like a bomb, or something worse. They haven't seen me yet. Waiting for your go."

"Stay put, kid. I'm almost there," Gabe's voice came through, strained but controlled. Each word crackled through the comm as his descent grew more desperate with every step. The basement door loomed ahead, and with a final burst of speed, Gabe slammed through it, the sound echoing loudly in the confined space.

Gabe quickly emerged beside John, his breath still heavy from the mad dash, but his sharp eyes instantly assessed the situation. Across the room, Emily's voice carried with a commanding edge, "Stabilise it now! If this goes off, everything we've worked for is lost!"

John's heart clenched at the sound of her voice so familiar, yet so alien in this context. His grip on his weapon tightened as the weight of his mother's words sank in, a confusing mix of anger and deep, unspoken pain. Gabe placed a firm hand on his shoulder, grounding him in the moment. It was a silent message of reassurance: *We're in this together.*

"We need to intervene now, John. Are you ready?" Gabe's voice was low and steady, a calm contrast to the chaos swirling inside John's mind.

John's jaw clenched, his grip tightening on his weapon. "Let's do it. For the timeline."

In sync, they stepped out from their cover, weapons lowered but at the ready. Gabe's voice cut through the hum of the temporal device and the murmurs of the VTI agents, sharp and authoritative. "Emily! Stop what you're doing. We need to talk."

The activity around the device halted, and Emily turned to face them. For a brief moment, her eyes flickered with shock and recognition. The sight of Gabe a man she had once trusted and her son, John, standing beside him, froze her for a heartbeat. But the cold calculation quickly returned to her features as she shifted her focus back to the device.

"John?" she whispered, her voice carrying a tremor of disbelief.

John's gaze locked on her, his hand shaking for a moment as the realisation that his mother was not only alive but deeply involved in something catastrophic settled over him. The pendant around her neck gleamed, a cruel reminder of the past an heirloom she had always worn. Seeing it now, on her, stirred a whirlpool of emotions within him loss, betrayal, anger. His grip tightened.

"Everyone, step back," John commanded, his voice hard with emotion. "Back away from the device, now!"

The VTI agents hesitated, exchanging uneasy glances. Emily, still in control, raised her hand. "Stand down," she ordered her team. The agents, though reluctant, complied, stepping back from the buzzing device.

Gabe advanced slowly, eyes trained on Emily. "Emily, whatever this is, you need to stop it. We can help, but you need to let us in."

Her eyes flicked between John and Gabe, and for a moment, there was vulnerability, a softness that vanished almost as quickly as it appeared. "You don't understand," she said, her voice low but insistent. "This isn't what you think. We're trying to prevent a catastrophe, not cause one."

"By risking everything?" John shot back, his voice sharp, anger seeping through the cracks. "You're playing with forces you can't control."

Suddenly, Sarah's voice crackled through their comms. "Gabe, John, the device is reaching critical levels. You have minutes before this thing blows. Shut it down, now."

Gabe responded into his comm without breaking eye contact with Emily. "It's her. It's Emily. She's behind this."

There was a stunned silence on the other end of the line, then Sarah's voice, tight with shock, replied, "Emily? John's mother?"

John's heart pounded in his chest as he kept his gaze on Emily, the weight of Sarah's words pressing down on him. His mother someone he had thought lost, now standing before him, complicit in something dangerous and world-altering. The pendant around her neck was just a symbol now, of everything stolen from him.

"Yes," Gabe confirmed grimly, his gaze never wavering. "But we're running out of time. The device is going critical."

Before Sarah could reply, another voice broke through the comms, cold and authoritative. "Emily."

The word seemed to echo, cutting through the tension like a blade. John's blood ran cold. He recognised the voice but couldn't place it. But from Emily's reaction, he could tell she knew exactly who it was. Her body stiffened, and for the first time, her hands trembled. Fear flickered across her face, just for a moment.

Gabe shot a glance at John, who met his gaze with equal confusion. "Sarah," Gabe demanded, his voice sharp, "who else is on this line?"

Before Sarah could answer, Emily barked another order at her agents, her hands flying back to the device. "Stabilise it now! If this detonates, everything we've worked for is gone."

John's pulse quickened. He had been pushed to the edge, and this was his breaking point. "Gabe," he growled, "she's going to blow it. We have to move."

Gabe nodded, his voice low but steady. "We'll deal with everything else later. Right now, we stop her. Are you ready?"

John's eyes blazed with resolve as he glanced at the pendant around his mother's neck one more time. "I've been ready."

They stepped forward, Gabe leading the way with his weapon lowered but ready, his voice commanding and clear. "Emily, stop what you're doing. We need to talk."

The air seemed to freeze as Emily looked up from the device, her mask of composure finally cracking as her gaze met her son's. For the first time, her voice softened, filled with something like regret. "John," she whispered.

But John's expression remained hard, cold. "Don't," he said sharply, his voice thick with years of anger and hurt. "Not now."

Emily hesitated, her eyes darting between her son and the device. "You don't understand," she said, her voice pleading now. "This isn't what you think it is. I'm trying to protect you, to protect all of us."

Gabe stepped forward, his tone firm but imploring. "Then explain it to us, Emily. Tell us what's going on before it's too late."

For a brief second, it seemed like she might, that she might actually let them in. But then, with a glance at the buzzing device, her resolve returned. She shook her head. "I can't. You'll ruin everything."

"You're about to ruin everything," John spat, his voice finally breaking with emotion. "I'm not letting you destroy the timeline, or yourself."

The room felt like it was on the brink of an explosion emotionally and physically. Mother and son stood on opposite sides of a line, the clock ticking down towards a fate neither of them could fully control.

This was no longer just about a mission. It was personal.

And time was running out.

Emily's hands hovered over the controls, her eyes darting between the flashing lights and the faces of her son and Gabe. For a brief second, the tension in the room felt like it had reached a tipping point, and John could feel his pulse pounding in his ears.

"Emily," Gabe urged one last time, stepping forward cautiously. "This doesn't have to end like this."

But before anyone could react, the device emitted a sharp, high-pitched whine, its vibrations rattling through the room. John's instincts flared, and his gaze snapped to the control panel. Something was wrong terribly wrong.

"Mom, stop!" John shouted, panic lacing his voice as he rushed towards her.

But just as his hand reached out, the device surged. A blinding pulse of energy crackled through the air, lighting up the room like a supernova.

Emily's eyes widened in horror, her hands freezing over the console. "No, no, no!"

Before anyone could react, the device overloaded, emitting a deafening roar as its internal components began to fail. Sparks erupted from the core, and the air seemed to ripple with the surge of temporal energy building inside.

"Get down!" Gabe yelled, diving towards John to shield him, but the warning came too late.

The explosion hit with brutal force a blast of temporal energy that tore through the room like a tidal wave. The walls buckled, and the floor trembled as the detonation lifted John off his feet, throwing him backwards like a ragdoll. The sound of shattering glass, twisting metal, and the terrifying groan of the building filled the air, drowning out everything else.

John hit the ground hard, the impact knocking the breath from his lungs as he slammed into a nearby pillar. His vision blurred, the edges of his world dimming as the overwhelming noise became a distant echo. Through the dust and chaos, he could barely make out Gabe, a shadow moving frantically amidst the debris.

The building groaned ominously as the shockwaves rippled outward, cracks spider-webbing across the walls. Chunks of the ceiling began to rain down like deadly hail.

John's head swam as he tried to push himself up, his body screaming in protest. Pain flared through his side, but his eyes locked on the centre of the room, where the device still buzzed, flickering violently as it neared critical failure.

Through the haze of smoke and dust, Gabe's voice pierced the chaos, faint but desperate. "John! John, can you hear me?"

John tried to respond, but the words were trapped in his throat. His body felt too heavy, his vision too blurry. He collapsed back to the ground, barely conscious, as the world around him spun into darkness.

Gabe, his ears still ringing from the blast, stumbled forward, eyes locked on John's crumpled form. He pushed through the wreckage, heart pounding. "John!" he shouted again, his voice cracking with desperation. The collapsing building muffled his cries.

Dust filled the air as the walls creaked and shuddered, the entire structure moments away from complete collapse. John's vision flickered images of his mother, the device, and Gabe flashing through his mind. His world was falling apart in more ways than one, and time itself seemed to distort as he drifted further into unconsciousness.

Gabe reached John's side, his hands trembling as he knelt beside him. "John, stay with me!" His voice was ragged with desperation. John's only response was a faint, unfocused blink, his consciousness slipping away.

Gabe's heart pounded as he assessed John's condition, his pulse quickening with the reality of the collapsing building. Dust choked the air, beams groaning under the weight of the impending collapse. Gabe knew he had only seconds to act.

Just as he tried to lift John, the ground trembled violently. A massive chunk of debris crashed down, slamming into the floor just feet away, the shockwave knocking Gabe off balance. His world tilted as he was thrown back, and before he could reach out, a steel beam fell between them, cutting him off from John.

A surge of panic overtook Gabe as he scrambled to his feet, calling out, "John!" But his voice was drowned out by the roar of crumbling walls. He could barely make out John's form through the dust his friend lay partially buried beneath the wreckage, unmoving.

Gabe's breath hitched, but he forced himself to stay calm. He needed to think, needed to act fast. If he couldn't move the debris, John was as good as gone. Yet, as Gabe clawed at the wreckage, it became clear he wasn't strong enough. The weight of the situation pressed down on him, as heavy as the rubble itself. There was no way he could get to John in time.

Emily's eyes locked onto John's motionless body, a cold terror clenching at her heart. The collapsing building seemed to close in around her, the groaning metal and collapsing beams forming a suffocating backdrop to the chaos. She saw Gabe trying to reach John, his desperate shouts barely audible above the destruction.

Her legs felt heavy as she fought to make her way towards John. Debris rained down around her, narrowly missing as she ducked and dodged the falling beams. A large piece of concrete crashed behind her, sending a plume of dust into the air. Time seemed to blur, each second stretching as the space between her and John felt like miles.

Emily lunged forward, her eyes stinging from the dust. As she closed the distance, her heart sank a massive piece of debris fell between Gabe and John, separating them. She screamed John's name, but the sound was swallowed by the chaos. She stumbled, barely catching herself as another violent tremor rocked the building.

Gabe turned to her, their eyes meeting for a brief, terrible moment. His expression mirrored her own a mix of guilt, helplessness, and terror. Emily forced herself forward, the urgency propelling her despite the danger. She tried to claw at the debris, but it was too heavy, immovable. The weight of the world seemed to hang on her shoulders as the final cracks echoed through the collapsing structure.

She could see John now, but he was too far, too still. Tears blurred her vision as she realised there was no way to reach him. Her heart screamed for her to keep trying, but her mind whispered the cold truth: they were out of time.

With a heavy heart, Gabe reached for his lapel, his fingers brushing the small, glowing Chronoverge pinned there. His hand trembled as he hesitated, the urge to stay and fight warring with the harsh reality before him. The dust, the rumbling collapse, the sight of John his friend, his brother lying unconscious beneath the wreckage. He couldn't stay. Not like this.

He activated the device, the familiar hum growing louder in the dust-choked air. Time itself seemed to slow as the decision solidified within him.

"I'll come back for you, John," Gabe whispered, his voice cracking under the weight of the promise. "I swear."

With one last look, he pressed the button. A brilliant flash of light enveloped him, and in an instant, he was gone.

John, barely conscious, glimpsed the flash of light through the fog of his fading vision. His mind struggled to make sense of it, the colours and shapes of the world blending into a chaotic swirl. He wanted to move, to reach out desperation clawing at him but his body was too weak. The darkness was closing in, swallowing everything too fast.

The last thing he saw before the blackness claimed him was the blurred figure of his mother, her face twisted in anguish. She was reaching for him, her voice a distant, fading echo in his mind, slipping further from his grasp with every heartbeat.

The sounds of the collapsing building the cries, the chaos faded into nothingness as John surrendered to the unconscious void.

Chapter Twenty

Gabe pressed the button on his emergency time hopper, bracing himself for the familiar, jarring shift. But this time, something felt off. Instead of the usual smooth transition through the currents of time, the world around him shattered into jagged fragments. His body was torn through the swirling vortex, battered by waves of temporal distortion.

The journey wasn't the controlled experience he was used to; it was violent and chaotic. For a moment, Gabe could feel the pull of the collapsing building, the intense heat of the explosion chasing him through the timestream. Then, with a gut-wrenching jolt, he was thrown out of the temporal flow, crashing onto the hard, cold floor of the LTC training facility.

Disoriented, his breath came in ragged gasps as the sterile, brightly lit medical facility swirled into view. The weight of the journey left him dizzy, and his body throbbed from the rough landing. Technicians and medics rushed towards him, their concerned faces blurring together as he tried to focus. His clothes were singed, his body covered in dust and debris from the explosion.

Gabe struggled to stay conscious, the rough landing still reverberating through his bones. His body was stiff, aching from the brutal journey through the timestream. Technicians and medics rushed towards him, their white coats fluttering as they moved with purpose. The sterile environment, with its sharp, antiseptic scent, clashed with the dust and debris clinging to him.

A familiar voice cut through the haze. "Gabe!" Dr Moore, the senior medic, pushed through the cluster of technicians, her eyes wide with a mix of shock and concern. Her gaze travelled from the burn marks on his clothes to the ash smeared across his face. "What happened? Where's John?"

Gabe blinked hard, his vision swimming. He tried to sit up but was met with a wave of dizziness that forced him back down. His head throbbed, and the words came out in a ragged whisper. "Explosion… massive… John's still there…"

Dr Moore's expression darkened, the fear in her eyes mirroring the helplessness Gabe felt. His body gave in, and the strength to keep his eyes open slipped away. The last thing he saw before the world faded was the worried face of Dr Moore barking orders to her team, the urgency in her voice punctuating the gravity of the situation.

As his consciousness slipped away, the medical team wasted no time, lifting him onto a gurney and wheeling him towards the intensive care unit. Dr Moore's voice was sharp as she issued rapid instructions. "We need full scans and stabilisation. Now."

Meanwhile, in the comms room, the hum of equipment mixed with the tense murmurs of the staff. The moment the emergency alert went off, Sarah had been notified. Her face was drawn with worry as she rushed to the scene, her mind racing with questions. There was no time to waste she needed answers, and she needed them fast.

The urgency in Sarah's movements belied the storm swirling inside her. As she rushed into the comms room, the blinking lights of the console felt like tiny, insistent pulses of alarm. Her heart pounded, her breath coming in sharp bursts as the dread settled deep in her chest. This was more than just a mission this was personal.

"Get me a status report," Sarah's voice sliced through the controlled chaos, but beneath the command was an undercurrent of barely restrained fear.

Dr Moore glanced up from her work, her hands never stopping as they moved over Gabe's unconscious form. "He's stable but unconscious," she replied, her tone professional but laced with concern. "He mentioned an explosion and that John is still there."

The words hit Sarah like a punch to the gut, but she couldn't allow herself to crumble. Not now. She clenched her fists at her sides, fighting back the wave of emotions threatening to surface. "We need a retrieval team," she said, her voice tight, but it lacked the sharpness she normally wielded so effortlessly. "Prep the team. We're going back to 2075. We have to find John and bring him back."

As the technicians rushed to synchronise their time travel devices, gathering the necessary equipment, Sarah stood frozen for just a moment, her mind racing. John was still out there, possibly injured or worse, and she was here helpless, stuck in the sterile halls of LTC. The memory of their last conversation flashed through her mind, the casual banter that had carried an unspoken trust. Now, that trust hung in the balance, tethered to a crumbling building and a mission gone wrong.

Her hands trembled as she activated her communicator, connecting with the team leaders. The sense of dread that had settled in the pit of her stomach grew heavier, threatening to drown her. But she couldn't afford fear, not now.

"We're heading back to the site of the explosion," Sarah instructed, her voice steadier than she felt. "Our primary objective is to locate and retrieve John. Be prepared for anything." She paused, swallowing the lump in her throat. "We won't leave him behind."

As the team assembled, the air was thick with tension, each operative acutely aware of the risks. Sarah could see it in their eyes the same worry that gnawed at her heart. But she pushed it all aside, burying it deep. They couldn't fail. Not this time.

After Sarah had finished giving orders to prep the retrieval team, she hurried into the operations centre, her eyes scanning the room for key personnel. She spotted Max and Lisa bent over a terminal, clearly having already heard some of the commotion.

"Max, Lisa," she called, her voice firmer than she felt inside, "we're heading back to 2075 to bring John back. You're both coming with us."

Max straightened up, his expression hard and determined. "You don't even have to ask. I was already coming." His jaw clenched tightly as if daring anyone to stop him.

Lisa nodded, her face pale but resolute. "We'll find him, Sarah."

As Sarah continued organising the team, her gaze fell on Jack and Anna at the far end of the room. Jack, the armoury expert, was briefing Anna on some equipment, but they turned their attention to Sarah as she approached.

"You two are with us," Sarah said. "This mission's going to need all hands, and your skills could make the difference."

Jack gave a sharp nod. "You got it. I'll grab the gear. Let's bring him home."

Anna's eyes flickered with both determination and nervousness. "I'm ready, Sarah. Just tell me where you need me."

With the team assembled and the time travel devices calibrated, Sarah felt the mounting pressure of the moment. "Everyone, prepare for time travel on my mark."

Max, Lisa, Jack, and Anna stepped into formation with the other agents, the tension in the air palpable. For a split second, Sarah's hand hesitated over the activation switch, her thoughts racing with all the worst-case scenarios. But there was no room for doubt.

"Mark."

With a synchronised activation of their devices, the team was enveloped in a brilliant light. The sensation of time travel engulfed them, the world spinning into a vortex of colours and sounds. Sarah's mind raced with a mix of hope and fear, praying they would reach John in time.

The light dimmed, and the team materialised amidst the ruins of the building in 2075. The air was thick with dust, and the sounds of distant sirens and crumbling structures filled their ears. Sarah's heart pounded as she scanned the debris, searching for any sign of John.

"Spread out!" she commanded. "Look for any sign of him!"

Max and Lisa immediately began moving through the wreckage, working in sync like a well-oiled machine, their connection palpable as they sifted through rubble. Jack and Anna checked the structural integrity of the area, using their technical expertise to ensure the rest of the team could search without triggering further collapse.

Sarah's eyes darted around, every second feeling like an eternity. She refused to let panic take over, focusing instead on the task at hand.

Finally, a shout came from one of the operatives. "Over here! I've found something!"

Sarah rushed over, her breath catching in her throat. Partially buried under the debris, a communicator lay cracked, its screen flickering faintly. It was John's a familiar piece of equipment that now served as a lifeline of hope. Her pulse quickened. The device, though damaged, was still functional, meaning John had been there, maybe still close by.

She knelt down, her hands trembling slightly as she carefully retrieved the communicator from the rubble. The cold, broken metal felt heavier in her hands than it should have, the weight of what it symbolised sinking into her chest.

"John..." she whispered, her voice barely audible, though the rest of the team was close behind.

Max and Lisa reached her side first, their eyes scanning the debris. "This means he's still here," Max said, the urgency rising in his tone. "We just have to keep looking."

Relief flashed through Sarah, but it was quickly dampened by the sickening realisation that John could be trapped under the wreckage. Injured. Running out of time.

"We've got a lead," Sarah said, her voice breaking slightly with emotion. "Let's keep searching. We're not leaving without him."

The team exchanged determined glances, their focus narrowing. John was still in the rubble that was the only possibility that made sense. He had to be.

But as they resumed their search with renewed intensity, the clock was ticking, and Sarah couldn't shake the gnawing fear that they might be too late.

The team continued their search, their determination unwavering. Every breath was laced with tension as they sifted through the wreckage, hands brushing past twisted metal and broken concrete, eyes scanning the layers of debris for any sign of life. They moved with a precision honed from years of training, but this mission wasn't just about duty it was personal.

Max crouched low, his hands shaking as he pushed aside a large piece of shattered wall, his thoughts racing. John wasn't just a teammate; he was like a brother. Every scrape of metal against stone felt like a countdown to something darker, and the weight of that pressure was almost unbearable. He glanced at Lisa, who, despite her calm exterior, wore the same strain in her eyes. They both knew what was at stake.

Lisa's voice, usually steady, cracked slightly as she called out, "We'll find him, Max. We have to." But even as she said it, doubt gnawed at the edges of her resolve. The destruction was overwhelming, the crumbling ruins a maze of jagged edges and shadows. It was easy to get lost in this sea of wreckage, both physically and emotionally.

Nearby, Jack and Anna worked side by side, their movements synchronised, driven by an unspoken urgency. Jack's usual playful demeanour was gone, replaced by a quiet intensity. His hands moved swiftly, his eyes narrowing as he scanned the debris for any clue, any fragment of hope. Anna, young but resolute, mimicked his focus, her heart pounding with the same unrelenting fear. The weight of what they were searching for who they were searching for pressed on them like a heavy fog.

"John wouldn't give up on us," Anna muttered to herself, pushing harder, her voice barely audible but filled with a determination that kept her going.

In the distance, Sarah stood, orchestrating the search with her characteristic control, but beneath the surface, she was unravelling. This wasn't just about the timeline anymore. This was about John about saving a friend who had been through hell and back, and who had been left behind in a situation far worse than any of them had expected. She clenched her jaw, her eyes scanning the shifting dust, every passing second a reminder that they were running out of time.

The air around them thickened with tension, the weight of failure pressing against their chests as every second bled into the next. The timeline was fragile every moment John remained missing was a potential fracture, a ripple that could dismantle everything they had fought to protect. But more than that, for Sarah, Max, Lisa, Jack, and Anna, this was a personal battle against a force that had threatened to take everything from them.

They were fighting not just to find John, but to preserve what was left of their fractured team of the bonds that had been tested but never broken. And with every piece of debris moved, every shadow checked, they reaffirmed that they wouldn't leave without him.

At the LTC medical facility, Gabe lay in a state of uneasy rest, his body and mind still recovering from the ordeal. The sterile smell of antiseptic and the soft beeping of machines surrounding him contrasted sharply with the chaos he had left behind. Every breath felt like a reminder of his failure to protect John.

The door to his room opened quietly, and Dr Malcolm Davis stepped inside, his face etched with concern and something deeper guilt.

Gabe's eyes fluttered open, blinking a few times to clear his vision. "Malcolm is John?" His voice was strained, raw from worry.

Dr Davis sighed, placing a reassuring hand on Gabe's arm. "We haven't found him yet, but we're doing everything we can." His tone was steady, but the uncertainty lingered between them.

Gabe's eyes filled with unshed tears. He turned his head away, overwhelmed by the crushing weight of guilt. "I should've been there. I should've protected him," Gabe whispered, his voice cracking with emotion. His mind replayed the explosion, the last moments he saw John, the split-second decision that still haunted him.

Malcolm shook his head gently. "You did everything you could, Gabe. There was no way to know how that would play out. Now we need to focus on recovering and planning our next move. We will find John. I promise."

The words hung heavy in the air, the promise of hope mixed with uncertainty. Gabe nodded weakly, but his heart was heavy with the weight of his failure.

As Dr Davis pulled up a chair beside the bed, his expression shifted from concern to something more serious something he had clearly been dreading. He took a deep breath before speaking, his voice lowering as if bracing himself for a confession.

"Gabe, there's something else we need to discuss," Malcolm began, his voice steady but heavy with guilt. "It's about the stagecoach ride."

Gabe's eyes narrowed slightly, a mix of curiosity and wariness crossing his face. "What about it?" His tone was cautious, but there was a familiar edge he had suspected something about this for years.

Malcolm took another breath, his hands clasped together. "I've been carrying this burden for a long time, and I need to come clean. I was part of the stagecoach mission. I knew about the orders that came down, and I played my part. But knowing what I know now, I realise that mission it was a significant part of what drove Emily from LTC."

Gabe's jaw tightened, his suspicions confirmed, but the admission still hit hard. "I figured you were involved, Malcolm. But why bring this up now? What difference does it make after everything we've been through?"

Malcolm's eyes met Gabe's, filled with remorse. "Because I need you to understand that I never wanted any of this to happen. I believed we were doing the right thing, protecting the timeline, following Anton's orders. But seeing the fallout Emily leaving, John caught in the crossfire I can't shake the feeling that we could have done things differently."

Gabe sighed, the weight of the moment pressing down on him. The constant struggle between loyalty to the mission and the human cost was something that had haunted him for years. "We were all following orders, Malcolm. Orders that came from the top, from Anton Lennox himself. But that doesn't change the fact that we tore a family apart. A family that now has a missing son."

Malcolm nodded slowly. "I've asked myself countless times if there was another way. If we could have protected John without causing so much pain. Emily's departure, her decision to take the VT-5500 and disappear into the timestream it all ties back to that mission. We pushed her too far."

The mention of the VT-5500 Emily's escape vehicle stirred something in Gabe. Emily had been a mystery ever since she left LTC, her actions now more devastating than ever. Gabe's eyes flashed with a mixture of anger and sorrow. "And now, John's out there, somewhere, lost because of the choices we made. He's been through hell because of us."

Malcolm's voice softened, earnest. "We'll find him, Gabe. I'm committed to making things right. Emily's actions, her disappearance it's all a part of the mess we need to clean up."

Gabe leaned back in his bed, his body aching from more than just the physical wounds. The tension in his shoulders eased slightly as he saw the sincerity in Malcolm's eyes, but the pain of their choices remained. "We've made a lot of mistakes, Malcolm. But we have to keep moving forward. For John."

Malcolm placed a hand on Gabe's shoulder, his grip firm, the weight of their shared guilt palpable. "We will find John, Gabe. And we'll bring him back. But for now, focus on your recovery. We need you at full strength for what's ahead."

As Malcolm left the room, Gabe stared at the ceiling, his mind racing with the implications of what he had just learned. He thought of John, trapped somewhere in time. He thought of Emily, a ghost they could no longer afford to ignore. The journey ahead was uncertain, but his resolve remained unbroken. For John, for Emily, and for the future of LTC, he would do whatever it took to bring them back together and uncover the truth behind the tangled web of secrets that had shaped their lives.

Outside the room, the LTC medical facility buzzed with activity, a stark contrast to the heavy silence lingering in Gabe's mind. He remained still, eyes on the ceiling, while the echoes of Malcolm's words reverberated through his thoughts. The weight of their shared history pressed down on him decisions made long ago that had led to this moment, with John lost in the chaos of time and Emily's choices haunting them all.

Gabe clenched his fists, guilt and determination warring inside him. The mission to find John and untangle the web of secrets from their past was far from over. They had only scratched the surface. But with each passing hour, the stakes grew higher, and the path ahead seemed more uncertain.

Hours passed as Max, Lisa, Jack, and Anna led the search team, combing through the ruins of the building in 2075. The devastation was immense, and every piece of rubble they overturned only seemed to amplify the weight of John's absence. The strain showed on all of their faces, especially Max, who was pacing the site, his frustration threatening to boil over.

"We can't just give up!" Max finally shouted, his voice breaking through the tension. "He's out there, Sarah. I know it!" His eyes were wide with fear and anger, his hands clenching into fists.

Lisa stood beside him, her jaw tight, but her eyes reflected the same raw emotion. "We've searched every inch. We're missing something," she said quietly, but with firm resolve.

Sarah's face was etched with anguish as she issued the final call. Her heart ached as much as theirs, but she had to balance that with the risks to the timeline. "I don't like it any more than you do, Max," she said softly, her voice betraying the strain she was under. "But we can't risk further contamination of the timeline. It's a direct order. We're pulling out."

Max's shoulders sagged, his fists unclenching slowly, but his face was still twisted with disbelief and anger. Lisa shot Sarah a look that was part frustration, part understanding. "There's nothing else we can do here," she said, though the words seemed bitter on her tongue.

With heavy hearts, the retrieval team gathered, activating their time travel devices one by one. The devastated scene of 2075 shimmered, the crumbling building fading from sight as they returned to the present. But even as the dust and destruction disappeared, the weight of their failure to find John lingered, like a shadow hanging over them.

Back at the medical facility, the soft whir of machines and hushed voices filled the sterile halls. Gabe lay awake, his mind still swirling with the revelations Malcolm had confessed earlier. The second part of their conversation hung in the air, unresolved and heavy.

Gabe shook his head slowly, the full weight of it pressing down on him. "Malcolm you don't know how hard this is for me. I promised I'd protect him. I gave him my word, and now I don't even know where he is."

Malcolm's gaze softened. "We will find him, Gabe. But you need to focus on your recovery. There are still a lot of pieces to this puzzle, and you're a key part of putting it together."

Gabe nodded, though the pain still clung to his features. "I'll get better, Malcolm. For John. For all of us."

Dr Davis gave Gabe a reassuring pat on the shoulder. "Rest up. We've got a lot of work ahead."

As Malcolm left, the room fell into quiet again, save for the beeping of medical equipment. Gabe stared at the ceiling, the weight of the past, present, and future pressing on his chest like a physical force. He thought of John, Emily, and the tangled web of secrets they were all caught in. The path ahead was fraught with danger and uncertainty, but Gabe's resolve was unbroken.

The retrieval team returned to the stark, sterile reality of the LTC facility. Though the crumbling ruins of 2075 were behind them, the weight of their failure clung to each member like a shadow they couldn't shake. The air felt heavier, thicker, as if every breath was harder to draw.

Sarah, still reeling from the emotional toll of the mission, barely acknowledged the team's return. She could feel the tension among them, the lingering hope that had now turned to frustration. But there wasn't time to wallow in defeat. She had to move plan the next step. Her responsibility, her drive, kept pushing her forward.

Her mind raced as she moved briskly through the corridors of the LTC facility. The sterile, high-tech environment seemed to pulse with the urgency she felt. She needed answers, a plan, something to cling to.

When she reached her office a sleek, glass-walled room that overlooked the bustling operations centre below the door slid shut behind her with a soft hiss, sealing her off from the noise and activity outside.

She approached her desk, her fingers gliding over the touch-sensitive surface to activate the secure communication system. The screen flickered to life, displaying a series of encryption protocols that took a few seconds to complete. Once the connection was established, the screen revealed a shadowed figure, though Sarah knew exactly who it was.

"Sarah," the voice greeted, steady but with an edge of tension.

She took a deep breath, preparing for what she had to say. "The mission didn't go as planned. Gabe and John engaged VTI operatives at the summit. And... we've confirmed one of them was Emily."

The silence on the other end was heavy, more telling than words. She could feel the shift, the subtle pause before the voice returned cool but tighter. "Emily."

Sarah nodded, though the figure couldn't see her. "There was an altercation. Gabe and John managed to disrupt the device, but there was a temporal explosion." Her voice wavered slightly. "Gabe's been retrieved, injured but stable. However, John's location... and his condition... are unclear."

Another pause, then a slow, measured response. "And the device?"

"Destroyed," Sarah said, her words clipped. "But it destabilised the timeline. We've recorded major anomalies in the historical data. The explosion caused significant damage, affecting key events. We're in the process of assessing the full scope."

The figure leaned forward slightly, his tone quiet but insistent. "And John?"

Sarah's grip on her datapad tightened. "We're regrouping. I've called a temporary halt to the search to avoid further timeline contamination. But we'll continue as soon as we stabilise the situation." She hesitated, then added, "We won't stop until we find him."

The voice softened, betraying a glimpse of personal concern. "Make sure you do. He's vital to all of this."

The screen went dark, leaving Sarah alone with her thoughts, the unspoken weight of Alexander's reaction hanging in the air. She stood, walking towards the window overlooking the operations centre below, her mind racing. The mission was critical, but the implications of what had just happened ran far deeper than any of them could afford to admit.

Gabe's slumber was deep, the kind of heavy sleep that comes after a storm of pain and exhaustion. The quiet beep of medical monitors was the only sound until an insistent knock at the door broke the peace.

"Gabe," a firm voice called out, sharp and steady, like it wasn't used to waiting.

His eyes fluttered open, and as his vision cleared, the door swung inward. Standing in the doorway was a tall woman, dressed in a sleek, dark suit. Her presence filled the room with authority. Gabe knew instantly who she was.

"The Vindicator."

His jaw tightened. He'd heard stories about her an agent of Lennox Time Corporation, brought in when things were about to get serious. Not the kind of person who showed up unless the situation was critical. Her reputation came with a whisper of fear among LTC agents. If she was here, it wasn't just a friendly check-in.

"You've got a meeting. Time to get up," she said, her voice carrying the weight of someone who didn't repeat herself.

Gabe rubbed his face, grimacing at the soreness that shot through his body. "So they've called in *you*?" he said, his voice laced with a hint of sarcasm but edged with respect. "Ain't that just peachy."

The Vindicator didn't flinch. "Get dressed," she replied coolly, her eyes steady and calculating. "We're on the clock."

Gabe grunted as he swung his legs over the side of the bed, every movement reminding him of the hell he'd been through. His ribs ached, and his body felt like it had been thrown through a time rift probably because it had. As he reached for his boots, his mind raced. He knew what happened when the Vindicator got involved things got cleaned up, fast, and usually without much regard for what got broken in the process.

"Where're we goin'?" he asked, slipping his boots on. The casual tone didn't hide the seriousness of his question.

"You'll find out soon enough," she said, a touch of finality in her voice. "But I suggest you prepare for something big."

Gabe eyed her for a moment, taking her in. The Vindicator wasn't just some pencil-pusher she had grit, the kind that came from walking through fire more than once. "Figured as much," he muttered, pulling his jacket on. "Ain't never simple when they send you."

She didn't reply, just gestured for him to follow. They walked in silence through the sterile, dimly lit corridors of the medical facility. Gabe couldn't help but notice the way she moved every step deliberate, eyes always scanning. He'd seen it before in soldiers who'd lived too long on the edge. She was trouble, but the kind you wanted on your side when the storm hit.

They reached a set of double doors, guarded by two stone-faced agents. At a nod from the Vindicator, the doors swung open. Inside was a small, dimly lit room with a table and two chairs, simple but heavy with expectation.

"Take a seat," she said, her voice soft but firm. "You'll be briefed shortly."

Gabe hesitated for a moment before lowering himself into the chair. "When you show up, things tend to go sideways," he said with a wry grin. "Should I be worried?"

The Vindicator gave him a hard look. "You should be ready."

As the door clicked shut behind her, Gabe sat back in his chair, staring at the empty space across from him. Whatever this was, it was big. And if the Vindicator was involved, it was about to get even bigger.

Gabe sat, his mind still spinning. The Vindicator gave him one last, unreadable look before turning and slipping out the door with a soft click. The silence that followed was thick, almost suffocating, but Gabe wasn't the kind of man to let the quiet shake him. He leaned back in his chair, eyes narrowing as he surveyed the empty room. Something about this setup gnawed at him like a calm before the storm.

Minutes passed. His fingers tapped idly on the table, the only sound in the room. Just as impatience began to creep in, the door opened again. The Vindicator reappeared, her presence as sharp as before, but now she held a small, metallic device. Without a word, she placed it on the table and pressed a button.

The room shimmered. Gabe felt the air shift charged, humming with energy and then the familiar pull of time travel gripped him. Only, this wasn't like any jump he'd experienced before. It was smoother, too smooth, like being slipped through a seam in time itself.

"We're moving," she said, her voice barely above a whisper, yet filled with authority.

Gabe braced himself as the room dissolved into swirling light and shadows. His pulse quickened, but he kept his breathing steady. This wasn't his first rodeo. Still, something about this jump felt different, like they were slipping between timelines rather than travelling through them.

When the sensation faded, they weren't in any place he recognised.

They stood in a long, sleek hallway lined with reflective surfaces that stretched on into what seemed like infinity. Gabe's boots echoed softly on the floor, but the air around them hummed with something unnatural like the energy of countless timelines converging in this one strange place. He felt his gut tighten.

"This some kind of temporal pocket?" Gabe asked, his voice low.

The Vindicator gave a curt nod, her eyes forward. "You're catching on."

He didn't reply, his attention now on the windows they passed. Glimpses of other eras, and other moments in time flickered beyond the glass, each one a slice of history that seemed frozen and alive all at once. The further they walked, the more Gabe felt the weight of this place. Whoever ran this operation wasn't just playing with time they were *controlling* it.

"This way," the Vindicator said, her tone softer now, more respectful of the space they occupied.

They reached a set of large, ornate doors. Without a sound, they opened, revealing an office that made Gabe pause. It was like stepping into a nexus, a centre where time itself was kept in check. Windows displayed different eras, constantly shifting, as if whoever sat behind this desk could pull threads from any point in history. The walls were lined with artefacts pieces from long-forgotten civilisations, relics that didn't belong to any one moment but spanned centuries.

Gabe let out a low whistle, though his expression stayed guarded. "Well, if this ain't somethin' straight outta a sci-fi flick."

The Vindicator said nothing, but he didn't miss the faint twitch at the corner of her mouth. Whoever they were about to meet, this wasn't just some ordinary briefing.

Gabe's boots clicked against the marble-like floor as he stepped further into the room. His gaze swept across the walls, a strange sense of unease settling in his gut. Artefacts from countless eras were meticulously placed, each one a reminder that the room's occupant wasn't just powerful he held history in his grasp.

At the centre of the room, behind a massive, polished desk, sat a figure that Gabe recognised instantly. Anton Lennox. His presence was commanding, his gaze sharp and assessing as he looked up from a series of holographic displays.

"Gabe," Lennox said, his voice smooth and controlled, though there was always that unmistakable edge, a coldness born from a lifetime of calculating every decision. "We have much to discuss."

Gabe swallowed hard, the weight of the moment pressing down on him like a freight train. He was still aching from the injuries, every movement sending a reminder of the chaos he had left behind. But the pain only fuelled his anger. Lennox, with his Soviet roots, was never one to waste time. Gabe knew well enough by now when the stakes were this high, the fall was a hell of a lot further.

"Please, take a seat," Lennox gestured towards the chair opposite him, his movements precise, almost mechanical. His tone made it clear this wasn't a request. "We have a lot to cover."

Gabe sat down, wincing slightly as he shifted in the chair, the strain of his injuries making it hard to hide the pain. His muscles ached, his ribs throbbed, but he wasn't about to show weakness. The Vindicator stood silently beside him, her watchful gaze never leaving the room. Lennox leaned forward, folding his hands on the desk, his expression as unreadable as ever, but with a sharpness in his eyes that spoke of a man used to surviving at any cost.

"First, tell me everything that happened in New York. I need to understand every detail."

As Gabe began to recount the mission, he couldn't shake the awareness of who he was talking to a man who had grown up in Soviet Russia, where survival meant sacrifice. Lennox had built the Lennox Time Corporation with the same cold precision he'd learned in his youth control the timeline, control history, no matter the cost. It explained the coldness, the way he could compartmentalise the loss of people like it was a necessary sacrifice in his never-ending war to protect time itself.

"After the explosion, I lost sight of John," Gabe continued, his voice strained with the memory, but also with the effort of sitting upright through the pain. "I managed to activate my emergency time hopper just in time, but—" He paused, unsure of what reaction Lennox would show regarding John. Would he care about the young man, or only about preserving the timeline?

Lennox's eyes darkened at the mention of John, but before Gabe could finish, Lennox cut in, his tone unflinching. "The Border Collie," he said, his voice sharp and insistent, like a man who didn't have time for interruptions. "Joe, I believe you called him. Is he safe?"

Gabe blinked, his frustration bubbling over. Of all the things "Joe? Yeah, he's fine. We left him at the safehouse before heading to the summit. Why?"

Lennox leaned back, a faint smile tugging at the corner of his mouth cold, calculated. "The dog is important, Gabe. More important than you might realise. His presence with you and John... well, let's just say it has larger implications. We must ensure his safety at all costs."

Gabe's fists clenched, pain shooting through his ribs as his anger surged. "You're worried about the dog when John is missing?" He didn't bother to hide the bite in his words. "Joe is all I have left right now. If you're suggesting I leave him behind or subject him to tests, you can forget it."

For a brief moment, Lennox's eyes hardened, that cold Russian pragmatism shining through. "You misunderstand, Gabe," he said, his tone like ice. "This isn't about sentimentality. This is about the timeline. Your attachment to the dog is irrelevant, but the dog himself may not be. We must remain cautious."

Gabe's jaw tightened, his whole body trembling with restrained fury and the pain gnawing at him. "I know what's at stake," he said through gritted teeth. "But John is missing, and you're talking about hypothetical dangers to Joe. If you try to take him away from me, I'll resign. I'll take Joe and leave LTC for good."

Lennox sighed, rubbing his temples like a man who'd carried the weight of the world on his shoulders for too long. "Gabe, this isn't just about the dog or John. You have to understand the bigger picture, like we did back in Russia." His voice dipped, colder now. "Sometimes sacrifices are necessary for the survival of the many. But I won't take Joe away from you." He paused, his gaze softening just enough to show a flicker of empathy, as if remembering what it was to care for something other than the mission. "I'll order you back to the safehouse in

1940 England. Monitor for anomalies, and keep an eye on Joe for any signs of temporal effects."

Gabe simmered, the pain radiating through his body as his fists clenched at the side. He took a breath, but his voice came out raw. "You care about the timeline, I get that. But John's still out there because of Emily. And we both know what happened in St. Louis." Gabe's eyes bore into Lennox's, daring him to flinch. "We both know how far she's willing to go. And now, we're caught in the crossfire."

Lennox didn't react immediately, but there was something behind his eyes, a shadow that flickered across his face, too brief to catch if you weren't looking for it. "Emily is not your concern, Gabe," Lennox said quietly, his voice losing some of that Soviet edge, but still firm. "Your focus is John, and keeping the timeline stable. We'll deal with Emily when the time comes."

Gabe leaned forward slightly, ignoring the sharp pain in his ribs. "We're past that. The time came when we let her slip away. When St. Louis happened. She knows what she's doing, and now John's caught in the middle. So don't tell me I don't have to worry about her."

Lennox's gaze hardened, and for a moment, the air between them crackled with tension, both men staring each other down. But Lennox was the one to break the silence, his voice low and controlled. "Emily is dangerous, but her connection to John is what makes this even more volatile. That's why you need to stay focused. England will give us the space we need to work. Keep an eye on Joe and remain vigilant. We'll handle Emily."

Gabe's teeth clenched, his body trembling from the weight of his injuries and the anger boiling just beneath the surface. He leaned forward slightly, ignoring the sharp pain in his ribs. "We're past that, Lennox. The time came when we let her slip away. When St. Louis happened. She knows what she's doing, and now John's caught in the middle. So don't stand there and tell me I don't have to worry about her."

Lennox's gaze hardened, the air between them almost crackling with tension, both men locked in a silent face-off. But then Lennox broke the silence, his voice low and controlled. "Emily is dangerous, but her connection to John makes this even more volatile. That's why you need to stay focused. England will give us the space we need to work. Keep an eye on Joe and remain vigilant. We'll handle Emily."

Gabe leaned back, exhaustion and pain etched across his features, but his voice remained steady and full of heat. "Fine," he muttered, his voice gravelly. "But I want updates on John, on Emily, on the whole damn situation. I ain't sitting in the dark anymore."

"You'll have them," Lennox replied, his voice as cold and controlled as ever. "Stay vigilant and keep Joe safe. We will get through this, Gabe. One way or another."

Gabe's eyes narrowed, his fists tight against the pain ripping through his body, and his voice dropped into a dangerous growl, laced with that unmistakable West Texas defiance. "Well, Mr Lennox," Gabe spat, tipping his hat just slightly in that signature way, "Let's just hope we ain't ridin' into a storm we can't outrun. But let me make one thing crystal clear. You keep jerking me around like this," he paused, locking eyes with the cold Russian, "And you can kiss my West Texas ass."

With that, Gabe turned sharply on his heel, the ache in his body barely contained by the sheer force of his anger and willpower. His boots echoed against the polished floor as he strode out of the room, each step driving home that he wasn't playing by Lennox's rules anymore. Lennox could take his timeline, his cold calculations, and his orders, but Gabe wasn't about to let any of them keep him from finding John. Not this time.

Outside, The Vindicator was waiting, her expression impassive, though her eyes followed Gabe with a flicker of curiosity. She gave a slight nod and motioned for him to follow her down the corridor. Gabe said nothing, his mind still simmering from the confrontation, his body protesting every step, but he knew the next move was already in motion.

As they reached the end of the hall, The Vindicator pressed a device on her wrist, and the world around them began to shift. Gabe barely noticed the click of the doors closing behind them he was already bracing himself for what came next.

The air seemed to ripple and twist, a kaleidoscope of colours swirling around them. Gabe felt the familiar weightlessness, the disorienting rush of temporal energy. He closed his eyes, focusing on the mission ahead and the promise he had made.

When the world finally settled around him, Gabe found himself standing on a quiet dirt road, the cool English air brushing against his face. He took a deep breath, grounding himself in the serene surroundings that contrasted sharply with the chaos he'd just left behind. The distant sound of birds and the rustling of leaves in the trees were a welcome change from the harsh noise of collapsing buildings and blaring alarms.

But despite the peace, Gabe's mind couldn't let go of the tension. He was miles away from New York, from the devastation, from John and yet, the weight of it all hung heavy around him, refusing to lift. This wasn't over. Not by a long shot.

His body ached, each bruise and wound a reminder of what he'd barely escaped. Yet, the stillness of the countryside felt like an eerie calm before the storm, almost unnatural in its quiet. He looked around, spotting the rustic cottage nestled among the rolling hills, the soft glow of light from within casting a warm, inviting contrast to the cold twilight settling over the landscape. It was the same as before unchanged, untouched by the turbulence of time. A haven.

But peace had no place in Gabe's world right now. The light from the cottage might've been warm, but it was a temporary comfort. His jaw tightened as he started down the path towards the door, knowing that his mission was far from over.

And until John was found, there wouldn't be any rest.

Chapter Twenty-One

Gabe sat in the cosy, rustic cottage in the heart of the English countryside, the crackling fire casting flickering shadows on the wooden walls. The atmosphere was quiet and still, a stark contrast to the tumultuous events of recent days. Joe, the loyal Border Collie, lay at Gabe's feet, his head resting on his paws, eyes reflecting the firelight as he watched his new master intently.

Gabe uncorked a bottle of fine 1876 Old Pogue Kentucky whiskey, the rich aroma filling the room as he poured himself a generous glass. He took a sip, savouring the smooth, smoky flavour that warmed him from the inside out. Leaning back in his chair, he glanced down at Joe and sighed.

"Well, Joe," Gabe began, his voice tinged with melancholy, "it's just you and me now, pardner. Can't say I ever expected things to turn out like this."

Joe's ears perked up at the sound of his name, and he gave a small, encouraging woof. Gabe smiled faintly, reaching down to scratch the dog's head. "I know, I know. We'll figure it out, somehow."

Gabe reached into his coat pocket and pulled out a cigarillo, its slim form a comforting weight in his hand. He struck a match and lit it, the tobacco crackling as he took a deep draw. The familiar scent mingled with the aroma of the whiskey, creating a nostalgic blend that reminded him of quieter times.

The fire crackled, filling the silence with its comforting presence. Gabe stared into the flames, his mind drifting back to the moment he had to leave John behind. The guilt and worry gnawed at him, making it hard to find any peace. Every flicker of the fire seemed to echo his doubts. He took another sip of whiskey, hoping it might dull the edge of his anxiety.

"John's a tough kid," Gabe said, as much to himself as to Joe. "He'll find a way to survive. I just wish I could've done more to protect him."

Joe wagged his tail slightly, his gaze unwavering as if he understood every word. Gabe chuckled softly, appreciating the dog's silent companionship. "You miss him too, don't ya? He was always good to ya."

The room fell silent again, save for the occasional pop and hiss of the fire. Gabe's thoughts, though, were anything but quiet. He tried to focus on the fire, but his mind kept drifting to John, to the moment he had to make the hardest call of his life. Leaving him behind had torn a hole in his gut that whiskey couldn't patch, and every minute felt like one step further away from finding him. But the dog Joe was a tether. A link to the past and to hope.

"Anton thinks I should keep an eye on ya for any effects from the time travel," Gabe mused, taking another sip of whiskey. "But I think he's missin' the point. You're more than just a subject for observation, Joe. You're family now."

Joe thumped his tail in agreement, a gesture that brought a small, genuine smile to Gabe's lips. He reached down to give the dog a pat, the warmth of the fire and the whiskey creating a fleeting sense of comfort.

The fire burned low, the room growing dimmer as the night wore on. Gabe leaned back in his chair, the weariness of the past few days catching up with him. He closed his eyes, allowing himself a moment of rest, knowing that tomorrow would bring new challenges.

Joe shifted closer, his head resting on Gabe's boot. The simple act of companionship was a balm to Gabe's troubled heart. As he drifted towards sleep, the last thought that crossed his mind was a silent promise to John, wherever he might be.

"Hang in there, kid. We'll find ya."

Suddenly, a strange ripple of energy swept through the cottage, distorting the air like a heat mirage. The room seemed to bend and flex around the disturbance, causing Joe to leap to his feet, barking furiously. Gabe jolted upright, fully awake and alert, his hand instinctively reaching for his revolvers.

The cottage groaned like the very walls were holding their breath. Every fibre in Gabe's body screamed to move, but he stayed locked in place, instinctively aware that this was no ordinary disturbance. His hand hovered over his revolvers, the room thick with the kind of tension that came before a fight or something far worse.

The air in the room grew colder, the fire sputtering as if struggling against an unseen force. A voice echoed through the distortion, faint and desperate. "John! Wake up!"

Gabe's heart pounded as he scanned the room, every sense on high alert. The flickering firelight cast eerie shadows, and the distortion coalesced into a dark, imposing figure, its breath visible in the cool night air.

Joe growled low, the sound vibrating through the tense silence. Gabe's knuckles whitened around his revolvers. The figure's presence sucked the warmth from the room, leaving nothing but the bone-chilling cold and the hollow sound of Joe's growls.

For a moment, the figure stood motionless, an ominous presence that seemed to absorb the very light from the room. Gabe's instincts screamed at him to shoot, to take control of whatever this was, but something held him back an inexplicable sense that this confrontation was not what it seemed.

Then, as quickly as it appeared, the figure moved a single step forward that brought it just close enough for Gabe to catch a glimpse of something startling: a pendant, identical to the one John's mother wore, dangling from the figure's neck. The sight sent a shockwave through Gabe, freezing him in place.

Everything in the room seemed to hold its breath, waiting for the inevitable clash.

And then...

Darkness.

The last thing Gabe registered before the world went black was a voice, distant yet eerily familiar, whispering his name with an urgency that sent a chill down his spine.